TASTE

a love story

TRACY EWENS

TASTE

a love story

*Happy
Reader!*

Taste: A Love Story
Copyright © 2015 by Tracy Ewens

ISBN-13: 978-0-9908571-5-0 (print)
ISBN-13: 978-0-9908571-4-3 (e-book)

Book design by Maureen Cutajar
www.gopublished.com

For Katlyn Day, my first.
I love you.
Wait, wait, best story ever.

Chapter One

Kara Malendar was a bitch. She hadn't planned on being one and hadn't always been one, but as she stopped during her mid-Saturday morning run, it was clear she must be the very worst kind of person. Catching her breath and taking a sip from the little water bottle fastened around her waist, Kara fixed her eyes across the street at Marco Polo. Men in blue jumpsuits were emptying the local Italian restaurant. Boxes, tables, and chairs were being loaded onto a large moving van with a cartoon kangaroo painted on the side. Tony and Pam Forte, the owners, were a husband-and-wife team. He was the business part and she was the chef. Pam was classically trained, or so Kara had read in the *About Us* portion of their website. She had always hated the term "classically trained" because it was assumed that was synonymous with great chef. Trained and great were two very different things in Kara's book.

She pulled her UCLA cap down low and sat on the bench just up the road from where the Fortes were saying good-bye to their dream. They'd been open a little over two years. Seventy percent of all restaurants collapsed after a year, so they were luckier than most. And who really knew why they finally decided to call it quits? There could have been several reasons Kara was not privy to, but as she took an even larger sip of water, she felt certain it was the scathing review she'd submitted six months ago to her employer, the *Los Angeles Times*. That had probably finished them off for good. "The last nail in the coffin," as her Nana would have said. Granted, Pam's linguini was overcooked and the wine pairing their sommelier had suggested was awful, but the atmosphere was wonderful, with old exposed brick and fantastic Venice-like lighting. Their bruschetta was on point. It wasn't clumsy or overblown. Very few restaurants could pull off bruschetta. Kara had been to Marco Polo a couple of times, but the night she went for her review, things were clearly not working in the kitchen and the critic in her pounced. She could have remembered their bruschetta and come back another day, but she hadn't. She'd listened to the nasty beastie that whispered in her ear. *The best survive*, it growled. *You're doing the California dining population a service. It's your job. No mercy*, the beastie had insisted. Her review was front page of the Food Section with the headline, "One Word Every Italian Chef Should Know—Al Dente."

Six months later, as Kara stood across the street sweating, her stomach knotted with something she didn't often let in: sympathy. She felt bad. They were human beings after all—the sleeves-rolled-up, worried-about-paying-their-bills type. She could have walked away, given them a break, but she didn't and that made her a bitch. Her reviews had power. That was something she'd loved, wielded even, over the years, but lately she wondered if instead of powerful she'd simply become detached.

As she watched the still-new-looking Viking range top being carried into the moving van, Kara tried to remember the last time she had even enjoyed a meal. Was it at a restaurant? Which one? It couldn't have been at home because she barely cooked anymore. The next question that popped into her mind could have been easily dismissed, but the knot in her stomach tightened, telling her she was onto something: did she even like food anymore? Sure, she knew all the check boxes: what made a perfect cassoulet or which microbrew went best with Wiener schnitzel, but that was just semantics. She used to love food: the sizzling pop of cooking, the blending flavors, the dance of a meal. Kara used to feel passionate about a lot of things, but now, as she slowly let out a breath, she realized she felt very little at all these days.

Oh, boo hoo, she thought, quoting her father as she stood and prepared to finish the last leg of her five-mile run.

"Boo hoo, you'll survive," was one of Senator Patrick Malendar's favorite pieces of parenting advice for her and her brother, Grady, whenever either of them complained. Turned out he was right—she and her brother had survived.

Kara took one more look at Marco Polo, shook herself back to indifferent, and put her headphones on. In the time it would take to finish her run, she would have forgotten all about the sad, failed Fortes. *They should have done better, worked harder*, she told herself as sweat soaked the brim of her cap. Kara started up the hill that would twist two more times before delivering her home. She wondered, not for the first time in the past few months, if who she'd become was who she was meant to be.

Logan Rye wasn't superstitious, but he did believe in good and bad energy or karma. People got back what they put out. For that reason, he was a little reluctant when Tony Forte called to tell him Marco Polo was going under and he would give Logan a great deal on anything he wanted. It felt like benefitting from someone else's misfortune, but Logan went anyway. He'd given the Fortes a more-than-fair price for the food processor and a few copper core pans. Logan was a sucker for copper. He hugged Pam, wished them both the very best, and left through the side door leading into the alley.

Apparently the universe didn't care about his more-than-fair price or his best wishes, because right before he stepped out of the alley, karma punched him in the face. Kara Malendar was sitting on a bench across the street, right in front of his truck.

Shit! He should have just wished Tony good luck over the phone and stayed home, but no, here he was taking a couple of steps back into an alley and hoping the only woman to have put his heart through a meat grinder hadn't seen him. Not that she would run over and throw her arms around him even if she did happen to notice him. Yeah, that fantasy died a long time ago.

She still had legs for miles and he was sure those same hazel eyes that used to crawl right into his soul were tucked somewhere beneath the cap she was clearly hiding under. Logan knew he would bump into Kara Malendar eventually. After all, he was a newbie restaurant owner; didn't her kind prey on his? No one wanted an enemy at the *LA Times*. He'd have to find his way to cordial, but that wasn't going to happen today. He wasn't in the mood and definitely wasn't ready.

He did allow himself one more look. She was too thin, too pensive, and even from a distance, a little sad. That part he hadn't expected. In the few short months they had spent together his senior year of college, she had never seemed sad—the opposite actually. Kara Malendar, or Winnie Parker as she'd been known to everyone in their cultural food exchange program, was a little shy at first, but then she simply exploded with color.

At the memory, Logan suddenly became aware of his heart in his chest. Her hair was pulled back now, but he remembered Paris and the gold streaks of curly blonde hair. Winnie wore bright peasant tops and no makeup. She was spectacular. He couldn't keep his eyes off her back then, and eventually they couldn't keep their hands off each other. Logan looked out from the alley as Kara stood and turned to leave. How could all of that breath-stealing, uninhibited sunshine turn into Kara Malendar, cynical food critic? It seemed a shame, but it wasn't like she cared what he thought anyway. Whatever game she had been playing in Paris was over a long time ago. He would admit it took him a while to forget the depths of her eyes and the silky curve of her body, but he had. Most women in his experience were game players, and Kara Malendar had proven herself a master.

Once he was sure she was gone, Logan crossed the street, loaded the box in the back of his truck, and by the time he arrived at his new restaurant his heart had settled down.

Entering his kitchen through the back door, he found Travis finishing up the pizza dough and mushrooms for the lunch crowd that would hopefully arrive in about four hours.

"Whatcha got there?" Travis asked as he floured, balled, and placed his morning's work in the dough boxes lined with parchment.

"Fire sale at Marco Polo." Logan put the box down in his office, which acted more like a storage room than anything else.

"Aw, man! Really?"

"Afraid so." Logan stepped over to the utility sink to wash his hands.

"Their bruschetta was the best. Shit, I had my last decent date there. Another one bites the dust. Make you nervous?"

"I'm not sure nervous is the right word." Logan dried his hands. "Gets me up earlier, puts me to bed later. I mean that's all we can do right?"

"And cook kick-ass food."

Logan laughed. "That too."

"So what do you think it was? I mean, I like to analyze this stuff. Figure out what they did wrong, so I can make myself feel better." Travis stacked the finished dough boxes.

"I don't know." Logan shook his head. "Who knows why anyone succeeds or fails? I mean shit, Applebee's is still in business. Nothing makes sense." He put pieces of the food processor into one of the dishwasher bins.

"True, but if you needed to make your favorite sous chef feel better . . ." Travis gave him a pleading look. "Help a man rest easy."

Logan shrugged because there was nothing he could say that would ease the constant uncertainty of the restaurant business.

"Oh come on, we both know you've thought about it." Travis turned, leaning on the counter now.

Logan sighed. "They never found their groove, I guess." As soon as the words came out of his mouth, he felt like he was jinxing himself, speaking ill of the unlucky. Because it was luck, wasn't it? He considered Marco Polo's demise as he broke down the box he'd brought in and the three others up against the wall from last night's wine delivery. No, he didn't believe in luck. Hard work—that's what he was raised on and he had to believe it's what separated his from the hundreds of other restaurants trying to succeed. Hard work, good energy, and great people who knew more than he did—those were the keys.

Travis was still looking to him for comfort.

Logan let out a steady breath. "Their parking lot was too small and the valet company they used kept screwing up. They lost customers because it was a bitch to even get in there. Their bartenders were inconsistent, and they had almost fifty percent turnover with their wait staff. I don't think their clientele ever felt like they knew the place."

Travis smiled, so Logan finished strong.

"And Pam's sauce was too sweet, too many carrots."

"There he is! I knew you had a list, my fearless leader. I feel better already." Travis wiped his brow with his forearm.

Logan smiled, walked into his office, and returned with two pages torn from a yellow pad.

"That being said, here's my punch list for this place."

He handed the pages to Travis and watched his ego deflate.

"The top ten are ongoing overall issues. Makenna is taking the lead on most of those, but I need you to deal with the last one. The left walk-in is a mess. I'm not sure what system you've got going on in there, but it needs to be redone."

Travis glanced toward the huge refrigerator taking up most of the wall behind them and nodded.

"The other fourteen items at the bottom are things I observed last night. When we all meet later, I'll go over those, but I wanted to give you a heads up. Most glaring, the eggplant on our bruschetta was overcooked, and I'm not sure what's going on with the grater, but the shreds of white cheddar on the spinach salad are too big. It's overpowering. We need to figure that out and tone it down by lunch today."

Travis read the list with wide eyes that traveled to Logan and then back to the list. He didn't say a word and Logan laughed at the look on his face.

"Okay, so back to work." He patted Travis on the back. "We don't want to be next." Logan left to turn the floor lights on. He'd cut some new flowers for the giant vase standing among the round tables. It was a tall copper pot really, and they tried to change out the flowers every few days. The last ones were all wrong, so Logan replaced them and noted which windows needed to be recleaned once Summer, their hostess, arrived in a few hours. He heard bins being dragged around and the opening and closing of cabinets back in the kitchen, along with Travis cursing. That was always a good sign that work was getting done.

Chapter Two

Kara was already in the office, tea brewing, by 7:15 the next morning. She was looking forward to trying the new white tea she'd picked up last weekend while she was at the beach. She was not, however, looking forward to sorting through the e-mails now on her screen. Her review of a new Thai restaurant in east Hollywood was trending, according to the all-caps title of an e-mail from Olivia Palm, her editor. Just as she clicked on the e-mail to read further, the woman herself was standing in the doorway of Kara's office.

"So, look at that, people are just as fond of your 'happy sunshine' reviews as they are of your always popular 'you suck' reviews," Olivia said, chewing her quinoa breakfast bar.

"Apparently." Kara tried for enthused as she sipped her tea, but truth be told, she hated that she was hailed for saying ugly things about people trying to make a go of it in the restaurant business.

"Was it painful being nice?"

"No, I can be very nice." Kara smoothed the blotter on her desk and glanced up as Olivia raised her perfectly waxed brow.

"Fine, maybe not nice, but I'm honest. They had fantastic pork belly, the place settings were immaculate, and the wait staff were perfect. Hands down the best Pad See Ew I have ever tasted and we both know I've done a lot of Thai in the last few years."

"True." Olivia chewed the last bite of her bar. She moved toward Kara's desk, threw her wrapper out, and took a seat, crossing her flawless stocking-clad legs. "So how's that piece on panettone coming?"

"Finished it this morning." Kara pulled the article up on her computer and pivoted her Mac screen so Olivia could see.

"Oh, that's a great shot." Olivia leaned her silk-covered arms on Kara's desk for a better look. It was a picture of the sweet holiday bread, fresh out of the oven. "Did Jeremy get those?"

Kara nodded.

"I'm telling you the man has a way with a lens," Olivia sighed in a way she really should have kept to herself.

Kara was again at a loss for a response. Olivia and Jeremy had a sort of friends-with-benefits relationship a few months back. The entire office knew about it, but Olivia never said a word. She just made suggestive references every time Jeremy or his work was mentioned. Whether Olivia knew she was doing it was anyone's guess. According to Braxton, their copyeditor and fact-check master, her sexual subconscious was likely at work.

"Yes, he does take great pictures." Kara turned her monitor back around. "I'm e-mailing this to you right now."

"Perfect. I want it polished and ready to run right after Thanksgiving. I'd like to do something each week leading up to Christmas and Hanukkah. Did you see Ed's review of that new English pub?"

Kara shook her head.

"Christ, it was god-awful. I understand that the kid is fresh off his hometown newspaper, but nowhere—never—do I need to see a picture of someone actually eating fish and chips. And who the hell describes tartar sauce as chunkalicious? Not a word."

Kara laughed and Olivia let out a dramatic sigh.

"Damn small-town amateurs."

"Olivia, Ed is from Chicago."

"A suburb—and did HR ever actually verify he hails from Chicago? Because I don't believe it."

"So, what did you tell him about the article?" Kara asked, pouring more tea.

"I told him to try again, to which he replied, 'What do you mean by that?'" Olivia sat back. "I'm on my way to his cubicle after I leave you."

Kara sipped her tea.

"Oh, did you notice Marco Polo finally bit the dust?" Olivia asked, checking her manicure.

"I . . . I did see that. Probably just as well." Kara tried to make sure her stupid heart was back where it belonged. The food section of the *LA Times* was no place for humanity.

"Agreed. It'll be a great location for a serious restaurant that knows what it's doing. Your review was spot-on, by the way." Olivia stood and smoothed out her leopard-print pencil skirt. "Well done. Now," she sighed again and brushed the ink-dark bangs off her face, "I'm off to give a hands-on 'try-again' demonstration to Ed from Chicago." She gave a dismissive wave over her shoulder as she sauntered out of the office.

Kara refilled her teacup and began reviewing the rest of her e-mail. Her phone vibrated with a text from her mother:

Reminder – you're expected at the Volunteer Thank-You this Wed. Please dress appropriately, preferably raspberry. It's your signature color! :) :) :)

Kara was pretty sure her brother had taught their mother to text. She would be sure to thank him for that "little slice of heaven," as their Nana would say. Texting had given their mother twenty-four-hour access for her passive-aggressive hinting. There was nothing the woman wouldn't say and now she could follow it with happy faces.

It was an election year, which meant the Malendars were expected to be out in full force and on their best behavior. Her parents had even hired a PR babysitter for her brother. Kara hadn't met Kate, the babysitter, yet, but judging by the way her brother talked about her, Kara was pretty sure that relationship was going from professional to complicated any day now. All Kara's mother had said about Grady's new keeper was that her name was too close to Kara's and it was confusing. As if a mother would confuse her daughter with someone else because her name was similar. "Does that happen?" Kara had wanted to ask her mother with more than a little sarcasm, but she hadn't because she was the obedient daughter, the one who followed the rules. Grady was the wild child of the family and while her brother was one of her favorite people, she often envied his courage. Instead of bold and brave, Kara had a chip on her shoulder she couldn't seem to shake. She decided a while back that being a bitch and distancing herself was easier than feeling. Feeling only reminded her of Paris and what was stolen from her.

Kara opened her desk drawer and pulled out the stack of envelopes she had labeled *Campaign*. They were all dated in the right-hand corner, with a black dot if they required formal attire. Wednesday's invitation was still unopened. Kara usually waited a couple of days before reading any political event invitations. That cut down on the time she had to second-guess and dread. Running her pearl-handled letter opener along the sealed crease of the envelope, she pulled out a single card.

Let's Celebrate You!

Kara rolled her eyes.

Senator and Mrs. Patrick Malendar would like to thank each and every volunteer—

—blah, blah, blah.

We will be hosting a happy hour and buffet-style dinner at—

She stopped reading and set the invitation down. After what her best friend, Jake, called a "deep cleansing breath," she picked it up again. Nope, nothing had changed—it still read the same. Her parents would be hosting their thank-you party at:

The Yard, a cool new local restaurant we've been hearing great things about.
The Yard is owned by hometown chef, Logan Rye.

Well of course, Kara thought, tossing the invitation back into her desk drawer.

The one person from her past who probably hated her to the core. Kara had heard about Logan's restaurant when it opened three months ago, but she had done a very good job avoiding everything concerning The Yard or Logan Rye up to this point. She'd left that entire mess behind in Paris.

"Out of sight, out of mind," she reminded herself every time she crammed some ugly thing to the back of her mind. She'd recently added the Marco Polo review to her mental back drawer, but now Logan Rye, a long-time back-drawer resident, was moving to the front of the class. Thanks to her parents. *Damn it!*

She replied to her mother's text:

I'll be there with bells on!! :) :) :)

Christ, she actually nauseated herself sometimes. Kara let out a slow breath, took a sip of tea, and turned to her computer monitor. She tried to focus on proofing her review of Two Guys Taco Shop, but she kept reading the same sentence over and over again, so she accepted that focusing on anything other than the invitation was a waste of time.

The weekend crowd flow was still a little patchy. Friday had been dead, but they were slammed on Saturday, which was strange because there was a local football game Friday and Logan assumed people would have—*Aw hell*, he thought, none of it made any sense.

He simply needed to do the work, keep getting their name out there, and make kick-ass food, as Travis liked to put it. Logan poured himself a cup of coffee behind the bar.

It was Monday morning, the start of a new week. He had spent yesterday in his garden, trying to clear his head and cultivating his own little farm. Although his father and brother would laugh their asses off if they heard him call it that. They ran a *real* farm—that's what they would say, and they would be right—but Logan's little piece of earth was still pretty impressive. What had started off as a garden had grown into something much more. Logan loved working the land and growing food. It seemed so vital, essential to who he was, and when most of his week was filled with Makenna barking at him to post more content to The Yard's Facebook page or figuring out why most of his servers were either stoned or obnoxiously enthusiastic, his garden was a refuge.

The carrots had come in beautifully and he now had more kale then he knew what to do with. He'd started some seeds for his next planting, and it seemed in another week or two, Travis would have the rutabaga he'd requested back in June. Travis had made Logan pork tenderloin with cider jus and rutabaga for his birthday and it was nothing short of amazing, so of course Logan wanted it featured on the fall menu.

Almost every thought in Logan's waking life was consumed by food—either planting it, sourcing it from somewhere that made him proud, or cooking it. He allowed a few hours for sleep, and then the rest of his "free" time was spent with his family, discussing, arguing, or doing his part at Ryeland Farms. He supposed it was a good life, but he was tired.

"Stupid douche bag."

That was all Logan heard as he set his coffee down and rounded the bar toward the front of the restaurant.

His sister, Makenna Rye Conroy, her long brown hair pulled into a knot, shouldered through the front door. Her muck boots told him she'd already been to the farm, most likely to help their father feed. The woman did more before noon than most people did all day. She was typing a message on her phone with one hand and in her arms she balanced a water bottle, folders, her purse, three large pieces of leather, and a pair of tennis shoes. She resembled a game of Jenga, and Logan wasn't sure if he should touch anything for fear it would all come tumbling down. She anchored one hip on the closest barstool, thumbing her phone and still holding everything.

"Did you want to me to take some of that, or am I the douche bag?"

Nothing, just more thumbing and a large exhale of breath.

"Kenna." He tried again to get her attention as he locked the front door.

"Hmm?" She finally dropped the contents of her arms on the bar in front of her. "Oh shit. Sorry." Realizing she'd put shoes on the clean bar, she moved them to the stool next to her, set her phone down, and turned to Logan.

"Rough morning?" he asked.

"No more than usual, why?"

"Well, you have what looks like"—he leaned forward and touched the glob on the shoulder of her black sweater—"chewed up . . . cracker, maybe?"

Kenna examined her shoulder, pulling the arm of her sweater forward to get a better look. "Oh yeah, Paige didn't want to go to day care this morning. There's some kid on the afternoon-session kindergarten bus who she finds, wait for it, 'intolerable.'" Kenna let out the tired laugh of a single mom in love with every detail about her daughter. "Can you believe she actually used that word?" She shook her head and grabbed a napkin off the bar to remove the glob. "We stopped at McDonald's on the way in. Did you know they still have animal crackers?"

"Do you feel any guilt feeding your daughter fast-food when your brother owns a restaurant?"

"Nope." Makenna looked at her phone again.

"Well, you should. Do you have any idea what the fast-food industry has done to our society? All it does is foster substandard—"

Makenna covered his mouth with the hand not zipping through her phone. "Shhh"—she set her phone down again—"no one wants to hear from your soapbox this early in the morning."

Logan stuck his tongue out and Makenna immediately dropped her hand, wiping it on her jeans.

"Eww, you're gross and still, like, five years old."

Logan laughed. "So, who's the douche bag?"

"Huh? Oh, right. This," she picked up her phone and began frantically trying to get something on the screen. "This douche bag left a review for us on Yelp and I quote, 'the waitresses are hot, but their onion rings,' spelled T-H-E-R-E, 'sucked. They were cold.' Frowny face."

"We don't have onion rings." Logan leaned over to look at her phone.

"I know. If you read the rest of this moron's misspelled review, it's clear he's talking about The Yard House. You know, the sports bar?"

Logan was confused.

"Please tell me you know what The Yard House is?"

"Of course I do. I'm just confused why we got their review. And are their waitresses really hot?"

Makenna hit his arm and Logan laughed.

"I have no idea, nor do I care. What I care about is that this re-view brought down our rating. I hate Yelp. There's no damn filter. Any idiot can go on there and leave crap. I'm okay with the legit ones if you don't like the food or the place was dirty, but if you're going to say our onion rings suck and give us one star, could you fucking make sure we serve onion rings?"

Logan said nothing. She'd been his sister for thirty years; he knew when to sit back and let her rant.

"Sorry, it's just that people use these sites, Logan. Some might even pass on giving us a try based on stars or forks or whatever. I e-mailed Yelp's technical support, but Lord knows how long that will take. It's the name. People are searching Yard House and stop at The Yard."

"Well, there's nothing we can do about that. They should correct it eventually, right?"

"Yeah, but it's not good to have this out there. We already have the one from last month. Remember the creepy toothless guy who left us one star and said he hated that we took over the lumber yard because he used to 'cop a squat' under the awning to keep himself and his grocery cart out of the rain?"

Logan laughed. "I loved that one. It's printed and up on my fridge at home. Made me almost want to build another awning somewhere. I'm still wondering how a homeless guy got to a computer and if he did, why would he take the time?"

Makenna's face was stone. "One star, Logan. We can't afford one-star anything at this point."

He sighed. Never in a million years when he was busting his ass at Margot's in Seattle and dreaming of his own place did he think these would be the things he would be dealing with. "I know, but we can only do so much. According to Summer—"

"Which one's Summer again?"

"The hostess, curly hair," he said.

She nodded.

"Anyway, Summer told me some woman was leaving last night and commented that she loved the food, thought the place was great, but our white napkins left lint all over her black pants. We're never going to please everyone, Kenna. We have to let some of this shit go."

"Able to let that one go were ya? How long did it take you to order the black napkins?" Makenna's thumb paused midair over her phone as she raised her eyebrows at Logan.

"Last night," he sighed and dropped his head to the bar. He told himself all the way home he didn't care that his napkins were white, but by the time he crawled into bed, he'd convinced himself the lady had a point, got back out of bed, and ordered the damn things.

"Yeah, that whole Zen, let-it-be shit only works when you're watching the sunset and even then only until the phone rings. That's why monks don't run restaurants."

"I suppose that's true." Logan finished his last sip of coffee.

"I'll follow up." Makenna walked behind the bar and pour herself a large Coke. "Both of these reviews need to be taken down. I'm on it. All part of the job."

"Breakfast of champions?" He pointed to her drink.

"You know it." She held her glass up in a toast.

Logan shook his head.

"Fine, I'll add some fruit." She grabbed a few cherries and a straw. Taking a very long sip, she closed her eyes in pleasure and was instantly energized, ready to go.

Watching his sister spring to life, Logan thought maybe he should ditch the coffee and return to the Mountain Dew of his college years.

"So, what are the fires today?" she asked and he handed her a page from his yellow pad.

Bringing Makenna on board was one of the best business decisions he'd ever made. She had the Rye family drive and she loved spreadsheets and numbers, all the parts he hated.

"We've got the senator's volunteer thing Wednesday night, unless they cancelled? Please tell me they didn't cancel." She started adding the items on his list to her own longer one.

"Nope, still on."

Makenna let out a sigh. "Thank God. That's going to be huge. Lots of people who haven't tried us yet, and because it's volunteers, it won't only be hoity-toities. Real people will be there too."

Logan laughed. "What does that mean?"

"It means the normal, eating-out population will be represented. We like them."

"And what about the senator's crowd?"

"Eh, they're good too. I mean an eater is an eater, but they're usually more trouble than they're worth. Shitty tippers."

"Wow, isn't that some kind of profiling?"

"Sure is."

"And you're okay with that?"

"Just calling 'em like I see 'em. I need to put this stuff away." She stood and loaded her arms again. "I have to go prepare myself before our new server shows up and starts complaining about how she needs more hours." Kenna rolled her eyes.

"I probably don't pay you enough," Logan called after her.

She threw her head back as she retreated into the kitchen, pushing through the large door. "Truth, the man speaks the truth!"

Logan laughed, wiped down the bar, and turned on the overhead speakers. Fallout Boy's "My Songs Know What You Did in the Dark (Light Em Up)" filled the restaurant. Travis would be there in about twenty minutes. Logan hummed the lyrics as thundering drums spilled into the dining area. He turned on the front lights and opened the screens to the patio. By the time the lead singer howled the chorus for the last time, he had some great ideas for the senator's event. He would serve their brisket and ask Travis his thoughts on which sides should go with it. By the end of the day, Logan hoped to have the menu for the senator's event nailed down and any thoughts about the senator's daughter pushed back where they belonged.

Chapter Three

Kara was on the Rose Bowl loop track by 5:30 Wednesday morning, her *Kick My Own Ass* playlist paused and ready as she
stretched and adjusted her laces. It was a clear, but chilly September morning. A group of cyclists passed and she pulled her sleeves
over her thumbs, squeezed the play button on her headphones,
and set out to clear her cluttered mind.

As she closed in on mile one, he was still in the forefront of her
thoughts. From the pictures and interviews she had read when
The Yard first opened, Logan was bigger now and even more sure
of himself than he was back then. The memory of the first time
she'd laid eyes on him would no longer stay where she willed it and
burst forward as mile two approached.

They had been paired up as partners at the Le Cordon Bleu
cooking school in Paris. They were both UCLA students and had
never met before, but there they were in white aprons at a classroom table thousands of miles away from home. It was strange
how things happened.

"Logan Rye," he'd said, extending his hand with an ease Kara
called "campus causal." She had noticed it when she arrived at
UCLA her freshman year. The walk, the talk, the way people greeted

one another—it was something she didn't have much exposure to in her eighteen years prior to college. Sure, her brother, Grady, had an ease about him, but it was still a bit studied, a bit calculated. It came from growing up as they had, in a fishbowl. After being at UCLA for two or three days, Kara learned there were people who carried themselves as if no one was watching because, well, no one was. It was heady and she loved it, at least from afar.

So, thousands of miles away from school and into her junior year, Logan Rye was that ease, that comfort. She shook his hand and noticed immediately that it was large, warm, and callused. Not a lot of artistic guys, working with food or otherwise, had callused hands. As she quickly glanced up at him, she realized Logan didn't look like the typical artist by a long shot. Even then, he presented more like a farmer than a budding chef.

"Winnie, Winnie Parker," she had replied. She no longer tripped over her introduction because she'd practiced it enough in the mirror. Although, Kara was still working on remembering to turn around when someone called out, "Winnie."

"Winnie, great. Nice to meet you." Logan opened his folder. "Do you have a lot of cooking experience?"

"No, first time in a cooking class. I've watched our family's cook—" Kara caught herself. "Cooking shows, my family watches a lot of cooking shows, but that's about it. How about you?"

"I've worked in a restaurant since freshman year of high school, picked up some things here and there, but I'm looking forward to some formal training."

Kara smiled. She wasn't sure what else to say or who she should be at that point.

"Of course, I can't understand most of what Madame Auclair is saying, even though I'm pretty sure it's English." He laughed, but quickly stopped when Madame Auclair cleared her throat and walked past their table.

Kara gestured to the proper place on the handout. They were going over the basics of their cooking tool set. Each student was given one and they were at "paring knife basics." Logan noticed where her finger pointed and nodded. Kara momentarily forgot her notations were in French. She found it easier to stick with one language when abroad, but realized they would be of no use to her partner.

"Wait, you speak French?" Logan asked before she could figure out whether or not she needed to hide that detail too.

She nodded, focusing on the knife grip Madame Auclair was demonstrating at the front of the class.

"Huh, that's cool." Logan grabbed his knife, holding it exactly right on the first try as if it was second nature. He began slicing in that rocking motion. He may not have looked like an artist, but the movement of his hands was a bit mesmerizing.

Kara had the grip, but the rhythm was different. It felt a bit odd because she'd always thought of chopping as up and down. Logan reached over, molded his hand over hers, and steadied her movement.

Now approaching mile three, Kara could still remember the moment he touched her, the minute her heart jumped in her chest like that of a child running to the window for a better look.

People rarely got close enough to touch Kara—certainly not some guy she had just met. She didn't know what to do back then, so she let go of the knife and it clanked loudly against the steel workstation. Logan laughed and returned his eyes to the handout propped up in front of them.

"Have you taken French for a while now?"

"Since junior high," Kara answered, leaving out the part that she also had a nanny growing up who spoke French and tutored her. "I don't speak it much anymore, but it does come in handy here." She smiled at him.

"Yeah, I'm sure it does, it being Paris and all." Logan's mouth curved into a grin she recognized as both sarcastic and sexy.

Their conversations continued like that—simple and uncomplicated—for a few days. They became partners, learned to work well together, and Kara found herself relaxed around him. Paris became this place where she could be someone else. She grew to love Winnie Parker, until—

Sweat dripped past her cap and into her face. Kara turned up her music, pushed through mile four, and kept going. The track was only 3.2 miles and she would normally be past done by now, but today she was running it twice. She could feel her breath control slipping, and her calves burned. This, she thought, was the reason she ran. The harder she pushed, the more she gave, and the fainter the memory. All she had to do was push and the feelings would disappear, too. If she focused on her feet hitting the pavement, she would forget about the other memories now clamoring to the top, all because she allowed one in. The day they spent in Montmartre, falafel, and the absolute unexpected freedom of kissing a boy at sunset. She had loved herself in Paris and was certain she had fallen in love with Logan. Everything made sense there . . . but then suddenly nothing made sense at all. Nothing seemed fair. That's when Kara became an adult and realized the limits of her life: what she could and couldn't have.

Her breathing gave out just as she finished the sixth mile. She stopped, put her hands on her knees, and tried to regulate. After a few breaths, she walked the rest of the way to her car, then pulled a towel from her bag and sat in the driver's seat for a minute.

She never heard from him after she left Paris and she certainly hadn't blamed him. After all, she'd left him standing in the lobby of his apartment building with nothing to hold on to but a lie. A few months after returning home, Kara wondered if he would call or e-mail, but he didn't and eventually she put Logan Rye away in a box with all her other souvenirs from her time in the sunlight.

Now eight years later she would see him again. He wasn't married, she remembered that from the article, but Kara was pretty sure Logan had learned his lesson when it came to her. He would keep his distance, she was certain, but he wouldn't need to worry. Kara was safely in her cage this time. As she started her car and drove home, she wondered for a moment what it would be like if she arrived at the Volunteer Thank-You event tonight as Winnie Parker, because she sure as hell didn't want to show up as Kara Malendar.

Finishing up the corn salad for Senator Malendar's event, Logan needed scallions from the front kitchen. Travis was flirting with two women at the pizza counter and sautéing at the same time. Flirting and cooking. Travis was a legend, Logan thought as he moved past him toward the pizza oven.

"Logan," Travis called out, adding a little pasta water to the sauce he was spinning over an open flame. "Logan here is the owner, ladies."

"Really," the brunette purred in a way that made Logan wonder if somehow his scratchy over-tired eyes and wrinkled shirt were sexy.

He smiled politely, grabbed some chopped scallions from the cold box under the pizza counter, and shook his head at Travis.

"What?" Travis whispered as Logan moved past him again. "They are totally into food guys."

Logan's brow furrowed. "Food guys?"

"Yeah, you know . . . us." He gestured between the two of them and Logan was amazed he managed a straight face.

"We're food guys? Jesus man, are things that bad out there in the dating world? You're using food?" Logan asked, laughing. Travis quickly plated his Bolognese, tossed the pan into the bin, and followed Logan to the back kitchen.

"Food is sexy."

"Is it now?" Logan shook his head again and started adding scallions to his corn salad.

"Those women are hot, man. When was the last time you went on a date?"

"A date? Travis, when was the last time *you* went on a date? I'm not sure you've ever actually been on a real date. Here's a hint—it involves a meal or sometimes even a movie." Logan added salt to the salad.

"I always cook for the women I sleep with, and nine times out of ten, we watch a movie in bed."

Logan laughed, tasted his salad, added some more pepper flakes, and handed a taste to Travis.

"That's perfect." Travis tossed the spoon into the dishwasher bin and continued his pitch. "So, are you saying you are not interested in taking those two lovely, willing, and able ladies to dinner?"

Logan was still laughing as he came back from the walk-in.

"When exactly would that date take place?"

"I was thinking tonight."

"After we close?"

"Yeah."

"At eleven?" Logan confirmed.

"Yeah, you in?" Travis asked and Logan was amazed.

"I don't even know how to help you anymore. No, I'm not in. One, I think my new rule is that I will not be dating the clientele. Two, to use a Makenna term, only a douche bag picks up a woman at eleven o'clock for a 'date.'" Logan held up air quotes for emphasis.

"Yeah, well Ken calls me a douche bag all the time, so I suppose the shoe fits. You're sure, man? The brunette is a gymnast." Travis wiggled his eyebrows.

Logan secured the cover on his salad and shook his head.

"Fine, miss out. I've got to get back out there before Todd burns the place down."

"You know Makenna hates it when you call her Ken, right?"

Travis took a quick look over his shoulder, scrunched his face like a kid on a playground, and said, "Yeah, that's why I do it."

As Travis left through the kitchen door, Logan heard him redirect his attention to his new audience. "Ladies!"

Food guys? Unbelievable, Logan thought as he unwrapped the briskets he needed to get into the oven.

Senator Malendar's reservation specified between 250 and 300 people. Makenna had searched the event on the senator's website so she could share it on The Yard's Facebook page. While she had been excited about new potential clientele, all Logan managed to notice was the wording, "Senator Malendar and family." That meant Kara would be in his restaurant in a little under six hours.

For a moment he thought she might not show, but if Logan had learned one thing about Kara Malendar, it was that her family and her responsibilities meant more to her than anything else.

He could respect that part of her because he knew all about family and responsibility. Hell, there wasn't much he wasn't willing to do or hadn't done for his own. So maybe things would be fine, maybe he would share the same space as her after all these years and—just like the pretty brunette at the bar—he would smile and know that he had little or no interest. He'd moved on; she'd moved on. Although Logan did happen to notice she wasn't wearing a wedding ring in the staff picture on the *LA Times* website. Okay, so he'd Googled her. That meant nothing. He was curious, it was two in the morning, he found himself unable to sleep, and he Googled her. That was just natural curiosity, he told himself as he closed the oven on his briskets.

Chapter Four

Kara walked through the huge metal warehouse-looking front door of The Yard a few minutes after six. Her mother had asked her to be fifteen minutes early, but she'd been having a small mental breakdown in her car only a few moments earlier, so Bindi Malendar would have to deal with fashionably late. It wasn't a breakdown actually; it was more of a power talk with herself, complete with some pounding on the steering wheel and maybe a few mock conversations with the rearview mirror. Alone. She may have been acting out both sides of said conversations.

Fine, a tiny breakdown, but she was entitled.

Seriously, what were the chances that her parents, the king and queen of the five-star restaurant, would choose this place? It was super inconvenient that the one night they decided to 'normal' up had to be at a restaurant owned by the very man who had made love to their daughter for the first time in her life on a rainy evening in Paris. God, she thought, closing her eyes toward the very end of her breakdown, please let him be balding or fat or out sick, because even after eight years, she could still see the stretch of his shoulders as he rested over her on his forearms. She still remembered his jawline, his hands touching her as he moved right through the center of her body and taught her what it meant to feel. A woman simply didn't forget memories like that, no matter how much time passed. The only thing she could do once it was all gone and taken from her was box it up, bury it deep, and remind herself at least once a year exactly where those types of feelings got her.

"Kara, darling." Her mother approached the moment she stepped into the bar area of the restaurant.

"Hello, Mother." Kara returned a kiss to her cheek.

"Isn't this place fun? So kitschy, right?"

Kara thought of places like Cracker Barrel as kitschy, but she supposed anything without silk wallpaper was kitschy to her mother.

"It's very nice," was all Kara could muster because, in truth, the smell of food was intoxicating. To her complete surprise, her stomach started to growl. Kara simply didn't crave food anymore. She attributed it to her job and constantly being around food, but clearly her body was trying to tell her something. Of course her mother heard.

"Oh my, someone's hungry. Well, eating will have to wait; your father and Grady are already out on the patio with all four volunteer coordinators. You are late." She took Kara's hand and led her through the bar. Kara barely had time to notice the gorgeous concrete floors and the exposed plumbing. The patio was through two enormous garage doors that had been rolled up. The Yard, at least from what Kara could tell while she was being dragged to yet another photo op, was incredible.

Out on the patio, Stanley, her father's campaign manager, tsk-tsked her for being late. She smiled and apologized as she usually did in Stanley's company. She kissed her father, rolled her eyes in tandem with her brother, and then fell in line as the snapping cameras captured Senator Patrick Malendar's perfect family. There were a few shots of the family casually laughing at absolutely nothing and then a couple more of them pretending to be ridiculously interested in something a volunteer coordinator was saying. Kara had never met the man before and yet there was a shot of her playing patty-cake with his toddler daughter. The entire thing was surreal and ridiculous, but it was the world her parents lived in and whether she liked it or not, that made it part of her world.

When Stanley finally moved on to shots of the senator and his lovely wife sitting with some of the volunteers, Kara and Grady were dismissed like schoolchildren.

"That was somewhat painless," Grady said as they both headed back into the bar.

"Not too bad," Kara agreed with a thick layer of sarcasm. "I think the highlight was you and Dad arm wrestling on the picnic table out there."

Grady laughed. "Yeah, I totally let him win. We do that all the time when we are out to dinner. You know, just me and my dad, two regular guys."

They both shook their heads at the absurdity of their situation.

"Hey, have you tried this food?" Grady asked as he pulled her toward the buffet. "This meat is incredible."

"Brisket, it's brisket." Kara glanced at the silver serving tray while Grady put some on a small white plate.

"That's what I thought it was, but this melts. It's unbelievable. Try." He held the fork up to her mouth.

Kara shook her head. "I'm not hungry."

"Sure you are. The way you eat, you're probably hungry all the time. Open up, sis. A girl can't live on tea alone."

He moved it closer to her lips. She could smell the spices and her stomach growled again.

"Fine, one bite." She opened her mouth and took the bite off his fork. Grady was right. It was perfectly braised. Her mouth exploded with flavor. Just the right amount of garlic, and was that chili powder? She knew it was only a bite of beef, but Kara felt her knees go a little weak. Not that Grady needed to know any of that. "It's good. Maybe a little dry."

Grady let out a sigh and then his eyes were drawn to a very pretty redhead entering the bar area.

"Eat something. I'll see you later." He handed her the plate.

"Is that the babysitter?" Kara asked.

"Kate, that's Kate." Grady smiled. Kara was certain she had never seen her brother smile that way before.

"I see, well, don't let me keep you then."

Grady was already gone.

She sat down at a high-top table in the back corner of the bar. The tabletops were made of what appeared to be wheel frames covered in glass. Sort of like the wagon-wheel table in their family ski cabin, but much nicer and less 1976. Kara set the plate down and stared at the food as if she were staring at the chef himself. She wasn't hungry. A growling stomach meant nothing. The smell teased her nose. She dipped a finger in the juice that pooled at the edge of the plate and brought her finger to her lips. Delicious. She glanced around as if she had something to be secretive about and grabbed a napkin rolled around silverware.

Putting the napkin in her lap, she breathed in the aromas and cut herself a small piece. Damn it, even the end piece was tender. It was the same—melting and tinged with heat—a perfect balance. Kara closed her eyes to the chatter and music of the bar and was aware of the cool utensils in her hands. She thought of him for an instant and then ate the entire plate of meat as if it was her first meal in years, each bite growing more flavorful than the next. Her stomach warm, she was lost in the sheer joy of eating. She set her fork and knife down and let out a deep sigh, then glimpsed up for the first time since she had taken the second bite. The crowd was laughing and buzzing, oblivious to her sitting in the corner. Had food ever been this good? She smiled, and as her gaze began to travel back to her plate, she saw him.

Logan Rye was watching her through the window of the exposed kitchen with a look of complete and total satisfaction. It was as if he had won a game she didn't know they were playing. Or had pleasured her in some way. Well, he had admittedly, but he appeared smug. Okay, maybe gorgeous, a little tired, pretty damn near edible himself, but smug all the same. The happiness her stomach had been enjoying only moments before turned to a knot of pissed off. Couldn't he have come out and greeted her like a civil human being instead of lurking from his kitchen while she shared a clearly intimate moment with his brisket? Lurking wasn't fair. Kara felt something she never ever felt anymore—vulnerable. She turned around, hopped off her seat, and carried her plate to find someone, anyone, she knew.

Grady and the babysitter, perfect.

"Kate, it is Kate isn't it?" Kara asked, still reeling.

Kate blinked wide-eyed at Grady as if Kara was some sort of dangerous animal and then nodded.

"Great, well I just wanted to say that my father is running for reelection to the United States Senate, not some county seat in the backwoods." Kara had never even met this woman formally, and she was dumping all over her, but she needed to be a bitch if she wanted to recalibrate.

"Kara, what's this about?" Grady asked.

Kara flipped her hair and put her plate down on the table next to them.

"I'm saying, who picked this place? I mean, this venue, this place, is not exactly up to standards. We're not playing in the farm league for Christ's sake." Oh, that was good, Kara thought. Could farm boy hear her from his lurking spot in the kitchen? She sure as hell hoped so.

Kate seemed like she was about to say something and then her mouth closed and even before Kate's face changed, Kara knew he was behind her. Eight years and her body still knew him.

"Aw, Kara. You say the sweetest things."

Christ, he still sounded like he'd just rolled out of bed, maybe off of some completely satisfied woman. *Jesus, Kara, get a grip!* As she turned, she pretended not to notice the tattoo—that was new—or the size of him or his sexy glasses. She pretended to be unfazed by the yumminess of him and simply rolled her eyes.

"Shouldn't you be back behind the counter, sweating or some-thing?"

Kara deferred to Grady hoping he would laugh or help her out, but he was looking at the lovely Kate who still had her eyes on Logan. Who could blame her?

"Well, you would know all about sweating in the kitchen, wouldn't you?" Logan shot back.

Kara stopped cold. No more games, no more comments. This was her father's campaign. There were important people here and she was to act like a lady at all times. She could hear her mother's voice in her head. She froze and hoped the warning stare she was sending his way would work.

"You're good on the counter too, if memory serves," Logan said.

Kara didn't know her next move as their eyes squared off. Just as she was about to resort to her pleading look, Logan's eyes softened. He smiled, but not at her.

"I'm Logan. Nice to meet you, finally. It's a pleasure hosting your dad at my place," he said, extending his hand to Grady.

Kara turned her back to them and grabbed a drink off a passing tray.

"Grady. Good to meet you," she heard her perpetually gracious brother say. "This is your place? It's fantastic."

"Thanks. It's a real labor of love." Logan looked around his restaurant and then his eyes landed on her again.

Her heart was out of control at this point. What if he said something to her brother? What if he mentioned Paris?

Get ahold of yourself, Kara. It's not like he's going to say, "Hey, did you know I once brought your sister to the point of waking up the neighbors, using only my tongue, and they screamed at her in French?" Kara laughed at the thought and snorted. Oh boy, things were certainly going downhill.

"Been open just over three months," Logan continued and thankfully shifted his focus back to Grady.

"Well done, man. This used to be something didn't it? Was it a garage?"

"Hardware store and a lumber yard."

"Right, I see it now. Cool building. I love what you've done. And the name, The Yard. Perfect."

"Thanks. Can I get you guys anything?"

Kara spun around to that smug smile on his face again. No way she was letting him win this. First he lurked and now he was enjoying himself at her expense.

"This food is atrocious," flew out of her mouth.

"No, it's not." He shook his head slowly and stepped toward her.

Damn it, damn it. Kara stepped back.

"I mean, seriously what were you going for here? The spices are all wrong, flat even." She continued down a path she desperately wanted to exit, but turning and running from the building was not an option. Bitch was her only choice.

"Nope, the flavors are right on and you know it."

"Maybe this just isn't my speed. My palate is a bit more sophisticated than backyard barbecue."

Logan raised his eyebrow and held her gaze. He was poised for her next move, still smug. Damn it, nothing was working.

"That is what you're going for, right?" She examined his restaurant. "Barefoot backyard meat grillin'? You pairin' this with some bathtub gin from the bar there, Logan?" she finished, mocking the casual comfort of his restaurant that she secretly loved.

Logan shook his head slowly, stepped into her again, and Kara couldn't move. He was so close she could feel his body heat as he reached past her and ran his thumb along the plate Kara had set down before she'd started a game she was already losing.

"Looks like you managed to get some of this atrocious food down after all. Empty plates don't lie." Logan brought his thumb to his mouth and sucked. "Damn near perfect spice, I'd say." He smirked and walked away. "Great seeing you again, Kara. Be sure to stop by anytime."

Game, set, match. Damn it!

She turned to find herself all alone in her humiliation. Grady and Kate had probably slowly backed away. She tried not to stomp—it was childish to stomp—and yet she found herself stomping very hard all the way to the ladies' room.

Well, that had been fun, Logan thought, pushing through the kitchen door from the bar. He could practically feel her glare on the back of his neck as she followed behind him and then cut into the bathroom. The warmth felt good, kind of like going outside on a summer day after being in the air conditioning. The heat was back, but Logan didn't mind. He'd always preferred crazy Kara. Crazy curly hair, crazy colors, crazy in bed. Logan smiled at the memory and then shook his head. *Get back to work, idiot.*

Once a liar, always a liar, that's what his brother, Garrett, had told him when he was thirteen and busted for smoking in the garage. It had been his first time and even though he had managed to throw the cigarette behind the woodpile when he heard Garrett coming, the smoke lingered. Garrett asked him if he'd been stupid enough to smoke, pushed him a little, and then leered at him and said, "Think before you answer. Once a liar, always a liar." Logan had fessed up, never touched cigarettes again, and remembered his brother's words to this day. He hadn't seen Kara coming the first time, but oh, he saw her for who she was this time.

He still wasn't sure why she was pissed. Was it because he'd seen her damn near having an orgasm over his brisket? No shame in that, it was great brisket. He'd smiled when she'd glanced up and caught him watching her. Why the hell she needed to then rip his food apart, he would probably never understand. He was the one who should be pissed, and even that was a long time ago. He gave up trying to understand Kara Malendar the day he learned her real name. None of it mattered now—he'd seen her, spoken to her—now it was done and time to move on.

The event was in full swing and it seemed like it was going well. That's what was important.

"What the hell was that?" Kara burst through the kitchen door clearly marked "Staff Only."

"Back so soon?" Logan barely spared her a glance.

Kara put her hands on her hips. She was in black jeans and some red-purple-colored blouse. What was that color, raspberry maybe? It didn't matter; in any color, she was still too thin and entirely too smooth. Her hair was smoothed down and tamed and there was even something smooth and staged about her movements.

"Cut it out, Logan. What are you doing?"

"Just playing the game, princess."

"Don't call me that." She gestured to the front of the restaurant. "I don't need anyone knowing my past."

"You mean your dirty past. Wait, does that make me the dirty little secret?"

Kara rolled her eyes, losing a little of her smooth.

"You're an idiot."

Logan laughed. "I must be doing something right because you're back here, all flushed and pissed. It's kind of hot, I don't mind saying."

"Look at me." She approached and put both hands on the counter next to Logan.

"I'm looking." He finished up sorting through cherry tomatoes, as if he and Kara were talking about the most banal thing. No way she would see that he was ruffled in the slightest or that he could see down her shirt to the lacy bra holding what he knew from experience were damn near perfect breasts.

"My family is here tonight. You have no right to go out there a . . . and say those types of things to me."

"Okay, but you can rip my place apart in front of important, possibly influential customers? How's that fair? I had to do something to shut you up. We've only been open a few months. A mouth like yours . . ."

No doubt Kara was biting the side of that mouth, most likely to keep herself from smacking him. He'd deserved it at that point, but he couldn't seem to stop playing.

"A mouth like that could get me, I mean my place, into trouble," he finished and then wiped his hands and turned to lean up against the counter.

"Is this some kind of game to you?" she asked.

He could tell she was trying to calm down.

"I don't do games, Kara."

"Neither do I."

"Oh, princess, you're the whole damn toy store."

"Please, just stop," she pleaded and he caved.

Logan let out a breath. "I'm not playing with you. I mean I was out there, but you were being . . . nasty. You're pissed because you had to be here and you were taking it out on my food. Not cool. By the way, I saw you scarfing down the brisket. Do they feed you in the ivory tower?"

Kara shot him a warning look and he could tell she was teeing up for some hysterical, crazy lady rant.

"I do not scarf."

Logan raised an eyebrow. "Sort of looked that way."

"I was hungry and . . . I don't owe you an explanation."

"True, but the food is not bad. It's damn good to be more specific. Make sure you mention that and stay objective if The Yard is ever chosen by your almighty newspaper for review."

"Your food is . . . decent."

Logan laughed. "Oh man, that's worse than bad. Decent is the kiss of death."

Kara smiled. He could tell she didn't mean to, but he eased them back into fun banter. He was still poking, just not as hard.

"Fine. Your food, at least what I tasted, was good. As for the review, you don't need to worry about that. You've barely settled in. I'm sure the *Times* won't be interested at this point."

Logan scratched the back of his head. "Okay, well that's good to know. I'm sure you'll let me know when I'm worthy. I've got work to do, so if you could . . ."

He gestured to the door and saw Kara flush with what seemed like embarrassment. She was being asked to leave and even though he didn't really know Kara Malendar, he guessed she wasn't used to that.

"Right. Fine. Well, please refrain from sharing childish references to our . . . whatever the hell that was." She turned to leave.

"Our time in the city of love? Our brief fling?"

Kara turned with a look that ordered him to stop. Yeah, Logan was never one for orders.

"Our little adventure, maybe? Oh, I've got it: our hot, steamy, up-against-the-wall, on-the-floor—"

He stopped when Kara left, flinging the door closed behind her, and then his body rumbled with laughter. That had been fun, maybe a little too much fun because at one point Logan wanted to push her up against the wall and hold her hands above her while he—

"We're stretching the tomato garlic salad, but we're going to need more pretty fast." Travis's voice cut into Logan's fantasy just in time. He handed up the salad.

"Perfect, I think they're loving us!" Travis was like an excited kid.

"I think so," was all Logan managed and then he went to the back sink to splash cold water on his face.

He was either stupid or needed to get laid because nowhere in his right, rational mind did getting anywhere near Kara Malendar make sense.

Once a liar, always a liar. Yeah, yeah. Shut the hell up, Garrett, Logan thought, soaking his face once more.

Chapter Five

*A*fter another busy weekend, Logan was up before the sun. He swam almost 4,000 meters in the hour he'd set aside for the gym. He wasn't much of a gym guy. He preferred getting his exercise outdoors, but lately it felt as if he spent every minute at The Yard, so an hour at the gym was all he could squeeze in. Logan needed to do something every morning to get his body going and his head together.

He learned the value of a sore and happy body in high school. At six foot three and two hundred and twenty pounds, he was the biggest swimmer for the Bedford High Eagles. Garrett had given him crap and used to shoot his Speedos across the living room at him, but his family was always in the stands cheering him on. When he went to UCLA, Logan got sick of being called "big guy," so he decided to use his size and play water polo. He loved the competition and camaraderie, but now that he was an adult, he appreciated the peace and quiet of simply swimming laps.

He was showered and throwing his bag into his truck by 7 a.m. He needed to be at the restaurant by 7:30 when the meat delivery arrived.

He turned the lights on in the kitchen, just as Anna and Lacey pulled up in their signature Mini Cooper delivery car. Both women were trained butchers, second generation, and local. They were old-school, from the way they treated their animals to the way they cut their meat. All of their animals were pasture raised and grew up naturally. It was slower, but it was fair, to Logan's mind. The things done to animals in the name of mass-produced food was sickening and he sought out like-minded vendors.

"Hey there gorgeous." Anna loaded up a cart with his meat order. Logan had recently started working with them and they delivered his order personally. He imagined after a while he would no longer get all the love and attention, so he took advantage of it while he could.

"How are my two favorite butchers?" He held the door for them.

"Pretty sure we're your only butchers, honey." Lacey smiled, pushing another cart through the door.

"We better be." Anna winked at him as she passed.

"How are things, ladies?" Logan asked and locked the door behind them.

"Things are good. We got a new sausage maker, which is sort of like a Tiffany box to us." Anna laughed loading the brown-paper-wrapped bundles onto the counter. Logan had been impressed the first time they had delivered. Their work was immaculate, right down to the way each package was wrapped, tied with white string, and marked with black wax crayon.

"We have a new apprentice. He's a little squeamish so far, so we've got him working the counter until he gets it together." Lacey helped load the last of the order. "And, we just started a new class."

"Yeah, we're calling it The Whole Hog. It's a class on, well butchering a whole hog. We go over how ours are raised, the humane way to slaughter, and how to cut properly and use the whole animal," Anna chimed in with an excitement that filled the kitchen.

"That's incredible," Logan said. "Are you getting many takers?"

"Three local butchers so far and two from out of state. The response has been fantastic."

"You're changing the world, ladies. Well, at least California."

"Hey, that's a start."

They all laughed and went over the order. They'd run out of chicken thighs and promised to add them to next week's order, but everything else was there. The lamb Travis had wanted Logan to ask about would not be a problem. Logan gave them each a cup of coffee to go and thanked them for doing what they do.

As they were leaving, Travis arrived. Logan fired up the music.

"Sorry I'm late. Man, let's just say handcuffs are not all they're cracked up to be," Travis declared putting his helmet away. Logan was about to beg him to stop speaking, when Makenna suddenly came swirling into the kitchen. She grabbed Paige's lunch box, kissed Logan on the cheek, and thanked him—for what he had no idea. Before he could ask her, she was gone.

"Any idea what that was about?" Logan asked Travis. Travis shrugged and another day at The Yard was underway.

"Olivia, I really don't think there's a story here. They've barely been open for three months and from what I can see it's a slow go." Kara sat on the opposite side of her editor's desk, feeling like it was a little too early in the day for this conversation.

"Didn't your father's campaign just have an event there last week?"

"Yes, but that was for the volunteers and if you ask me, it was a little lowbrow, if you know what I mean." Kara was desperately trying to appeal to the snob she knew her boss to be.

"No, I don't. It looks like a very cool place. I'm excited about what it's bringing to downtown and you should be too."

"Right, I am." Kara sighed internally. She wasn't going to win this one. "I'll go there tonight and work on a review. I should have something for you by the end of the week."

Olivia twirled her glasses as she perused her computer screen. That was a sure sign of brainstorming. *Damn it!*

"I want a feature."

"What?" flew out of Kara's mouth.

Olivia's head popped up; she seemed a little startled at being questioned, let alone so enthusiastically. Kara smiled, mouthed a "sorry," and tried to collect herself. She bit down on the tip of her pen hoping that would help calm her anxiety.

"Listen, I know he's not your speed, but this guy lives at 920 Seco Street: 2009 winner of the Pasadena Historic Preservation Award," Olivia continued moving her mouse around for more information that Kara already knew.

"He has an urban farm," Olivia added.

Knew that, Kara thought, and bit harder on her pen.

"That's very 'in' these days, trending." Olivia swirled her mouse on its pad.

Kara hated that word, "trending." She loved technology, but some of the lingo made her feel like she was back in high school. Olivia loved the lingo, so Kara smiled and nodded in feigned interest.

"From what I'm told he's a good-looking guy." She clicked a few more times. "Holy Shit! Kara have you seen this guy? He's hot." Olivia quickly turned her monitor to Kara, and there—in however many pixels—was Logan Rye wearing jeans and a plaid button-down shirt. No glasses this time. It was taken at The Yard and he was leaning on the pizza counter. He had an easy smile and the camera perfectly caught the natural wave of his thick brown hair and those light whiskey eyes that were rimmed in a darker shade.

"Kara, I want this guy."

Me too, she thought. "I mean I used to, but certainly not anymore, that's just..." Kara realized she had said that out loud. *Where the hell was that pen?*

"What did you say?" Olivia asked looking at her like she was wearing last year's Ferragamos.

"I was saying that I've met Logan Rye and I'm not sure he'll have time for a feature. They are pretty busy. And with Election Day coming up, I've got a lot—"

"New restaurant, *LA Times* wants to do a feature on you. I'm guessing he'll make the time. I want you on this. I've already put this in Harold's ear. He likes it. So if the big boss likes the idea, and I like it, you need to like this. K?" Olivia smiled and just like that Kara would be spending at least a week—

"Let's do a three-part series." Olivia folded her hands on her desk, as if she could not have been more pleased with herself.

Make that several weeks with Logan Rye, Kara thought.

"We need to get this on the front page of our section before some other paper or magazine or God forbid one of those damn foodie bloggers gets ahold of him. I want pictures, the whole deal."

"Don't you think you should talk to him first?"

"I'll call him right now." Olivia put her hand on her phone.

Kara took that as her sign to leave.

"Let's talk more about this at our one o'clock. Oh, and close that door on the way out, hun."

Kara walked out of Olivia's office, poured some tea, and sat in her mesh, ergonomically correct chair. Kicking her heels off under her desk, she got comfortable and did something she hadn't imagined herself doing when she woke up this morning. She Googled Logan Rye. This time it was in broad daylight, not tucked into the covers of her bed on her iPad. Then she searched urban farming. She also found several articles on 920 Seco Street and read the incredibly romantic background story of Bill and Rosemary Barbus. Kara made notes and started to put together some preliminary questions. If she had to do this feature, she was going to do it well. She learned that urban farms and even communal gardens were expanding and had, in fact, been around for years. She began to feel a little overwhelmed as she read about heirloom seeds and the differences between conventional and organic farming. She rubbed her eyes—it was time for a break. She was prepared with some research so she didn't look ridiculous, but now she needed to prepare emotionally.

She decided to meet up with her friend Jake for lunch.

After Kara had finished giving Jake the backstory on Logan Rye, well most of the backstory, she asked Jake what she should do.

"Is this a trick question?" he asked, biting into his gyro and wiping his mouth. "Write a damn good feature, that's what you need to do. I mean look, you had a fling with this guy in Paris. Sounds like a great memory. Sure it ended badly when the Wicked Witch made you come home, but most things end badly." He took another bite, sipped his iced tea, and continued.

Kara loved Jake's rants. They were like power talks.

"You're in a job you hate most of the time."

"I don't hate my job." Kara sipped her water.

Jake took her hands across the table.

"Honey, you're a food critic who barely eats. After your shitty review of my all-time-favorite Vietnamese restaurant, I'm beginning to wonder if you even have taste buds."

Kara shook her head and pulled her hands away.

"All I'm saying is, now's your chance to do something different. I don't see the problem. You're not in love with this guy. I get all the 'you got to be yourself with him,' yada yada, but there's no going back to Paris. You're a grown woman Kara, and you need to figure out a way to be in your own skin. Be you, ya know?"

"Are you sure you're just a plumber?"

"Sweetie, there's nothing 'just' about being a plumber. We are literally the person everyone calls when the shit hits the floor."

Kara laughed. She'd heard that joke before, but it was funny every time.

"I watch a lot of Dr. Phil, or I should say I listen to a lot of the guy. Almost every damn afternoon appointment I go on, Dr. Phil is on the television. He's a big deal. Cotton thinks he's hot." Jake rolled his eyes at his husband's crush and finished the last bite of his gyro.

"So before we conclude the emergency lunch," Kara said, "how's Eloise since she got her tubes put in?"

"Much better. Doctor says they will dissolve or fall out on their own and we haven't had an ear infection in two weeks. Brilliant."

"I can't believe she's going to be three next month." Kara took the napkin off her lap and set it on the table.

"I know, right? It's crazy. She's all signed up for school, just waiting on the uniforms to come in."

"Are you doing okay with sending her off to school?" Kara asked.

"I have to be. It's a great school and with things picking up at work, we would need to send her to day care. This is the best thing. Can you believe they teach Mandarin in pre-kindergarten now? Frickin' Mandarin!"

Kara laughed. "She'll be smarter than all of us by the time she gets out of kindergarten."

Jake's phone vibrated. "Okay, sweetie, I need to get to my next appointment. Put your big-girl panties on and write something sensational."

Kara touched his hand to slow him down for a minute. "Thank you."

"Anytime." Jake leaned over to kiss her. "I love you. It's your turn to pay," he confirmed, getting up from their booth. "Call me and let me know how it's going." And then he was gone behind the tinkling bells of the swinging front door.

Kara paid the bill, took a mint from the little bowl by the register, and pushed out into the afternoon sunshine. Jake was right. This was an opportunity. She wasn't some lovesick child; she was an adult, a respected professional even. By the time she pulled back into the parking lot at work, she was ready to tackle Logan Rye. Well, maybe not him, but at least his restaurant.

Chapter Six

The Rye family met at the same diner every Wednesday morning. It was the family-business meeting to go over where things were on the farm and now at Logan's place. In sickness and in health, they arrived at the second leather booth near the window every Wednesday at 6 a.m. sharp. Schedules, routine, it was the fiber of Logan's family. As a grown man, he recognized it was the way they survived when it was suddenly just the four of them.

Logan's father, Herbert Rye, seemed about two days from his monthly haircut, Logan noticed as he entered Libby's Little Breakfast Place. He was listening intently to something Garrett was telling him. Most likely something about their crops or else he was complaining about their distributors. Logan slid in next to his dad and sure enough caught the end of Garrett's lecture.

"The thing is, it's tragic because most Americans have no idea anymore what a real damn tomato tastes like."

Their father nodded and added cream to his coffee.

"And then this guy asks me the shelf life of our tomatoes."

Herbert laughed. "What'd you say?"

"I told him we could can them for him if he was interested in shelf life."

"Lo, your brother's a funny guy."

"Isn't he though." Logan met his brother's eyes. "Morning."

"Morning," both men replied in unison just as the only female of the Rye family arrived. Makenna was holding file folders stacked on top of her laptop. She was in jeans, muckers again, and what looked like the same flannel shirt their father was wearing. Her long brown hair was still wet and piled on her head. She smiled a morning-before-her-large-Coke smile, and Paige, already dressed for school in jeans and her green sweater with a cow on the front, ran behind her mother and right into the waiting arms of their father.

"Donk!" Paige exclaimed.

"Well hello there, angel. Let me take a look." He pulled her out of their hug as if surveying her. "Yup, you're beautiful even this early in the morning."

Paige kissed his cheek and settled into the booth between her Donk and her Uncle Rogan. Kenna shook her head, set her laptop down on the table, and pulled her bag off her shoulder. Paige rested her head on Logan's shoulder.

"Good morning, Uncle Rogan," she whispered.

Uncle Rogan. Logan couldn't have asked for a cooler name. Paige had trouble saying the "L," and for a while Kenna gently corrected her, but Logan liked it. Eventually, Kenna stopped trying to change it and even though Paige could now say his name correctly, he was still Uncle Rogan. It pissed Garrett off, of course, because he wanted a nickname too. Paige called their dad Donk, which no one could figure out. Makenna thought it had something to do with when she was very little and their father would carry her around on his back and say he was a donkey.

"Good morning, gorgeous. Why are we whispering?" Logan touched the top of her little head.

"Because Momma gave me the look."

They both looked at Kenna who was now searching her bag for something.

"It's the look Momma gets when she's tired in the morning and needs a drink." Paige was still whispering, but the whole table, even Makenna, erupted in laughter as Logan tickled her.

"Sweetie, you should probably add that Momma needs a drink of Coke when you tell people that. Otherwise, I sound like a lush."

Paige nodded as if she knew exactly what her mother was saying and then rested both arms on the table. Garrett recognized his cue and rested his arms on the table in the same way on the opposite side of the table.

"One, two, three, go," Paige counted out on her tiny pink-tipped fingers and then locked eyes with her Uncle Garrett. The staring contest had begun. Garrett came out strong, puffing his cheeks up and trying to get Paige to break, but she was not budging. How she managed to stare for so long without blinking, Logan would never understand. It almost seemed painful. As had happened dozens of times before, Garrett sneezed, Paige declared herself the winner, and Garrett pretended to argue with her until she climbed under the table and into his lap.

"How'd you get so good at that?" he asked her, kissing her button nose.

"My handsome and . . . what was the other word again?"

"Virile."

"Right, my incredibly handsome, virile, and favoritest uncle taught me," Paige announced and again the table, including Libby who had come over to bring Kenna a Coke, laughed. Paige giggled and disappeared under the table.

"Gentlemen." Kenna nodded with some flair as Paige appeared at her side and climbed into her arms.

"Ladies," they all replied together, raising their coffee cups and smiling at their baby sister and her daughter. It was a greeting that went back to when Kenna was little and used to come to the breakfast table in her nightgown, *Bear in the Big Blue House* slippers, and morning hair.

"Bless you, Libby." Kenna took the first sip of her morning Coke.

"You're welcome, honey." Libby put her hand on Paige's shoulder.

"Miss Paige, we are shorthanded behind the counter this mornin'. Would you mind helping me out while Momma has her meeting?"

Paige jumped down from Kenna's arms and put her hands on her hips.

"Sorry guys, Libby needs me. Carry on." Without even a backward glance, she took the order book Libby handed her.

Makenna mouthed, "Thank you!" to Libby, and Paige walked away.

Kenna didn't miss a beat. Knowing Paige was in good hands, she handed each of them a stapled packet of papers and slid in next to Garrett. Logan got two packets. Somehow he didn't think that meant he was lucky. Just looking at it made him tired. He'd never been a numbers guy and definitely not at six in the morning.

"Okay, if you look at the second page, you'll see that the farm did well this month and that's before we add in the Fall Festival revenue for next month. Our first weekend of the pumpkin patch was a huge success and brought us back in the black, even with the tractor and blade maintenance expense from September."

She glanced up and all three of them were staring into their papers in a sort of trance. They said nothing.

"Well?"

"So, we're making money?" their father asked.

Before Makenna had a chance to answer, Libby's oldest daughter came over to refill their coffee and take their order. Pancakes, pancakes, pancakes, and chocolate-chip pancakes with whipped cream for Kenna. Logan was surprised the poor girl even wrote their order down the way she was ogling Garrett.

"How can you eat that crap?" Garrett asked Kenna.

"What? I'm only adding some chips to mine. It's like a handful of chocolate. I skipped dinner last night. Wait, did you just wink at Libby's daughter? Christ, who winks anymore?"

"Um, a lot of people wink." Garrett appeared bewildered. "I wink. She's cute."

"She's barely out of college."

He gave her his "What's the problem?" look.

"You're thirty-four," Makenna added.

"And?"

"Ugh, men are disgusting."

They laughed and Garrett bumped her with his shoulder.

"I'm just kidding, Ken."

"No, you're not and don't call me Ken. I'm not a man, in case you haven't noticed."

"I always call you Ken."

"Travis calls her Ken now too and she hates him," Logan said.

"Hate is a strong word." Kenna looked up from her spreadsheets.

Interesting.

"So we're making money?" their dad tried to redirect.

"Dad, yes, the farm is looking good. We're managing our money well and if we keep this up there will be reserves to buy another cultivator early next year."

"That's great news." Their father flipped his packet of papers closed.

"Yeah, when we do that, I found this guy who refurbishes old equipment. I'd like to try him first, see what he has. Some of the older models are actually better. They're tested in operation," Garrett said.

They all agreed Garrett could handle the purchase when the time came and Makenna filled Garrett and their father in on The Yard. It was doing incredibly well and was poised to make a profit in only its second quarter. Logan wasn't sure why good news tended to make him more nervous; it must have been the whole negative and positive energy thing again. After a round of coffee cup and Coke glass clinking to celebrate the good news, Libby, accompanied by Paige—who was now wearing a frilly apron—dropped off their breakfast. Paige paused for a moment so she could kiss her mom on the cheek. Kenna beamed and they all put away the money talk and passed around stories, gossip, and thoughts on the upcoming holidays. To no one's surprise, Garrett shared that the ballet teacher he'd dated for all of six days didn't work out. That led Makenna to ask the question that silenced the table.

"Dad, have you ever thought about dating?"

Garrett got the same look on his face he used to get when Makenna would ask him to pick up some tampons on the way home from work when they were younger.

"What? Why the hell would he want to do that?"

"Oh, I don't know. He's a man. He's been single for over twenty years. What do you mean, 'why?' You date half the damn female population. Why should Dad be any different?"

"Yeah," their father added with a smile, "why should I be any different, lover boy?"

Garrett shook his head and poured more syrup on what was left of his pancakes.

"Okay, are you serious, Dad?" Logan asked.

"I'm just giving him a hard time. Kenna, I can't say I have thought much, or think now, about dating."

"Really? I mean don't you want to have someone to be with, someone to love and, you know, be physical with?"

"Holy hell! Do we need to be having this conversation?" Garrett looked like he was in pain. "I'm kind of visual, Ken and some of this shit I can't unhear."

"Oh, grow up. I'm just curious. It's been the four of us for so long. I'm simply talking about Dad's individual life."

"And I appreciate that, honey. It's nice that you still think of your dad as a human being. Truth is, I'm busy. I like what I do and sure I get lonely sometimes, but I have a full life. I've got you guys."

"You get lonely?" Logan asked.

"Sometimes."

"Well, give one of us a call next time that happens. I'll take you to a movie. Can this little talk be over?" Garrett pleaded looking at Makenna.

"Jesus. Fine. Let's talk fertilizer." Makenna handed her glass to Libby's daughter for more Coke.

"Now that's a great idea." Garrett finished chewing his last bite of pancakes. "I'm thinking we need to look into something different for those new avocado trees we planted. They look pathetic and we planted them with that great compost. They need a boost of something. About fifty percent of the leaves have fallen off."

"I don't think that's the issue. Ricky was telling me the other day that he thinks they're not getting enough drainage. He was thinking too much compost," their dad added.

And just like that, Logan thought, the conversation turned. He sat back and considered his sister, who was now looking at her phone, and he couldn't help but think that she was putting the dating topic up for herself instead of their father. It had been over five years since Adam died and Logan was sure his sister got lonely, but she never said a word. He thought it was probably a great sign that she was even thinking about dating. As if she knew he was watching her, Makenna glanced up. Logan tried to find something in her eyes, but she smiled quickly and returned to her all-important e-mails.

No one answered when Kara knocked on Logan's front door at 920 Seco Street later that morning. His truck was in the driveway, so she walked around back. Logan was on the side of the yard, standing in a large planter, and Sweet Baby Jesus, it was far too early to see Logan Rye, complete with morning hair and stubble, reaching across a planter. She hadn't had time to put up her hard outer shell yet, and there he was: T-shirt riding above the waistband of faded jeans spotted with dark soil and that damn tattoo winding up his arm and crawling into his short sleeve. Kara caught herself wondering if it continued on to his chest. Did it wrap around his back? It was as if his body heard her, because Logan turned and began digging or hoeing or whatever it was called. The muscles of his back bunched and released about a dozen times before she realized she was staring like some stupid high school girl. *Get your crap together, Kara.*

She reached into her purse, pushing past some sand and the pebbles of glass she'd collected last weekend during a trip to Zuma Beach, and found her pen. Stepping closer to Logan, she cleared her throat; he turned and lifted his arm as the sun hit his eyes. She would never be able to explain it to someone, but Logan was like the earth that he was working, solid and real. Even when they were in Paris, before she knew who he was and what he did, Logan was this farm. Maybe that's why when their eyes met for the very first time, she saw something she didn't recognize but knew she wanted. He was the opposite of who she was back then. Even the way he sat in a chair or ate a sandwich was different. He was warm from the inside out.

But that was several years and one big lie ago. This was now, as Jake had put it, and the Logan walking toward her didn't feel all that warm anymore.

"Kara." Logan nodded and stepped in front of her.

"Logan, thank you for agreeing to meet with me. Any ground rules we need to go over before we get started? Is this even a good time for you? You look pretty busy."

"Irrigation pipe broke. I was fixing it." He wiped his hands on a rag he pulled from his back pocket. "Rules, yeah, I have one."

"I'm all ears."

"The scene in my kitchen a couple of weeks ago, I'm not up for that if we're going to be working together for a few weeks now. Basically, I just want it to be clear that I don't do women anymore."

Kara's head tilted in confusion, and sarcasm got the best of her. "Really? Hmm... I didn't see that coming, but if you're gay that's—"

"Not what I meant. I'm not gay." He twisted the greased rag in his hand. "I don't do the dance around, please like me, what are you thinking, woman game. Not my thing these days. I don't have time for it."

He had an edge. Kara didn't think it was just her this time. He seemed like he had things on his mind.

"Oh, well then we will work beautifully together because I don't do the look at what a stud I am and you'd be lucky to have me, but I'd like to screw around for another five years, guy game. Not my thing. No time."

"Great."

"Perfect."

Kara noticed the bead of sweat dripping down his neck, into that little dip right below his Adam's apple. She let out a slow breath and sat down on a concrete bench.

"Well, in the interest of moving on—as my editor already told you, the *Times* is interested in doing a feature on your new restaurant and more importantly your philosophy on farm to table and the local food scene."

Logan smiled. "This is killing you, isn't it?"

"You have no idea." Kara focused back down on her pad. "Anyway, I'd like to start with your place here, some history, and how you've revitalized this particular urban farm. Then I'll do a separate piece on the restaurant concept, the work that went into it, and surviving in the food world."

Logan laughed.

"Something funny?"

He shook his head. "No. Food world. I like that."

"Great. That will be followed by a piece on your family's farm and your hometown roots."

"I'll need to discuss that with my dad, make sure he's on board, but the rest sounds fine. A little painful, but good for the restaurant, so I'm in."

Kara nodded and closed her notes. "Okay, well if you have time maybe you could show me around."

"I have time." Logan lifted the hem of his cotton shirt and wiped his face. Kara knew it was for her benefit, his way of being all farm boy to what he considered her princess, and it worked. She was sure her face flushed as her eyes dropped to his—*bad eyes*, she scolded herself.

"Where should we start?" Kara asked, clearing her throat again.

"Well, it's all about composting, so let's start with the soil and how we got things back together when I bought the place." He gestured for her to walk in front of him.

She started toward the back of the property and marveled at the organization and the beauty of a garden this size. When Kara was growing up, her mother had paid people to keep up the gardens around their house, and she was pretty sure they once had a cook who kept a small vegetable garden, but it was nothing like this. This was incredible and the smell of the earth—minerals she guessed—drew her in. She'd once read that your body responded to the things it was lacking—the nutrients it needed. The life growing all around pulled at something in her.

"Kara?"

She glanced over her shoulder. Logan had stopped and picked up some of the black soil.

"This isn't going to be a puff piece, is it? I mean, there aren't going to be any pictures of me holding a damn shovel or anything, right?"

"I don't write puff."

"Yeah, I know. I've read your stuff."

Kara was taken aback, but looked down instead of at him while she gathered her attitude.

"But I seem to be your least-favorite person these days," he continued, "so I just want to make sure I'm not wasting my time here only to be humiliated."

"Right, well, I have a reputation. My boss gave me this assignment and it's a feature. I won't be blowing this. You'll come across however you present yourself. I'm honest, if nothing else."

"Really? Not my experience." His face was unreadable.

"Oh Christ, Logan. Let it go. I didn't tell you who I was in Paris because I couldn't and . . . well, I didn't want to be the person I was. You certainly never came after me to ask questions, so let's leave it in Paris, okay?" She took a deep breath. It felt good to finally say something about their past, even if it was merely a fraction of what buzzed around in her head. "And you are not my least-favorite person," she admitted.

"I'm not?"

"No." She faced him. "Maybe in the top five."

She smiled, and so did he. It was a real, genuine, smile. Probably the first time she'd seen him smile like that since they'd shared a kitchen and began slipping into blissful lust with each other. He used to look at her and smile in a way that made her believe in the entire crayon box, not just the black and white of her world. She grew to believe things were possible and eventually she saw herself dancing in his eyes. Barefoot, in the rain, dancing.

"So"—Logan rubbed the soil between his fingers—"this is where it all starts. The soil is key and when I bought the place, things had pretty much dried up. It took me about two months of constant composting, tilling, and troubleshooting before I planted anything."

"Is all of this from seed?"

"Yeah." He dropped the soil and brushed his hand on his jeans. "There's this great seed bank in Petaluma. Used to be an actual bank. They have everything. I also like Baker Creek if I'm looking to get creative. They're out of Missouri and I'm like a kid with their catalogue." Logan laughed and Kara wrote a few notes down.

"Can I use these names?"

"I'm sure you can. The exposure would be great for them. Baker Creek has these tiny Thai eggplants. They look like green peas, but they're eggplants. So cool. I put them in a red curry with chicken." Logan's love of food radiated off him. "That was one of the specials the first week we opened."

"Red curry? Interesting. What would you call the cuisine of The Yard?" Kara asked, reading from her notes and trying to keep to her structure.

Logan laughed.

"What?"

"I have no idea what the cuisine of The Yard is."

"That's a legitimate question, Logan. People are going to want to know how to classify your food, what they're getting when they come to your place."

"Can't they just show up? You know, it's called The Yard. Doesn't that say show up? It's a barbecue one day and maybe a Cajun feast the next. There's also room for fresh lemonade and sandwiches. A yard with twinkling lights could be a wedding or a fancy event, too. I like it all."

"I suppose, but at some point you'll need to define it. Do you have a set group of recipes?"

"No."

Kara regarded him.

"Recipes? Come on Kara when did we ever follow—"

Logan seemed to catch himself. He stopped talking and his eyes shifted away from her as if he'd been too caught up in something. He took a breath and started again.

"I mean we have our standard menu that we set every quarter. Those are offered every day, but we don't use recipes." His eyes met hers. "Travis and I work on everything for each menu together. We test and build the whole thing in the kitchen."

Kara found herself a little light-headed listening to him, watching him pace back and forth, hands moving with his words. She was grateful for her notebook because she needed little breaks to find her balance.

"Okay, let's save some of this for the middle piece which will actually focus on the restaurant itself. Tell me about your place. Like, what are these?" she asked gesturing to the planter right in front of them.

"That's kale. Dwarf Blue to be specific. I'm harvesting that now. We use it in our chili, which is on the fall menu. We'll also put it in mashed potatoes with some variation of our meatloaf. Travis is really into bison these days. He wanted a bison meatloaf, but we need to watch that flavor for most people."

Logan stopped. "Sorry, I'm rambling. What was the question again?"

"You were just talking up the kale." Kara smiled, feeling playful, if that was even possible anymore.

He laughed. "It's hard to separate what I do here and the restaurant. They sort of go hand in hand. There's also a smaller garden onsite at The Yard. Did you notice the garden when you were there for your dad's thing? Probably not, you were too busy being pissed."

"I wasn't pissed. I just don't like airing my—"

Logan held up his hands in surrender. "Let's not do this again."

"Fine. Okay, so tell me some of the other things you're growing right now and how they correlate to your fall menu."

They went around most of Logan's expansive yard, every inch dedicated to growing something. Carrots and peas, he explained, were ready and would be included in their stew and a split pea Travis liked to do with a ham hock. He showed her his herbs and three different types of garlic. All of it was heirloom, when he could find it, and organic. Kara knew enough about food to be impressed. Logan even had a large flower garden that supplied daily flowers for his restaurant. He cut them himself and brought them in every few days. The term "labor of love" was thrown around a lot in the restaurant world, but this, what Logan was doing, truly was that. Everything he grew and used, including the vendors he worked with, needed to be in line with his beliefs about sustainability and food integrity. Kara put her hand to her stomach, unsure if she was hungry or simply dizzy from him.

"We currently have five kinds of tomatoes, all heirloom and all delicious." He picked a small cherry tomato and handed it to Kara.

She rubbed her thumb over the deep red surface.

"Try it."

"I'm not hungry, but thank you." She handed it back to him. "They are beautiful and I'm sure they're—"

Logan put the tomato in his mouth, closed his eyes, and chewed. "God, I never get tired of the flavor. It's like you can actually taste the sun in them, ya know?"

Kara didn't know, but his eyes met hers again and she wondered if he could see the want. She hadn't expected it, but her stomach fluttered again. It was clearly hunger, almost a craving.

"I'm sure they're delicious. They look beautiful."

Logan held her gaze for a beat longer than was comfortable and then turned to the house.

"So, this is 920 Seco Street, used to be 251 Las Robles." He gestured to the house and grinned as if he was introducing an old friend. The edge she had noticed when she first arrived was gone; the exhaustion in his eyes softened.

"Oh, that's right. It was moved," Kara said, flipping the page of her small notebook. "I pulled up some history back at the office, but tell me a little about it. What makes it special for you?"

"I could talk your ear off about this house, so I'll try to stick to the top three reasons I love it," he said. "Greene and Greene built the house about a year after they started their architecture firm back in 1895. They were starting out, new and uncertain, kind of like me. I like that."

He walked up the three steps of the white-painted porch and held the screen door open for her. She walked in and stumbled a bit as she tried to take in the honey wood floors, the sunny yellow and white colors of his home. She steadied herself by grabbing a small wooden chair. It was one of four chairs tucked around a round wooden table a few steps from the side entrance they'd already walked through. Kara ran her hand along the curve of the wood. She needed a minute, so she asked a question.

"What's the second thing?"

Logan stood in front of the couch. It had a cream-colored slipcover and Kara found herself wondering where he got the couch. Did he pick it up at a clever little secondhand furniture store one Sunday morning after breakfast with his girlfriend? Had she helped him decorate? Was she everywhere in the tiny house and Kara didn't even know?

"Kara?"

"Oh, sorry. I was just looking around. Sorry." Kara looked back down at her notebook. "So what was your number two again?"

"The design. It's practical, but there are little touches, a few pocket doors, some glass knobs, that give it detail. I like the clean lines with a little twist."

"Spice," Kara added without even realizing she was speaking.

"Exactly. It's a solid meal, hearty, but with a little spice."

Their eyes held and there it was again, the pause that was heavy with memories. Logan broke first this time.

"And the last thing is a tie between the basement—which I still haven't decided what to do with yet—and the story of Bill and Rosemary Barbus."

"I read a little about them. They seem like lovely people."

"They are, well Bill passed away a few years ago, so I didn't get to meet him, but he's everywhere in this house. They bought the house for a dollar. Can you believe that?"

Kara shook her head in disbelief.

"Rosemary is still a docent down at The Gamble House. She comes over every month or so and I make her lunch. Great people and an incredible love story. Her energy is, well it's special." Logan looked like he'd caught himself sharing too much again.

"Sounds like Bill and Rosemary are more important than the basement."

"Yeah, probably."

"I know you did a lot with the gardens or urban farm, but what about the house? Did it need a lot of work?" Kara tried to remember she had a job to do.

"Nothing." He walked to the front window that opened out onto another small porch. "It needed nothing. Bill worked every day on this house and the love practically pours out of it. I wouldn't change a thing, so I just maintain his work."

Kara noticed the hardwood floors, buffed to a high shine, but the planks were a little misshapen in some areas, proof they were cut by actual human hands. The entire house felt like its own person, as if it had taken on bits of the lives of its former inhabitants. She had read about Rosemary and Bill and as silly as it sounded, she felt like she knew them, too. The house wasn't specific to them now that Logan was in the space, but it felt like history and years of love, day to day. Kara watched Logan as he walked to the large wood banister and ran his hand along the polished surface. She lost her breath. She was drowning in the house, in him—pulled under by the unexpected weight of feelings that left her more confused by the minute.

"This is the spine of the house." His voice startled her a little, and Logan laughed. "Still jumpy, huh, princess?"

He ran a hand up the banister and Kara walked toward the staircase.

"Everything seems to culminate right here." He gestured for her to walk up the stairs ahead of him. She brushed past him and even though it was just the two of them, it suddenly seemed crowded. She could feel the heat of his body, smell the sweat on him, and it mixed with the comfort of the house, sending her senses into overdrive. Kara stopped, not sure she should continue up the stairs, but then she saw the pictures along the wall. Different frames; some pictures were black and white, some color. She went up a few steps and took in images of the Rye family.

"That first one is all of us." Logan stepped up next to her. "That's my dad, my brother, Garrett, and Makenna, she's the baby. God that was taken a long time ago," he added with something in his voice. "So strange how you can have a picture in your house, pass it every day, and rarely look at it."

She turned her head and he was right there. The sun was coming through the large glass window of the massive red front door. It brushed copper through his hair and highlighted the contrast between the white of his T-shirt and the tan skin of his neck. Kara suddenly felt more than she was prepared to feel when she first woke up that day and willed herself to treat this whole thing as just an assignment. On some days, the little affirmations she told herself in the morning seemed downright impossible as early as noon. This was clearly one of those days.

"Your mom?" Kara asked, surprising herself by managing to stay on topic.

Logan shifted and Kara could hear the creak of the stair below him. "I was almost eight in that picture. She was gone by then."

"Oh," Kara whispered at the realization and then felt her stomach turn. "I'm sorry. You were so young. How did I not ask that question when we were in Paris?"

He laughed, of all things, and Kara was suddenly uncomfortable.

"What?" she asked.

"There were a lot of things we probably should have asked in Paris, don't you think?"

She nodded. "I guess the details didn't seem important then." She stepped back down the stairs, deciding she'd had enough for one morning.

"Don't you want to see the upstairs?" he asked.

"I need to get going, but I would like to see your kitchen. Did you change it when you moved in?" Kara knew bringing the conversation back to food or his kitchen would rescue her from what felt far too intimate.

"I did, so I guess I lied before when I mentioned that I hadn't changed anything. It wasn't a complete remodel because I have the kitchen at The Yard, but," he paused as they walked into the kitchen and he turned on the lights, "I changed out the appliances and the countertops."

"More wood," tumbled out of Kara's mouth as she walked further into the small kitchen and noticed the well-used surface, one section still coated with flour. She touched it with the tips of her fingers.

"Yeah, sorry about that. I didn't have time to clean up when the pipe broke and I had a geyser in the yard."

"What were you making?"

"Bread, we don't seem to ever have enough of it at the restaurant. I never realized when we decided to put bread on the tables, but holy shit, people can pack it away."

They both laughed.

"Your kitchen is smaller than I imagined, but I like that you kept with the design of the house."

"Size doesn't really matter."

Kara looked up to find him standing in the small entry of the kitchen, his hands overhead, gripping the molding, and a wicked smile on his face that promised trouble.

"Very funny." She hoped she wasn't blushing.

"I thought so." He smiled and dropped his hands from the

molding. "But seriously, it's true. As long as I have counter space and there's a place for everything, I'm good."

"Well, it's a great place, Logan." She turned to take in the feel of his home one more time. "I think I have enough for the first piece and anything else I need, I'll get online."

His gaze traveled over her as if he saw something new, or old, Kara couldn't tell. "Can I make you lunch before you go?" His voice was a little raspy.

"No, thank you. I'm not hungry and I don't think that's a good idea. Things are almost pleasant between us," she joked. "Let's leave it there."

"Are you ever hungry, Kara?"

Their eyes met and she felt the weight of his question. *What does that mean?* She wasn't going to answer him because something shifted in his eyes and things were suddenly about her—not a topic she liked to discuss. Kara put her notebook in her purse, and Logan walked her to the door.

"Thanks for the tour," she said, not able to meet his eyes.

"You're welcome. Make me look good, princess."

"I'll do my best." Kara was now certain she was blushing again.

She got into her car, drove around the corner, and pulled over. Then she took a deep breath and tried to collect her thoughts. The few months she'd spent with him in France had taught her so many things. What she wanted, and eventually, what she wasn't allowed. He was playing with her, and that was all. The house, the stories, those were in his world, not hers. She needed to remember that.

Chapter Seven

The annual Halloween craft cocktail contest was a bit of a tradition in Pasadena. Local bartenders and some from Los Angeles competed for the coveted onyx shaker. Sage Jeffries, lead bartender for The Yard, had competed last year and lost to "some guy who made a damn milkshake in a martini glass," as she put it. That explained why nearly two weeks before Halloween and shortly after they opened for lunch, Logan was sitting at the end of the bar, taste testing drinks while trying to remain sober.

"I've narrowed it down to two drinks. This first one"—Sage pushed an orange drink across the bar to him—"is a Zombie. I used the juice we froze from those blood oranges you brought me back in July. Even though it's frozen juice, I think that's what sets it apart."

Logan sipped and tasted apricots, rum—lots of rum—and the orange juice. "It's good, strong, and I can taste everything. It all goes well together. I get the rum, and is that apricot brandy?"

Sage nodded, surveying him with her odd bartender sense. He wasn't sure what she was looking for, but he must not have given it to her because she reached over with her silver spoon straw thing, took a sample of the drink, and shook her head.

"Too much apricot and shoot, I can't get the grenadine right." With that she swiftly removed the glass, as bartenders do, and dumped it.

"Hey, that was good. Why can't you just—"

"This one," she cut him off, "is ambitious. I'm calling it Mrs. Hyde." Sage moved a purple drink toward him that was smoking. It was beautiful, but he was almost afraid to drink it.

"How do you get it to—"

"Just a sliver of dry ice," she cut him off again.

Sage did that a lot and Logan was used to it. Sometimes when he was with her he found himself pausing and waiting for her to finish his thought for him. He turned the drink by the stem of the glass; it was a work of art. Sage was staring at it and Logan pointed to the purple crystals that rimmed the martini glass.

"Purple sanding sugar."

He nodded and then pointed to the sprig carefully placed in the drink. He recognized it. "Lavender from our garden?"

She nodded, still looking at the drink, assessing her creation.

Logan sipped and just as he was about to tell her it was an herbal explosion that he loved, his brother sat down next to him.

"What are we playing here?" Garrett asked, putting a pair of work gloves on the bar.

Sage glared at him like he had just come into her perfect, lovely bathroom and left the seat up.

Logan set the glass down carefully.

"What's with all the tension? Sage, can I get a beer?" he asked almost dismissively and then turned his barstool to Logan. "I dropped three boxes in the kitchen: more tomatoes and some avocados. The brussels are small. I'm not sure what happened this time, but maybe they'll taste good. That's your department. Let me know, and if they're shit we won't put them out at the market this weekend."

Sage threw down a square cocktail napkin, placed one of the mugs they used for kids on the bar, and proceeded to pour Garrett a root beer. She threw out the bottle with a loud clink and turned to help another customer who sat down.

Garrett looked at Logan who was already laughing.

"Is... there something I'm missing here? What's crawled up her ass?"

"We were going over her entry for the cocktail contest when you—"

"Barged in." Sage whirled back to them after making what appeared to be a modified gin and tonic for the new guy at the bar whose wife had just joined him. "That's what you did, Garrett, oh clueless one. I served you a root beer because you're like a child." She turned back to the wife with a big smile and poured her a Coke from the guns at her waist. She was then back at Garrett, smile gone. "Does it ever occur to you that people are doing things when you make your entrance?"

"Wow, I'm... sorry?" Garrett was less than sincere.

"Do you at least have my lemons?" She pointed toward her fruit bins behind the bar.

Garrett smiled and Logan remembered why his older brother always got the girls when they were growing up. He had a confidence that had nothing to do with how much his watch cost or even how much he could bench press. Garrett Rye worked hard and that sort of radiated from him. He wasn't there to impress anyone, didn't need to.

"Oh, sweetheart, now that's a loaded question," his voice hummed as smooth as any liquor Sage had behind the bar.

She was flustered, having walked into a game Logan was certain she didn't know how to play. Sage was a bartender, but she hadn't been on long enough to get that edge a lot of them collected. She was one of the sweetest people he knew, but she wasn't a pushover and didn't like being embarrassed. She met Garrett's eyes and said nothing about the lemons. Smart girl.

"Isn't this a public place? I made a delivery and came to talk to my brother. I'm sorry you were playing"—he gestured to her drink still sitting on the bar—"girly cocktail time, but some of us have work to do."

"You're going to want to try this before you say that." Logan slid Sage's creation over to his brother.

Garrett inspected it. "The damn thing is purple and is that a little flower? Yeah, I'll pass."

Sage reached over, took his gloves off the bar, held them up, and waited.

"Oh, come on. Those are my favorite pair."

She picked up scissors in her other hand and smiled. Logan's sides hurt from laughing.

"Shit." Garrett pulled the lavender from the drink and downed it in one gulp.

Logan saw it in his eyes before Garrett even opened his mouth.

Garrett blinked up at Sage. "What the hell was that?"

She smiled, handed him his gloves back, and walked away.

Logan put his arm around his brother. "That, dear brother, is a Mrs. Hyde."

"She sure as hell is." He gawked at Sage, clearly stunned that a little "girly drink" packed such a punch.

Garrett left a little while later after Logan made him a sandwich for the road.

Logan fixed a stopped-up sink in the ladies' room himself because the online maintenance service they used said it would be about two hours before they could get out there. He'd need to look at that contract; two hours might as well have been six with a packed restaurant. Finally, after calming Travis down because a customer sent back his spinach salad, saying the bacon pieces were too big and she preferred bacon bits, Logan made his way back to the bar.

Sage had pulled her short dark hair to the side with a clip and was talking with two guys about last night's final game of the World Series. Logan sat at the end of the bar again and she made her way over.

"Shall we resume our testing?" Logan asked, even though he already knew the answer.

"Nah, I've decided."

"Mrs. Hyde?"

She nodded.

Logan smiled. "Good choice."

"It's a pain in the ass to make, but I think it's worth it." She smiled and turned back to her customers.

Logan headed to the kitchen and had to wonder whether Sage was talking about the drink or his brother. He wasn't sure how long it would take Garrett to figure out Sage was in love with him.

Kara could feel fall in the air and, more importantly, she'd begun counting the eighteen days until Election Day, or as she and Grady like to call it, Independence Day. She had agreed to be with her parents on the big night and at the celebration that same evening, or if it was a close race, the following evening or possibly two. Two or three elections ago, there was a runoff and maybe even a recount. It lasted forever and the celebration wasn't until the following January. Grady likened that year to being on parole. Their life wasn't that bad; sure they fed off each other and made it worse than it really was, but they both knew it wasn't any worse than other family obligations.

Of course, the press rarely covered normal family get-togethers and adult children were not often instructed what to wear. There were certainly worse things in life, but election years were rough. Grady drew the short straw this year and was much more active in the campaign, so Kara had to take Thanksgiving at the local shelter. It was after Election Day, but it would be the last event she would need to attend until her parents' annual open house in February. She would have time to enjoy her holiday out of the spotlight. Now if her father lost, that would be a different story and not one Kara wanted to think about on such a beautiful day. She closed the calendar on her computer and pulled up the review she'd been working on.

Noodle houses, or more specifically, ramen houses, had been around for a long time, but they had experienced a huge renaissance in the last five years. Kara reviewed two places in LA last year that were awful. Mushy-noodled, overcooked-pork, runny-egg awful. She wrote her reviews and told the truth. Maybe the second one was a little mean because she'd poked fun at the name: it was called Silly Noodles. How could she not comment on a name like that? But after today's lunch, those two harsh reviews were distant memories.

Kara spent a half hour at Kanpekina Ramen, which she learned meant Perfect Ramen. A bold statement she thought at the time, but now that she'd been there, she had to agree. The place was small, only a handful of tables and a few seats at the ramen bar, but it was clean, streamlined, and the people could not have been nicer. They served Hakata-style noodles that were perfectly cooked—they were just the right degree of chewy and sat in a milky broth. Noodles and broth were equally important in ramen dishes, because one without the other ruined the whole experience. She ordered hers with egg. It was perfectly done and the presentation was excellent. They even placed pickled ginger and some mustard greens on the side.

Kara had savored her usual three bites and they were exactly as the name implied: perfect. The owner had been a little distraught when she got up and left most of the meal behind, but she had what she needed and there was no need for any more. She was there to examine the mechanics, the structure of the meal. It wasn't about enjoying food. That wasn't her job.

Driving back to the office, she turned up the music and found she was a bit giddy that she'd be able to write another great review. Her reputation as a tough critic was well earned. In the past, she'd been downright ruthless, but lately it was as if someone had opened a window. She wondered if the restaurants were getting better or if she was simply better. She liked to think all of her reviews had been fair, but as she pulled onto the freeway, she suspected much of the past few years had been fueled by resentment and missed opportunities. That wasn't a pleasant thought, so she shifted her focus back to her current review. All she could do at this point was move forward.

"Well?" Olivia asked as she walked by Kara's office about an hour later.

Kara was typing her review and selecting pictures she wanted from the few Jeremy had sent her. She gave Olivia a thumbs-up, hoping that would keep her walking so Kara could finish her work. No such luck.

"Really? That good? Thumb all the way up?"

"All the way." Kara finished typing her opening sentence and looked up from her computer. "It was fantastic."

"Nice. Busy?"

"I got there early, but there was a line out the door when I left and I can understand why. You know, it's simple to serve good food. I think it's when people try too hard or try to offer too many things, that's when things go wrong. I loved it."

"Great!" Olivia looked down at her legs as if she was checking for a run in her stocking. "Speaking of simple and good, how's the first article on Logan Rye?"

Kara decided Olivia always sounded like she was undressing a man when she spoke his name, or maybe she reserved that for men she thought were good-looking.

"It's going well. Jeremy is down there now getting a few shots of his place. I asked him to get the tomatoes too. Logan has five different kinds and the colors are incredible."

"Well, if anyone can capture it and make it sing, it's Jeremy." Olivia was doing it again. *Yuck!* Between her oozing Logan's name and the thought of poor Jeremy singing, Kara wanted to take a shower.

"True, he is a good photographer. I should have the first section of the feature to you in a week. I've set up an interview for tomorrow with the preservation society. They have some wonderful information on the house that I think will be a nice touch. Is it going to make the front of the section?"

"Not sure. I'll have to see how good it is." She smiled, stood, and left Kara's office.

Kara couldn't quite figure Olivia out. She sort of roamed the office and stopped at everyone's spot like a queen bee. She loved meetings and team building, and yet she never saw her doing much.

Kara knew it was strange that she worked at a newspaper. The media had never been kind to her, but she supposed it was a case of "if you can't beat 'em, join 'em." A therapist could probably have a field day with that one, but Kara avoided therapists.

She stood in her stocking feet, ran to the kitchen for some tea, and then decided the ramen house review could wait. She pulled out her notes on Logan's house and laid them out around a picture of 920 Seco Street in the center of her desk. She loved the door of Logan's house and quickly texted Jeremy to make sure he got a shot of just the door. Maybe she would use that as a metaphor for something. Jake had been right—it was fun doing something different, something a little more creative.

The time she spent at Logan's place wouldn't leave her. She was trying to be objective, but all she truly wanted to write was that his urban farm was one of the most wonderful spaces she'd ever experienced. That so many people threw around the words "warm" and "organic," but nothing compared to 920 Seco Street. She obviously couldn't gush like that, the *Times* wasn't big on gushing and she wanted the feature to make front page of the section. She held up the picture she'd printed off the Internet, the one of him leaning on his bar. Of course it would be a professional coup for her, but Logan deserved to be front and center. An odd feeling of pride and protection seemed to seep into her pores. Even though she would now admit it was entertaining trying to outwit him, she knew he didn't trust her. She could see it in the quiet moments. Feel it in between the jokes and the digs.

There was a time he once trusted her, but that was long gone. Kara couldn't fault him for it though—she wasn't sure if she had ever actually trusted anyone. She should probably look into that therapy, but instead she opened a text from Jeremy of Logan's beautiful door and got back to her story.

Chapter Eight

*L*ogan signed off on the tile bill for the bathrooms. They were done, finally. Bathrooms, he'd read in some trade journal, were very important to the success of any restaurant. Unreal, he had thought at the time. Time spent sweating over the menu, eating spaces, lighting, music, and sometimes it came down to the bathrooms? Hey, who was he to argue? He had bills to pay, so if it was bathrooms his customers wanted, he would give them great ones. He'd built a sink in the middle of a huge table saw left over from The Yard's days as a hardware store. It was mint green and solid steel. The plumber thought he was nuts when he'd requested they cut a sink into it, but the customers loved it. The male customers that is, because it was in the guy's bathroom.

The women's bathroom had a huge hammer sign with four dozen tiny lightbulbs that had hung outside the store since 1939, until he paid far too much to have it removed undamaged, cleaned up, and repaired. It lit up the ladies' room at night and was another discussion piece among diners. He had to admit it was cool. It brought a nice energy to the place—good mojo as his father would say.

Bathrooms done. Now if he could just figure out the small table in the corner of the restaurant that Summer dubbed "the love corner."

She could spot couples falling in love, or celebrating love, a mile away. The Yard had only been open a few months and they'd already had two proposals in that corner. The lamp that currently cast a dim light over the lovebird perch wasn't right. It was too shiny and while the actual light was fine, he wanted something with character. Another space that still needed work was the private dining area they used for large parties. He wanted a chandelier-type thing, but definitely not some fancy crystal mess. He wanted something unique.

"Morning," Makenna called as she pushed through the side door holding her keys in her mouth and a big box.

"Need help there?" He took the box before she answered.

Her keys fell into her now free hands and she dropped them and the purse from around her shoulder into one of the empty booths by the door.

"Fall menus finally came in. Printer called me this morning so I swung by after I dropped Paige off."

Logan set the box down on the pizza counter and opened one of the clear-wrapped stacks.

"They turned out great. Sage's handwriting is perfect." Makenna was now standing next to him.

Logan scanned over the long, cream-colored piece of card stock, through the "Starters" section, and all the way down to the "Finish Up," where they listed their two reoccurring desserts: Banana Pudding with Handmade Vanilla Wafers and Chocolate Cake with Italian Cherries and Vanilla Cream. They were the only two desserts Logan knew how to make when they first started out. He'd never been good in that area and his father always said, "Stick with what you know." Logan now had a part-time pastry chef. She made a featured dessert each morning and had taken over the pudding, the cake, and most of the bread, although Logan still loved making bread. There was something essential about bread that he found gratifying. Looking over the menu, *his* menu, written in his bartender's perfect box lettering, his heart warmed with pride. *This is good work.*

"I'm pretty sure we caught any mistakes, but have everyone look at it and let me know. Oh, I wanted to show you Paige's Halloween costume." Kenna grabbed her purse. "I took a picture when we tried it on last night."

Makenna found her phone and began flipping through her pictures. Logan leaned in.

"Wait," Logan cried, but Kenna kept flipping. "Were you naked in a few of those pictures? You're into that?"

"Oh yeah, I'm all about the naked shots. I send them to all of your friends. Thinking about starting a newsletter." She hit Logan with the hand that wasn't holding her phone.

He laughed. "A newsletter. That was a good one."

"Ooh, here it is." Kenna turned her phone. "Isn't she a sweetie cakes?"

"An owl!" He grabbed the phone, feeling all mushy that Paige was getting so big. It was hard to believe Makenna had her almost six years ago. She and Adam were married their senior year in college and Paige arrived less than a year later. Logan's dad was nuts for his first grandchild and Paige was the most beautiful baby Logan had ever seen. Makenna and Adam had been pretty wild in college, but once Paige was born, they were great parents, took her everywhere. Adam worked for a boat designer. Three weeks after she was born, he was working a boat show and didn't want to spend the night in Newport, away from Makenna and Paige, so he started home just after one in the morning. It was only an hour-and-twenty-minute drive, but he fell asleep behind the wheel. His car hit the median, flipped, and Adam was killed instantly. Makenna had called Logan at three in the morning the night Adam died, sobbing that she, "sensed he was gone," even before the police called. Logan was living in Seattle, but he flew home in time to hold his sister as she collapsed in a corner of the emergency room. It was a horrible time—one of their worst, he thought now, looking at another shot of his adorable niece.

"So cute, right? She's really into that National Geographic channel these days, made me follow them on my Instagram."

Logan laughed and noticed, as he had lately, that his sister's eyes were less vacant. Over the past few months, Makenna seemed better. Logan was certain that Paige had saved his sister. Structure, love, and a "have-to" attitude were what picked Makenna up off the floor.

"That's awesome," Logan said. "Where did you get the costume?"

"I made it."

"You made this? When, between three and four in the morning?"

Makenna laughed.

"Well, Paige helped. Lots of feathers." She held out her hand and Logan handed back her phone.

"Nice job, Mom." He pulled her in and kissed her forehead.

"Yeah, well you know, I have to make up for the McDonald's somehow."

"True."

They both laughed.

"Text me that picture, will ya? I'm going to put it up at the hostess station on Halloween."

"Okay." Kenna flipped her thumbs along the screen of her phone and then threw it back in her purse. "Done. I need to get going because I've got payroll to approve and I have to pick up our third-quarter tax reports from the accountant." She leaned up and kissed her brother on the cheek. "You giving out candy at your house next week?"

"I'll be here, but I'll leave a basket out. Since it's on a Saturday we should hand out candy here and Travis wants to make popcorn balls."

"Travis knows how to make popcorn balls?" Makenna asked, moving toward the door.

"He does. He's dressing up too. He won't tell me what his costume is, so I'm already scared."

"I love Halloween."

"Me too. Hold up, I'll walk out with you. I want to go to a few places and look for a new lamp for that corner."

"Oh yeah, that one sucks." She stepped out the front door.

Logan shook his head and locked the door. "Never one to mince words, are you Kenna?" Why didn't you tell me when I put it there?"

"You didn't ask." She waved and got into her car.

She was going to be all right, he thought. Hell, she'd been all right for years now, but she was his baby sister. She'd lost her mother when she was barely five and then her husband. He wanted more than all right for Kenna; he wanted to see her silly happy again someday.

The lamp in the window at zenDeluxe on Holly Street was perfect for "the love corner." It was an old brass desk lamp, but the shade was an incredible mosaic of glass pieces. It had a Tiffany lamp feel, but it was more weighted and each piece was a different shape. He fell in love with it on sight, but the store didn't open until ten. Logan needed to be back at the restaurant to get ready for lunch, so he called the owner when they opened. The woman told him the lamp was the only one they had and that each piece was unique. The shade was made from sea glass and hand designed and assembled in Pasadena. Logan was sold. He paid for it over the phone and texted Summer to have her pick it up on her way to work. Happy with the sale, the shop owner and Logan exchanged niceties, and he invited her to come by for lunch sometime. He explained that he wanted a piece for the restaurant's private dining area, and asked if she could provide the name of the artist. The owner, Jill, promised to look up the artist and get back to him.

Summer arrived with the lamp, and by the time they opened for lunch, it was in the romantic corner and it was perfect. Something about it sitting at the table reminded him of Paris. He and Kara had gone to an exhibit on Émile Gallé and his influence over Louis Comfort Tiffany, the designer of the Tiffany lamp. It was a brilliant exhibit and on the way back to Kara's apartment it had poured rain. That was the night they . . . People were seated and the hum of lunch filled the space, but the lamp stood there, holding his memory. That was the night they made love. They weren't exactly "in love," but there wasn't an actual word for what two people did in between sex and making love, so he was going with "made love." It had been more than sex. He had peeled her out of her wet clothes and then reached back and pulled his own shirt off. Her hair was soaked and water droplets sparkled on the eyelashes of her playful face. She'd pulled him onto the bed as she fell back, giddy with the day they'd shared and so damn beautiful . . . Logan closed his eyes in the middle of his busy restaurant because he could still see the pink in her cheeks, feel her cold rain-soaked lips.

It had been his first time with Kara, but her first time ever. Kara, or Winnie back then, seemed to be checking off a lot of firsts during her time in Paris. Logan's twenty-three-year-old self had been more than thankful he got to participate in many of her firsts. He wasn't sure when he'd sorted through those memories and turned them into "some girl I met in Paris," but it had been quick. Sort of like the immediacy of putting your finger in your mouth after cutting it on a sharp blade to stop the bleeding. He'd put her away that fast. She had made it pretty easy when he'd walked into her apartment a few weeks later thinking they were heading to lunch, only to find two guys in suits standing over her as she packed her things. She had told him they "came to collect her," which at the time he thought was such an odd thing to say. Once she told him her real name was Kara, everything else went kind of fuzzy. She was the daughter of US Senator Patrick Malendar. Some crying happened after that and then, "I'm sorry, so sorry," was all she'd said as the men escorted her through the gate and into a waiting black SUV. He never saw her again.

Logan could still hear the clinking of dishes and the laughter of his guests. Years apart should have dulled his feelings, but there was something about the lamp. Damn if it didn't remind him of Winnie Parker in all her vivid colors.

"I'm here to see Travis, but he's pretty busy in the kitchen right now. Do you mind if I sit in the bar and have some tea while I wait for things to die down?" Kara asked tapping his shoulder and scaring the crap out of him. What were the chances that he would be in some kind of Paris trance and she would just show up? She was standing so close he could smell her perfume. It wasn't flowery—more woods and spice. He had no idea what it was, but if a smell could be dangerous, that one was.

"Shit," he exclaimed, louder than an owner should during his lunch rush, after being startled. Logan smiled an apology at the two people sitting closest to him at the pizza counter, took a deep breath, and turned.

"I'm sorry," she said.

"Don't be." He glanced one more time at the lamp and then turned to the very real, present-day, Kara. "I'm fine. Sure, you can have lunch while you wait."

"I'm not—"

"Hungry," Logan interrupted her. "Right, when *do* you eat, princess?"

Kara said nothing, but took her bottom lip between her teeth and Logan's eyes dropped to her mouth. He cleared his throat and met her eyes.

"I got a new lamp." He turned toward the bar.

"I can see that. It looks great there."

"Yeah." He looked at her. "Much better."

Logan followed Kara into the bar and by the time he'd put out his first fire of the afternoon—the broken ice machine—things were back to normal. There was no Paris, no rain, and all was right with the world. Kara worked on her laptop while she waited for Travis, so Logan slipped some bread, a board of cheese and soppressata, and some olive oil on the table. She ate. He wasn't sure she even realized she was eating, but she was. On his way back to the kitchen, he smiled, oddly thrilled that she had at least remembered how.

"So how did you meet Logan?" Kara asked after she and Travis finally settled at a table in the bar. The lunch crowd was starting to die down and Travis pulled up a stool.

"How did I meet Logan, you ask?" Travis was purposefully loud enough for Logan to hear him in the kitchen. "Well, I stole his girlfriend."

"That's a lie," Logan said from behind the wall. "I hope you have a fact-checker at the *Times*."

"See, he can't come out here because someone has to cook while I'm talking with you." Travis was like a child planning a prank. "So anyway," he said a little louder, "Logan is quite the ladies' man. He goes through them like nobody's business, but me, I'm a little more stable. I'm a settle-down kind of guy."

"Is that so?" Kara was enjoying their game.

"Yeah, so this woman wanted something more stable and Logan had like three, maybe four on deck."

Logan appeared behind the bar, sizzling pan still in hand.

"What the hell is wrong with you?"

Travis laughed.

"This is for the restaurant. There's no time for your sick delusional stories. I'm the ladies' man, me?" Logan raised his brows.

Travis shook his head. "Hey man, I'm only trying to be honest here."

"Really, well maybe you should tell Kara all about how handcuffs work, or what was her name, yeah Sheila and the duct tape. Yes, Trav, tell Kara all about how your ladies' man friend here had to pick you up at the emergency room after you had an involuntary body wax."

"Hey"—Travis looked around—"that was traumatic and private. I can't believe you would share that with our lovely guest."

Travis eyed Kara, who was loading some salami onto a piece of bread.

Where did this food come from? Dear God, this olive oil is incredible.

"Behave." Logan shot him a playful warning glare. "I've got more stuff, my friend. Don't make me lay your shit bare." He pointed the frying pan at Travis and both men laughed. So did Kara because they were fun to watch. Between their show and whatever delicious cheese she was currently eating, she almost forgot she was there to work.

"Fine." Travis held his hands up in surrender, but when Logan disappeared again into the kitchen, he leaned in. "Don't tell him I said this, but he's honestly the best human being I've ever known."

Kara took a sip of water because the sincerity in Travis's eyes was a little unsettling.

"Wow," she tried to lighten the mood, "he must really have dirt on you."

"I'm serious. If you are writing an article on this place, on him, you need to know that. The man lives by a set of ethics that are just . . . he's a great friend and an incredible human being."

For a moment, she wasn't sure what to say. She was supposed to be objective, but part of her wanted to say, "I think you're right!"

Fortunately, Kara kept that part of herself under control. Besides, she barely knew the man he'd become. Travis must have seen something in the way Kara was looking at him because he moved on.

"So, what do you want to know?" he asked, reaching over and popping an olive into his mouth.

Kara started from the beginning and asked again how the two of them had met. Travis explained that he met Logan when they both worked in Seattle under head chef Benji Paradis. They were young and those were the days of killing themselves in the kitchen and then hanging out at the bar until closing.

"Well, that was my plan anyway. Logan would go along and then spend the whole damn night studying for his online classes."

"Classes for what?"

"Anything he could get his hands on. By the time we left Seattle, he had another damn degree in restaurant management."

Kara took notes and Travis told stories about their escapades, the endless months that went into planning and getting the restaurant to where it was now. He gave some examples of how they put together their menu, and he told a funny story about a melon salad he'd never make again. Kara found Travis to be much more boy next door under his bad-boy surface, but he did finally admit that he was, in fact, the ladies' man of the two of them.

"Although, Logan wasn't a monk, let me say that."

"Sure I was." Logan came back out of the kitchen, pulling an apron over his head and throwing it at Travis. "We've got to get ready for dinner, so your interview is over, celebrity chef."

"Aw, we were just getting started."

"I'll bet." Logan poured a glass of water from one of the pitchers at the server station. "Orders are current except for the one pizza that's got another couple of minutes. It needs the greens salad and it's out."

Travis stood up and shook Kara's hand. "It was a pleasure meeting you. I'm sure we will talk again very soon."

She laughed and Logan popped Travis with the towel he was holding.

"Get to it, Romeo. We don't want burnt crusts."

"Thank you, Travis," Kara said, "it was informative and entertaining."

He stepped into the kitchen and Logan took the seat across from Kara, dipped a piece of bread in some oil, and put it in his mouth.

"That oil is great." She finished the last bite of bread on her plate.

"Unfiltered. The monks make it."

Kara laughed.

"No, I'm serious. We get it from one of the monasteries. They make small-batch oil, unfiltered and you're right, it's so nutty and smooth. I'm hooked. Can't use anything else."

Kara made note of the oil on her pad.

"Travis spoke very well of you."

Logan snickered, but when he saw she was serious, his eyes warmed.

"There's more to Travis than he lets on."

"I can see that."

"Comes from a big family, played high school football. His mom still sends him cookies."

Kara smiled.

"He's one of the very best people I know. I'd trust him with my life."

"Huh, he said the same thing about you."

"Well, we've been through a lot." Logan looked down at the empty cheese board in front of her and Kara wanted to ask for more detail about what they'd been through, but instead she opted for a joke.

"It seems you two have been through a lot of women too."

"I thought you said you weren't hungry?" Logan ignored her comment, which was probably just as well.

"Oh, yeah, well I guess I was." She glanced at him, but found herself not ready to meet Logan's smile. It wasn't his smug smile, but this one was uncomfortable too. "Mind if I ask you a couple of questions?"

"One condition."

"And what would that be?"

"Nothing about my past. I'd like to focus on right now."

This time, their eyes met and Kara wasn't sure if he was asking her not to discuss his other women or his past with her. Neither were topics she wanted to cover, so she agreed. Instead, she asked him why he chose the hardware store for his restaurant and learned Logan had grown into a man who cared about preserving the world he lived in and he believed in reusing and recycling when possible.

"Why would I build from scratch when I can add on to the history of this place, give it new life?" he asked. "This would have been demolished for some strip mall eventually, but now it's a restaurant, a place for people to gather. Kind of like the hardware store it was before. One honors the other. I hope someday when The Yard is past its prime that someone will come in and change it up. Layers, I like layers."

Kara nodded. She agreed, but didn't want to say so. She took notes because any more than that distant act would feed the yearning she felt every time he shared more of himself.

"Last question, do you believe in big farms? I mean you must since your family has run one for generations."

"I believe in anything as long as it's responsibly run." He stood and put their dishes in a bin behind the bar. "I'm not against big. There are a lot of people on the planet. I'm against sloppy, lazy, and just plain wrong."

"Can I quote you on that, Mr. Rye, because that was a great line?" She grabbed her keys and then standing, she slung her bag onto her shoulder.

"Sure." He handed her a box.

"What's this?"

"A surprise."

"Logan, I don't need—"

"I know," he interrupted, and Kara could have sworn he looked concerned, "but just take it."

She took the box.

"Now go." He smiled. "Enough questions, I have work to do."

She waved to Travis, and upon being questioned by the hostess about her hair, Kara told the beautiful young girl that she too had naturally curly hair, but she had it blown out most of the time.

"See, I need to do that. My name is Summer by the way." She touched her curly auburn hair a bit self-consciously.

Kara leaned over the hostess station, not concerned about the waiting crowd. "Don't touch one hair on your gorgeous head. You don't want straight hair," Kara urged, meeting her eyes. "Trust me."

Summer smiled and Kara knew that, despite her advice, the young woman would spend countless hours with a flat iron. She would have to figure it out on her own someday. Women rarely took advice, preferring instead to learn as they went along.

Kara climbed into her black BMW, but before she shifted into drive, curiosity got the best of her. She popped open the folded closure of the brown cardboard box Logan had given her. Rich, deep chocolate cake with cherries. In the stillness of her car, Kara sighed and picked up the plastic fork that was in the box. The cake was so moist, just the right amount of cocoa and the zing of cherry puckered her lips. At the last bite, she rested back and closed her eyes. Her stomach was warm and full. She opened her eyes, picked up the last few crumbs with her finger, and put them in her mouth. She smiled. No one was watching her. As she pulled out of the parking lot, she felt something she barely recognized: satisfied.

Chapter Nine

The Yard ran a food truck once a month down at Irwindale Speedway. Logan grew up watching the races with his family. His brother Garrett was into racing in his twenties, but not so much anymore now that the farm kept him busy. Once a month Logan broke out his best short ribs, pulled pork, and burgers for the race crowd. It was his way of bringing good, wholesome food to places that up until recently only offered pizza pockets or bad hot dogs. Todd, their new apprentice, had asked to work the truck with him.

Logan loved that a lot of the same race fans had known him since he was a kid. They supported every restaurant he worked at on his way up into his own place. They were family—show up and smile even if it's raining or hot as hell family.

Logan was inside the truck and trying to remember why he'd agreed to bring Todd, who was leaning up against the stainless-steel counter that ran the back length of the truck, texting with a big dumb grin on his face. Logan didn't want to know what that conversation was about, but he did pound on the cutting board that had four onions the guy had yet to slice. Startled, Todd slid his phone into his back pocket.

"Right, sorry bro, I'll get on these criers right now. There's just this girl who won't leave me alone and—"

Logan held up his hand, indicating he didn't want to hear one more word of Todd's story and pointed back to the onions, or "criers" as Todd like to call them. Logan maneuvered around him to grab more napkins and then turned back to the grill. Logan's dad was sitting outside at one of the picnic tables they'd set up, waiting for his burger and talking to Eddie, "the plastics guy," as his father called him. Eddie was a rep for the company that supplied the farm with all its feed buckets and lockers. The two men went all the way back to high school together.

"Herb, your son is quite a cook there," Logan heard Eddie say as he slid his father's burger onto one of their homemade buns.

"Thanks, Eddie. Yeah, he's really making a go of it. Have you been to his restaurant yet?"

"Oh yeah, Bev took me there for my birthday last week. I had that cauliflower in cheese for an appetizer. Holy Moses, I told Bev I didn't even know I liked cauliflower."

Both men laughed and Logan smiled as he wrapped his father's burger and stepped up to the food truck window.

"Hey, Eddie."

"Logan. Good to see you down here at the races. Don't want to lose you now that you're a damn master with that cauliflower."

"Not a chance. It was nice to see you on your birthday. Thanks for sharing it with us."

"Thanks for that pudding and the candle. That was nice of ya."

"You're welcome. Can I get you something tonight?" he asked, handing down the paper-wrapped burger to his father.

"What've you got there, Herb?"

"Burger, he grinds the meat himself."

"No shit?" he asked looking at Logan.

"No shit, we get the chuck and sirloin from our butcher every week. About eighty-five to fifteen ratio, depending on what they have."

"This isn't one of those damn gourmet burgers is it?"

Logan shook his head. "Just salt and pepper. When the meat's that fresh, you don't need to do much else."

"Sounds good. I'll take two: one for Bev, one for me. Both medium."

"You got it." Logan turned to the grill.

"You don't get much of a chance to see the show from in there," Eddie called to him in the truck.

"No, but at least I can still hear it." Logan packaged everything up in a small box and threw in some napkins and peppers from the garden he'd recently pickled. He knew Eddie loved peppers.

When Eddie reached for his wallet to pay, Logan stopped him. "It's on the house. Consider it an extended birthday celebration."

"That's awful nice of you, Logan. You've got a good boy here, Herb."

His father nodded with his mouth full. Logan promised to cater Bev's fiftieth birthday party next year and Eddie headed back out to watch the races.

Todd finished the onions and seemed ready to actually work, so Logan left him at the window while he loaded the two small refrigerators at the back of the truck with more bottles of water.

"Oh, yes please. Prime cut heading our way."

Logan shook his head, but then laughed. "Is it sad that I know you're talking about a woman? Prime cut, huh? Well, you can go ahead and take this one, just behave." Still crouched down at refrigerators, Logan shot him a warning look.

"Not a problem, man. I got this."

Todd turned to the window. "Hey there, darlin'. What can I get you?"

"Wow, are you from the South?"

Logan stopped at the sound of the familiar voice. Todd's prime cut was Kara Malendar. Oh, this was going to be good. He stayed out of sight and listened to the show.

"No, I'm from Sacramento. Why?"

"Oh, no reason. I just think Southern gentlemen are the only ones who can pull off little nicknames for women they don't know without sounding sleazy."

"But I said I wasn't Southern."

"Exactly. I'll have the burger."

Logan cracked up and Todd turned to him, looking like a man who had just been taken down a notch, maybe two. While Todd fixed her burger, Logan moved toward the window.

"Hello, Kara," Logan heard his dad say. He'd met Kara briefly when he'd come into The Yard for lunch. Herbert Rye never forgot a pretty face, Logan thought smiling, as he remained out of sight.

"Hello, Mr. Rye."

"Oh, please call me Herb."

"Sorry, can't do that. I would never hear the end of it from my mother."

She must have smiled because from Logan's view, he could see his father was smitten. Couldn't actually blame him. Kara's smile could be pretty potent.

"Well all right then. Burgers are good tonight."

"That's what I hear."

"I didn't know you were a race fan."

"Well, I'm not really. I'm here with my brother, Grady, and some idiot . . . I mean a very special guy he thought I should meet."

"Ah, blind date?"

"Unfortunately, yes."

"Might want to get a beer with that burger."

Kara laughed and walked back to the window. Logan could finally see her. Tight jeans, a thin orange sweater that left little to the imagination, and short black boots. Boots with super high heels at a racetrack. Logan smiled. Her hair was down, curly, but pulled off her face in some braid he didn't understand, but the whole look woke him right up.

"I might." She laughed again as Logan's father threw out his wrapper.

"I'll be back, Lo. Kara, try to have a good night."

"Thank you." He could see her neck stiffen as she turned to find Logan looking down at her.

"You're the famous burger?"

"Well, not exactly. I make the famous burger. Blind date, huh?"

"Don't start." Kara grabbed some napkins.

"What? I was just going to say that this is a surprise, princess."

"Yeah, well Grady likes this sort of thing." She looked over her shoulder toward the track as the announcer riled up the crowd.

"I knew there was a reason I liked him."

Kara handed up her money and Logan took the burger from Todd—who was now cowering in the corner of the truck like a neutered dog—and handed it down to her.

"Is that for you, or did you walk all the way over here in those boots to get your new honey a snack?"

Kara shook her head. "Very funny. It's for me."

"Good to see you eating, even if it is my food."

"I eat." She shifted from one of those heels to the other. "And, I didn't know it was your food. Why isn't the name on your truck? Why didn't Grady tell me when he sent me over?"

Logan could almost see the lightbulb go on behind Kara's eyes. Grady must have caught on that the blind date was not going well, so he sent Kara to him. He was running on about three hours of sleep, and curly, sexy Kara Malendar was exactly what he needed. "Thank you, Grady," he almost said out loud.

"We recently finished refurbishing the truck. The name goes up next month," he explained instead.

"And what's wrong with my boots?" she asked, putting her free hand on her barely there hip. Kara needed two burgers, he thought. She still didn't look like she ate enough. For a moment, Logan wondered why and then he stopped. Not his circus, not his monkeys. That was his new life motto, but he was allowed to tease the monkeys. That was just good fun.

He leaned out the window and peered down at the boots and the woman wearing them. A smile spread across his face.

"Nothing."

Kara shook her head. "You've passed annoying now. It seems like you're only decent when we're talking about food."

"Probably." Logan fixed the condiments in front of him and wiped the small metal shelf.

Kara appeared to be gearing up to say something but must have changed her mind. Logan's aching head was thankful for that. She turned to leave.

"Have a good night, princess. Enjoy that date, oh and the burger."

Kara put her hand up to wave and one finger in particular barely shot up a little taller than the others. Huh, who would have thought, and this close to Election Day. Must be the racetrack dust rubbing off on her.

Logan laughed.

"He was a perfectly nice guy. I don't think you gave him a chance," Grady said two races later.

"Where did you find him?" Kara asked.

"He's Josh's brother."

She had no idea who Josh was, let alone his brother.

"Josh, we were friends at Stanford? He runs my ... I think he runs that Roads Foundation, you know the big one?" Grady suddenly appeared uncomfortable, but Kara let it go.

"Your friend runs a foundation like Roads and his brother still collects baseball cards?"

"What?" Grady asked and started to laugh.

"He shared that little tidbit with me when you went for your pretzel. The man is thirty-three, just recently moved out of his parents' home, and bought his first house. The highlight, the best part of owning his own place according to him, was having a spot for his card collection. Takes up his entire guest bedroom apparently." Kara sipped the last of her water and threw the bottle into the metal barrel.

Grady was still laughing. "Are you kidding me?"

"Would I make this crap up? So, thanks for introducing me to that little gem." She was now laughing with him.

"Sorry about that, but at least I got you out to the races. Pretty cool, huh?"

"It is." Kara stopped and looked back one last time at the lights cutting through the air still thick with dust from the last race. "It was surprisingly cool. I might come back."

Grady raised his eyebrows as if he was still holding out hope for Josh's brother.

"Alone. I might come back alone." She smiled. "Or with my favorite brother."

Kara hooked her arm in his as they left the track, heading toward Grady's car. She had suggested getting a driver for the night, but Grady argued that it messed with his innate manliness to be driven to the alpha of all sports, a racetrack. Fortunately they'd met "the blind date" at the track, so there was a quick handshake when he left right before the last race, claiming his allergies were acting up. Blind Date was going to stop by his mom's because she made him this great herbal tea. Dear God, as if Kara didn't have enough reasons not to date.

"Did you see Logan?" Grady asked, opening the car door for her.

"You know I did. You sent me to him." She grabbed the door and closed it. She heard Grady laugh as he walked over to his side.

"How was that?" He put his seatbelt on, still smiling.

"It was fine. A good burger."

"Is that all?"

"Yup."

"Huh. Something's up with you two. Are you ever going to tell me how you know him?"

"I already told you. We both went to UCLA."

"So you met him in class?"

"Sort of."

"Can I get a little more?"

Kara sighed. "I'm going to tell you where I met him, okay, but you need to be an adult and refrain from giggling. Can you do that?"

"I do love a good giggle, but I think I can control myself." Grady stopped the car amid the huge bottleneck of traffic leaving the track.

"Okay, try hard." Kara took a deep breath. "I met Logan in Paris."

Grady looked over and she could see he was trying to control himself, but probably wouldn't succeed.

"Paris your junior year? The year Stanley made you—"

"Yes, that Paris." She hoped the conversation would die there. She should have known better.

"Cooking school. Ah, that makes sense. He was part of that cultural thing."

"Yes."

"Huh. Were you two... friendly? Because at the volunteer thing it seemed like he might have known some things about you."

"We were friends."

"And?"

"And then he found out who I really was, that I was lying, and I was leaving. When Mom's flying monkeys came to collect me, it all became a bit ridiculous."

"I thought Dad's flying monkeys brought you home."

"Whatever, I always blame everything on Mom because, well she's easier to dislike."

Grady laughed.

"Anyway, I never heard from Logan again."

"Until now."

Kara nodded. "Right, until now."

"And you're writing this article or these three articles about him and his place."

"I am."

Grady was quiet as he finally made it out of the gate and turned onto Speedway.

"What?" Kara asked when he snickered.

"Oh, nothing. Just sounds like the setup for a really good romance."

"Yeah? And you watch a lot of romance?"

"I'm all about romance these days, little sister."

"Great. Well, let's stick with your romance because I'm more of an action film girl myself or maybe one of those moody, tragic, but somehow life-affirming, indie stories."

"Like one where the woman is pent up for so long that she finally breaks free and becomes a Vegas showgirl or a high-end hooker?"

Kara laughed. "Yes, exactly like that. I'll take one of those, except no hooking. I feel like I lack the skill set for that job."

"Well, as your brother, that is good to hear. Enough of your sad little indie flick, let's get back to my sweeping romance. Kate and I are going away for the weekend. Last weekend before the big Election Day."

"Thank God. How do you think it's going to go? I can't imagine Dad not doing what he does."

"Me neither. He'll win. It's close, but he'll pull it out, always does," Grady said with that same inherent tension his voice usually held when he talked about their father.

"So, you and Kate are . . . good?" Kara asked, changing the subject.

"Think so. She's . . . well she's special." Grady's face was so warm and unrehearsed that Kara was taken aback.

"You love her."

"I do."

"And you're okay with that?"

Grady shrugged. "Okay or not, it plowed me over like a truck, so here I am."

"Is she okay with all of our crap? Our delightful dysfunction?"

"I think it helps that it's her business, so she knows a fair amount about bullshit. Every family has shit, Kara. Ours may be a little more public, but we are certainly not unique."

"I know, but the public part makes it seem like we are." Kara looked out the window as they pulled onto the freeway.

"I suppose it does, but there's no way around it."

"No way under it," she added, smiling at him.

"No way over it." Grady changed lanes as they approached their exit.

"I guess we'll have to go through it," they both exclaimed in concert and then laughed recalling the lines from a book their Nana read to them when they were little.

Chapter Ten

Kara woke up the Monday before Election Day to her brother's face on the front page of the *Times* and the *Pasadena Tribune*. Overnight, it was everywhere. Her brother, known more for his partying than his substance, was the founder of the Roads Foundation, one of the largest philanthropic organizations in California, possibly the country. He'd started it with some friends from Stanford and for fourteen years had kept it a secret, from his family, even from her. Kara's first reaction, upon hearing the news late last night via her mother's text message, had been pride. There was more to Grady Malendar than he, or the rest of the world, allowed. She was proud because the Roads Foundation gave millions of dollars every year to local organizations of every size and shape. He did all of that without any recognition, which was pretty great because their entire life had been about public displays and recognition.

Her second reaction—hurt. That he hadn't shared it with at least her, that he didn't trust her to keep his secret. Kara knew on some level that he must have had a reason, but growing up, it had been the two of them in the sea their parents threw them into. She would have thought he could completely share himself with her, but then again she certainly didn't share everything with him. Kara sat on the couch with her tea and hit mute on the television. She wasn't interested in anything the talking heads had to say.

She texted Grady to check on him and got a response that he was "up to his ass," and he would call her later to explain. By the time she got in to work, the Roads Foundation dedication of the new police resource center was airing on the flat screen in their lobby.

"Kara, I e-mailed you messages from reporters who have been calling all morning." Their receptionist looked up, more than a little sheepish. "Do you want me to keep doing that or tell them something specific and leave you alone?"

"You don't need to give me the messages. Please just say that I have no comment." Kara briefly touched the counter for balance. "Thanks and I'm sorry for the craziness."

"Not a problem."

She walked into her office and Olivia was already standing by her window. "Holy crap, honey. Your gorgeous brother isn't just a pretty face after all." She turned toward Kara, brimming with curiosity.

"I guess not." She set her bag down and took out her teacup, desperately wishing Olivia would learn some boundaries.

"I'm surprised you're in. Don't you guys need to do some kind of family huddle? Although, I'm sure since this is good news and the election is tomorrow, there's no huddle necessary."

"Olivia, did you need something related to work? Because if not, I'm not terribly inclined to discuss my family's private business, even if it's a bit more public this morning. If there's going to be a 'huddle' as you put it, it will be during my off hours and you won't be privy to the details."

Kara took her jacket off and hung it on the back of her chair. When she glanced up, Olivia was in complete shock. Either that someone spoke to her that way or that she didn't think Kara had any bite.

"Well, I guess you told me. Sorry to disturb, your majesty. I merely thought since your family is usually all over the place, that they were part of the general dialogue."

"We are not all over the place. The media likes to have fun with us because of my father's job. There's a difference. And 'the general dialogue'? I'm not even sure what that means."

"Kara, what the hell has gotten into you?"

Kara took a deep breath because something bubbled beneath her surface. Sure she and Grady mocked their family, but they rarely tolerated anyone else trying to do the same. It was a tribe thing, Grady had once said. "I'm sorry. Under normal circumstances, we work well together, even gossip or talk current events. I'm just in the unique position that every now and then the people I love are the current event and then it's not so fun. I'm simply reeling from all of this, so I'd like to get to work, if you don't mind."

"Understood." Olivia let out a breath. "I'm sorry too, for the huddle comment. I don't know your life and my therapist often tells me not to judge."

Kara laughed off some of the tension. "Olivia, you're a food editor—your whole life is about judging. How does that work with the therapist?"

Olivia shook her head. "I know. That's what I kept telling him. But then we started sleeping together and the whole thing is just a mess now. I'll leave you. You don't need my drama on top of your own." She walked out with her over-the-shoulder wave.

"By the way"—she peeked her head back in—"I always like Bitchy Kara best, but Bitchy Protective Kara—she's fantastic."

Kara shook her head as Olivia continued down the hall.

The woman was strange, no question, but Kara liked her for it.

She worked the rest of the day on a piece Olivia wanted her to write about cranberry sauce. She'd approved the final proof of the first part of Logan's feature and was working on the first draft of his restaurant piece. She kept herself focused even though the phone kept ringing. Publicity of any kind made Kara nervous, and just as she was hoping her brother was okay, he texted her.

Are you mad at me?

No

Ooh, short response, you're mad.

Kara smirked and responded.

I'm not mad. Well done, by the way. Proud of you. I love you. I wish you would have told me, but I'm sure you'll have a very good explanation when you take me for pepper jack grits at Lo Lo's because that's what it'll cost you.

That may have to be after Thanksgiving. I've got stuff to settle here. Let's let the vultures calm down.

Okay, I understand, but you are totally doing the Thanksgiving dishes.

Aw, that's cute. I love it when we play normal family. How about I help the caterers pack up?

She laughed and texted back.

Deal! Are you pissed at Dad?

There really aren't words.

Will you forgive him before Thanksgiving?

Probably.

I love you.

Love you too.

Kara put her phone back in the charger and for some reason started to cry. She was sure it was a release of the tension she'd had since she woke up, but maybe it was also that the people she loved were out there, under the microscope all of the time. Ever since she was little, any time she saw reporters, her hands would start to shake, especially when they shouted. Why did they always have to shout? She'd gotten better as she grew older, but the vultures got better, stronger, too.

As expected, Senator Malendar won the election. Kara surveyed the hotel ballroom and recognized only a handful of people. She took a deep breath and smoothed her hands over the snug-fitting wool dress that hit right above her knees. It was plain, sleeveless, and even with the gray four-inch heels she wore with it, she still felt like a child. Her mother had picked out the dress and it was delivered by messenger to Kara's house the night before the celebration. She had been so insulted, so pissed, that she vowed there was no way in hell she would wear it, and yet there she was. Kara stuck with mineral water because if she drank too much, she might punch California State's Attorney Beacham in the face. He kept pinching her cheek and telling her, he couldn't believe how much she'd grown. She tried to deflect, as her father had taught her, tried to talk about his dog, but nothing worked. She wanted to scream that she was now thirty years old and well past pinching age.

Just as she was about to make a break for the bathroom, her mother took her arm, smiling for any roaming photographers. Kara smiled too; it was instinct. Part of her training growing up: how to smile in different situations. How to jut your head out a little to look thinner. How to position your body for the most flattering full shot. It was all in there somewhere rattling around in her head. Most of the time she simply responded like a trained soldier. Nothing worse than a bad photo, God forbid.

"Kara," her mother greeted, kissing both of her cheeks, "you look stunning."

"Thank you, Mother. Congratulations."

"Oh, thank you, dear, but your father deserves all the credit."

"No, no, he would be nothing without you, Mom." Christ, this was like watching the same movie over and over again. Kara could predict the moves, the dialogue.

"Well"—she adjusted Kara's necklace—"that's nice of you to say. I just knew this dress would look great on you. Signature color." Her mother touched her on the nose. It was a gesture that felt ridiculously juvenile between two grown women.

Again, she wanted to scream that she was no longer a child. That she was out of puberty, owned a home, oh and by the way, she fucking hated the color raspberry. Instead, Kara smiled and sipped her mineral water.

"I was thinking we could do some Christmas shopping once things . . . Oh, dear, could you excuse me for a minute?" Her mother didn't wait for a response before she was gone. Kara watched her hug and compliment and hug and small talk all night.

She did have some memories of her mother when she was younger. When she still had bad hair days, before she became a professional senator's wife. She used to garden before she hired gardeners and the Malendars used to eat pizza in the living room and watch episodes of *Friends*. They were a family, and they still were in the important sense of the word. It was just different, more collected and put together. Kara laughed at that thought as she finally snuck away to the ladies' room.

She returned in time for the last round of congratulatory speeches and dessert. Her father stood to thank everyone for their support and then shook several people's hands. By the end of the night, he would shake every hand in the room. That was her father's thing. He knew the people who worked for him. He was actually a great senator and had helped to move the boulder that was politics in the right direction.

"Hey there, you ready to dance with your dad?" Her father came up next to her, still smiling and waving. Kara was pretty sure he never stopped smiling or waving.

"Is it my turn?"

"You're up."

"Cameras ready?"

"Come on, Kara. It's not really that bad."

"No, it really is." She smiled to ease the truth. Everything was a staged photo op, but the senator was still her dad. "I'm only kidding, Dad. Of course I'll dance with you."

He smiled and took her hand. "Thanks, honey." He spun her on the dance floor as Kara began to hear the "oohs" and "ahhs" that usually accompanied most private moments with her father.

"Wait, what are you thanking me for?"

"For a lot of things. I know these campaigns are tough on you guys and, well thank you for putting up with it. Sincerely, thank you."

Kara brushed his jacket and smiled. "Well, if you're sincere, then you're welcome. Have you talked to Grady yet?"

His face fell. "No."

"Don't you think you should?"

"I do, I know. I'll go see him tomorrow."

"Thank God it was an early call this year, right?" Kara tried to change the subject.

She had learned in her years as a Malendar that there was no point discussing the who did what to whom or the why. Her father won the election on the back of his son's hard work. It was probably necessary to ensure his win, but it was wrong. Kara knew and from the look on her father's face, he knew it too. With nothing left to say, it was time to fall into the "let's talk about other elections" part of the evening. "Remember the year you had the runoff?" Kara asked.

Her father laughed his politician laugh as he continued to turn her around the dance floor past the photographers. As her Nana would say, "it is what it is."

Chapter Eleven

Ryeland Farms had been hosting the Fall Festival since before Logan was born. His roots ran deep and this was often a source of inspiration for him. At some stupid hour of the morning, he and Garrett had finished moving bales of hay for the hayride. No matter how many years they did this, it seemed like they always left the hay for the last minute.

One of his fondest memories growing up was sitting out on the bales in the moonlight, and drinking beer Garrett snuck from the garage refrigerator, where their father kept his stash. Logan learned how to throw a punch and how to unhook a bra on those hay bale nights. Valuable information was shared between brothers who had no idea what they were doing or where they were going in life. Back then, the only thing certain in their lives was that chores would come the next morning. Logan smiled at the memory as the Fall Festival opened and visitors started pouring into their farm. He watched his brother lift a little boy up and down on one arm while giving the kid's parents directions to the petting zoo. Logan grew up loving the farm, but Garrett *was* the farm. He knew every last acre. He probably kept a running mental list of every crop, every animal, and what needed to be done at any given moment.

Logan watched as people filled up the main parking lot, many of them pulling their children in wagons. He saw her in the crowd, well actually he saw her wild hair, bundled in some kind of golden nest at the base of her neck, first. He'd just turned to check on the roasted corn and the sight of her soft in the setting sun, wearing jeans and a wide, beautiful smile as she watched the face painting, almost knocked him to the ground. She saw him too and her eyes traveled over him in that way they'd started to lately, sort of like she was undressing him. Logan wasn't complaining, but when her eyes grew that smoky, it made it very hard for him to remember why steering clear was his best option.

Kara glanced toward the entrance and then ordered her eyes to look away from the sight of him in a baseball cap, as if his "I work with these hands" image needed any help. A light gray T-shirt and the flannel he wore open, finished up every fantasy, farm or otherwise, that Kara had. The man jumbled her, but when he turned those golden earth-god eyes on her, she slipped past jumbled and straight into stupid.

She reminded herself this wasn't some high school field trip and walked over to get a very adult beverage. Handing the tall woman at the wine booth five dollars, she took a little plastic glass of some local Pinot she'd heard of, but had yet to taste. She sipped and leaned against a low wall of hay while she finished watching Eloise get her face painted by a woman with dreadlocks and a starfish tattoo on the back of her neck. Jake and Cotton were still taking pictures.

So this was a fall festival, she marveled. She had been to a few farm-themed birthday parties and even a wedding that took place on a vineyard, but this was more farm than she had ever experienced. Kara loved fall, and as she waved to Eloise, who turned and ran back toward the ponies with a very impressive cat face painted over her cherub cheeks, Kara realized she liked farms too.

She bought a roasted corn, finding herself suddenly hungry again. As she lifted the buttered corn to her mouth, she felt him. Jake and Cotton were over with the ponies and Kara knew the warmth behind her could only belong to Logan.

"You're cold." He stood next to her.

"No, I'm fine. I'm just adjusting to the setting sun."

"Is that real? Adjusting to the setting sun?" Logan asked laughing.

"Um, yes. The sun is going down and my body is adjusting to . . . not having the sun. Christ, why do I sound so stupid around you? No, Logan, I am not cold, but thank you." She bit into her corn and tried to catch the dripping butter as it trickled down her chin. When she glanced over, Logan's eyes were fixed on her mouth. Even when neither of them appeared to be trying, the energy was palpable. Kara wasn't sure if it was the festival or the excitement of fall, but she wanted to pull that flannel off of him, run her teeth up his—

"See, that was a shiver. You are cold and it's only going to get colder once the sun goes down."

Before she could figure out a way to tell him the shiver had nothing to do with the temperature, he was taking off his flannel. Kara averted her eyes, searched for something else to focus on. Suddenly, the corn in her hand felt awkward.

"I have a jacket, but I left it in the car. I can go and—"

Logan took her wrist to keep her from moving away.

"You parked in the side lot. That's a hayride or a pretty long walk. It's just my shirt, Kara. I'm not in it—take the damn thing."

He dropped the shirt over her shoulders and the chill was gone. She handed him her corn and slid her arms into the warmth that lingered in the fibers. The collar was thick and skimmed her cheek. She knew it was stupid and cliché, but she did it anyway.

"Did you just smell me?"

Kara closed her eyes and decided he was messing with her, flirting with her, something, and she was going to something him right back.

"Hmmm, sure did," she purred, slowly opening her eyes and taking back her corn. "You showered today, farm boy."

Logan laughed.

"I did. Washed the dirt off just for you."

"Oh, I bet. I'm sure it had nothing to do with the brunette in the paint-on jeans who was smiling at your . . . corn a few minutes ago." She took another bite.

Logan seemed to suck in some extra air as Kara dabbed at the corners of her mouth.

"Paint-on jeans. Huh, I'm not seeing a whole lot of room in your jeans."

"Please, I can breathe in mine. Hers are, well let's just say she has a steady pulse. I know because I can see it from here." She savored the last bite of corn and threw the cob in the barrel lined with a black plastic bag.

"Tight jeans look good on a woman." When Kara turned back, his eyes traveled the length of her legs. *Good God, was there something in farm air?*

She stumbled. His look was heated, an "I'd like to strip you out of those tight jeans" look. Kara recognized it from years before when Logan couldn't get enough of her and he had literally peeled her out of her jeans on the floor of her tiny Paris apartment. She had a bed that folded out of the wall, but they were on their lunch break during Egg Week at Cordon Bleu. There had been no time to pull the bed down, and the need threatened to burn them both alive. Their bodies dropped to the floor shortly after her jeans. They were a tangled mess of carelessness and passion. It was . . .

"Kara?"

Christ! Her cheeks were warm and for what seemed like an eternity, she couldn't forget the look on his face back then as he made fast, urgent love to her . . . how desirable he'd made her feel. Her insecurities, her sheltered and proper self had fallen away with each pulse of his body and she'd been so empowered. She could hear the music at the festival and Logan's voice in the present call her name, as she begged the memory to let her go.

When she finally pulled herself back, Logan was watching the dance floor, smiling.

"What?" she asked because he looked smug again, damn him.

"Looked like you were pretty far away there, princess. Where'd you go? Montmartre? Your apartment? Mine? The storage pantry? Wherever you just went, I was there with you. I could see me in your eyes. Touching you . . . I was there, wasn't I?" he said softly into her ear as they both stood side by side watching couples dancing to a local country band.

Her knees softened. Maybe it was the wine, she lied to herself and then finished the contents of her little plastic cup in one last gulp. "Very inappropriate," her mother would have criticized. "Ladies never gulp." *Oh zip it, Bindi*, Kara thought.

"We were at my apartment, lunchtime, during Egg Week," she said without a filter. It just slipped from her lips because he was right. He was there, touching her. She saw no point in pretending.

Logan's smile broadened, as he continued looking at the dance floor. He brushed his hand past hers, briefly touching her. "Yeah, I've replayed that one a few times."

She took in a deep breath and tried to collect herself. "I wasn't replaying, it was only when you mentioned—"

"Let's dance." Logan took her hand and they walked into to the area cordoned off with hay.

It was a slow song, but she followed him and slid into his arms anyway. Maybe it was the farm or the lilting romantic sound of the fiddle or his shirt. Whatever it was, Kara wanted to stay right where she was. She was a young woman, an ordinary woman with a tiny glass of wine on an empty stomach, unless she counted the corn, dancing with a tall handsome man. She rested her cheek on his chest and did something she hadn't done since Paris—she let Logan lead.

"So are you and painted jeans dating?"

Logan laughed and rested his head on top of hers.

"No."

"Used to date then. There's no way she hasn't seen you naked, not with the look she was giving you before."

"Then you must have it too."

"Have what?"

"The look. You've seen me naked, remember?"

"I do." She felt playful. "I have very clear memories when it comes to that particular subject, but I don't have the look. I erased that a long time ago. It's a dead giveaway and sort of an amateur move. Every woman knows you have to get rid of the look."

His chest rumbled harder. "You're something else. I plead the fifth."

"Yeah, well she's clearly still ... into you." Kara pulled back a bit to catch his eyes.

"Pretty sure her boyfriend would disagree." He gestured as they moved into a faster two-step and sure enough, painted jeans was wrapped around a large guy in a cowboy hat.

"Oh, well, hopefully he doesn't notice the look."

Logan laughed again, the song ended, and they both walked off the dance floor. It was dark now and the entire festival was lit by either bonfire or clear bulb lights that hung above from trees and between the barns.

Jake appeared next to them with his own little plastic glass of wine.

"You two looked good out there." He kissed Kara on the cheek and nodded to Logan.

Logan introduced himself and extended his hand.

"Really good to meet you, I'm Jake."

They shook hands.

"Glad you could make it."

"How many times has Eli been on the ponies?" Kara asked.

"I've honestly lost count. We couldn't get her off the black and white one the last time. I'm sure we will hear pleas for a pony all the way home."

"That's great. Happy to help," Logan joked.

"Yeah, she and Cotton went to get some more kettle corn. It's their second trip, although I'm pretty sure Eli's fallen asleep on his shoulders." Jake looked toward the food area. "This is an amazing place, Logan. Your family is great, too."

"Thanks, it can be a handful and so can they."

"Did you grow up here?"

"Sure did. I'm a farm boy through and through." He bumped Kara's shoulder. She laughed and then caught herself, but by the time she looked back at Jake, he was already giving them both the "aren't you two cute" look.

"Okay, well I'll leave guys to it. I'm thinking of trying out the bouncy thing. Can adults do that?"

Logan and Kara laughed and Jake was gone.

"He seems like a nice guy. Good friend?"

"My one and only. Well and Grady, but he's my brother."

"Jake is your only friend?"

"Yup and Cotton, but that's through marriage. Jake is a plumber."

"That guy in the sweater vest is a plumber?"

"Yup, he gets that look a lot from people, but he's actually very well respected. Third generation. He likes to tell people he's a plumber without the coin slot."

Logan laughed, clearly getting the reference to plumbers' frequent wardrobe malfunction.

"We met when he came to give me a quote for some work on my house. He also did a lot of work in my backyard, all the plumbing when I was building my . . . I mean . . ."

"Your what?"

"Oh, nothing. I lost my train of thought there for a minute. Anyway, we met when he was working on my house. I love him; he's family." Kara walked toward one of the barns. She wasn't sure where they were going, but her body followed his. She was so aware of his every move that it was almost painful, sort of like she had an itch out of reach and if she could just reach up a little farther . . .

"Why do you only have one friend?" Logan asked, picking up a cup that had been left on the ground and throwing it away.

"My life is complicated."

Logan laughed. "What, like which car to drive?"

His laughter grew louder and Kara was lost in it. She wanted to touch him, so she did. As soon has her hand made contact with his chest, her control slipped further. She tightened her hand on his shirt.

"You know what you need, Logan Rye?"

"Oh, we're using last names now. What's that, Kara Malendar? What is it I need?" He smiled and even though her face was pleasantly numb, the feel of his body, the tilt of his head, and the humor in his eyes, finished her off.

She grabbed his shirt tighter and pulled him into the breezeway of the nearest barn. She was doing this. She was going to show him exactly what he needed, but by the time they were alone, her nerves chased away her fuzzy wine buzz. She chickened out, let go of his shirt, and they stood in the silent barn lit only by the glow of the outside festival.

"Kiss me, Kara."

"What?"

"You heard me. Stop looking at me like that. I can't take it anymore. Make your move, or I will."

She laughed. "I'm not sure what you're talking about. I'm not looking at you any—"

Logan took her arm, and then the other one, and pulled her into him. The words she thought she had were gone and she tried to steady her breath.

"Here's the thing. You look at me and I like it. I look at you too, but now I want to touch and so do you. It's stupid, I know that."

"Why is it stupid?'

"Because I'll kiss you, taste you, and then you'll destroy me. You're like some huge storm that just rolled overhead."

"Did you just say I'm huge?"

Logan grinned, heated and sexy. He was still holding on to her. "A hurricane—that's what you are. Beautiful, out of nowhere, cool rains on a hot day, incredible storm. I want a closer look, I want to close my eyes and soak the whole damn thing in, but I should know better. There's dust and wind. Shit, people get killed in hurricanes."

Kara had been around smooth talkers all her life, but Logan's jumbled, breathy words as he ran his hands up her arms, were almost eloquent and he again pulled her closer as if that would somehow give him his next breath. He was so close, pushing her to admit things she wasn't sure she could. She had far too many people in her life pushing her. At least with Logan, she could push back. She could try.

"I am not a tornado, I'll have you know that—"

"Hurricane."

"What?"

"I said you were a hurricane, not a tornado. Big difference."

"Whatever, I'm not that and while your ego clearly needs its own room right now, I have no intention of kissing you."

"Suit yourself." He held the back of her neck, tilted his head.

Her hands went to his chest and clung to him like magnets. She could feel his breath on her skin. His eyes narrowed and the deep gold was mesmerizing. Despite her very best efforts, Kara's eyes fell to his lips: full, moist, and wanting. Logan seemed to settle in. Was he waiting for her to protest, to slap him? She was going to disappoint him then because she couldn't move.

"Close your eyes," he said.

"No."

Logan smiled and it reached his eyes. What was already sexy became an older, scarier version of familiar. She knew his lips, knew he would take her right out of her skin with the simple slide of his tongue. Kara brought her hands to his shoulders and allowed herself to feel the muscles beneath his shirt. A sigh escaped her lips. She wasn't closing her eyes; she wasn't about to be taken.

"You close *your* eyes," Kara instructed in a tone that almost disguised her racing heart.

Logan licked his bottom lip, smiled, and closed his eyes. She noticed his lashes. They were bleached on the tips. He stood before her rough, worn, and yet a little vulnerable with his eyes closed. He was beautiful and Kara hesitated for a moment as she admired him.

"Exactly how long do you want me to—" Logan's words fell as Kara gently put her lips on the dip of his neck, the part at the end of the suntanned, corded muscle, and moved toward his shoulder. She could feel his pulse pounding.

"Shhh." She slid her other hand into his hair, kissed along his stubble-lined jaw, and then found herself at his mouth. The anticipation of his lips was unbearable. It hung in the air between them. She waited one more beat and as her own eyes softly closed, she heard him moan and she was ready to "make her move," as he'd said. She kissed him and his arm snaked around her waist. Their lips strained and then Logan was taking over, driving the kiss. She let him. She knew better than to interfere.

Unlike most men Kara had dated, Logan seemed perfectly happy to stay in the kiss forever. As he tilted her head for better access, her hazy mind acknowledged that nothing had changed between them. It was as if they had been transported back to Paris, standing in line at the Louvre on their day off, his fingers making tiny circles under the hem of her T-shirt. His hands had driven her so crazy that day. The same hands were now on her face and all she could do was hold on and move with his lips. Her fingers closed around the fabric of his shirt as he gave it his all. *Good Lord, the man could kiss.* Soft and then nipping. He seemed to love lips and tongues, her tongue in particular at the moment. She was about to surrender completely when he pulled back.

"Shit," he whispered, his lips barely off of her.

Kara's eyes flew open and she pulled away. In that moment, she demanded that every insecurity threatening to come bubbling to the surface stay right where it was. Maybe he didn't feel what she felt. Maybe he was just screwing with her for leaving him. What the hell was she doing in a damn barn?

This is not your life, she reminded herself, *and now you've given him the upper hand, genius.*

She turned to walk out of the barn and Logan followed. They walked in silence for a few steps, nothing but hay and gravel crunching. She wanted the safety of her car. A full moon lit the entire farm and the crowds began making their way toward the front parking lot. Rows and rows of crops that seemed to go on forever were laid out in front of her as she walked toward the side entrance where she'd parked. It was magical, even though every instinct in her told her to leave. She could smell the smoke from the fires still burning at the festival. Taking off the shirt he had loaned her, she welcomed the shiver of the night air, recognized it as reality.

Still walking, Kara handed the shirt back to Logan. He grabbed her instead and pulled her to the side of the barn.

"What the hell is wrong with you?" He kissed her again. This one felt reluctant and then frustrated.

Their eyes met for one quick look, pooled in moonlight, and they went back under. When his hands moved down her back, Kara knew she needed to leave before she made a fool of herself. She yanked free.

"I thought it was shit. Do you often go back for more shit?"

Logan shook his head. "You honestly think I meant that kissing you was shit?"

"You said, and I quote, 'Shit.' Not exactly what a girl wants to hear." Kara pushed the hair out of her face.

"Pretty sure I'm never going to understand you, princess." He followed her again as she approached the side gate.

"I told you not to call me that."

"I know you did. Back to the kiss, 'shit' can mean a lot of things. It amazes me that someone who prances around like you do needs to have—"

She turned on him, pushed his chest. It didn't move. "I do not prance."

Logan lifted his finger to her lips. "A woman who carries herself like you do, as if any man on the planet would be lucky—"

She'd had enough, interrupted him again, and continued walking. She was not going to stand there, moonlight or not, and have one more person tell her who she was and what she was lacking. Logan followed, but gave her space. When they reached the fence, he opened the gate for her and walked the rest of the way to her car. Kara beeped the lock open, took the little purse she was carrying on her wrist, and threw it in the car. She steadied herself and turned to him.

"Goodnight, Logan. Your family's farm is . . . well, it's truly lovely. I'll have some great material to work with for the third piece of the article."

He nodded and held the door open as she got into her car. She turned the engine and he knocked on her window. She rolled it down.

"Did you put your seatbelt on?"

Kara scrunched her forehead in frustration and pulled the strap across her chest.

"Good. Strapped in. Now, 'shit' can mean a lot of things. In this case, in my case, I would have gone with 'holy shit,' but forming two words at that moment was damn near impossible."

Their eyes met and Kara's breathing eased down from angry.

"'Shit' in that situation," Logan continued, "meant I'm in trouble, or shit I'm on the edge of the storm and I just got knocked on my ass." He bent down, rested his arms on her window. "I can't figure you out, Kara Malendar, but kissing you . . . Hell, I could do that for at least a few days straight."

Kara wasn't sure how to respond to that. She simply stared at him as he stood and patted the top of her car.

"Night, Kara. Drive safe." He started to walk away.

"Hey." She finally found her words.

He turned back, still looking thoroughly kissed in the moonlight, and she smiled.

"You're shit too," she said.

Logan let out a full-bodied laugh and Kara realized she liked him—liked who he was as a person. Every part of her body wanted him, and that was wonderful, but above all he was a good man. Before she got out of the car and jumped him again, she drove home.

Chapter Twelve

*K*ara knew it was only a matter of time before Jake would want some one-on-one time with Logan. When she reminded Jake that they had just met at the Fall Festival last week, he had countered with, "I know, but that wasn't good question-and-answer time. Besides Cotton hasn't met him yet." The look on his face told Kara there was no point in arguing, which was why they were currently sitting in the large black leather corner booth at The Yard. Logan was busy, but Travis must have given him a breather because he came over to take their order and "chat," as Jake liked to call it.

"Logan," Kara said as he approached the table, "you've already met Jake, my best friend in the world, and this is his husband Cotton." All three waited for the usual puzzled look over Cotton's name, but Logan just came right out with it.

"Cotton, is that a family name?" Logan asked.

Cotton, who was a very tall, slender Southern man, laughed and gave his standard answer.

"According to my parents, I was named after Cotton Mather, who was a minister involved in the Salem witch trials. It's beautifully ironic that their son grew up to be a gay man, don't you think?"

Logan laughed and Kara swore it filled the space around them. Maybe her draw to him was rooted in Paris or that kiss or the fact that he was so damn sexy with his disheveled hair and glasses. Maybe it was because of how fun it was to watch him in his element. He seemed tired, but tired was working for him. Kara must have been staring at him while he and Cotton talked farmers markets because Jake cleared his throat. Kara turned to him and he wiggled his eyebrows. She shook her head while Logan and Cotton continued in animated conversation. Jake nodded his "watch this" nod.

"So, Logan"—Jake put his hand on Cotton's shoulder—"sorry to interrupt, but Kara tells me you two met in Paris?"

Logan hesitated and deferred to Kara for direction, but she gave him nothing. She wanted to see him handle this one.

"Y—yes we did. We were both part of a food and culture exchange program through UCLA." Logan was polite and probably hoping that would be the extent of the curiosity. If so, he was so very wrong.

"Really, so tell us, is our girl here a good cook? She never cooks for us."

Kara chewed a bite of her salad that had been delivered amid the conversation and knew exactly where Jake was going.

Logan smiled.

"I like your friends, Kara." He dropped into a squat so he was level with, and resting his arms on, the table. "Yes," he answered, this time catching Kara's eyes. "She was a great cook. She was a natural, especially with the spices. She was always great with spices."

Kara held his look in a dare.

"Is that so? Spices always seem like the sexy part of cooking. Am I right?" shameless Jake asked.

"Yes, very sexy." Logan smiled, playing along. "Kara always was pretty sexy."

Kara should have probably warned him that he was heading into Jake's trap, but she was looking forward to watching him squirm. Besides, the way he said sexy, the way he looked at her, brought back delicious memories of his mouth kissing hers, his hands on her. There were worse images. Kara sat back and enjoyed her salad.

"So what happened with you two? I mean, I know about Kara's charade, but why didn't you call her up?"

And BOOM, just like that Logan needed to check something in the kitchen.

"Maybe you should take it easy on him. Seems like a nice fella," Cotton said.

"Damn, did you see him run? Kara, what did you do to the poor man?"

Kara laughed as she watched Logan sort through orders or pretend to at least. He glanced over at her, his face unreadable.

What had I done to him? She'd actually never thought about it. She was too wrapped up in her own mess, and then he never did call and she merely chalked it up to a fling. Granted he was her very first fling at the age of twenty-one, but she'd always believed she was the only one who had blossomed and loved their time in Paris. For Logan, it had just been . . . what had it been for him? How had she not thought about his side of things? Kara wasn't sure what that made her: either dumb or self-absorbed. Or a bitch.

Logan eventually came back to the table to face the music. He met Jake's eyes, clearly ready with his response. "What happens in Paris, stays in Paris."

Jake laughed and Cotton clapped. Logan had survived the interrogation and the rest of the evening was spent enjoying roasted vegetables, incredible salt-and-pepper shrimp, and a flatbread pizza with a mushroom medley none of them had ever had before. They shared and loved everything. Logan eventually had to return to the kitchen, but Kara peeked in to say goodnight as they were leaving.

"How'd I do?" he asked, pulling plastic wrap over a huge metal bowl.

Kara laughed. "You were great. Very nice navigation."

"Christ, I had to step away to figure that one out." He shook his head. "But they're both great guys, I can see why they're your friends."

"They are the best." She hesitated, feeling a little foolish. "Well, I won't keep you. Thanks for the great dinner. The article comes out tomorrow, so I'll e-mail you a copy."

"Okay, great." He wiped his hands on a towel and walked toward her. "Goodnight." He leaned in like he might kiss her, but then didn't. Kara turned to leave and found her courage.

"Logan."

"Yeah?"

"Did you ever wonder about me after I left? How I dealt with leaving you or Paris?"

His brow furrowed. "I think, well, I meant what I said to Jake. It stayed in Paris. I'm sure you didn't think of me and I didn't think of you—it was just over."

"Right. Yeah, that's what I thought too." Kara turned to leave again, not sure why she was so hurt. She should have felt better hearing he never thought about them again. But she could practically feel her heart break a little, right along the same familiar scar tissue. "Goodnight, Logan."

"Night, princess."

Chapter Thirteen

*L*ogan couldn't sleep. He lay in bed, staring up at the exposed ceiling, counting the beams of wood in an effort to distract his thoughts. It was definitely not working. He had volunteered earlier in the week to help switch pastures for the chickens at the farm. Even though he enjoyed working with his family and being around the animals now and then, he was dead tired. The comfort of his childhood bed was doing nothing to lull him to sleep. He kept replaying that damn question over and over again.

"Did you think of me after Paris?" What the hell kind of question was that? One minute it was a fight, the next minute he was kissing her, and now this. Those eyes when she'd asked him were still killing him. What was he supposed to say, "Oh, yeah, I thought about you all the time, Kara and how you dropped me without even a glance back"? No way that was happening. It was bad enough he'd kissed her, but up until tonight it had still been a game—a sparring, flirtatious game. There was no point in discussing things you couldn't change.

In hindsight, the kiss was probably a bad idea, especially because it was at the Fall Festival at the farm, so now even the smell of hay reminded him of her. Logan closed his eyes and then opened them again. He yanked the wool blanket under his chin because just like when he was a kid, the damn house was drafty. Every time he closed his eyes, he saw her, tasted her. He wanted her all over again. Two or three years it took to get his shit together and suddenly he was worse off than he was the first time he'd laid eyes on her. Spending time with her had only made the want worse. Logan threw the covers off, pulled on his jeans, and went into the kitchen.

It was three o'clock in the morning and he needed to do something, so he made coffee. An hour later his family woke to biscuits and gravy and Logan felt better. Kara Malendar was now put back behind everything else in his life, where she belonged. She was some girl he met in Paris. Not some irresistible woman he needed more than the first time.

"Holy shit, you should get all stupid for a woman more often." Garrett walked into the kitchen pulling on a long-sleeve shirt.

How the hell did he know? Garrett's big brother radar annoyed the crap out of him.

"This looks great, sad little lovesick man. Thanks for breakfast."

"It's four in the morning. Doesn't your mouth need to warm up?" Logan set the bacon on the table.

"Nope." He poured some coffee and took a seat at the large scarred wooden table. "Course, I actually slept for a few hours. You should try it sometime. Makes a guy much more agreeable."

"You're agreeable?" Logan raised his eyebrow.

"I'm usually pretty agreeable until someone pisses me off."

"Which happens when? Right after you brush your teeth?"

Garrett laughed and snatched a piece of bacon. There was enough food to feed everyone, twice.

Makenna shuffled in next, boots on but not yet laced, and her hair was pulled through the back of a Dodgers cap.

"Mornin'," Garrett said, helping himself now to the full breakfast.

Kenna waved on her way to the refrigerator. She cracked open a Coke, poured it over ice, and kissed Logan on the cheek. He thought he heard her mumble something about breakfast, but it was best not to engage her before her first full glass of caffeine. She'd always been that way. In high school, Logan would have it already poured on the days she usually burst into the kitchen yelling about how she hated having brothers and how they'd better stop touching her stuff. On those days, her hormones joined her at the breakfast table; that's what their father used to say, which only pissed her off more. Logan learned early from his sister that the last thing women wanted to hear when they were hormonal, was that they were hormonal. It was a piece of information that helped him as he went out into the dating world.

Makenna cupped her glass as if it was a favorite stuffed animal and Garrett was almost through his first round of breakfast when their dad came into the kitchen. He was in his "uniform" as they liked to call it. Dark Levis, white T-shirt under a plaid flannel shirt—which became a plaid cotton shirt during the warmer months—all tucked in with a belt. His father's belt buckle was brass with wheat stalks and a tractor. Logan remembered as a kid he and Garrett would sneak into his bedroom after they thought he was asleep and try his belt on. Holding it up and sticking out their bellies as far as they could, only to have the whole thing fall to the floor with a pretty loud clank. That usually woke their father who gathered them both up and threw them on the bed for "tickle torture."

Logan smiled now at his father. Herbert Rye placed his cowboy hat on the seat next to him. Even at four in the morning he was freshly shaven. Always freshly shaven.

"Where's the only cute member of the Rye family?" Garrett asked.

Makenna pointed up as she spooned some eggs on her plate indicating that Paige, who had her Uncle Garrett wrapped around all of her fingers, was still sleeping.

"That's where sweet angels belong." Garrett's pillowy voice had them all looking at him.

"Pretty sure I was feeding the chickens when I was six." Makenna shook her head at her brother.

"Yeah, but that was just you." Garrett leaned over and hit the brim of Kenna's cap. "Paige the Magnificent is different."

"It's nice to have you home, Logan," their father said, grabbing some breakfast.

"Hey, what about the rest of us?" Garrett asked.

"You don't cook for me." Herb smiled and placed a napkin in his lap.

Garrett feigned insult and huffed as he stood for more coffee, smacking the brim of Kenna's cap again on his way to the coffee-maker. She flipped him off and so began morning breakfast at the Rye house. Logan leaned back on the counter to enjoy the moment. This was where his heart belonged, and he was so grateful for his life. He guessed that came with age, because there was a time when he resented practically everything. Not anymore though. Their mother hadn't won when she'd left them, and that was all that mattered.

That morning Kara pulled up her article and read it as if she hadn't read it over dozens of times before submitting it. She liked pretending she was the reader, with a fresh set of eyes, although that was virtually impossible. Even after an article was in print, she still hesitated at the spots that had given her a hard time while writing it. Those bumps never really went away, but when she finished reading her first of what would become three articles on Logan, she had to admit it was good. Front page good, which was thrilling. She'd managed to capture the feel of Logan's place and a little bit about the man. There was a nice lead-in to the second part about The Yard, but she didn't give too much away. The writing was tight, the pictures were great, and nowhere in there had she hinted that she had once climbed, and occasionally still wanted to climb, Logan Rye like a tree. *Well done, Kara.*

She e-mailed it to Makenna and Logan. He texted her about an hour later asking her to meet him for dinner. Kara hesitated. Sharing the article with him was one thing, but dinner? She was still a little uneven after the stupid question she'd asked him. She blamed it on Jake when she'd talked to him this morning. It was his fault for making her feel all warm and fuzzy and for bringing it up in the first place. He'd laughed at her and then suddenly had to go. Typical.

Sure, I'll see you around 6.

That's what she texted Logan. She thought it sounded casual, no mention of her "oh please tell me your deepest feelings" moment back in his kitchen. She was over it and he would need to get over it too, if he even cared. Damn it, she sounded ridiculous. *Just drop it, Kara. Go back to being playful.*

They did so well when things stayed playful. She had a busy day ahead of her and then she would stop by The Yard to celebrate her article. Light and easy, that was Kara's new motto, she thought as she rearranged some photographs for her article on trussing a turkey.

The pastures were moved by noon. After lunch, Logan and Garrett chopped some more wood for their dad because his pile was getting low. At some point he remembered showering, but it was all a little fuzzy. Logan was back at the restaurant in time to help prep for dinner and meet Kara to talk about her article. Kenna loved the feature, but something about it was bugging him. They would be closed for Thanksgiving and the Friday that followed. He would sleep then. Right after he served turkey dinner to hundreds of people in Pasadena's Central Park on Thanksgiving Day. He'd started working with Homeless Services last year, even before The Yard opened, and Ryeland Farms had been a sponsor since the event started. This year Logan had agreed to cook some of the meal and most of The Yard's staff would serve. But that was tomorrow; right now he needed more eggplant. Travis was manning the stove, so Logan agreed to chop. Chopping could actually qualify as moving meditation in his book.

He took a break between the first dinner rush and what they all hoped would be the second wave to sit with Kara.

"Optimistic? You called me optimistic." Logan set plates and napkins on their table.

He'd read the feature, and he wasn't trying to be picky or cast out negative energy, but optimistic wasn't exactly a badass word. Maybe his ego expected her to paint him as a badass, not . . . Peter Pan for Christ's sake.

"I did. What is wrong with that?"

Logan served her a slice of the mushroom and goat cheese pizza and some of the salad he'd made for their meeting. He'd stopped asking her if she was hungry. He now knew she was. After grabbing a couple glasses of water from behind the bar, he sat across from her at the corner bar table where he'd tucked them so the entire place wouldn't hear their conversation. Privacy was not easy in Logan's life either these days, although his lack of it had more to do with snooping relatives and employees than reporters and photographers.

"It makes what I do sound . . . simple, childish. Children are optimistic. It's hard enough getting people to see that growing their own food, knowing where their food comes from, is not some backwoods, hillbilly agenda. That good nourishing food, humane food, is basic. It's a simple, basic right."

"I said all of that. I used more quotes in this first piece than I've ever used. Partly because I'm not quite sure what you're always talking about."

He caught the joke but didn't smile. Kara looked concerned, and it wasn't that he disliked the article. It was well written, but as he continued to flip from the first page of her article to the second page, back and forth, back and forth. The words "optimistic" and "hometown" popped out at him like too much balsamic vinegar. Too syrupy and sort of like a novelty; here today and gone tomorrow. Maybe these were his own issues, nerves, or whatever. He'd never had something so in-depth written about him, his home, and what he believed in. There on paper it just felt odd and a bit foolish.

"And what's this 'Logan Rye not only grows his food, but he has recently learned the value of foraging'?"

"What is wrong with that? You have. I'm not sure why you are getting so worked up. The article was well received. The *Times* loves the tone. Logan, it's just a peek into you and what you believe in as a chef and a man. It wasn't meant to be all-inclusive."

Kara seemed a little offended, so he backed off and by his second piece of pizza he decided all publicity was good for the restaurant. Kenna was thrilled, so he needed to relax.

"It's not your article. Your writing is fantastic; I guess I'm not into all of this. I do what I do. It makes sense to me, and yeah it's how I think the entire country should eat. We'd be better for it, but reading this. I don't know, it makes me sound . . ."

"Like a different kind of guy, with a unique 'optimistic' vision for the world. A man who works hard, not only growing food, but also making delicious meals? That is who you are. If you wanted my article to paint you as some cool, mainstream, food-off-a-truck chef, I'm sorry. You're not that guy."

"Food-off-a-truck chef," he repeated and laughed. Sometimes she surprised him with her one-liners. No other woman made him laugh like she did, except maybe Kenna, but he was often the butt of her jokes. "That's a good one. I might need to keep that for myself on the days when I'm wondering how the hell I'm going to keep this all together. I still hate the word 'optimistic'."

Kara shook her head. "It means someone who thinks all things are possible. Like it or not, that is you, Logan. At least when it comes to food."

"What's that supposed to mean?" he asked because her comment seemed like a departure from the current conversation, like she was about to launch another "feelings" question his way without warning.

"Exactly what I said. You're a little jaded in other areas of your life, but when it comes to food, you're inspiring."

"Well, it's hard to have much else when I'm living at this place. Were you looking for me to inspire you, Kara?"

She laughed. "No, I'm fine, but thanks for that offer."

"You sure?" He leaned across the table and touched her hand.

He liked debating with her, tossing things around. He felt better and she was back to playful. It was nice having someone to talk with. Oh, who was he kidding? It wasn't just having someone, it was nice having her, watching her defend her work and then brag about him until he felt pretty damn badass even with the Peter Pan word. He cared about her and with the exception of that one moment the other night, things were light, fun. Just the way he needed them to stay.

"Never been more certain in my entire life. Back up, farm boy."

He didn't move, held her hand.

"There's something about the way you say that." He stood and moved to her side of the table. He could feel her nervous energy as the game played on.

"Is that so?" She met his eyes. Damn, the woman could go from sweet to dangerous in seconds.

"Conjures up all sorts of fantasies—farm boy and uptight princess. Has a nice ring to it, don't you think?"

"Oh yeah," she moaned and he knew it was for his benefit. Logan felt the game turn in her favor. She slid off her stool until their bodies were touching. The bar was pretty crowded; no one was watching and he noticed Kara didn't even look. Progress, he thought. He wasn't sure what had gotten into her, but when she ran her hand up the buttons of his shirt, he instantly felt like a damn teenage boy. "Were you thinking we could . . . take a roll in the hay? For old time's sake?" she whispered in his ear.

No question, she was screwing with him once again, but he still couldn't resist. He cleared his throat to make sure he didn't squeak his answer like a sissy, as Garrett would have instructed.

"Princess, just say the word," was his response. Short, cool, he thought it was well played until her hand snaked around to his ass.

Kara patted him as if he were a toy, her toy. Then she picked up her purse and patted him on the shoulder. "There you go being optimistic again, farm boy." She flashed him a not-on-your-life smile and walked out of his restaurant. Her clicking heels carried away his favorite pair of legs and her own ass, which looked to be getting bigger and healthier. He grinned, shook his head at her through the bar window as she passed to the parking lot, and then he laughed all the way back to the kitchen.

Chapter Fourteen

The morning before Thanksgiving, the *Pasadena Tribune* ran a story featuring a picture of Kara dancing with Logan at the Fall Festival. The article questioned how she could be objective when she was "clearly in a relationship with the owner of The Yard." Her feature had only been out a week, barely enough time to be proud before the vultures swooped in. She should have been outraged, hurt, insulted, but instead she was simply reminded of the world she lived in and prepared to give Olivia her resignation. That didn't happen. When she got to work that morning, Olivia pulled her into her office and closed the door. "Those fucks! You just ignore these morons, honey. I've already spoken to Harold and he could give two shits about their piece. I mean, it's a clear grab at attaching themselves to your great feature, and it will backfire."

Kara didn't often cry, and never in public, not since 1995 when she was photographed with ugly-cry face at a veteran's memorial service. But if she had allowed herself to cry, it would have been right there in Olivia's office. Her embarrassment and humiliation at being called a fluff had all come rushing forward as soon as Olivia offered her shoulder, but Kara kept it together. She thanked her and turned to leave.

"Oh, and if you are sleeping with that delicious man, honey, more power to you."

Kara laughed.

"At some point you have to ignore the haters or they'll eat your soul," Olivia added as Kara walked out.

She was pretty sure they'd already reached her soul, and long before the Pasadena Tribune food section jumped into the ring. For the rest of the day she worked on the second Logan article and tried to put the *Tribune* out of her mind, even though her phone didn't stop vibrating. She eventually threw it in her purse. She'd promised Logan "no fluff," and yet there the two of them were, splashed all over some other paper as just that. Kara made tea, called Jake for one of his famous talks, and by the end of the day she had silenced the voices in her head telling her she'd never be good enough.

"Did you see this?" Makenna asked, walking up to Logan while he was waiting for Travis to give him a side of fennel salad to complete the order for table twelve.

"I really hate when you start a conversation that way." Logan eyed the order tickets clipped in front of him.

"Yeah, I know, and I was waiting for you to have a break, but I don't think it's coming, so look at this." She held the newspaper in front of his face.

"Whoa, get that out of here unless you want to spend some quality time with the health department next week. Just let me," he paused as Travis handed him the salad, "finish these next two and I'll meet you at the bar. Go try and cheer Sage up. She's still pissed she lost the Halloween cocktail contest again."

"But—"

"Go away, Kenna." Logan leaned around her. "Drop the pizza for seventeen, Matt. And what the hell is taking so long on the potatoes for eleven?" He returned to the rhythm of his work. Everything else could wait.

Makenna huffed and left the kitchen.

After about an hour and some words with their apprentice, Todd, who was now sporting a blue streak in his already too-long bangs, Logan entered the bar area, looking for Makenna. She normally sat at the bar and talked with Sage, but it was packed, so she was at one of the tables by the window with her face in her laptop. He grabbed some coffee from Sage and sat across from his sister. Her fingers were typing frantically. She said nothing and pushed the newspaper across the table to him. It was the *Pasadena Tribune*, their food section. The headline read *Malendar Plays Favorites* and below the headline was a picture of him dancing with Kara at the Fall Festival.

"What the hell is this?" Logan asked.

At the sound of his voice, Makenna finally stopped typing.

"Read it." She returned to her laptop.

"After the glowing praise Ms. Malendar, food critic for the *Los Angeles Times*, received for her first of three feature articles on Logan Rye, it seems clear objectivity is not her primary concern," Logan read. "While the article was engaging and we mean to take nothing away from Mr. Rye or his accomplishments, one has to wonder how Malendar can write anything more than a fluff piece when she's so clearly 'involved' with the subject matter."

Logan set the paper down and ran a hand over his face. His eyes burned.

"So, there you have it. Great publicity one minute and God only knows what now."

"This is bullshit. Anyone who reads this will see it for exactly what it is."

"And what is it, Logan?" she asked. "Because we're all in this. We all have something to lose here."

Logan took a deep breath and reminded himself this was not important; this was a stupid article that would be gone as quickly as it arrived. Negative energy and he would not let it piss him off.

"The feature the *Times* ran last week was great. People have mentioned it, hell you framed it and hung it on the damn wall." He pointed to the article near the bar. "It was, and still is, a good thing for us. This"—he flicked the paper—"this is trash and it's not going to affect what we do here."

Makenna shook her head. "I sure as hell hope you're right, because I know I say it all the time, but everything has to be better than perfect at this phase of the game."

"I know, and I'm getting as close to perfect as I can." He touched her hand. "Now, I've got to get back to work, so throw that crap out. Go pick up my niece, bring her some real food for dinner, and get some sleep, you look like shit."

Makenna laughed and wiped under her eye with her middle finger letting Logan know she was his number one fan, sort of. He popped his towel at her and went back to the kitchen.

Part of his job was to manage and keep an even head. That was what he'd tried to do with his sister, but as he rounded the corner into the back room, his heart was racing. He wasn't all that concerned about the *Tribune* article. Few people read the food section for anything more than reviews, even fewer read past the stars indicating good, better, best. Logan had agreed to the *LA Times* piece at Makenna's urging, but he'd never thought it would have a sink or soar effect on their restaurant either way. So, this new article wasn't that big of a deal for him, but it was for Kara. It's not like they were really "involved" as the article stated, but he knew her well enough to be humiliated for her. He believed in his work and if anyone took issue with the quality of his job . . . well he'd spent most of his life making sure that never happened. He wondered if he should call her, but what would he say? Then Travis called him to the window and the next time he looked up, it was closing time.

Chapter Fifteen

Senator Malendar and his family worked the lunchtime shift at the St. Christopher Homeless Shelter on Thanksgiving morning. As expected, Kara and Grady were there being dutiful children. Grady brought Kate, his fiancée, with him. Kara liked her—she saw that Kate was good for her brother. He deserved someone, she thought, smiling at the two of them as the family emerged for a brief meeting with the press. Kara stood tall in dark slacks and a raspberry sweater. She found her focal point, a traffic sign, to keep her gaze "up and interested" as her mother had trained her. Her father fielded questions, her mother flashed a toothy grin, and Grady held Kate's hand. They were almost done; Kara had just started thinking about cranberry sauce, when the question zinged past her ear.

"Senator, any comments on your daughter's relationship with Logan Rye?"

Kara's eyes moved away from the safety of her traffic sign to Grady who shook his head in disgust. She had told her parents about the article and assured them it was not a big deal, but standing there, unable to leave without looking like she actually had something to hide, it suddenly felt like a big deal.

"Griff, I'm not sure what 'relationship' you're referring to." She could see aggravation creep into her father's eyes. "As you know, my daughter is a food critic for the *Times*. She's writing a three-part piece on Mr. Rye, his family, and his new restaurant. She has been spending some time with him, and any swirling rumors are simply that, rumors."

"Sir, with all due respect, with the new farming regulations up for discussion this term, are you aware that Ryeland Farms supports the farm-to-table lobby that's putting a lot of pressure on big businesses in Pasadena and Los Angeles?"

Bingo. That's why she, and Logan for that matter, were suddenly so important. Politics, it always came back to politics and let the casualties fall where they may. All she wanted was to get in the damn car and away from the vultures, but then her father laughed and she was able to take a full breath.

"Oh, come on. Are you seriously linking this article to some other sinister plot to influence farming decisions? Just stop. Believe me, things are far more complicated than just one farm or one farmer. Now, if you'll excuse me, I'd like to finish the holiday with my family."

"Okay, maybe that was a stretch, but do you think the rumors are true?" another reporter chimed in.

"Kara, are you and Logan involved?" another reporter shouted before the first question was even answered. Kara could tell they were entering what her father's campaign manager, Stanley, liked to call a "feeding frenzy." It was where the press, failing to get an answer to what they wanted, began throwing anything out to get a rise. Kara started walking toward the car.

"Okay, that's enough," Kate interrupted and stepped in front of the senator. She was a PR executive for Bracknell and Stevens and had helped Kara's father win the recent election. Kara was sure she was stepping in for damage control before her father gave the reporters a sound bite he would regret by the time he got to the car.

"Kate," three reporters called out in unison, and then one continued, "we thought the election was over. You part of the family now?"

"Soon to be, Griff. Now, what's this about? The Malendars have spent their afternoon giving back to their community. They're ready to go home now."

"Kara," another reporter addressed Kara directly and held up the *Tribune* article, "do you have a comment? As a journalist, should you be this involved with the subject of the piece you're working on?"

Kate put her hand on Kara's shoulder, indicating it was time for her to leave. Kara glanced at Grady who smiled and gestured for her to keep moving toward the car.

"This is ridiculous. Don't you guys need to get home for turkey?" Kate tried to deflect.

"Oh come on, Kate. Do you have any thoughts you'd like to share?"

"I have lots of thoughts, Griff, but you probably won't like any of them. You guys are absurd. Hey, Happy Thanksgiving."

"Grady, how's it going? Are you and Kate enjoying being engaged?"

Grady said nothing as he waited for Kate to finish.

The reporters turned and began moving toward Kara as she followed her father to the car. She felt like a damn child again, unable to speak, not allowed stick up for herself or her job.

Kate pulled Grady and stepped between Kara and the four men approaching for one last jab.

"I'll say we're enjoying being engaged, right babe? I mean why bother with Kara's little dance when I can tell you all about the endless stamina that is her brother. Dear Lord!" Kate began fanning herself and it worked. All four men turned. Kara caught Kate's quick smile as she ducked into the black Lincoln Town Car. When the door was about to close, she heard her brother.

"Well, you know I hate to brag, but let's just say we're not getting a lot of sleep," Grady added wrapping his arm around Kate's waist.

"Damn it, Kara," her father launched right in as soon as they were in the safety of the car. "I've told you that you need to be careful."

She felt foolish, certainly not for the first time in her life, but she was getting sick and tired of being treated like the same awkward girl she'd been growing up.

"Do you have anything to say? I mean they do have a point. The farming stuff was just politics, but as a reporter—"

"Dad, I write food reviews and the occasional feature. This isn't Pulitzer Prize-winning stuff here. I danced with him at a fall festival. It was innocent; it was fun. I promise fun will never happen again."

"I didn't say you couldn't have fun." The light of his phone screen illuminated. "Wait, hang on, I need to answer this." He began typing.

"Who is this young man?" her mother asked, giving her what Grady called "the death stare." When they were little he used to hum the Darth Vader theme when their mother would leave the room. God, how she needed him right now.

"Logan Rye." Kara looked out the window. "Not that it's any of your business," she added softly.

"Excuse me?" More death stare.

"I said it's not any of your business. I mean, if you'd read my article you would know all about him. The damn election is over and I'm thinking I can talk, work, or dance with whoever I want at this point."

"Whomever, Dear."

Kara shook her head. "Actually, no one uses that anymore, Mom. Whoever is perfectly acceptable now."

"Well, I don't like it."

"Of course not."

"I don't like your tone either. Patrick, do you have anything to say?"

Kara's dad was still on his phone.

"I think she's right, Bindi. I mean I would prefer not to have been ambushed back there, but she can do what she wants."

"It's not ladylike. It's certainly not becoming for the daughter of a US senator. You should remain professional at all times."

Kara took a breath, her focus still out the window, and wondered why the hell she hadn't brought her own car. She began wondering a lot of things, like why she hadn't said anything back there to those reporters. What was wrong with her? She just froze and stood there like a little girl in knee socks and patent leather shoes. Anger simmered and all she wanted was to get out of the car. She cracked the window, but it didn't help.

"Do you even know anything about this boy?"

"'Boy'?" Kara laughed. "Logan passed 'boy' a very long time ago, Mother."

"Oh well, look at you all grown up. I hope things don't go the way of your other men. And dear Lord, I hope you haven't taken pictures with him because when this blows up, I don't want your father left dealing—"

At that, her father chimed in. "I think that's enough, Bindi. I'd prefer not to think of my daughter in, er, compromising positions on Thanksgiving. As she explained, it was simple dancing and having fun. She has to deal with what it means professionally. Now let's let it go." He redirected his attention to his daughter. "Kara, how do you think that went? Good turnout, I thought."

"It was a homeless shelter, Dad. Good turnout?"

"Right, well, you know what I mean. Stanley just texted me, wants to know how it went. I think it went well. You?"

"It did. I think it was a noble use of your valuable time."

"Are you being a smart-ass again? I'll have you know that your father—" her mother stopped as her father's hand squeezed her knee.

"What's gotten into you?" she continued at a whisper, clearly unable to help herself. Kara wanted to roll her eyes. Scream. Any reaction seemed better than none, but "none" was what she was used to. "It's not enough that I had to deal with Grady's antics, now all of a sudden you're having what, some kind of sexual revolution?"

Kara laughed. "Mom, you seem awfully interested in my sex life."

"Only if it shows up in pictures."

"There are no pictures."

"Well, you haven't had the best luck with men."

"Fully aware of that, Mother. Can we be finished now?" Kara asked.

"Yes, fine, if you're sure you are being careful."

"All my life, believe me, all my life."

"Well, that's good to hear. Now, we've invited a few guests to Thanksgiving."

Just like that her mother was back on task. Kara was grateful that the interrogation portion of the program was over and the car was once again filled with this and that, gossip and table settings. It seemed like there was always talk of table settings. Kara smiled, as her mother fixed her father's hair. Despite the general yuck factor of public life, when her parents were alone, they seemed genuinely in love. Kara wasn't sure how that was possible. It wasn't a love she imagined for herself, but it somehow worked for them.

Logan rang the bell and asked himself again why he couldn't simply keep his distance.

Kara opened her door in gray sweatpants and a white, tight-fitting T-shirt that read "finisher" next to some marathon logo. Her hair was smoothed down, but off her face, which appeared recently cleaned of makeup he was sure she'd worn for her parents. He preferred undone Kara much more. For a moment, he felt like he was backstage at some production, looking at the actors after the curtain dropped.

"Hey, nice place you have here." Logan waited for an invitation.

"Hi. Why are you here?" she asked, letting him know she was not in the mood for much.

"Grady called and told me what happened. Makenna had a little flip out last night, so I thought we could hide out together. Since we're that crazy dancing couple now."

"It was nothing really. Stupid." She paused for a minute and then it seemed like her hard exterior was softening a little. "But then there were the reporters and Thanksgiving dinner at the Malendar house. I'm just so tired of it all." She shook her head and gave a small laugh. It sounded like a pity-laugh in Logan's book. "I took my pies to go."

Still questioning why he was there, he had the strong urge to comfort her. "Can I come in?"

"Are you sure you want to? There could be reporters lurking."

He stepped into the entryway. "I'll take my chances."

Logan took in Kara's sprawling house. Lots of white, clean-cut furniture and space, blank space. Like its owner, Kara's house was refined, beautiful, and nothing was out of place.

"Should I take off my shoes?" he asked, smiling at her.

"Shut up. I like tidy."

"I can see that. I mean this is gorgeous, love the windows, but I'm not going to lie. It's a little intimidating."

"Stop, can I get you something? I really did bring home pie."

"What kind?" He intentionally threw his coat over a chair instead of on the designated hooks that held Kara's coat and umbrella. Controlled, that was the word; the entire place was under control. The mischievous kid in him was begging to jump on the couch.

"Apple and pumpkin. Homemade."

"Your mom?"

"My mom's cook."

Logan laughed. "I'll have pumpkin and some coffee if you've got it." He followed her into the kitchen. "I'll help. I like the sweatpants, by the way."

Kara shrugged. "I wasn't expecting company."

"Am I company?"

"You're a visitor, maybe an unwelcomed one," she joked, "but yes, you are company."

She handed him the French press and Logan began scooping coffee into the glass cylinder.

"So I thought it was a good one," he said.

"What?"

She was cutting the pie.

"The picture of us. It was a good shot. I would have preferred one with my hand on your ass—now that would have been something, right?"

Kara didn't laugh. She stopped cutting and looked at him.

"Oh, come on. It's not that big of a deal. Grady mentioned Olivia was fine with it. I know today was probably a nightmare for you, but it's not like we were actually rolling around in the hay."

"Do you want pie? Because if you do, zip it."

Kara sat on the couch, legs tucked under. Logan sat next to her, pushed the plunger on the French press, and poured himself a cup.

"Coffee?"

"No, thanks." Kara covered her cup. "I drink tea."

"Right, I knew that." He smiled at her and tried to hold her eyes, but she handed him a plate with a slice of pumpkin pie.

Logan took a bite.

"Hmm, this is great pie." He took another bite.

"It truly is." Kara left hers untouched on the table.

"My God, this crust is definitely butter, so good." He noticed she wasn't eating.

Logan lifted his fork to her mouth. Kara sipped her tea, didn't budge. He held his ground. Kara shook her head and opened her mouth.

"Good, right?"

Kara nodded and then smiled. He picked up her plate and set it in her lap.

"Don't make me eat alone, princess."

After sitting in silence for a few bites, Logan had to say something.

"So, are we going to talk about this?"

"What's there to talk about?" Kara put her fork down and reached for her tea.

"Kara."

"What? We danced."

"And?"

"And . . . you kissed me."

Logan tilted his head.

"Fine, I kissed you, we kissed. It was . . ."

"Hot?"

Kara laughed.

"It was 'holy shit,' as you put it, and it was private. Mine. The whole night, the dance too, was mine and then it was stolen, taken from that place in me. Thank God they didn't get everything on camera. I should have known better."

"How? Why would you think someone at that festival was going to be lurking around taking pictures of you?"

"Because they just are, it's how things work."

"What's it like?" Logan asked.

"What's what like?"

"Being Karaline Malendar."

It occurred to Kara that of all the questions she had been asked in her life, no one had ever asked that one before. She wasn't sure how to answer.

"It's, well, it's like being in any other family. I guess."

"I doubt that. I've danced with a few women in my time and no one took my picture without my knowledge. Garrett can be stupid, but he's not climbing anything that's going to end up on YouTube."

"You know, I'm not really into the whole, 'Oh poor Kara, she's been in the public eye all her life.' It's very first world, as Grady would say." She let out a half laugh. "'It is what it is,' my Nana's famous line. I'm sorry you were involved and that it touched your life. That's unfortunate and I apologize."

"Why are you apologizing? It's like you're giving me some kind of prepared speech. I could give a shit if people see me dancing with you or kissing you, but I'm not being put on the spot like you or your dad are. Was he pissed?"

"No. Well, he was a little annoyed at being bombarded on Thanksgiving, but he's used to it."

"And so are you, right?"

"Right," was all she said.

Logan could see the pain, way in the back, but she didn't want to discuss it and he didn't want to make it worse, so he moved on.

"Okay, well that's settled, so do you want to play backgammon or Scrabble?"

"What?"

"Thought we'd play a game."

Kara appeared almost stunned at the simplicity of it. God, he loved surprising her with the simple. It was his way of easing her mind, gathering her close to him for a minute until she felt better.

"I need more tea. How do you know I even have games?"

"You have games. Do you still have that leather roll-out back-gammon set you bought in Paris? God, we played that thing every night for like a week straight, remember that?"

Mid-laugh he caught her eyes. She stood between the living room and the kitchen staring at him, as if she was trying to reach him. A tear slowly traveled down her cheek. Logan went to her and pulled her into his arms.

"Hey, it's okay."

"I know. It's fine. I'm—" she took his face and kissed him. It was so tender, fragile, he was almost afraid to return it. But when she eased his mouth open and took more, he stopped thinking and joined her in erasing whatever pain caused that tear. Kara pulled back; the look on her face was so vulnerable that his heart squeezed and in that moment, he wanted nothing more than to keep her from all the gar-bage that went along with her life. He felt an unrelenting need to keep her safe. "Thank you. For checking on me, for kissing me, and for Paris. After everything, I never had a chance to thank you."

"You're welcome. Anytime, princess." Even though he felt like someone was squeezing his chest, he still tried for light.

Kara laughed, quickly wiping her tears. "Backgammon is in the chest next to the couch. I'll get more pie."

"You might want to bring both pies out here with two forks. It's probably going to be a long night while I kick your ass. Do you remember my mad backgammon skills?"

146

She continued laughing and his heart turned over at the thought that he could do that to her again. Even with everything now swirling around in their adult lives, he could still give her a few moments of Paris.

Chapter Sixteen

*L*ogan spent the following Saturday trying to make up for being closed Thursday and Friday. He had hoped to restore some of the lost revenue mainly so he wouldn't have to listen to Makenna, but it wasn't meant to be. Yesterday had been slow, probably because most of the shoppers collapsed and slept right through the weekend. Logan was fine with a slow day. It gave him a chance to restock, catch up, and he and Travis spent some time doing what they loved—creating. It had been a productive day and now he was enjoying a Sunday morning in his garden, but he was still dreading seeing Makenna Monday morning.

She had suggested serving a Thanksgiving-type dinner and leaving the restaurant open, but Logan just couldn't do it. Maybe some places were fine profiting from Thanksgiving, but if the whole of his success hinged on that kind of crap, he'd rather close the doors. She then begged him to do a quick eats menu on Black Friday and he declined again. He didn't believe in the crazy commercialism of it.

"Besides," he had told her, "our staff needs a great time to be with their families. We've been going nonstop."

"This is business, you get that right?"

"I do, but—"

"No buts, Logan, numbers don't lie. You have a wine inventory that needs to move, we have bills."

"I know that. I'm not nine, Kenna. We've got Christmas Eve — first time I won't be on the farm for Christmas Eve. There's a sacrifice for ya."

"Dramatic and not true. You missed Christmas altogether in 2008. You were living in New York and snowed in, remember?"

"Shit, you're like a walking time line."

Makenna had smiled. "So, you've missed Christmas Eve before and you'll miss it this year. I love the candlelight thing you're doing and the menu looks incredible. That should be a great night. Already sold out."

"Right, so we've got that and then Restaurant Week, which is almost fourteen days, so that should be a huge bonus. Two of those nights we're bringing the sommelier from Twisted Tree. He's a big deal and their vineyard is local, well Lake County, sort of local."

"Great. All good news and I understand wanting to close on Thanksgiving, but Friday is a mistake."

"Well, it's a mistake we are going make."

"Did you see where I put that on the budget? Revenue loss?"

"I did and it can't always be about money, Kenna."

"At this point it needs to be about money."

"Nah" — he had closed her laptop and pushed it toward her — "that's what I have you for, numbers lady."

Makenna had shaken her head and returned to her books, but Logan just knew she would be flashing her spreadsheets in the morning, reminding him that they were a business. He knew she meant well, had his best interests, but sometimes the woman gave him angst.

He wasn't going to let it bother him. Life was good. He was going to head down to the farmers market in about an hour to bring his dad and Garrett breakfast. They didn't always work the markets, but this one was part of a Shop Local Fair the city was putting on, so they decided to man the booths themselves and talk up the farm and local produce.

Focusing on one or two things sometimes helped because if he took on the whole damn thing, he'd be sucking his thumb. The entirety of what he was trying to do with the farm and restaurant was too much sometimes.

Kara spent the morning at the beach and met Jake and Cotton for lunch. They hit some garage sales and she came home with three lamps. One of them was old and needed electrical work, but they were perfect, just needed a little TLC. She answered some e-mails and spent the rest of the day doing laundry and watching movies. As the closing credits rolled for *The Last of the Mohicans*, she again told herself it was all about Daniel Day-Lewis and his raspy voice when he tells Madeline Stowe he will come back for her under that waterfall. It really was all about that scene under the waterfall. The desperation in his voice, now that was romance, she thought.

Kara loved movies and after she'd folded her towels she turned on *The Bourne Ultimatum*. It was the first movie she and Logan had seen in Paris, and at the moment in the movie when Jason Bourne decides not to shoot the guy in the fuzzy hat during the opening scene, Kara was lost in the memory of a much younger and a far less sure of himself Logan Rye.

They'd been in class just over three weeks and had each made what Madame Auclair considered a "passable" French omelet. It was Friday and Kara—Winnie as far as Logan knew—was packing up her bag to leave class.

"Do you like movies?" Logan asked.

"I do." Kara remembered her hands were a little jumpy because a guy usually had one thing in mind when he asked a girl that question, didn't he?

"Please don't tell me you're into foreign films."

Kara smiled and caught his eye for a moment as she put on the straps of her backpack.

"I'm not into foreign films."

"Romance?" he asked, moving around their work stools and grabbing his phone and pencil.

"I'm not sure there's a woman alive who's not a fan of at least a few romantic movies, but I really like action. The more car chases and kicks to the mouth, the better." She smiled and made her way out of the classroom. Logan was right behind her.

"Seriously, you look like you do"—his eyes roamed over her quickly—"and you like action movies?"

"What does that mean? I look like I do?" Kara asked as he held the door for her and walked out into what had become the familiar hum of a Paris afternoon.

Logan walked next to her holding only a notebook with a pencil tucked into the spiral. He dodged people going in the opposite direction of the narrow street toward Kara's apartment.

"I just meant that you"—he paused to step down off the curb and let a woman with a stroller pass—"I mean, what I was trying to say was you're"—Logan flattened himself against the rail of the bridge they were now passing to make room for a man carrying an extra-large box. Kara heard him exhale behind her and then she heard footsteps as he ran to keep pace with her. She remembered being so nervous that what would come out of his mouth would be either wonderful or awful. Both prospects scared her.

"Winnie!" Logan stopped and called her name. She'd been in Paris long enough that she had almost become Winnie. She turned and he was on the other side of the narrow street she had just crossed. The light had turned and they stood there on opposite sides as cars rushed in front of them. That was the first time she'd noticed how tall he was, his body. It was the first time in three weeks she'd actually stopped, unafraid to look at him. Maybe it was the safety of being on opposite sides, she didn't know, but the look on Logan's face was a bit like Daniel Day-Lewis's face in *The Last of the Mohicans*. She hadn't known that even existed, that kind of unspoken want, in real life. The crosswalk lit up and Logan walked toward her, in between a man on a bike and a woman in a short brown skirt listening to her iPod. Even now, sitting on her couch eight years later, Kara remembered every detail.

When he finally reached her, he was short of breath, not from the walk across the street; maybe the look in his eyes was taking most of his breath, because Kara was certain it was taking hers. He put his hand to the back of her neck and kissed her, right there on the uneven sidewalk of Rue de something just as the sun began to set. His hand was gentle and his lips were cold and minty. She remembered touching his shoulder and kissing him back. She would never be able to recall how long the kiss lasted because time seemed to stop. She was aware of the things around her, but as her mouth parted and Logan swept his tongue across hers for the first time, Kara felt nothing but him. It was an incredible sensation for someone like her who up until that moment had only touched people, men included, in a very proper, orderly fashion. Even her dates and at-the-door kisses had been almost rehearsed. The one boy, a prom date she had cared about in high school, humiliated her, so after that, Kara was careful. But there was nothing careful about Logan or his kiss. When he pulled back he kept his hand on her neck, his fingers moving to feel her hair.

"You're beautiful." His cheeks were flushed. "That's what I meant back there when I said 'looking like you do,' that's what I meant."

Kara smiled. At the age of twenty-one, she had been called many things, mostly well mannered, or even elegant, but no one, let alone a breathless boy with golden-brown eyes, had ever told her she was beautiful. She believed him that day.

"Thank you." She felt an overwhelming need to be honest about something. "I like you too."

Logan had smiled a glorious smile that touched the sides of his face as he took his hand from her neck.

"Do you want to go see a movie? *The Bourne Ultimatum* is playing tonight, I checked," he asked.

"I would," was all Kara could say at that point. It was a perfect moment and she knew even back then she would remember it forever.

"Thank God." Logan let out a breath. "I'm not sure I've ever worked so hard or been so damn nervous asking someone out."

They both laughed and Kara kissed him again when he walked her home after their first movie in Paris.

Sitting on her couch now, Kara was surrounded by the memory and was so grateful that in that moment when Logan first kissed her, she had no idea how things would unravel only a couple of months later. She was happy they had that moment and she would carry it in her heart forever. Things were different now, but if all it took was watching Matt Damon kick some ass for her to travel back to a time of firsts, when things were simple, she wasn't going to complain.

Chapter Seventeen

The *Pasadena Tribune* article hadn't hurt Logan's restaurant one bit. In fact, over a week later it proved a huge boost. People loved what they called the "romantic picture," and started showing up for lunch and dinner hoping to see Logan and Kara together. It was bizarre, but Makenna was happy and Olivia was thrilled, so Kara went along with it. Olivia wanted the second part of the feature out as soon as possible, so Kara arrived at The Yard bright and early the following Monday morning to get pictures of Logan, the restaurant, and his staff before they had to start prepping to open. She had just finished helping set up the prep guys in the kitchen when she came around to the server's station.

"Great, can you pull your shirt out?" the photographer asked Logan who was set up in a mock exchange at the kitchen window.

"What?"

"Your shirt, we need it out."

"Why?"

"Because it looks better. It goes with the scene."

"What scene? This is my scene and it says tucked shirt."

The photographer brought his camera to his hip and appeared to be looking for Kara. She was now standing right behind him.

"I'm not sure what you want me to do here, he doesn't want to take his shirt out," he complained to Kara.

Logan started to laugh, and when Kara was about to say something, Jeremy, the lead photographer, walked over.

"What's going on over here?" Jeremy asked his guy who suddenly appeared a little less sure of himself.

"He doesn't want his shirt out?"

"Okay, well this is his restaurant. The article is about him, not about your fashion advice. Go outside to the garden and take pictures of things you don't have to interact with." Jeremy rolled his eyes and swung his camera around to take over.

"Thanks, Jeremy." Kara stepped back prepared to watch him work.

"Yeah, sorry about that." He leaned forward and moved the stack of cloth silverware rolls out of his frame. "All right you crazy defiant shirt tucker, let's get this over with, shall we?"

Logan and Travis, who was now on the other side of the service window, laughed and Jeremy got his shot.

"That's it." He took a few more shots of the pizza counter and one of Logan's tattooed arm, which Kara was sure he would keep for his own portfolio.

"Really? We're done?" Logan's shoulders relaxed.

"Piece of cake. Thanks for your time. That's a great tat."

"Thanks, man." Logan bumped Jeremy's fist.

Kara always wondered how men managed to assess each other and connect with such ease. She'd watched her brother and his friends and even men in a corporate professional environment. Her father even fist bumped some of his colleagues and voters. Why didn't women fist bump? Why was her gender so in need of knowing everything about each other, sniffing around? Life would be so much easier, she thought, if women just fist bumped.

"That's a fleur-de-lis, isn't it?" Jeremy asked as both men walked toward Kara.

"It is." Logan twisted his arm to see the back where Jeremy was pointing.

"Kara, check out this tattoo." Jeremy leaned in for a closer look.

The tattoo again, as if she hadn't noticed, thanks for bringing it up, Jeremy. Believe me, I'd like to see that tattoo and everything else it's connected to, she thought, but did not say. Instead, she gave her best neutral face as her eyes settled for Logan's beautifully defined swimmer's arm.

"The fleur-de-lis is crumbling and look at the heart with the lock on it. Really cool, man."

"Thanks. I got that one before I left Paris."

Kara followed the design on Logan's arm, and then she met his eyes, which were on her, but not willing to give any answers. The fleur-de-lis was a famous French symbol. Usually represented the kings, queens, and . . . princesses. There were strands of curling hair swirling around the crumbling symbol. It was beautiful. Before she could say anything, Logan was walking Jeremy and the rest of his crew out to their cars.

As he walked back from sending them off, Makenna ran up from the back office.

"Are they gone?" she asked looking out the bar windows. "Shit, I wanted them to get a picture of the two of you."

Logan wrinkled his brow. "What?"

"Since we are getting such a great response from that article, I thought we could play it up a little, maybe even put a picture on our upcoming Valentine's Day menu. You know that's going to be a huge night for us, we're nearly sold out already."

"Without the picture? We are nearly sold out without the picture, huh, it must be about the food then." Logan ruffled Makenna's hair. "You're nuts."

"Well of course it's about the food, but people genuinely like you two. When are you guys going to accept what's going on and be a thing?"

Makenna looked at Logan and Kara, both of them expressionless.

"Did you want to take this one?" Logan turned to Kara.

She shook her head. "Nope, it's all yours."

"We're not a thing," he said.

Kara thought it was well delivered, even a little stern, until Makenna started laughing in his face. After a few seconds, she patted him on the back and then disappeared into the back room without another word.

Logan shrugged. "She's sleep deprived."

Kara smiled, still wondering if she, or rather what they used to be, was somewhere in the swirling colors of Logan's tattoo.

Kara returned to the office after the photo shoot for some afternoon meetings and to look at the proofs. She was back at The Yard later that evening and stole a few opportunities to speak with Logan's pizza guys and even some of the now regular patrons. Her story was shaping up, which was good because Olivia wanted to see a draft in her e-mail first thing in the morning.

After closing, Kara sat at the pizza counter while Logan went into the kitchen. Neither of them had eaten dinner, and her stomach growled when he came back with his hands full. She'd accepted that she was hungrier and eating more these days. Logan sliced a loaf of crusted bread, poured olive oil in a dish, and put the combination up on the counter in front of her.

"Okay, we have chicken left over from lunch and these green beans need to be used, so it's cold chicken and my green beans. Any takers?"

"Sounds good." Kara pulled apart a piece of bread.

"Did you hear Makenna bought Paige a bike for Christmas?"

"I did." She finished chewing. "Handlebar streamers and all. God, bike Christmases were always the best."

"Christmas is better when you're a kid. I think it's the toys. Once you start moving into clothes and electronics, it's just not the same." Logan sliced the chicken and layered it on the small platter.

"That's so true. I'm not sure when my childhood ended and I moved into that, but I think it was my swing set. I remember I used to live on the swings in our backyard. Always with bare feet. Oh, and I never wanted my hair brushed back then, never had the time." Kara cradled her teacup and crossed her legs. "I can still feel it. The grass on my toes and the sound of the chain swinging back and forth. The whoosh on my face as I pumped higher and higher."

She shared her story and somehow never felt foolish around him. Something about Logan, when they were alone and not volleying back and forth, made her comfortable, as if she was wrapped in a blanket. He walked around to her side of the counter, put a piece of bread in his mouth, and sat down with a bowl of green beans. He began pulling the ends off and looking at her, listening as if she were the most interesting person on the planet.

"I loved that swing set, flying through the air, up near the trees in our backyard, but still holding on."

Logan smiled and her heart thumped in her chest. The man could smile.

"Anyway, I seem to have lost the point of the story."

"What happened?" Logan asked, still trimming the beans.

"What?"

"What happened to the swing set? I mean, is it still there, in the backyard?"

Kara watched his hands move from bowl to bowl and remembered the point of her story.

"It was just gone one day. They took it down because it was rusting and we were getting too old and whatever other perfectly adult reasons my parents came up with. I got home from school, I must have been in the 5th grade, and it was gone. Dead grass outlining where my childhood used to be. I guess I grew up after that. Started shaving my legs, wearing dresses."

"Just like that?"

"Well, I'm sure it wasn't just like that, like the same day." She gave an unnatural laugh. "But when I look back on it now, it sure feels that way. Strange how something like a swing set can change things?"

"It is." Wiping his hands, he took both metal bowls back into the kitchen. "I guess my swing set was a dump truck."

Kara sipped her tea and waited for him to share himself.

"It was yellow. One of those real metal ones. You know, before they started making everything plastic for safety or whatever?"

Kara nodded and Logan took a frying pan, brown and black from use, off the stack next to the range top, lit the burner, and added a large swirl of olive oil. Watching him cook or do anything in the kitchen was like watching a dance. At some points his movements were slow and easy; at others, frantic and passionate. He added shallots and swirled the pan over the flame.

"I think I got it for my fifth birthday. Brand new and shiny. My Pop Pop, Dad's dad, gave it to me." He watched as the pan sizzled. "I loved that truck. I took it everywhere. It was dented and repaired, and I remember putting tape on the plastic windshield over and over again." Logan laughed.

Kara finished her tea and went into the kitchen.

"Do you still have it in a box somewhere?" she asked, sliding behind him to get more hot water.

"No." He added the green beans to the pan. "My mom, she was . . ." Logan seemed reluctant, eyes on the pan. "She threw it against the wall when I was six."

Kara put her hand to her mouth. Logan paused for a minute, let out a breath, and then returned to the rhythm of his pan.

"Why?" Kara finally asked, returning to the counter.

"She was vacuuming. Not exactly the domestic type." He smiled. "She must have been pissed my dirty truck was in the house." He switched the flame off.

"Anyway, at least it dented the wall before it broke into three pieces," he said eventually, turning the beans out onto a white oval dish. "I cried. She threw it out. It was all very poor-baby tragic." He laughed, sort of.

"How old were you when she," Kara hesitated, not quite sure how to get the word out and equally confused about why she needed to know, "died?"

"Garrett was eight." Logan's expression seemed strained, as if he wasn't sure what to say.

Of course, she didn't know what it was like to lose her mother in grade school, so she just listened.

"I was almost seven and Makenna was five," he continued.

"So . . . right around the same time you lost your truck?"

"Yeah."

"What happened, had she been sick?"

He put the beans and the sliced chicken up on the counter and walked around to take a seat again. Logan put a small plate in front her and gave himself one. He served the beans, with tongs, onto each plate and then the chicken.

"Dad bought me a new one, a truck, with a new windshield and plastic body." Logan reached over the counter for two wineglasses. He poured a deep, rich burgundy wine. "Yeah, I never touched the new one. Wasn't the same."

Kara pushed her tea aside and took one of the glasses from him. He handed her a fork and then picked up one of the beans off his plate and took a bite.

"Does that mean you don't want to talk about it?" Kara asked with a small smile as she sipped her wine. "I'm pretty well versed in the art of the dodge, so I recognize it."

Logan smiled, not giving in. "I'm sure the truck was donated or given away at some point. I moved on to my bike and baseball cards. That time was over." He took another bite and Kara dropped it. He didn't want to talk about his mother or her death and she couldn't blame him.

"Hmm . . . not bad, but you're the expert," he teased.

Kara rolled her eyes and took another bite of the most delicious green beans. Crisp and cooked perfectly, but she would keep that to herself.

Logan held up his wineglass for a toast and Kara joined him.

"Okay, so here's to the sad tragic demise of our childhoods. May there be enough olive oil to ease the ache."

They sipped and Kara laughed. There was a glimpse of pain in

Logan's eyes that she had never been given access to before. They held in that moment for a breath and then it was gone. She saw him as a child with his truck and the fear of losing not only his favorite toy, but also his mother.

Chapter Eighteen

Kara was at the restaurant early the next morning, mainly to show Logan the photographs she'd selected and to ask a few more questions Olivia had e-mailed her last night. She wanted them added to the article, and even though Kara felt she had finished the second article, she knew better than to argue with Olivia. The Yard didn't open for lunch for a few more hours, so she'd agreed to ask while Logan started the prep work. She went to grab the folding chair under the clock in the kitchen and noticed a Daniel Tiger lunch box. She recognized him from the PBS show Eloise watched.

"Is this your lunch box?" she asked, smiling at Logan who had started sharpening knives.

"Nah, although it is pretty sweet." He smiled. "That belongs to Paige. They must have left it. Just set it on the floor."

Kara did and then scooted the chair closer to where he was working.

"Okay, so tell me about people who have inspired you in the industry, mentors?" She held her pencil at the ready.

"Wow." Logan put the sharpener away and wiped down the knives. "That's a broad question. When I was in high school I worked at

Subway one summer with a manager who told me a sandwich worth making was worth making right. He also taught me that tomatoes tasted better at room temperature. Both valuable lessons I still use today."

Kara stopped writing. "You want me to go back to my editor with a Subway manager as your culinary influence?"

"Not fancy enough? Fine. My father has taught me everything I know about hard work. Get up early, sleep hard, and don't whine. No one is coming to save you."

"Excuse me?"

"Oh, that's the Rye family fight song." Logan laughed. "All right, I'll get serious. Chef Trevor Brant at the Fairmont taught me about cooking good food fast. He told me to create it and then let it fly. Also to take responsibility if what I made was shit. Madame Auclair, who I know you remember, taught me sauces, how to cut meat, and the importance of presentation. And then I guess, Greg Rast from Tableu. He was an incredible all-around chef. I learned braising and that a salad dressing should be simple. I mean this is a crazy question. I've learned from everyone I've worked with and I continue to learn. Just last week, Bernie, our pizza guy, showed me that our sausage had too much fennel seed and not enough pepper flakes. He was right. We changed it, and that was only a few days ago. I guess that's why I love this job. It's constantly changing and I'm never going to know everything. It keeps me on my toes. I like that."

Kara was no longer writing anything. She didn't need to; she would remember this conversation. Logan was fun to watch in the kitchen. His hands continued to move as he put pasta through a press and laid out sheets for what she assumed would be some kind of ravioli.

"Christ, I need a nap after that question. Are we almost done? Can I get an easy one next while I cut these out?" He held up what appeared to be a cookie cutter.

"Sure." She glanced down at her questions, none of which looked easy. She noticed Daniel Tiger looking up from the lunch box next to her with his sweet little eyes. She had her next question. "Did you have a lunch box when you were a kid?"

"I did." Logan didn't seem fazed by the change of topic as he turned the large strips of pasta into disks. "Did you?"

"Yes."

"Did you make your own lunch?" he asked.

"What do you think?"

At that, Logan looked up.

"Your mother?"

Kara gave him the "try again" look.

"The cook?"

Kara touched her nose indicating he got it right.

"Ah. Yeah well, I made the lunches. Actually, Garrett had hot lunch, but I made lunch for Kenna and myself. After a while, I made lunch for Dad too. Now, he had a cool lunch box. You know the metal ones, they're like a blue color, with the matching Thermos?"

Kara smiled and nodded.

"That thing was indestructible and so damn manly. It was like the alpha male of lunch boxes. My dad even called it a lunch pail." They both laughed.

"What kind did you have?" Kara asked.

"First and second grade, I had the equally manly Curious George lunch box." He cleaned up the pasta scraps and left to get something from the walk-in refrigerator. "Then third and fourth grade," he continued, returning with two covered bowls, "was Spider-Man. That one was awesome because the plastic handle was a web." He set the bowls down. "I must have become super cool sometime around fifth grade because from then on out, it was a paper bag. It's a shame." He pulled out a pastry bag. "I kind of wish I had one now, except not the little plastic Thermos that came with it. One day of forgetting to rinse out the milk and those things were nasty."

Kara laughed. "How do you remember these things?"

"I don't know." Logan twisted the end of a full pastry bag. "Lunch boxes—lunch for that matter—was a priority in my childhood. What kind of lunch box did you have?"

"I don't remember my early ones, but I do remember having a Hello Kitty lunch box at some point. It was retro and metal.

Grady used to beat on it with his cereal spoon in the mornings when we were eating breakfast and I would get so mad at him." Kara smiled and Logan stopped piping some kind of meat filling into his pasta disks and met her eyes. "Other than that, I think they were just patterns or different colors. I do remember having one with built-in ice packs. That was kind of different, but the thing weighed a ton."

Logan laughed.

"Okay, since that one wasn't so painful, let's try favorite lunch sandwich?" Kara asked.

"That's easy." Logan finished up and set the pastry bag aside. "Peanut butter and jelly—actually, Smucker's strawberry jam. You?"

"Bologna with Miracle Whip on white bread. Oh, and a Kraft single."

Logan stared.

"What?"

"Sorry, I didn't see that coming, princess. I was thinking chicken salad with walnuts and grapes on a baguette."

"Very funny. I don't like walnuts and I'll have you know I had connections in the kitchen when I was growing up. Beatrice, our cook, loved me. She used to give Grady whatever our mother ordered for lunch, complete with carrot sticks. He threw his lunch out as soon as we got to school anyway and ate pizza pockets, but Beatrice set me up. There was a special part of the fridge and the cupboard where she would hide my lunch supplies. I even got Fritos for a while until my mother found one of the bags in the trash. Then it was back to fruit, but always bologna."

Logan smiled, wiping his hands and walking to the end of the counter. "She snuck you junk lunch?"

"Yes!"

"Do you still eat Fritos?" he asked.

"I eat for a living now, so I don't eat much in my free time anymore. Food is not as fun as it used to be."

"You eat my food."

"I do." She held his gaze.

"Is that some kind of compliment?"

"Maybe?"

"Huh, look at us getting all philosophical over lunch and lunch boxes." Logan was now leaning on the counter in front of her.

Kara stood up and closed her pad.

"Are we done?" He moved toward her.

"For now." She stepped back.

"No one's here, princess. You're looking at me like that again."

"You're delusional. I'm thinking about . . ."

"Yes? Please be specific."

Kara laughed, probably blushed, but when he moved into her again, she didn't back away.

"I'm thinking about my story and how I'm going to convince Olivia that lunch boxes are something for the *Times* crowd."

"Is that all?"

"Yeah, that's about it." Her eyes betrayed her and dropped to his lips. Her pulse jumped.

Logan put his arms around her and pulled her against him as his lips brushed hers. Just then, they both heard a wailing voice thunder through the kitchen door.

Holding his motorcycle helmet, Travis came through the door belting out a really bad version of AC/DC's "Highway to Hell."

"Oh, shit!" He was still yelling until he took his headphones out. "I'm sorry. I didn't"—he looked at Logan who had moved away from Kara by that point—"I didn't know you were coming in this early. I was going to do the—" he broke off when he saw the finished ravioli on the counter. "You did them?"

Logan nodded.

"How was the filling? It looked good last night, but I was a little worried it would be dry this morning." He took his bag off his chest and set it down with his helmet. "Hey, Kara. Sorry about . . ." He gestured between her and Logan.

Kara waved and turned to put her notebook away. She needed to get going.

"The filling was great." Logan gestured toward the finished ravioli. "Smooth enough for the bag with the large fitting, but nice substance. We'll have to try some out." He held Kara's arm as she made her way to the door.

Travis diverted his eyes, grabbed Paige's lunchbox off the floor, and headed out to the front. No doubt to put some music on. Kara rarely saw Travis without some kind of soundtrack.

"Are you leaving?" Logan asked.

"I need to get into the office, put this into draft form, and get two other reviews finalized for Olivia."

"Good or bad?"

"One of each." Kara smiled.

"Hmm, getting a little soft?"

"You'll just have to read and find out." She moved closer to the door.

"Do you want to come back for lunch? I'll make you the special."

"Which is?"

"Pork Milanese salad."

"Seriously?" Kara sighed. "I'll be back around one. I think you're trying to fatten me up, farm boy." She walked past him out the door.

"Trying," was all she heard as the door closed between them.

Less than an hour later, Makenna came spinning into the kitchen with Paige in hand.

"Paige the Magnificent, is that you?" Logan scooped his niece up onto the counter.

"Uncle Rogan!" She giggled. "Mommy forgot Daniel Tiger again. I need him for lunch."

"Absolutely, I'm pretty sure I saw him . . ." Logan looked over to where Kara had been sitting, but the lunch box was gone. Before he had a chance to look around, Kenna came whirling back toward them.

"Got it. Let's go, sweetie. Give Uncle Rogan a kiss, we're going to be late."

Paige planted kisses on both his cheeks and one on Logan's nose and then she was gone, giggling under her mother's arm.

"I'll be back."

Before he had a chance to tell her to relax, the door closed behind them.

Later that day at lunch, Kara sat at the pizza counter again and could hear the whispering of a couple next to her.

The damn newspaper, she thought.

She found that the more time that went on, the less she cared. Still noticed, but cared less.

"Would you like to go see the trees on Christmas Tree Lane?" Kara asked as Logan moved around the kitchen full of boiling pots and sizzling pans. He took something in a tiny ladle and added it to one of the pans and then lifted it and swirled it over the flame.

"Are you asking me out on a romantic Christmas date, princess?"

Kara shook her head. "No. It's just a really cool place and I thought if you hadn't seen it we could . . . Oh, forget it. I was trying to be nice."

Logan handed the pan he was holding to Travis who nodded and took over as if they spoke some secret language. Logan crossed to the counter where Kara sat working on her laptop. She was trying hard now to bury her face behind the screen. He wiped his hands and leaned up on his end of the counter with his arms flexed.

That tattoo—Kara could not get it out of her mind. She was now pretty sure it went past his shoulder. It was like a teaser trailer, but she wasn't allowed to see the whole movie. The damn thing was driving her nuts. Logan poked his head near her computer.

"Hey, could you come a little closer. I never excelled at gymnastics."

Kara leaned in, still not smiling at him even though he was pretty damn cute in his apron and glasses.

"You're not wearing contacts?"

"I took a break, they hurt my eyes. Could you ask me what you just asked me one more time?"

"It's not a big deal. Forget it." Kara took a look around the restaurant, certain they were starting to draw attention.

"Any reporters?" he teased.

"Shut up. Get back to work, farm boy."

"Damn, I can't get past how hot it is when you call me that."

"Yeah, well try."

"Come here."

"No."

Logan laughed, dropped back down into the kitchen, and then disappeared into the back. Kara was trying to figure out where she was in her notes, when the chair she was sitting on suddenly spun around and Logan stood between her legs. She didn't have time to protest or look around. She barely managed to grab a breath before he was kissing her, hard and completely. He was nothing if not thorough. Kara went to that happy fuzzy place she always did when he touched her. His tongue swept through her mouth, leaving sensory devastation in its wake, and then he pulled back and kissed her again, but gently this time.

"I would love to go to Christmas Tree Lane with you. I'll bring the blankets, food, and the truck. I can get out of here tonight by eight. Pick you up at nine?"

Kara nodded and he smiled and left. As he walked away, the entire restaurant, including the kitchen, broke into applause. He held up his hand in victory and all Kara could do was laugh. He wanted to kiss her—must not have seen much resistance from her—and so he did.

It wasn't until a few minutes after the clapping died down that Kara even thought about the fact that someone could use that moment against her family again. But this time, she found she didn't care.

Chapter Nineteen

John Woodbury, founder of the city of Altadena, California, planted 150 deodar trees along what later became Santa Rosa. Christmas Tree Lane was now considered a historic landmark and was in the US National Register of Historic Places.

Lying back on the blankets Logan had put in the bed of his truck and looking up at the strands of colorful lights, Logan was grateful to Mr. Woodbury. The trees were huge and the cool night air chilled Kara's cheeks. She was all bundled up and could not have been more beautiful. He handed her a paper cup of hot chocolate he'd picked up on his way to get her. He wasn't sure whether to look at her or the lights, but as he leaned back and warmed his hands on his own paper cup, he felt like a kid again. It seemed lately he felt that way around her.

"When John told his brother he wanted these trees planted, do you think his brother should have told him he was crazy? Do you think he should have mentioned it made more sense to build the house and then put the trees in? I mean, things fell out from under the housing market like what two or three years later and the guy never got to build his house." Logan was still looking up at the enormous trees.

"But then we wouldn't have the trees—we'd just have some other oversized house. I think it was romantic. He came home from his trip, wanted the trees, so he planted them." Kara scooted closer to him.

"Yeah, but don't you think the brother should have been honest with him? I mean he had to have known John's plan didn't make any sense."

"Honesty." Kara let out a breath. "No one really wants honesty. It's a sound bite or a catch phrase, but real honesty is tough. There's backlash."

"Is that why you steer clear of the whole telling the truth business?"

Kara turned to look at him as their heads rested on the same pillow. She gave him what he clearly recognized as a warning, sipped her cocoa, and brought her focus back to the twinkling night.

"I remember the time I read some article in college about dysfunctional families." Kara picked at the cardboard sleeve around her cup. "It outlined the roles in dysfunctional relationships and ways to deal with and fix those issues. I called my mom."

"Oh boy." Logan was already cringing for her, the young girl she used to be.

"Yeah, I told her I wanted to have lunch with both of them."

"Where was Grady?"

"He was at school. I called him and told him. After."

Logan touched her arm. "Probably should have done that first?"

"Yeah, hindsight, right? Anyway, I brought the article."

Logan braced himself. He knew where this was headed.

"So, after my 'little presentation,' my father ordered another Scotch and my mother didn't speak to me for almost a month."

"There are varying degrees of honesty."

"I know, but I thought I was helping. I thought they didn't know and if I could just show them . . ." Kara started to laugh, noticing some cars as they drove past. "Jesus, I only wanted something I could touch, something to explain the void. Why we acted the way we did."

Logan said nothing. They continued to admire the enormous trees dripping in multicolored lights.

"We normally go to Hastings Park for lights." He was not so subtly changing the subject because even in the dark he could hear the sadness in her voice. "I mean we did when we were kids. This place is better."

"I think it's better because of the story." Kara turned to him.

"Yeah, I guess that's usually the case. The story—the history adds to things."

She set her cup down and crawled on top of him and Logan lost all ability to speak. He gazed up at her wild hair tucked under a knit cap. Her cheeks were pink and the Christmas lights, mixed with the stars, veiled the whole scene. Logan had to focus on breathing.

"Was it something I said?" he asked when she leaned down and touched his face.

"No, I think it's just you and these trees. It's the blankets and being tucked in here with you. Logan?"

"Yeah?" His heart warmed his chest.

"Would you like to make out in the back of your truck?"

He laughed and pulled her under him so quickly she squealed. There she was laughing, relaxed, and he was certain the look in her eyes was the very best thing he'd seen in a long time. Before it disappeared with the rest of the Christmas magic, he kissed her. Out of sight, in the darkness of a December evening, just as she'd asked, they made out in the bed of his truck.

"Did you used to wait up for Santa when you were a kid?" Logan asked as he drove Kara home.

"Sure. Grady was in charge of keeping us both awake. This one year, we filled our bathroom sinks with ice and if one of us started to fall asleep we'd have to go put our face in the ice bath." Kara shook her head. "He's always been a little nuts."

Without looking over, she could tell he was smiling.

"Despite all his crazy ideas, we never made it. We fell asleep before Santa came, every year. Did you wait up?" she asked.

"I know this is going to sound nuts, but I was the first one in bed."

"Seriously?" Kara was more than a little surprised. She figured Logan, Garrett, and Makenna were all dedicated Santa watchers.

"I know. It's weird, but I didn't want to do anything that would make him change his mind. I used to get so pissed at Garrett because he was always thinking up booby traps or weird stuff and Makenna was like his little helper." He enjoyed the memory.

"So you went to bed early? How did you fall asleep? That was the hardest part. The excitement of it all, that's what got me."

"I don't know. We'd get in our pajamas after dinner, watch *How the Grinch Stole Christmas*, the old cartoon version, and after that I went to bed. I told myself if I didn't fall asleep, there was a chance I'd still be awake when Santa came and I'd miss out."

"Maybe it was The Grinch. That's a pretty powerful, don't-mess-with-Christmas message." She smiled and glanced over at his face in the glow of the dashboard light.

"Maybe." Logan laughed.

"Did you leave cookies?" she asked.

"Of course, and carrots for the reindeer."

They rode, listening to the faint Christmas carols on the radio, giddy in their childhood memories. It occurred to Kara that both she and Logan were rooted in their families. Sure they were different, but there wasn't anything she wouldn't do for hers and she knew he felt the same way. Every family had traditions; her Nana had always said they were "the glue that held a family together even when we couldn't stand each other." She was right.

Maybe it was the holiday season, maybe it was that she had just made out with Logan and had hot chocolate. She wasn't sure, but Kara knew one thing for certain as they turned up her street. If she ever decided to make traditions of her own, if she ever wanted to bake cookies and tiptoe around her house putting presents under a glowing Christmas tree in the middle of the night, she wanted that with him. She had never been sure "normal" was possible for her, but she had feelings now that were impossible to ignore. They told her that things could actually be exactly as they should be in her life. There was no one size fits all. She and Logan could have their own story. It could be that she would wake up tomorrow morning in the throes of a panic attack, but at that moment none of her feelings scared her. They seemed more natural than most things in her life up to that point.

"Thank you," she said.

"You're welcome." Logan turned off his truck. "I had a great time."

"Me too." She turned and he leaned across to her.

The cab of his truck was warm and when Logan's lips touched hers, Kara sank into the most luxurious kiss. Her hand touched the side of his face and he shifted closer. She wondered if she would ever tire of kissing him. Had Bill and Rosemary Barbus tired of each other when they were growing old together in what was now Logan's house? Kara didn't think so; she was certain they had moments they weren't happy and maybe even some scary times, but that was life, wasn't it?

Logan came around and opened the door of the truck for her. As she slid down his body and her feet hit the driveway, she wanted to invite him in, wanted to wake up wrapped in him, but she hadn't been with a man in a very long time and all the questions came flooding back. How would this change things? What about her job? What if it didn't work out or he felt differently than she did? Just walking to the door, she could already feel her previously predicted anxiety attack, so in the end she kissed him goodnight and that was it. His cold nose touched her cold nose and Kara wondered if maybe she was a little too old for Christmas wishes.

Chapter Twenty

Kara turned in the second part of her feature on The Yard before she left the office early on Christmas Eve day. Olivia seemed pleased and of course, noticing the photography, made another awkward sexual reference to Jeremy and his "great angles." Kara had thought about bringing this to Olivia's attention on more than one occasion, but just as when someone has spinach in their teeth and they say they want to know, it's still super awkward when someone actually has to tell them.

They sat in Olivia's office and exchanged Christmas gifts, well, their version of Christmas gifts. Every year they bought each other obscenely expensive shoes. Their mutual affection for shoes had started back when Olivia interviewed Kara for the job. Kara was coming from *Los Angeles* magazine, where she wrote a small column on desserts for their food section. She also had a blog on food where she took recipes and scaled them down for the single woman. "Rather than having to cook something for four," Kara explained in the interview, "single women can go to my blog and see recipes tailored for one." Olivia had liked her, but she expressed concern that Kara didn't have enough experience and she also wondered if the Malendar name would create issues.

"I can do this job," Kara had said. "I'm writing about food, it's not like this is politics, so my family shouldn't be an issue."

Olivia agreed, but was still hesitant. "I don't want to hire someone who, let's face it, doesn't really need the job, only to have you up and leave in a year."

Kara still didn't know what got into her that day. She'd been desperate to have something for herself, so she blurted out, "Keep my shoes. If I leave before a year, they're yours."

It was the most absurd thing she had ever said. She was certain she'd lost the opportunity, but when she stood to leave Olivia asked, "Are those Ferragamos?"

"Yes." Kara had been so nervous. "I just bought them yesterday for the interview."

Grady was always telling her to "go for it." In these situations, her Nana liked to say, "Grab that bull by the horns," and when Olivia Palm, editor of the food section for the *Los Angeles Times*, held out her hand for Kara's shoes, she knew she'd made them both proud. Kara had left the office wearing the pedicure flip-flops she'd kept in her purse that day and got her tortoise-colored Ferragamos back on her one-year anniversary.

"Such a shame," Olivia had said, giving them back to her. "Would have made me a very nice Christmas present." And that was it, the idea that started it all. Kara and Olivia had exchanged six pairs of obscenely expensive shoes since and Kara's seventh pair, Jimmy Choos in gunmetal suede, was sitting on the seat next to her as she drove home. Olivia had slipped into her new Michael Kors black leather booties, with silver zippers up the back, before she'd even left her office. Kara liked traditions, and this one was fun. Traditions truly did have a way of bringing people together, even if those people were as different as Kara and Olivia.

Midnight Mass at St. Andrew's Church in downtown Pasadena was a tradition dating back to when Kara was five and Grady was six. Their parents had a Christmas Eve party every year, so Nana took them for the day, then to Midnight Mass, and then home to their beds before Christmas morning. Now that Nana was gone, she and Grady went every year, not because they were particularly religious, but because their Nana was and it was tradition. As Kara climbed in the car Grady had sent for her, she remembered going to church as a child in velvet and tights. Her Nana wore a fur back before fur went the way of cigarettes. Kara loved church, even as a kid, mostly because it was just the three of them. Their grandfather had died before they were born, so all of the memories were of Nana alone. She lived in a beautiful old home only two blocks from where they grew up, so Kara and Grady spent a lot of time with her. When Nana got sick, she moved into a smaller condominium and eventually watched her Wednesday and Sunday service on the television. She would have the programs mailed to the house and Kara remembered propping her up with pillows and playing pretend iron while Nana prayed the rosary and Grady asked questions about the stories in her Bible.

Her rosary was purple. It was funny, the things you remembered, Kara thought as she and Grady walked out of Midnight Mass into the cool crisp air of Christmas Eve. Both of them cast their gazes to the stars. It was a clear night.

"Do you think she's up there?" Kara asked Grady.

"Probably not," he said and Kara laughed.

"I can always count on you to be honest, right?"

He laughed too, buttoned his coat, and put his arm around her as they walked to the car.

"I think she's somewhere—you know her spirit. I can feel her sometimes."

"Me too." Kara slid into the car as the driver held her door open.

"Hot chocolate time," Grady declared as the car pulled out on its way to one of two twenty-four-hour drive-thru coffee shops, and the only one that used milk and piled whipped cream on their hot chocolate.

Kara took a deep breath and settled back into the leather seat. "I love that feeling. I don't get it every year, but this year, it was there."

"What feeling?"

"That sense of goodness, it's kind of an innocence, I guess, when we walk out of church and into Christmas."

"I think it helps that St. Andrew's is a beautiful church. I remember when we were little, I used to look up at those chandeliers and imagine swinging on them."

Kara laughed. "You've always had a thing for climbing, haven't you?"

"I guess, but I know the feeling you're talking about. It's the essence of what you want Christmas to be. It's the choir and the bells, the warmth of familiar people and then the stars."

"Nana loved the choir, remember?"

"Yeah, and she had the worst voice." Grady cringed. "Remember sitting next to her and she'd break out into 'Oh Come All Ye Faithful'?"

They both laughed.

"And," Kara was almost crying with laughter, "it was like she had no idea how bad it was. She was all loud and proud. That was the best part."

"I don't think she cared."

"She didn't give a—"

"Rat's ass," they both said together and the laughter started all over again.

"Or sometimes it was a donkey's ass, she liked that one too." Kara leaned into her brother.

"Or if she was really being dirty, like the time her neighbor complained about her animated reindeer being in the front yard and she said—"

"I don't give a flying fuck," they both bellowed and exploded with laughter. Tears and snorts, just like when they were children.

Kara dabbed her eyes, "Oh my God, I forgot about that one. Why was it flying? She was truly something."

They both got hot chocolate with the works, which included a drizzle of chocolate syrup, and rode home.

"Do you miss her?" Grady asked after a while.

"Yeah, I do." She reached out to hold his hand.

The car dropped Kara off at home and as she went up the walkway to her house, she stopped, feeling the cool breeze that rustled through the trees and across her face. She closed her eyes.

"Love you, Nana," Kara whispered into the night air and then went inside and turned on her very own Christmas tree. She had never bothered to get her own tree before, but this year felt different. She got into her pajamas and fell asleep on the couch by the glow of Christmas lights.

Christmas Eve dinner at The Yard had gone well. The entire restaurant, even the bathrooms, was lit by candles. When Makenna had suggested it, all Logan could think about was frantically calling the fire department when some kid knocked a candle into the bathroom trash. But when he woke up Christmas morning, he had to admit it was something special. He did make sure most of the candles were in huge hurricanes for safety reasons, but the candles lined on the pizza bar were open and the look as they melted through the evening was his favorite. It was kind of like inviting a few hundred friends for dinner over the course of the night. They served carved ham, homemade rolls, a standing rib roast, and Swedish meatballs, one of Travis's family recipes. Sage made apple cider and hot chocolate, spiked for the adults. Logan's family came by for dinner and Paige fell asleep in one of the booths. It was a great night, a shining example of the reason Logan did what he did. Good people, good food, prepared in a way that was at peace with the world around him. He had had that vision in one form or another for as long as he could remember.

Because they'd stayed open until eleven on Christmas Eve, he'd thought Kara might stop by and was annoyed with himself for even caring. That had started to happen a lot lately. He caught himself thinking about where she was or what she was doing, probably because they spent so much time together. That's what he told himself anyway. Being disappointed when she didn't show up Christmas Eve was ridiculous. She had her life and he had his. He liked it that way and the feeling of needing someone, needing to know where they were, was not a place he was ever willing to go again.

Logan walked out to his kitchen, made some coffee, and sat by the window. It was overcast with a prediction for rain, a rare thing in southern California. He planned to eventually make his way up to the farm for dinner and gifts, but for now most of the day was his. He contemplated going back to the restaurant when his doorbell rang.

He opened the door to Kara, standing in her pajamas, Uggs, and some hat with balls hanging off it. Crazy-haired Kara—his favorite. She was holding bags and he could smell the food.

"Merry Christmas!" She looked down at her boots as if she was second-guessing her outfit. "If this is too weird, tell me and I'll turn right around, but I went to Midnight Mass last night with Grady. I was thinking about my Nana and I had a great time with you at the Christmas trees," she took a breath, "and I just thought, we like each other, we're friends. I'm waking up on Christmas morning, so are you"—the hand not holding the bags was gesturing back and forth—"there's no reason that I shouldn't go over and say, Merry Christmas, so here I am."

He should have played it cool, been like, "Oh, hey Kara. Thanks for stopping by, but I'm on my way out. Merry Christmas to you too." That's what he should have done. That's what any sane man who had already been dropped by a woman who still cared what her parents thought, what the entire damn country thought of her, would do. Once a liar, always a liar. He should have listened, but he didn't.

"This is weird," she said, while he was arguing with himself, and then she turned to leave.

He grabbed her so quickly the bags flew out of her hands and onto his couch by the front door. He kissed her, kicked the door closed, and kept kissing her. Urgent and very Christmas morning.

She moaned or sighed, it was something, so he took more. His hand was under her flannel snowman pajamas which was another mistake because her skin was so soft that his hands wanted just as much as his lips were getting. *Good God, Merry Christmas*, he thought as they dropped to the chair. He was careful not to smash the food because it still smelled incredible and even in his lust haze, food was important.

Kara pulled back and swallowed. "So it's not so weird." Her eyes asked for more than Logan was sure he could give.

"That you wanted to come over?"

"Yeah."

"No, it's not weird." He kissed her gently this time. Maybe it was the PJs or the look on her face, but he suddenly felt very big bad wolf. "I'm glad you came over and brought whatever's in those bags." He walked over to the couch, picked up the bags, and put them on the table.

Kara was still standing at the door, flushed and beautiful.

"Oh, so we're not going to?" She gestured between the two of them. Logan couldn't help it—he laughed.

Kara huffed, which made her all the more adorable.

"I—did you? Wait, was that why you came over? For?"

Her face turned pink and she turned toward the door. He wrapped her in his arms.

"Kara Malendar, was this a Christmas booty call?"

"No." She squirmed, but he held tight.

"You totally want me. You wanted to unwrap me like a Christmas present. Take advantage of my totally innocent holiday mood."

"You are an idiot—I want no such thing." She hit his arms, again with no luck. "You're the one who grabbed me. I just wanted to come over, sit in our PJs, and enjoy some fresh-out-of-the-oven galettes. You are the one who wanted me. Couldn't even wait for me to put my bags down before you were all unwrapping me."

"Wait, did you say galettes?" Logan picked her up and took her to the table. She had stopped fighting and was now laughing. A good sign, he thought.

"You're fun, farm boy. I'm glad I came over."

"Me too, princess. Now tell me where you got fresh galettes on a holiday." He set her down on a seat.

"Well." She opened up one of the bags and pulled out delicious yummy cheese and fruit pastries.

"Oh God, is that one pear?"

"Yes, yes it is."

"Where, Kara, where?"

"My parents—"

"Had them flown in from Paris?" Logan turned to get coffee and tea.

"Very funny, that was a good one and very close."

Logan turned and gave her his best "Are you serious?" look.

"My parents have Christmas morning breakfast catered by Maison Giraud."

"Of course they do." Logan laughed bringing plates and napkins.

"Their cook loves me and I swung by their house before they were even up and stole us breakfast."

Logan kissed her again.

"And to think you almost smashed everything for a Christmas booty call," he said.

Kara balled up one of the paper bags, now that the assorted pastries were safely on the table, and threw it at him.

She sipped tea curled in his dining area, which opened up to the garden. He drank his coffee next to her. They both shared the most delicious galettes either of them had had since returning from Paris and told stories of their favorite Christmas mornings. There were no presents, no dressed-up, mature grown-up talk, just the two of them and a whole lot of feeling Logan had no idea what to do with. One thing was for sure—she crawled right inside of him and spoke to a part of him that he didn't share with anyone. That scared the shit out of him, but at that moment, on Christmas morning in her silly hat, she looked harmless. But looks could be deceiving.

Chapter Twenty-One

*K*ara had been volunteering to decorate the Rose Bowl Parade floats with her parents for as long as she could remember. When she was a little girl, she loved it and now as an adult she respected the tradition. As with all traditions, some years were easier than others, but she believed that showing up was often what held things together. At least that's what she told herself as she received yet another lecture about her hair on the drive over to the floats. She'd left it curly because she wanted to and her mother, of course, did her best to squash any defiance to the standard. Kara was already feeling the weight of her family and when her mother handed her a coffee, she just about lost her mind. She didn't drink coffee; her mother knew that and yet it was expected she would, because that's what Bindi Malendar wanted. Kara wondered if her mother ever found herself in a situation where she didn't get what she wanted. She took a deep breath and found it difficult to flash the perm-a-grin so early in the morning. She was truly slipping.

"I don't know why you don't schedule a standing appointment for a blowout every couple of days," her mother added as they pulled up to the floats.

Kara shook her head, took a few pictures with her parents and the grand marshal for the parade, as was tradition, and then left to get lost among the floats. She was assigned to work on the giraffe, so she smiled at the other volunteers, confirmed that yes she was really the senator's daughter, and then got to work.

There was no point in fighting, even though she'd had a wonderful Christmas morning with Logan only two days earlier and even though under the giant Christmas trees a few nights before that, she'd believed in so much. She needed to come back to earth. This was her life and there was "no point beating a dead horse," as her Nana would say. God, she missed her.

Logan didn't have much time. He needed to get back, but Kara had mentioned she was volunteering to decorate the floats for the Rose Bowl Parade, and he wanted to see her among all those flowers. It took him a while, but he found her adding greenery on a huge flower giraffe. He grabbed a bunch of roses tied together with string, sitting on a stack of similar bunches, and he hoped no one would miss them. She was in jeans, a UCLA sweatshirt, and Converse. He walked toward her. She hadn't seen him yet, and when Logan got closer he noticed her face was fresh and alive as she laughed at something an older lady on a ladder higher up on the giraffe float was saying. The look on Kara's face reminded him that he'd always wanted to give her flowers.

One morning in Paris, back in 2007, they'd walked toward the West Bank. They'd started that day in his bed, his arms wrapped around her as the morning sun peeked through the insanely small window of his one-room flat. It was Sunday and they didn't have class or anything planned. Winnie wanted to see the Marche aux Fleurs. The bird market was also held on Sundays, so Logan kissed her nose and carried her piggyback up the River Seine toward croissants and tea.

Standing among all the floats now, Logan remembered that so much of his time in Paris felt like he was moving toward something complete, real.

They had walked through all the potted flowers and plants that were only there on Sundays. Every other day it was more of a traditional cut flower market. Sundays were special. Logan had bought her a teacup rose bush meant for a garden, but she kept it in her apartment. She'd bought him a birdhouse woven from straw. They'd kissed among the fragrant blooms and held hands all the way back to his apartment, where they practiced cooking until they fell into bed again. That Sunday would be marked on his heart forever as one of the greatest days of his life.

The thought jolted Logan and reminded him he'd put those feelings away for a reason. He wasn't in Paris anymore, but he was in his hometown and a very gorgeous and very real Kara Malendar had just noticed him, so he finished walking toward her.

"These are for you."

"Thank you." She took the flowers and held them to her nose.

"Not quite as spectacular as the last time I gave you roses, but this is pretty cool." Logan looked around at the hundreds of people assembling floats for the iconic parade.

He could tell the moment she realized the exact memory because it filled her eyes.

"That was a great day too," Kara said, "and the croissants were better than anything we have here."

"True. God, I wanted you back then Kara. Still do, it turns out." Logan was very satisfied when Kara's cheeks blushed and she walked him away from the big giraffe.

"Are we afraid there might be reporters here?" he asked as she pulled him faster.

"First we're making out in the back of my truck and then you show up for a Christmas booty call." He was laughing now because he was definitely going to hear it once she got him away from the crowd. "Can't quite figure you out."

"Right back at you, farm boy. Will you please keep your voice down?" Kara turned on him, but lost her fight to contain that incredible smile. She was happy, so he kept teasing.

"So any thoughts on when we are going to revisit one of my all-time favorite Paris memories, princess?" Logan wiggled his eyebrows.

The look on Kara's face was priceless. He couldn't tell if she was more shocked or turned on. The lust was in her eyes for just a moment longer and then it was gone. She glanced around and he could tell she was doing damage control again. After having her picture all over the paper, he couldn't blame her, but she grew downright icy, so he backed away.

"Do you ever think about ignoring all of it? Doing what you want to do? Letting them take the damn pictures?" he asked her.

"No."

"Huh." Well at least she was honest, he thought.

"It's great that we're friends, but—"

"Friends?" Logan laughed. He could keep his distance in public, but there was no way in hell he was her friend.

"Well, whatever we are." She was still walking away from the crowd.

"Are you having a hard time . . . nailing down exactly what we are?" he asked moving closer to her.

"No." She stopped and turned to him. "I'm not. I wanted you when I came over for Christmas. I was in a great mood, ready to . . . you know, and you fed me instead. So now you show up here and in the middle of all this, in public, and you're asking me if and when I want to have sex with you?"

Kara took a breath and Logan prepared for the rest of the storm because it was coming.

"I'm confusing? It's not me. I have no problem nailing things down; I simply don't want to air my life in front of everyone. You seem like you want to push that limit. This time around you know exactly who I am, Logan. This"—she gestured to all the floats—"this is my life."

"This is your parents' life."

She laughed. "Oh Christ, please don't pretend you can teach me anything about this world. I know it like my next breath. Their world is my world. It's one big puzzle, so there's your precious honesty." She turned and walked behind one of the flower shop trucks. Once she was out of sight, she reached over and pulled him with her. "It's not pretty and there are days it downright sucks, but if you want me like you say you do, you have to know this comes with me. I won't pretend it doesn't anymore."

"Kara, I'm not asking you to pretend."

"But you are, every time you comment that I'm looking around, every time you try to get a rise out of me in public. You're asking me to be something I can't be. So"—she pulled him into her body—"you be you and I'll be me."

"Sounds like a deal. I'm glad I dropped by," he joked, trying to lighten what had suddenly become pretty intense.

She laughed, looked behind them, and then kissed the hell out of him right there in public, well behind a huge semitruck, but close enough. Hadn't she just asked him to back off? Logan wondered if she was kissing him because he'd pushed her over the edge, or if the cage she was in was simply getting too small. He kissed her back and pushed her up against the flower truck with a little more force than he'd expected. Then, right when he thought he had the upper hand, she pulled back from their kiss a little breathless and a lot sexy. She held his chest and smiled no doubt at the look of shock on his face.

"So, I'm sure I'll show up at your door again someday. Try not to blow it next time, farm boy." With that, she walked away, back into the sea of floats and flowers.

Logan laughed and then walked back to work. The woman was going to destroy him; there was no question now.

Chapter Twenty-Two

Dine LA Restaurant Week ran from January 23 to February 6. Logan had worked some variation of restaurant week three times at two different restaurants. It was always exciting and hectic, but this was different. This was his: his name, his food, and his to fail if things didn't go right. Most restaurants didn't participate their first year in business. "It takes some time to establish and settle once a new restaurant is opened." That's what a couple of his mentors had advised when he called asking for guidance. Guidance he promptly ignored.

"Okay, the guy I know at Fresco told me they're doing a beef short rib too, as a starter. He wouldn't give me the details, but I've eaten there and I'm guessing they're working the same ragu as when they run it as a special. It's good, not as good as ours with the celery root puree, but good. I think we should steer clear of the ribs and change it up." Travis sat up on the counter.

"Geoduck carpaccio," Logan said. "Remember Benji's chowder when we were at Margot's? Geoducks—he used to say they'd make great—"

"Carpaccio, yeah, yeah I remember. Great idea, let's do that."

"Garrett has a friend up in Bodega Bay. Fisherman, crabs, and this year he has geoduck clams. Fresh and simple."

"Perfect," Travis said with the enthusiasm Logan loved in him.

"I'll see if he can get us some by Thursday to prep and run a few taste tests with you before we go live on Friday."

"I think it's what we need. The taste is mainstream enough, but it's different. Perfect. I'll even make some fritters with the bellies. Remember when Benji did that?"

Logan nodded along with Travis's excitement.

Travis gave him a high five. "Done deal! What's next?"

Logan started flipping through his yellow pad and Travis sighed.

"That thing never seems to get any smaller."

"Tell me about it. Do you think we should have some type of loyalty program? Maybe with the wine?" Logan asked.

Before Travis opened his mouth, Makenna came into the back kitchen, grabbed a stack of mail off Logan's desk, and said, "Yes, we should, but nothing cheesy. I'm meeting this guy next week."

"Oooh, you got a hot date, Ken?" Travis asked.

Makenna glared at him.

"As I was saying, this guy next week runs a local promotion company, social media, giveaways, all the crap we hate. He says his company can handle it. I like their website and some of the other restaurants he's worked with are really impressive. You know that pie place that just went in on Third?" Makenna asked.

"Pie? That's all they do?" Travis asked.

Logan could tell his sister had had enough. She walked over to Travis and stood between his legs.

"Travis," she spoke almost like a kindergarten teacher.

"Yeah, Ken?" He sat casual and unflinching.

That was until Makenna put one hand on each of his thighs and leaned into him. Logan had known Travis a long time and the look on his face was priceless. He was nervous.

"Logan and I are trying to have a grown-up conversation," Makenna continued. "So why don't you go play . . ."

Travis smiled; his eyebrows wiggled and Logan could actually see the game change in his favor.

"Play with myself?" He raised his eyebrows.

Logan couldn't help it—he burst out laughing and Travis jumped down, sliding into the small space between Makenna and the counter. She quickly moved back as if she'd been shocked. Logan was rooting for his sister, hoping she'd make a comeback, but when Kenna turned to him, her cheeks were scarlet. Game over. She picked up her bag and her laptop.

"You're a moron." She spun around and Travis was still laughing.

"Oh, come on. That was a good one. It's all in the timing, Ken. Hasn't anyone ever told you that? You paused—it was fair game."

Makenna shook her head and glared at Logan who willed himself to stop smiling.

"I have an interview with Kara in a couple of weeks. Paige has a birthday party, so Kara agreed to meet me there. I guess she's moving on to the last piece about the farm and she wants to ask me some questions because I work both?"

"Makes sense." Logan tried not to notice Travis who still had a smart-ass grin on his face.

"I've got bills to pay and I'm ordering that new whiskey or Scotch, whatever it was that Sage wanted, today too. I'll be in the front if you need me."

Travis opened his mouth, but before he could say a word, Makenna held up her hand and walked out.

"She's something else," Travis said, and Logan caught the look in his friend's eyes. It was a flicker of something he recognized in himself lately.

"She's my sister."

Travis's head jerked up as if he was startled out of the dreamy look that watched Makenna leave. "What? Oh Jesus." Travis busied himself with the asparagus. "I know. I was just having fun. Ken, believe me, Ken is not my type." His eyes didn't quite meet Logan's and damn, he was blushing now too.

What the hell?

Makenna turned on some music and Sarah McLachlan filled their space. Travis rolled his eyes at her selection and Logan laughed the whole awkward thing off. There was nothing between them. Travis and Kenna hated each other; Logan kind of liked it that way.

"Speaking of Kenna's interview, what's up with you and Super Hot Food Critic Lady?" Travis asked.

"Why?" Logan tried to tone down whatever stupid, weird, guilty thing he was feeling.

"Well, we're friends and you never get any action, so you're kind of boring. I just thought since you were finally lusting after someone there might be some good stories."

Logan turned to face him.

"Oh, there's no one else here, man. Give it up, you're totally into her." Travis continued chopping as if what he was saying was perfectly understood.

"You're wrong." Logan turned to grab cream out of the walk-in.

Travis followed behind him and held the door open as he returned.

"Please, I can't read her debutante vibe yet, so I'm not sure if she's into you. But, you, my friend, my boss, you are into her. That kiss right out there on the floor? Yeah, you've never done that before. Totally blew the whole 'not dating the clientele' shit right outta the water."

Logan whisked and added cream to the large silver bowl in front of him.

"Stop. That was for the customers. Ever since that article, they love the idea of us as a couple. We were just playing that up." He was no longer able to make eye contact.

"Oh, right, sure. So that was all business out there. Got it."

Logan could tell he wasn't buying it, but he just kept whisking. That was his story and he was sticking to it.

"Hey, Makenna," Travis called to the front of the restaurant.

Shit! Travis was bringing in backup.

"What?" she yelled, clearly still annoyed.

"Logan," he called back to her, "totally into the foodie lady, right?"

"Oh yes, in a bad way." She came around the corner with her laptop and a piece of red licorice clenched between her teeth.

"What the hell are you two smoking? Kara is writing an article on me, on us, our place. It's great for business if we appear to be a couple, as you yourself said Makenna."

Makenna nodded.

"That's it, I mean I'm sorry to let you down, but there's no me 'being into' anyone. Now, I'm pretty sure we have stuff to do."

"Just as well." Makenna was still typing away on her laptop. "She seems like a massive bitch to me."

"What? Jesus, Makenna, you don't even know her. She's not like that at . . ."

The words were out of Logan's mouth before he noticed they were both waiting him out, like kids on a playground hoping some bonehead would take their dare. Logan was clearly the bonehead in this scenario.

Makenna bit off a piece of her licorice. She chewed and, smiling, pointed the rest of her red twisty at Logan as she walked back to the front of the house.

"I love you, Makenna." Travis was back to laughing. The guy could be really annoying.

"No problem," she called.

Logan shook his head. "You two are idiots."

Travis just smiled.

"Can we please get back to work? Geoduck clams, carpaccio, thoughts? Do you have anything productive, like job thoughts, in there Travis?"

"I do. I think the carpaccio is a great idea. It's a definite showcase dish. I think if Garrett can get us those clams we will be a hit."

Logan nodded, grateful to be talking about something other than Kara.

"I also think you need to lock those legs down and take that woman on a proper date. You know, a meal or a movie, or hell, just get her into your bed. That is if you ever actually use the damn thing."

"Great. Thank you for that valuable input." Logan dried his hands and threw the towel in Travis's face. "We open in two hours. Summer will be here in"—Logan glanced at the large round clock above the entry pass from the kitchen to the serving window—"twenty minutes. Mushrooms are already done, but you're going to need to finish this sauce for me. All it needs is cheese," he continued, taking his apron off.

"Where're you off to?"

"All this talk about Restaurant Week made me remember the chandelier over the private dining area. You know that lamp I bought for the dark corner?"

"Lover's cove?" Travis wiggled his eyebrows.

Logan laughed—he couldn't help it. "Anyway, I love that lamp and I want to see if we can commission the artist to make the ceiling piece for the private dining room. You know, like a chandelier, but better. According to Jill at zenDeluxe, the artist uses sea glass and repurposed brass lamp bases. I was thinking it might be cool if she could use some of that old green bottle glass we saved."

"The stuff from the garage door panels?"

"Yeah, maybe incorporate some of that into the design."

"Great idea. Who's the artist?"

"Not sure. She was supposed to call me back with the name, so I'm going to give her a call now."

Logan walked out to the bar, grabbed a phone, and called zenDeluxe. After some paper shuffling, Jill, the owner, came back on the line.

"Sorry, here it is. We are expecting two more pieces from her next week, but you wanted something special if I remember, right?"

"Yes." Logan grabbed a piece of paper from the bar register.

"Okay, well I'm not sure if she does commissioned work, but give it a shot. The artist's studio is on the grounds of her private residence and her name is Winnie Parker —"

Logan froze and almost dropped the phone as Jill kept talking in his ear.

"So, did you get that e-mail address, or do you need me to repeat it?"

"I know her, um, know it. Thank you."

Logan hung up, told Travis he might be late for lunch, and grabbed his keys. He wasn't sure what game she was playing this time, but he wasn't going to be left standing in some lobby, that was for damn sure.

Kara loved a new year. She'd made a pot of tea and was grooving around her studio to R. Kelly's "Ignition." It was her feel-good song. R. Kelly had just gotten to the "toot toot, beep beep" and Kara was rolling as his lyrics suggested. She dropped into her chair and wheeled up to the counter space that took up an entire wall of her studio. Her hands were in the air, she was in full dance club mode, when the lights blinked off and on again. She turned and immediately started patting her hand on the counter for the remote to the stereo because Logan was standing in the doorway. The look on his face was one of shock, similar to the look she'd left him with in the lobby of his apartment a little over eight years ago in Paris.

"Christ, Kara, what are you doing?"

"Well, I'm dancing around my studio, what does it look like I'm doing?" She tried for casual in contrast to the thundering in her chest.

"Winnie Parker designs lamps now?"

"She does." Kara held her ground. There was nothing else to do at this point.

"What is this?" Logan moved toward her. "Some kind of game?"

He surveyed her space as if something on the walls or sitting on her work table would give him answers and explain why she was once again standing in front of him as Winnie Parker. He wouldn't find any answers; those needed to come from her.

"You're not going to understand."

"Try me."

"This is who I am," she attempted a start.

"You mean, this is who you are when no one is looking? You're a grown woman. What is so wrong with just being you—one you—if you even know what that is?"

"No. You don't get to do this to me, this holier-than-thou, farm boy shit. I know who I am. Maybe I just don't choose to share it with you?" Kara stood face-to-face with him.

"See? Games." Logan's eyes changed and he backed off.

"Goddamn it, Logan. Stop poking and joking, like what I'm doing has anything to do with you. We're not even a defined . . . thing, so what makes you think you can barge in here and make me feel foolish."

He turned to leave.

Kara sat, prepared to let him. She saw no point in stopping him; there was no way to make him understand. Her heart took her back to the Christmas trees, the time they'd spent together. This was past Paris, and if she let him walk out, she would never know what came next. She took a deep breath and tried to share herself.

"When I was seven, I cut my own bangs."

Logan stopped, let go of the doorknob, and turned back around.

"It was, of course, a mess: crooked and choppy. Mother was livid. It was the morning of some event we were supposed to go to. I don't remember what it was, but I remember my dress. It was blue with this eyelet overlay." Kara touched her shoulder as if she were touching the dress and then shook her head. "Anyway, I wanted to be pretty. I remember wishing I could walk through those doors and have everyone say what a beautiful daughter Senator Malendar had."

"You were seven?"

Kara nodded.

"I'd just watched some documentary on Coco Chanel. I wanted to be different like that. So, I cut my own hair, thinking bangs were exactly what I needed. My mother almost left me at home. I was an embarrassment. I looked ridiculous, and even her stylists couldn't fix it, that's what she said. My father insisted that I go. There were about two dozen reporters when we stepped out of the car." Kara picked her cup up off the counter and sipped her tea, still not looking at him. "Two of my cousins were with us. Sixteen and eighteen, blonde, both gorgeous, or at least I thought so at the time."

"Kara."

"Most of the picture captions wondered what my stylist was thinking, but there was one, this one"—Kara stood, her back straight as if she was facing off to defend her younger self—"it was some stupid society rag. They led with a picture of me standing by my mother. The headline was 'Ugly Duckling.'"

"Jesus." He moved to her, but Kara held up her hand. She grew suddenly cold, as if letting in any emotion might sink her.

"When I was twelve I got braces. For over a year, it seemed like every picture they took of me had my mouth opened and I'm pretty sure there were a few where I had food from lunch still in my braces. My mother made me carry this tiny toothbrush around to avoid such embarrassments, but they managed to catch me anyway."

Logan said nothing. There was nothing to say; she simply wanted him to understand.

"My junior prom date, a guy I had a huge crush on, sold his story to the local paper. Not only was it intimated that I slept with him on prom night, but he hinted I was kinky. That led to the headline . . ." She watched him, knowing he could figure it out.

Logan shook his head, "'Kinky Kara'?"

"You've got it." The pain spilled out of her small laugh. "All this crap, and plenty more, can be Googled for fun. My entire life—awkward, out of sync, every mistake from zits to bad dates—is there for the world to see. I'm not saying the world is all that interested anymore, because thankfully since I've been in hiding, there's not much to report."

"Can't your parents get some of this shit taken down? Aren't there laws?"

"They tried in the beginning, but when that didn't work, they put it on me. It became my responsibility to look perfect, act perfect. 'Don't give them anything' became my life motto. I accepted it and became what I needed to be. I'm not telling you this so you can feel sorry for me. I've led a very privileged life, I know that, but that's why I don't share. I know who I am. I've spent years working on the me who lives behind closed doors."

"I'm sorry. I didn't mean to—"

"You don't need to be sorry. You didn't know. I get that it's weird and I seem like I'm screwing with you, but I'm not used to this."

"Used to what?"

"You. What you are, your family. I want . . ."

"What do you want?"

"I want to trust that what I'm feeling is right, safe, but I'm always reluctant to share. So, you see, I'm not playing games, Logan. I'm just keeping myself safe."

"I understand."

"We both went to UCLA at the same time. I didn't know you, and you didn't know me. I was very good at being invisible my first three years." Kara sipped her tea again, aware of the warm cup as she cradled it in her hands. "I went to Paris for the exchange, where we met, because it was an election year and there was some buzz, according to my father's campaign, that I was having an affair with my Humanities teacher."

"Where do they get this crap?"

"Freshman year, I was expected to pledge a sorority. Kappa Kappa Gamma. My mother was in Kappa, so were all of her friends, blah, blah. Anyway, I didn't rush because I didn't want to join a sorority, but that pissed some of the Kappa girls off. I was labeled a snob. Being called a snob by a sorority was really quite an accomplishment." Kara tried to smile. "The whole thing was stupid, but I'm sure that's where the slutty Kara rumors came from. To be honest with you, I'd learned to ignore most of it, but this one—the affair rumor—prompted Stanley, my father's campaign manager and an all-around asshole of a guy, to decide that I needed to be sent away."

"So that's why you went to Paris?"

Kara nodded.

"But then why were you dragged back home?"

"Story blew over. Turned out my Humanities teacher was sleeping with half of the Kappa house. The heat moved off me and my mother ordered me home to help with the campaign."

"They just move you around like that?"

"Not as much these days, but yeah I guess to someone else, I'm still moved around. But after Paris, things changed."

"What changed?"

"I did. I stopped going to office hours with my teachers, took some classes online if I could, and I learned. I basically learned how to handle things."

"By locking yourself away?"

Kara laughed. "I'm not locked away, Logan. I have my job. I attend the functions I need to, and I have this." She gestured to her studio.

"Hidden."

"Safe." Kara turned from him and set her empty teacup on the counter.

Logan walked past shelving underneath a massive pen-and-ink print of a wave. There were four or five table lamps in progress and a large art deco column lamp without a shade.

"What goes into your creations?"

"The lamp bases are antiques, most of them, and the rest is sea glass. I collect it." Kara gestured to her work counter, which was old wood and scattered with pieces of sea glass.

"Is this driftwood?" Logan ran a hand along the smooth surface.

"Yes, several pieces actually. Put together by a friend of mine, Oscar. He's a surfer. He makes boards and he made me this from pieces I collected."

"You collected?"

"Yes. Pretty much everything in here has been touched by me in some way."

Logan glanced back at the print.

"You?" he asked walking over to get a closer look.

"Yes, that's me too," Kara said, with what almost seemed like embarrassment. "I took an art class a few years ago. That was my final project. I thought it turned out nicely, so I put it there."

"Nicely? Kara, it's incredible."

Logan took a closer look.

"I can tell it's a wave. I love the broad strokes, but what makes up the shore here? Tiny letters, are those Japanese?"

"Very good." She seemed a little more comfortable with him in her space.

"What do they say?"

"It's a letter my Nana wrote to me when I graduated from college. It's a personal note about being strong. I didn't want people to read it, but I wanted it included, so I decided to put it in a different language. I thought the Japanese letters went well with the wave. Grady actually had it translated for me and then I made those letters the beach under the wave."

Logan stood there struck dumb with surprise. He'd known Winnie Parker and he had even learned bits and pieces of Kara Malendar, but the woman wringing her hands as she shared herself was something altogether more. Winnie's joy and energy mixed with the insight and maturity of Kara Malendar. All of that sprinkled with a need to connect, create. It was staggering and all Logan could do was continue drinking her in. He turned back to her work counter, needing some relief from the intensity. He needed to hear her laugh.

"Is that a welder?" he asked raising and lowering his eyebrows.

And there it was, her laughter filled the studio.

"It is. The smaller one is a soldering gun. I use both of them for my pieces."

"Yeah, you do. Do you wear tiny shorts while you're welding, because my teenage mind remembers a poster with that exact image."

She laughed harder and Logan felt the world right.

"No tiny shorts."

Logan snapped his fingers in feigned disappointment. He finished his self-tour of her space, was surprised to see *Moby Dick* on her bookshelf and even more surprised when she mentioned it was one of her favorites.

"I loved your lamps the minute I saw them." He sat down in the big armchair under the window near her books. "Did you see it in the restaurant?"

"I did." Kara dropped down on the floral couch across from him.

"And you didn't say anything."

"What did you want me to say? I don't advertise what I do, Logan. The fact that you happened to buy one of my lamps—that it spoke to you—was wonderful. There was nothing for me to say."

Logan shrugged in agreement. She had a point.

"I was incredibly flattered when I saw it," she added with a smile.

"Oh, yeah?" He joined her on the couch.

"Yeah."

"So, the name Winnie? Where does that come from?"

Kara smiled. "My Nana's name."

"Ah." He nodded. "Hey, was that R. Kelly I heard when I came in?"

Kara smiled as he turned to face her.

"It was. I'm a pretty big R. Kelly fan."

"Really?"

"No, not really, just that song, 'Ignition.'" She rolled her hands in a steering wheel motion, "Toot toot, beep beep. It's one of the songs on my Roll That Body playlist."

"Okay, any chance we can listen to the rest of that playlist?"

Kara laughed, leaning into him.

"My God, look at you." Logan suddenly grew serious.

She put her hands to her hair, eyes wandering to her silky pants with purple-and-orange swirls. Her feet were bare, hair piled at her neck with a pencil. "What?"

Logan reached forward and ran his finger along the strap of a tank top peeking out at the neckline of her oversized sweater.

"You're beautiful," fell out of his mouth before he had time to remind himself women were nothing but trouble.

Kara smiled. "Actually, I'm not classically beautiful. According to my mother's stylist, my eyes are too big for my face, my nose slants to the right, and don't get him started on my feet." Kara lifted her foot up like a toddler.

He slid his hands around her waist, pulled her into him, and held. Logan enjoyed sex as much as the next guy, but everything that went with it was almost as good. Every time her body met his after they'd been apart for a while, the feel of their connection was something that never got old.

"You, the whole of you in this space. You're playful, comfortable. This is who you are when no one is looking. It's beautiful."

"Thank you. You're pretty beautiful too." She touched her nose to his.

"Yeah? How's my nose?"

She kissed it on the tip. "It's cute."

"Cute, huh?"

Kara nodded and Logan kissed her.

Chapter Twenty-Three

*E*loise chased after the cat with two of her party guests as Kara helped clean up the wrapping paper from her birthday party. Jake and Cotton had a beautiful home in the bungalow district that they restored from the ground up.

"Can you believe my mother actually came to a party? And she was somewhat civil." Kara sat in one of the kitchen chairs.

"Gay is in now, honey, I'm sure Momma Malendar plays up her daughter's gay best friend every chance she gets." Jake rinsed off plates and put them in the dishwasher.

Kara had never thought of it that way, nor had she heard Jake say it quite like that. "So that's what our relationship is? You're a trendy accessory?" Her tone was serious and Jake shut the water off and turned to face her.

"Oh blazes, cut it out, of course not. I'm not even talking about us in private. I'm just saying it's a convenient benefit and that way it's . . ." Jake had talked himself into a corner.

Kara had seen him do it before and she recognized the look. "What? That way it's what?" she asked.

"Allowed." Jake touched her arm. "That's what I was going to say, but that's not exactly—"

"Allowed? I'm allowed? Is that what you think?"

Jake shook his head, but Kara knew that was exactly what he thought.

"I'm an adult, Jake. I do what I want."

"I know you do, of course you do."

"Oh my God! You think I'm a puppet. That I'm . . . them?"

"Honey, settle down, that's not what I said."

"Please don't bullshit me. You never have, let's not start this now."

"All I'm saying is you follow protocol with your parents. I understand why, and I'm not judging. I get it."

"And if gay wasn't in?" Kara asked.

"Our friendship would be harder. Kara, come on. There's an image to uphold. This isn't anything new. I'm relieved your mother likes me and that your father finds value in our friendship."

"Jake! Jesus!"

"What? I'm not saying we wouldn't be friends. We might just have to closet it up like . . . well, like the rest of you."

Kara felt the cold punch of honesty. Jake had dealt it many times before, but this one stung a little more.

"Your real laugh, your color, your glass, you, Kara. We both know that you don't let that you out very often."

"I'm just private."

"I know and I understand that, but you've mastered hiding the best parts of yourself. I've gotten to see them and I'm not saying you're only friends with me because your parents like me."

"Good." Kara found herself a little defensive as Eloise came running into the kitchen. Jake quickly changed the subject and they settled back into the festivities.

Driving home, Kara knew he was right, but knowing something and doing something about it were two very different things. She had been hiding for so long, she wasn't sure how to be found. By the time she pulled into her driveway, she had replayed the last time she'd done anything completely spontaneous without thinking. Maybe it was time for some spontaneity; it was certainly time for less thinking. She sat in her car and with the help of her mother's always present, always annoying, voice in her head, Kara ran through all of the reasons why what she was about to do was a massive mistake. She kicked her mother out of her thoughts and backed out of her driveway on her way to being found.

It had been a good night. They sold out their tasting menu for Restaurant Week, received endless compliments on the carpaccio, and all tables were full until almost 10:30. Logan and Travis were exhausted. Makenna's face hurt from smiling and if she gave out their social media information one more time, she told Logan, she was sure she would run screaming into the parking lot. Sage cut her finger about two hours into the night, but now there was so much lime juice in, it was numb. Doors locked, they all helped clean up.

"Did you see the guy at table four who kept stuffing bread into his wife's purse? It was like one of those weird couples on *The Love Boat*." Makenna leaned on the broom.

Logan and Sage stared at her, expressionless.

"What? Don't you guys have Hulu? Paige and I watch *The Love Boat* all the time."

They both shook their heads.

"You guys suck. I can't help it if my single-mother life isn't exciting." Makenna swept under the bar tables. "And if I'm not up to my boot in chicken shit, I'm in the shower or at a PTA meeting or here. When am I supposed to become exciting?"

"Speaking of exciting, did you see the guy sitting at the bar alone during happy hour? Black sweater?" Sage asked while she rehung the glasses behind the bar.

"Oh, yes I did. He was hot. It's been so damn long." Makenna leaned up against the bar. "I'm so tired, and I really need to shave my legs, but good God, yes, I thought he was lovely."

"Me too," Sage hummed in agreement.

Logan looked up from rolling silverware.

"Ladies, did you two want be alone?" He laughed.

"Oh, shut up," Sage said, "it's so much easier for men."

"Really? How do you figure that?" he asked.

"If a man wants to get laid, he just goes to a bar and picks someone." Sage wiped down the back bar.

"Yeah, if a woman does that she's a slut, but a man picks up a woman and sleeps with her, doesn't even need to know her name, and he's a damn hero," Makenna chimed in.

"You know, I was in the back, doing all the work"—Travis pushed through the door from the back kitchen—"and I heard parts of this conversation. Was someone talking about me?"

"We were discussing man-whores, so yes, Travis you fit that category." Makenna swept into the dustpan and slid past him to empty it.

"Man-whore is a harsh label, Ken. I prefer being called a field researcher."

Logan shook his head as he gathered up the rolled silverware and brought it to the server's station.

"You're going to want to back away slowly." He passed Travis. "You're outnumbered."

"Nah, these ladies love me."

Sage threw a towel in his face and Makenna laughed.

"Oh, and now on top of everything else I'm running around doing things half-assed, Paige tells me yesterday no one makes lunch like Uncle Rogan." Makenna put away the broom as Logan came back into the bar.

"That's my girl. Great memory too, I mean, when was the last time I made her lunch?"

"What are you talking about? You make her lunch at least two or three times a week. Every time I forget her lunch box here, the next morning it always has what she's now calling 'a gourmet lunch' in it. So, thanks for that."

"Kenna, I'm not making Paige's lunch. You do forget her lunch box all the time, but I haven't been putting anything in it. I just assumed you picked something up on those mornings."

Makenna sat down on one of the barstools. Sage was now cleaning out her fruit and olive bins and Travis had gone back into the kitchen.

"Let me get this straight. You're not filling Paige's lunch box with sandwiches made on homemade bread and giving her some kind of fruit salad she talks about nonstop? You're not responsible for why my daughter now makes me buy hummus?"

Logan shook his head, trying to replay some of those hectic mornings.

"Well, then who the hell is?" Makenna asked.

At that moment, Travis came out of the kitchen holding his bag and helmet.

"We're all good back there. If you don't need me for anything, I'm gonna take off." He rounded the bar.

Makenna was still dumbfounded, but Logan figured it out as soon as he saw Travis making his getaway.

"He is." Logan was just as shocked as his sister was about to be.

"What?" Disbelief hit her eyes.

"Travis—he's making Paige's lunch."

She laughed. As Travis walked past her toward the door, Logan nodded to his sister.

"Wait," Makenna said and Travis stopped just short of his escape. She walked over and stepped between him and the door.

"Is that true? You make Paige's lunch?"

Travis smiled and Logan could see him trying for casual, but it was no use. Douche bags didn't make lunch to help out frazzled single moms. Man-whores didn't make fruit salad complete with heart-shaped strawberries for little girls to brag about at the lunch table.

"It's not a big deal. Sometimes I notice you forget her lunch box. Instead of leaving it hanging around, I throw a sandwich in it, save you a trip in the morning." He moved to go around Kenna who was still dumbstruck.

She tilted her head up because Travis was almost the size of two of her. Sage and Logan were both silent, like they were watching two animals on one of those National Geographic shows Paige loved so much.

Makenna watched him, seemingly trying to figure him out, and then she went up on her tiptoes, leaned her hand on his chest, and kissed him on the cheek.

"Thank you."

Logan could see Travis's chest moving in and out, but other than that, there were no signs of life.

"Now that you've spoiled her, she's instructed me to forget her lunch box every night after school." Makenna's voice was soft, almost gentle.

The whole scene was a bit surreal.

"You're welcome, and let Paige know I'm taking special requests," Travis finally said.

Makenna laughed. "Oh, you are in big trouble now."

Travis's face warmed, and Logan wasn't sure why it didn't make him uncomfortable to have his best friend locked on his sister that way, but it didn't. The energy between the two felt genuine, so real, that Sage literally sighed and rested her arms on her bar.

"It's good trouble." Travis moved past her. "Goodnight guys." He glanced back toward the bar. "'Night, Makenna." The words hung between them for a beat, and then he was gone.

Makenna stood staring after Travis, then sat down and said nothing.

Before Logan could get up and lock the door behind Travis, Kara came through the front door.

"I know this is a bad time, that you're closed and probably tired, but I needed—" Kara stopped when she saw Makenna and Sage. "Oh. Hi. How'd everything go tonight?" she asked.

"Great." Sage looked at Makenna who was already collecting her things.

"We were just leaving." Sage pulled her bag from behind the bar.

"Right, I've got to get home." Makenna slid past Logan and left out the front.

Sage was right behind her and Logan turned to lock the door.

He followed Kara back into the bar and closed the blinds on the three windows. She was clearly upset and he thought it best to wait her out.

"I'm trying to find myself."

Logan turned and tried not to look confused.

Kara laughed.

"I guess I shouldn't have started with that. Eloise had her birthday party today."

"Oh, that's great. How old is she?"

"Three."

"So, you must have hung out after the party?" Logan was trying to make conversation until he could figure out why she'd shown up at 11:30.

"Jake said I hide and that I only do things or associate with people my parents approve of."

Ah, Logan thought, *now we're getting somewhere.*

"Do you want some tea? I can see if we have some in the back."

"I don't want tea."

"Okay, well I'm sure Jake doesn't know what it's like dealing with the press or all the other crap. Do you want to talk about it?"

"No, I don't want to talk."

"Right. Sure, come here." Logan took her into his arms.

"I need you. I'm at your door again, Logan." She looked up at him. Her eyes told him exactly what she meant, but he needed to clarify before he made an ass out of himself.

"What does that mean, Kara?"

"It means so many things, and I don't want to figure them all out right now. I just want you to find me, Logan. See me."

She put her hand on his chest, and he stopped.

"Make your move, Logan, or I will."

He smiled at his own words being thrown back at him in a much sexier voice.

"Well, normally I would say ladies first, princess, but I think I'll take this one myself." On the last breath, he kissed her.

Chapter Twenty-Four

"Last chance to call this off." Logan held her as they stumbled into the kitchen.

"This is a bad idea, right?" Kara tugged at his shirt. "Take this off."

"Probably one of our worst." He pulled his shirt over his head.

"Oh dear God, it does go onto your chest." Kara ran her hands up his tattooed arm, along his collarbone, and down his stomach.

Logan unbuttoned her blouse. "Kara, things are great right now and I don't want you to do this and then regret . . . Oh Jesus"—the silk blouse fell off her shoulders—"forget it. Best idea I've had in a long time, maybe even ever."

He backed her up until they hit the wood counter of his kitchen.

"I want you to know that I recognize the cliché here, that I cook and I'm getting ready to devour you on the kitchen counter. I get it and while I'd love to lay you down and love you all over my actual bed, I never seem to leave this damn place, so kitchen counter it is."

With that, Logan swiped his arm across the counter and sent steel bowls and tomatoes flying. He pulled her in and his body pulsed, as his breathing became urgent. His hands dug into her sides as he lifted her onto the counter and then reached behind her to knock the last couple of bowls out of their way. Gently laying her back, he slid her body up the counter and removed her jeans. As he ran his hands up her bare, long legs he realized she'd been eating. Her body was glowing. It was nourished and so damn sexy, he thought he was going to lose his mind. He undid the buttons of his jeans and hoisted himself onto the counter. Slowly crawling her body, he kissed soft skin he recognized from a distant memory, now fresh and different. Kara's hands went into his hair, caressing and then pulling. He could feel her need as he kissed his way past her stomach, to the dip in the center of her chest.

She sighed and reached for him. "Logan."

"Right here, princess. At your service." He gave her a wicked smile, still hovering over her body.

Kara laughed. "Get up here." She tugged on his hair.

"Hang on, I just got to one, well two, of my favorite parts."

He teased his way around her body and slowly brought her from playful to near crazy. The things the man could do with his tongue, she thought as her hands clung to the sides of the wooden counter. Logan moved as if he had all the time in the world, as if they were on some tropical island instead of the massive counter in the middle of his kitchen. He met her eyes, smiled and her body hummed. She couldn't take her eyes off him.

"I . . ." was all that came out as he took her mouth again and finally pressed his body against her. Resting his weight on his forearms, Logan moved her hair out of her face, held her, and continued kissing her lips, pulling, dipping. He moved to her neck, behind her ear, and then he bit her earlobe. He seemed to know exactly what she craved.

"You remember me," fell out of her mouth, breathless.

Logan's gaze locked on hers.

"There are some things a man never forgets. Your body, what turns you on and has you panting my name. Yeah, I'm never going to forget those things."

"I . . . I don't pant."

Kara didn't have time to say anything before he was gone again, kissing her hip bone, the back of her knees, and then he slowly removed the only thin strip of silk that was left on her body. Her body lifted toward him as he kicked off his own jeans and remained suspended in some sort of plank above her. Kara was never a fan of structured exercise, but if what Logan was doing actually was a plank, she could certainly get into that. He kissed her again, and then they slowly slid together. As he began to move, she felt as if her entire body might simply melt into him.

"Okay, maybe I pant a little." She was fighting for breath and he smiled, eyes hazy as if he recognized her again. He wanted to tell her something, but instead he moved one last time and they were both gone.

"Do you remember the first time we . . ." Logan paused as if he wasn't sure how to say it.

"Had sex?" Kara added, shifting into him and smiling into his shoulder.

"Yeah." He laughed and pulled her closer, balancing them both on the counter he would never look at the same way again.

"It was my first time, of course I remember it."

"Which I still don't understand. How did you make it to twenty-one without someone . . ."

"Have you seen my life? Not a lot of college guys clamoring to be a part of that mess." Kara kissed his shoulder.

"Well, I didn't know your mess."

"And wasn't that so wonderful?" She leaned against his chest and with each passing moment, the present was outdoing the past.

"I guess it's all how you look at it. We were in sort of a bubble."

"It was a great bubble, and that night in your tiny little apartment was the most spontaneous thing I'd ever done. I'd only known you forty-seven days."

"You counted?" He'd wanted her from week one, but even he hadn't counted.

"Sure, when I was berating myself for being reckless."

Logan laughed.

"I got over it though. Turned out I really liked sex, so thank you for that."

"You sure did. And you're quite welcome. I'm sure you've gone on to bigger and better things." They both laughed.

"I've actually become well versed in 'me' time."

Logan nearly rolled off the counter at the thought of Kara and—Christ, he'd never run that particular fantasy.

"I . . . you got me. I'm speechless. All sorts of great new images are flooding my mind, but I can't find my words."

"What? It's perfectly natural to . . . help yourself in that department. Besides, I gave up on group play once my parents pulled me away from . . ."

"From what?"

"From the sunshine." Kara sat up and slid off the counter.

He joined her and jumped back into his jeans. As she buttoned her shirt, he turned her to face him. "I'm sorry, Kara."

"For what?"

"For not seeing what all that did to you. I was so busy being pissed that you weren't who you said you were, I never thought about you."

"We were young and why would you? I did lie to you."

"True."

She swatted him and pulled her jeans up.

"Could we revisit the sex thing for a minute?"

She laughed. "Sure."

"Since metaphors seem more comfortable here, when was the last time you had . . . group play?"

Kara busied herself as if she was avoiding his question.

"I'm hungry, are you hungry?" she asked.

"I am. I'll make us something. Kara?" He lifted her chin and their eyes met. He knew her answer before it came out of her mouth. *Holy shit!*

"Stop looking at me that way. You don't understand my life and when I left Paris I decided it was easier to shut down."

"I'm not looking at you any way." But he knew it wasn't true. He tried to erase the pity from his face, but that was what he was feeling. In what world did a woman so full and breathtaking hide herself away like that?

"And don't do that stupid Hallmark movie scene where you tell me you're honored."

Logan belly laughed and she joined him.

"There's nothing to be embarrassed about." He pulled out two pans.

"I'm not embarrassed."

"You look a little pink in the cheeks there, princess."

"Shut up. Make me something to eat, farm boy."

Logan was more than a little stunned that he was the only person Kara Malendar felt comfortable sharing the deep, hidden shiny parts of herself with. It was indeed an honor. A brilliant sunrise kind of honor, but there was no way he was going to tell her that.

"So, this self play"—Logan decided to move on for both of their sakes as he came back from the walk-in with butter and cheese—"are spectators allowed to watch?"

She laughed and threw a mushroom at him as he grabbed her around the waist and pulled her into him. Right before he kissed her for the hundredth time that night, a feeling washed over him, the one men write stupid poems and love songs about. He took to her mouth deeper and ran one hand up the side of her body, under her blouse, to the warm, well-loved curve of her breast. She reached up and took hold of the back of his neck and Logan didn't care anymore if she was going to destroy him; it didn't matter. He wanted to touch the sun, feel her warmth. That was all that mattered. Men throughout history had made the same stupid mistake and he was going to join them. He just hoped what he had to give would be enough.

By the time they pulled apart again, the butter had softened. They made grilled cheese sandwiches. Logan swore by his blend of cheeses, thick crusty bread, and a grainy mustard Travis made in-house every week. Kara's version was her take on brie and granny smith apples, with the fig jelly the restaurant had on hand for their charcuterie.

"Nice to see you in the kitchen again." Logan popped the last piece of grilled cheese into his mouth.

"Well, it's a great kitchen." Kara smiled and sipped her wine. "It's beautiful, so personal. Not exactly the school kitchens, huh?"

"You mean the assembly line from *I Love Lucy?*"

Kara laughed. "It so was. Remember when that guy—I don't remember his name—fell asleep during the browning butter demonstration?"

"Victor!" Logan added laughing.

"Dear God, no one ever fell asleep in class again."

"I'm pretty sure it took him a week to get that butter out of his hair. Remember he had that long ponytail that Madame kept telling him to—"

"Tuck up, tuck up," they both called out, now tearing up with laughter.

Wrapped around each other, in one of the large booths, the plan was to head back to Logan's place. But as the lull of sleep pulled them in, their bodies softened into one another. Kara lightly touched the colors of Logan's arm.

"What does all of this mean?" she asked, tracing her fingers along the lines of his tattoo.

"It means a lot of things," he said, barely awake.

"Am I in there somewhere, Logan?"

"Of course you are," he replied unable to filter what he was saying because he was halfway in a dream. "All men get tattoos of the women who break their hearts, princess."

The last thing he remembered was her kiss.

The next morning, Logan was warm and sleeping better than he had in months when he heard Garrett's voice calling him. His foggy brain was beginning to process where he was and whose naked body was tangled around him under a blanket, but it was too late.

"Well, it looks like someone had a slumber party." Garrett's voice resonated through the empty restaurant.

Logan flew up, banging his shoulder on the curve of the table. He and Kara were still tucked into the large back booth.

"I needed to make bread," Logan offered as a pathetic, half-asleep explanation.

"Making bread. Is that what you kids are calling it these days?" Garrett asked as Logan finally opened his eyes enough to glare at his obnoxious brother. Garrett was laughing, but at least had the decency to turn his back as Logan slipped into his jeans and Kara, wrapped in the blanket, tried to tiptoe someplace safe.

"Morning, Kara." Garrett smirked as she walked past him, eyes down, waving as she quickly passed. Logan shook his head and walked over to his brother.

"Enjoying yourself?"

"You know, I really am." He patted Logan on the shoulder. "Produce is in the kitchen. You better get to work. From the looks of the kitchen, seems like a lot of bread was made last night." Garrett continued laughing all the way out the door. Logan smiled because his brother was sure due for some kind of karma; he just hoped he would be around to see it someday.

Chapter Twenty-Five

*H*e should have felt weird that Grady and one of his best friends, Peter, were having lunch at the bar, especially since Logan had recently taken Grady's sister right on the counter in the next room, but it felt as normal as just about anything. Grady and Peter grew up together and seemed more like brothers than friends as they sat arguing over which movie they considered Al Pacino's best.

There was that brief moment when Logan came around the corner to relieve Sage, so she could deal with a phone call. His eyes met Grady's and Logan wondered if he had "Holy Crap Your Sister is the Hottest Thing on the Planet" plastered all over his face, but it passed and now he was putting white plates and a pizza in front of both men.

"So how was she?" Grady asked and Logan nearly knocked their drinks across the bar.

"Excuse me?" Logan tried to swallow.

Peter steadied his teetering beer glass.

"Easy there, Logan. Maybe you need a beer," Grady said.

"She was good," Peter answered because apparently the question was directed at him and not guilty-I-know-your-sister's-'O'-

face Logan. "I mean, I think Sam likes what she's doing with her dress, so thanks for handing us off to one of your ex-girlfriends."

"Girlfriend is a really strong word. One I hope you'll refrain from using around Kate. We went on a couple of dates and she wasn't my type."

"The woman designs wedding dresses. I could have told you she was not your type." Peter laughed.

"Wait, but aren't you engaged now?" Logan asked filling up a soda water for the out-of-towner who sat at the end of the bar reading.

Grady smiled and Logan couldn't believe how much his face changed. He'd met Kate, before Grady had proposed, and she was a knockout, but Grady had it bad.

"I am, yes I'm very engaged."

Peter rolled his eyes and put his arm around Grady. "Logan, I wish you'd known this guy before he found the love of his life. Then you would be able to truly appreciate the transformation. He's a goner."

Logan laughed and Grady just nodded and raised his drink to toast.

"So how about you?" Grady asked Logan. "Have you made peace with my sister yet?"

You could say that, Logan thought, but didn't say.

"I, yeah, she's . . ." *Holy shit*, he couldn't speak. *Get it together.* "She's fine. We're fine."

Grady grinned at Peter and then they both looked at Logan. *Damn it.*

"Okay, so everything is . . . fine?" Peter asked.

Logan nodded and wiped down the bar. They were directly across from him and Sage still wasn't back. There was nowhere to hide and he wondered if he should look at them because he could feel their eyes on him. *Shit, this is ridiculous.*

Grady's eyes honed right in on him.

"Holy crap, Pete. He's sleeping with her. Do you see it? Right there, the weird twitchy thing his eye is doing. Dead giveaway for sleeping with a guy's sister."

Logan stopped wiping the bar, looked at Peter who was nodding and smiling, and then he did the stupidest thing he could remember doing. He put his hand to his eye. It was right up there with the grade school game, "You've got something on your shirt. Bah, made you look." That stupid.

Grady burst out laughing first and Peter was right behind him.

"Oldest trick in the book, man. Wow."

Logan shook his head, said nothing, and checked over his shoulder for Sage. Grady reached around and patted him on the back.

"So" — Grady straightened and cleared his throat — "what are your intentions with my sister, Master Rye."

Peter and Grady laughed and seemed to expect Logan to join in, but he didn't. He was too busy peeling the label off a beer bottle he'd collected from a vacant seat at the bar and wondering when things got so damn complicated.

"Any advice?" he asked after his new friends had settled down.

"Advice?" Peter repeated.

Logan nodded and threw the empty bottle out and the clank of bottles hitting other bottles echoed through the bar. He stared at both men. They must have realized he was serious because they both seemed concerned.

"On women in general or the one you're currently in . . ." Grady paused to consider and Logan shot him a look that begged him not to go there, "in . . . volved with?"

"Mine, I mean the one, yeah, your sister." Logan shook his head in embarrassment. This was rough.

"Well, it goes without saying she's a handful." Grady turned to Peter who agreed and took another sip of beer.

"But . . ." Logan met his eyes and Grady had a smile he hadn't seen yet. He would later understand it was Grady's big brother smile. "She's one of my favorite people. She's a fantastic light of color in a, well, a less than fantastic world."

"It's hard for me to figure out who the hell she is. One minute she's cold, proper, Kara and then she's—" Logan could feel his heart, physically feel it, throbbing in his chest. "I saw her studio. I had no idea. Again, something she didn't tell me."

"Yeah, Kara's not a big sharer," Peter added.

"But if you've seen the glass lair, well that's something, man. Our parents don't even know she designs those lamps."

"Help me understand that. I don't get how you can be around people, spend time with them and there are all of these things they don't know about you."

"Selective vulnerability," Grady said. "We all do it."

"I don't." Logan almost pulled his words back because he'd forgotten that he was a liar too. *Is lying by omission the same as being a liar?*

"Oh, sure you do. No one spills all their shit the first time they meet someone or even a month in. You're kidding yourself, Logan. Kara's not that different than the rest of the world. People hide and lie to themselves and others all the time. I get that you need her to be real or honest, but it seems like she's working on it for you."

"For me?"

"That's the way I see it. Kara had it a little harder than I did growing up. She chose the good girl, always behave, and do what's expected route."

Peter nodded to Logan in agreement.

"That shit will kill you," Grady continued, "or at least mess you up pretty bad."

"I guess. That's the thing, I don't know because I don't live in that world. I really don't want to. Kara and I are having a good time. I guess that's all I need to worry about."

"A good time. Right." Grady smiled at Peter.

"If you say so, man," Peter added.

"What?"

"Nothing." Grady sipped his beer. "If you ever decide to move past a good time, here's my advice. One of my favorite pictures of Kara is from when we were little. It's this picture of her on Easter morning. She has her basket, it's morning, and her hair, which was lighter than it is now, is all over the place. Crazy hair and warm face. Her smile is mischief and sweet. It's framed on the wall in my house. Anytime someone sees it, they can't believe it's Kara. That's how she wants it and quite frankly so do I. Crazy-haired Kara isn't for everyone. She's special. You've been given a gift not many people get—to my knowledge even fewer men. You get to see crazy-haired Kara. Even better, she loves you."

Logan felt the shock in his face as he started to correct Grady, but Grady ignored him and continued.

"You've got to just hang on to crazy-haired Kara. She's the best, and man, you've brought her back to all of us. She's bolder and braver with you by her side. The rest of it's bullshit. She knows it and she plays along. She has her whole life. That doesn't make her phony. That doesn't mean you don't know her or that she's not genuine. She's one of the most genuine women I know, when she allows herself, when she's safe. Just keep her safe, Logan, and you'll spend your life with crazy-haired Kara."

Logan felt a lump in his throat and was thankful when the guy two seats down ordered another round.

"That was beautiful, man," Peter mocked Grady and then pretended to wipe a tear.

"Wasn't it? Probably better than half the shit you write." He shoulder checked Peter, hard.

All three men laughed and Logan nodded to Grady that he understood. It didn't make it any easier, but it was clear. She loved him, that's what Grady said, and on some level Logan knew. He hadn't planned on this. The banter, the teasing, maybe even a little more, but then she was supposed to bolt again. That's what he knew, what he expected. But she wasn't going anywhere and Logan couldn't figure out how to let Kara in, because Grady was right. They all had parts of themselves, lies they'd told, that they didn't plan on sharing.

As Kara approached Boone Park, she could see Makenna stroking the top of Paige's head as she talked with other mothers and their little girls. Paige had a birthday party and Makenna had little or no free time, so Kara agreed to meet her at the park for their interview. She smiled as she got closer and Makenna waved, indicating she would be right over.

Kara took a seat on one of the benches. Hanging overhead was a huge oak tree. The sunlight trickled through tiny leaves and she lifted her face to the blue sky. The tree was a massive twisting of trunk and limbs. She squinted her eyes and wondered how many generations of children and mothers this tree had seen. How much laughter or how many skinned knees? Kara wasn't often around young children except for Eloise, and even then it was mostly school productions, birthdays, or holidays. She had once kept Eloise overnight while Jake and Cotton went to a convention. She had to take her to a play date and was given a behind-the-scenes look at the elaborate network of parents and their children. Being part of that seemed like it could be an incredibly supportive network of men and women all going up the same stream, but according to Jake, it was much more like high school all over again.

"Whose child is better, smarter, going to a better camp," Jake said, "but there are cookies and juice boxes to disguise the fangs and nails." Kara could see that now, looking over at the gathering of young girls and their moms with cell phones out. She wondered if there was a prototype mother, kind of like debutantes. Was there a certain standard or code of conduct and was anything outside that mold considered odd or out of place? She knew that Jake and Cotton dealt with close-minded people all the time, but they were two gay men raising a little girl. Their situation was very different than the average suburban family, but Kara wondered more about slight differences like disability, divorce, and finances. Did those move you from one clique to another?

She caught a glimpse of Makenna who was smiling and nodding like all the other moms as she tried to break away from the group and move toward Kara. Were these women her friends? Did they know Makenna had lost her husband and her mother? Did they treat her differently because she was single or even because she worked or was raised on a farm? Kara was raised by someone similar to the squeaky-clean blonde in the green cardigan and the floral headband. Bindi Malendar always sat at the popular girls' lunch table and while Kara had not been nearly as polished, she'd made judgments in her past that she was no longer proud of.

Makenna walked toward her looking a bit frazzled now that her back was to the mommy's club. Kara took out her pad and decided she would stick with her prepared questions.

"I'm so sorry. I mean how many damn pictures of her last trip to Hawaii does she have on that phone?" She plopped herself down next to Kara who laughed.

"So, she's not your friend then?"

Makenna glanced back at the moms.

"My friend? Yeah, no. We all have kids who go to school together. That's about where it ends."

"I see." Kara looked at her.

"I guess that was a little harsh. They're nice women and they do a lot for the school. I just, well, I have a different life. I work and usually have some kind of mud or hay or food on me. You'd probably fit right in over there." Makenna smiled.

"As fun as that sounds"—Kara crossed her legs—"I've spent plenty of my life around perfect women. It's far too stressful."

Makenna laughed. "So, I've never actually been interviewed. What am I getting myself into?"

"It will be painless, I promise. I simply want your perspective on The Yard, and what it's like working with your—"

"Do you like him?" Makenna asked, cutting her off and suddenly looking like a protective sister.

Kara wasn't that surprised. She had been around Makenna enough at the restaurant to know she was blunt. She wasn't exactly rude, but she seemed like a woman who had little time or tolerance for bullshit. Kara considered the question and went with honesty.

"Yes, very much," she admitted, "but these articles aren't about whether I like or dislike your brother. They are about his work and more specifically The Yard, which is such a huge part of what you do."

Makenna was giving that "I'm not really hearing you, finish up because I have something to say" stare.

"That's why I asked to meet with you." Kara tried to redirect, but it was useless.

"The thing is, the Rye family is a little—Oh, what's that stupid word Garrett's psychologist girlfriend used to call us?—enmeshed. Right, that's a fancy way of saying we are up in each others' business." Makenna smiled.

"Garrett already shared the sleepover story?"

Makenna nodded.

"Shit." Kara covered her mouth, remembering she was around children and then promptly felt bad. "Sorry."

Makenna laughed. "I'm sure these kids have heard much worse. Don't let the headbands fool you."

"Makenna, I'm hoping to get these interviews done. What goes on in my private life needs to stay there. Things tend to get out of hand when I discuss things."

"I'm not going to share any of your secrets—none of us would. We don't operate that way. I'm looking out for Logan. You seem very nice, but this restaurant is his world right now. I mean, we are all in it up to our elbows, but it's his dream. I'm not trying to be nosy or get all Tony Soprano on you, I just want him to be happy. There's no one on the planet who deserves to be happy more than Logan. He's taken care of all of us since he was a little guy. The man is exhausted and I'm happy he's getting a little action, no offense."

"None taken."

"It's just that it took him a while to refocus after you the first time."

Kara's heart woke up and she was suddenly aware of it in her chest. "What?"

"When you two split up in Paris. That was kind of a tough time for him. He wandered around a bit, spent some time in Seattle, and then eventually came home with razor-sharp focus about what he wanted to do and who he wanted to be. I don't want to see that go anywhere."

Kara said nothing and Makenna tilted a little trying to catch her eyes.

"Kara?"

Their eyes met.

"I'm sorry. I can be a little up front sometimes. I'm not saying you're messing with him. Well, maybe I am. You have all of this other stuff in your life and it seems very glamorous, but also pretty complicated and I want to make sure Lo is not caught in the mess. Ya know?"

Kara didn't know what to say. She was still spinning a bit at hearing Logan even reacted to her leaving, let alone had a difficult time.

"I understand what you're saying." Kara turned to her. "I'm not messing with your brother, Kenna."

It was a bit of a standoff, Kara thought. Two women who clearly cared about Logan in different ways: one was the simple and powerful love of a sister and the other was anything but simple.

Kara tried to explain. "I care about him. I've always cared about him, but I'm not stupid. I realize our lives, our families, are different. Logan isn't looking for any more than what we have right now and so—"

Makenna tilted her head in confusion, "Oh wow, don't kid yourself. Please, if you honestly believe that, you know nothing about him. The man is all about roots and commitment. He may be blowing something else up your skirt, but that's just protection. You left him, do you get that? Do you see the connection?" she asked.

Kara was completely lost now. "I didn't leave him. I had to go home. I'm a little shocked by all this because honestly, Makenna, your brother doesn't seem that traumatized."

Kenna shook her head. "That's not how he works. Logan picks up, dusts off, and makes dinner. He always has, but when he met you in Paris, he was like a kid. I guess the kid he never got to be. When we talked to him on the phone, he went on and on about the things he was learning and everything he saw in Paris. We knew he was in love. You can just tell. Ya know?"

"Yeah, I do," Kara said, barely above a whisper.

"I'm not blaming you. I know that you probably have your own set of family issues, but he never talked about it. When he came back it was all business and that guy we talked to in Paris was kind of gone. Dad thinks Logan probably has 'abandonment issues.'" Makenna put up air quotes, laughing a little. "Our dad watches way too much Oprah."

Kara smiled, thankful for some relief in conversation because she felt like someone was sitting on her chest.

"Abandonment issues?" she asked.

"Well, Dad said when Mom left that Logan did the same thing. He didn't fall apart even though he was only seven. He just organized and started cooking. Sort of the same thing with you."

"Kenna, I can't imagine how hard it is to lose your mother at such a young age, but I don't see how her dying has anything to do with me being summoned home from Paris." Kara took a very deep breath and wondered how her simple interview had gotten so off track. "Listen, I don't know. Maybe you're right and I'm sorry about that. Logan and I are . . . I honestly have no idea what we are, but he's a grown man—"

Kara stopped talking because Makenna was now looking at her as if she was crazier than she actually was.

"Is that what he told you?" Makenna asked. "That our mother died?"

"Yes." Kara instantly felt something was wrong. "Well, I'm not sure if those were his exact words, but we were looking at pictures and he said she was . . . gone." She caught the look on Makenna's face.

"Oh Christ. She's not dead, is she?"

Makenna shook her head.

"She left him." Kara put her hand to her mouth and remembered her rule about tearing up in public. "She left all of you?"

"She did." Makenna looked out at the playground.

"I didn't know. I guess I just assumed, but he didn't correct me."

"She might as well be dead." Still staring out, she grew suddenly cold. "I'm sure it was just easier for him, or he didn't want the pity. We're all pretty allergic to the sad little pity look you're giving me right now." She laughed.

Kara shook her head, tried to find a different look, as if that was possible.

"Anyway, wow, this took a dark turn, huh?"

Kara laughed and turned to touch Makenna's hand. She was a little shocked, but didn't pull away.

"This is really none of your business. I'm sure Logan would say that too, but I can tell you this: Logan was taken from me too. I didn't leave him and now that we are . . . around each other again, I will be careful. That's all I can promise." Kara looked as far as she could into Makenna's golden eyes. They were almost Logan's eyes, but with more green.

She let out a deep breath. "Good, he's one of my favorite guys, so even though he will be majorly pissed, I'm glad I asked."

Kenna uncrossed her legs and checked on her daughter who was now squealing with her friends as the birthday girl opened her presents.

"You know, gone or dead, people still don't know what to do with you." Makenna was still looking toward the party. "It's such a strange thing. I mean, we all have grief, but when something tragic happens, it's almost like it reminds people it could happen to them. I don't know."

"What are we talking about now, Kenna?" Kara was trying to be gentle.

Her eyes were a little glassy as she let out a slow breath.

"I like you Kara Malendar."

Kara smiled and took her hand because it felt natural and honest to touch her hurt rather than pretend it didn't exist. "I like you too Makenna, very much."

Both women sat, holding hands, in nothing but the buzz of children at play for a couple of minutes. She wanted to tell Makenna she knew about her husband. That she had read about the "devastating loss for the Rye family, owners of local Ryeland Farms" in the newspaper. That she had wanted to reach out to Logan and his grieving family she had never met, but didn't know how back then. She wanted to tell her how proud her brother was of her and that she knew a little bit about being alone. Certainly not on Kenna's level, but underneath all the details, alone was alone. Kara wanted to say so many things to the woman sitting next to her, but she didn't. She just left it alone, grateful for the connection.

She eventually got around to her interview questions when Makenna stood up and said, "Enough of this, let's go get some coffee so I can tell you how horrible it is trying to manage three mule-headed men."

They spent an hour, Kenna with her coffee and Kara with her tea, splitting a piece of banana bread. She shared some great insights about Ryeland Farms and Kara had no idea they'd added on to the farm twice in the last five years.

As expected, things led back to Logan and the restaurant. Makenna explained she felt it was Logan's sense of taste, "his ability to know the flavors people want before they even know," that set The Yard apart. Kara told her they spent two weeks at Le Cordon Bleu creating what Madame Auclair called, "a discriminating palate."

"Yeah, it could be that." Kenna held open the door as they left the coffee shop to pick up Paige. "Or it could be he found that everything comes to life when you have someone to share it with."

Kara smiled and met Paige who was all dark hair and freckles like her mother, but her smile was different, unfamiliar, and Kara knew she was seeing little pieces of the love Kenna lost so many years ago. As she drove home, Kara felt jittery. It was the feeling of connection, sharing someone's energy, and she'd forgotten how exhilarating it could be. She would need some time to sort out everything she and Kenna had discussed, but it was nice to have things to sort and even nicer to have feelings.

Chapter Twenty-Six

*Senator and Mrs. Patrick Malendar cordially invite you
to their home in celebration of the New Year
and all the promise it holds.*

The invitation was pinned to a board in Kara's kitchen. It was on
a beautiful light moss card stock and the font was twirly, but
soft. Had she been one of the other hundreds of recipients of this
invitation, she might have been impressed by the luxury of it and
the perceived friendliness of welcoming friends in the aftermath
of a busy holiday season. It was gracious, but Kara knew the only
reason her parents were hosting an after-the-new-year open house
was because Senator George, the other US senator from California, and his wife, "always did a Christmastime open house and
holiday craft boutique," according to her mother.

Kara remembered because her mother's "nose was out of joint,"
as her Nana would say, years ago when Bindi Malendar was forced
to reschedule her holiday extravaganza.

"His wife is some kind of crafter, can you imagine? I guess she's
a retired schoolteacher. Heaven save us," her mother had jabbed
after a couple of mimosas at Easter Brunch. Steven George had

won the seat left vacant by Henry Chartcraft who had backed out after a heart attack reminded him he was in his eighties.

"I'm not sure what this boutique is like, but I guess it's throughout her house and all of the money goes to animal charities. Of course it does," her mother had continued, her rant complete with eye rolling and that low "people might hear me" voice she used.

Kara had met Bethany George, the senator's wife, and thought the event sounded kind of lovely, but she was certainly not going to say a word back then.

"Anyway, she then says we can have ours the week after. First of all, your father is the senior senator and even if we agreed to that, it would put us too close to Christmas Eve. It's ridiculous. I'll just do something elegant after the new year," her mother had said, smoothing her napkin on her lap and flashing her smile with a splash of sinister.

That year, they had started their after-the-new-year tradition, and six years later, Kara was still asked to attend. As she ran her hand across the embossed lettering, she could hear her mother's catty tone. All of that rested beneath the lovely invitation. Nothing was ever at face value. Even invitation paper had stories that protected an image.

Kara walked out of her kitchen, looking down as her black peeptoed heels clicked across her slate tile floors. She stopped in the entryway and checked herself one last time in the mirror. Black A-line skirt, just past her knees, and a cashmere turtleneck. It was a beautiful sweater, but the damn thing was raspberry and it matched the toenail polish she'd had applied yesterday. She wore the woven pearl bracelet her father had given her for her twenty-first birthday and the pearl earrings left to her when her paternal grandmother passed away. Her hair was straightened, smoothed to a silky flaxen mane, and swept to the side with a small pearl clip. Just a hint of lip color. Kara pulled in and let out a slow steady breath.

She'd looked the part of a senator's daughter since she was old enough to shave and now at thirty, she was a perfectly constructed shell of a woman. Kara knew it was the reason she didn't date a lot. The media attention was a nuisance, but there was more to why she hadn't settled in with some rising VP of whatever at ABC big corporation, who would load her up in the car every season and head to their house on Coronado. It wasn't only the cameras she'd tucked herself away from, because on some level she knew that guy—the Brad, Alex, or Sebastian—would be the final piece. Once that piece slid into place, after the fabulous Hotel Bel-Air wedding, complete with hundreds of her parents' closest friends, Kara would be her mother. A younger, hipper, Bunko-instead-of-Bridge-playing accessory.

Kara laughed at herself. All of this introspection from a damn invitation. She needed to stop thinking this way if she was going survive the evening. She grabbed her purse, dimmed the lights, and the doorbell rang. That would be her driver. At least she had the backbone this year to get her own car.

She opened the door to Logan in a dark navy suit and plaid shirt opened at the collar. He was showered, shaved, and incredibly handsome. While Kara was looking for her words, Logan beat her to it.

"You look beautiful. Did you do something different to your hair?"

"Thank you. Yes, it's a side sweep thing. Why . . ."

"Why am I here?" Logan asked smiling and Kara noticed the navy blazer brought out something different in his eyes.

"Yes, why are you here?" she asked.

"Because it was time." Logan walked past her into the entryway. Kara was still confused. She peered out the door: no driver.

"Excuse me?" she asked and closed the front door.

"You've been to the farm, you came to the races, and you deal with me always being at The Yard. It's time I did something."

"That wasn't for you. It was part of my job and the races were a blind—"

"Right, can I make my point here, princess?"

Kara held up her hands for him to continue.

"If you can get dirty and be in my world, work or not, I can join you for an evening in yours. There's also the hope that after this party you will feel the need to thank me into the wee hours of the morning."

His look was playful and Kara smiled.

"I like your world. I don't mind being there and this"—she ran her hands along her skirt—"is not my world. It's my duty, my one of six off-election-year events of my parents' choosing. I think it's very noble of you, but you're going to want to get back in your truck and run." She smirked. "As Grady likes to say, 'You want no part of this shitstorm.'"

Logan smiled and she was touched that he was in her doorway offering.

"All the same, I think I do want in. You'll be there. I'm all set, and besides, on my way up to your door I sent your driver home."

Kara shook her head.

"Do you ever not get your way?"

"Oh, it happens all the time, princess. An awful lot when you're around, now that you mention it, but tonight, I'd like to be there for you. If you don't mind. Should I have worn a tie?"

Kara loved him. There it was. She had no idea how she was going to bring up his no-longer-deceased mother or how they were ever going to get past the games she was born into or the heartbreak of his childhood, but standing in her entryway, all of that seemed doable because she was in love with Logan Rye. He loved her too. He wouldn't be there willing to tackle a shitstorm if he didn't. Kara kissed him, took his hand, and the two of them headed to his truck.

They arrived at the Malendar home and Logan wasn't sure "home" was the right word. It was massive and on close to twice the land his house sat on, gardens included. The things he could do with this much land. He would get rid of all the grass and have a separate—

Christ, take a break, Logan told himself as the gates closed behind them and they followed the circular drive.

With the exception of a few survival tips, as she put it, Kara had been quiet the entire drive. He had no idea what was going through her mind and hoped his being there would help, not create more stress for her. She was all polished and beautiful, but caged was what came to Logan's mind. She looked like a prime turkey, all decked out. Logan would keep that little metaphor to himself though. He'd learned at a very early age that farm comparisons, no matter how well intended, did not go over well with women. He once told his lab partner, freshman year of high school, that her hair reminded him of Penelope. When she'd asked who Penelope was, he had very proudly explained that she was their finest mare. His very pretty lab partner changed partners the next day.

Stopping in front of the valet, Logan turned to Kara. She gave him a small smile and accepted the hand of the kid who helped her out of his truck. The guy seemed like he hadn't seen an actual truck in a while. Logan glanced over at the lot on the side of the house and understood why. Not a truck to be seen. If that was a 1969 Porsche over there, and he was pretty sure it was, Garrett would be losing his mind. The valet handed Logan the ticket.

"Thanks." He joined Kara at the base of the stairs leading to the front door and placed his hand at the small of her back. He was relieved when she relaxed.

"You're sure you want to do this? It's not too late." She looked up the huge staircase as if she was seeing it for the first time.

Logan had seen glimpses of polished, proper Kara Malendar, but this seemed a little extreme. He would admit it was a bit intimidating and he wasn't sure how this woman and R. Kelly-dancing Kara could exist in the same person.

"Are you okay?"

"Sure, I'm fine." She took his arm.

"Is there something I need to know about tonight? You seem awfully uncomfortable. Is it that bad?"

"No." She patted his arm. "It will be fine. I'm just tired." She gave a little smile and Logan took in another breath, then let it out slowly as they approached the door.

"I hope the food is good at least."

Kara laughed and right then and there he understood that she needed him.

"Logan." Senator Malendar crossed the room. "So glad you could join us. Happy New Year."

"And to you, sir." He shook Kara's father's hand.

"Sweetheart." He turned his attention to his daughter and kissed her on the cheek. "You look perfect."

Kara smiled and returned her father's kiss.

"Well, I'm sure perfect is exactly what she was going for, Dad." Grady joined them and shook Logan's hand.

He leaned in to kiss Kara. "Jesus, sis, are you trying to get rid of this guy? Why would you do this to him?" he asked at her ear. Kara laughed and Logan saw her entire face change. Grady did that to her every time.

"I volunteered." Logan smiled and put his hand at Kara's back again. Sometimes it felt as if he was keeping her from falling over.

"Guys, will you excuse me, I need to mingle," the senator said and before any of them could respond, he disappeared back into the crowd.

"You volunteered," Grady repeated. "Brave man." He put his arm around Logan. "We are going to need to get you a drink. This is not for the weak of heart and should never be undertaken sober."

"Wait, I drove." Logan laughed as Grady pulled him away from Kara.

"Mistake number two, my friend." Grady gestured to his sister that they would be back in a minute. Logan turned as some guy approached Kara and her face became animated.

"Who's that?" Logan asked as Grady brought him to the bar.

Grady glanced over his shoulder. "That is our mother's latest pick. He's thirty-four, Georgetown graduate, new to my father's staff, and an analyst, whatever the hell that is. He likes to play golf and probably eats chia seeds and yogurt, give it up for Stew."

Logan laughed at Grady's introduction, but then his eyes were right back on Kara who was laughing too and touching Stew's arm.

"His name is Stew?"

"It is"—Grady handed him what looked like Scotch, really nice Scotch—"and it's spelled like the comfort food, so you two have something in common."

He could tell Grady was trying to defuse his growing anxiety, but Logan grew less and less amused the more time Kara spent taking with this guy.

"Um, does you mother not know that we are, Kara and I are . . ." *Christ, what were they?*

"Together?" Grady helped.

"Yes, thank you, together. Does she not know that? Has Kara not mentioned that we—" He turned to look at Grady who was doing a pretty crappy job of keeping his face neutral. "Oh, that's it. She hasn't. No one knows."

"I know."

Logan's face felt warm, and even though he was trying for "Oh, that's cool. We have an open thing going on," he was sure Grady read the shock all over his face.

"Kate knows and Kara's friends know. It's just the parents are a different animal altogether." Grady sipped his drink.

"So when your dad greeted me at the door?"

"Totally surprised to see you and even now is probably trying to figure out why you're here."

"Shit." Logan finished his Scotch in two gulps as Kara stood still looking at the asshat's phone. Something was funny, but that stifled, stuffed-inside funny, and Logan was about to find out what.

Grady made a feeble attempt to keep him at the bar, but Logan was on his way to his date. *That's right, Stew, my date.*

As Logan approached the lovely couple, Kara sent what looked like an SOS to Grady.

What the hell? Was Grady my damn babysitter now? Not in this lifetime, princess.

"Logan," Kara exclaimed in that country club tone that he couldn't tolerate, "this is—"

"Stew, yeah I already know. Nice to meet you, man."

Stew shook his hand, but seemed surprised and just as Logan decided that he couldn't care less, the Scotch hit him. Hard. One thing about the Rye men, they tended to be lightweights, okay maybe that was only Logan because Garrett was a damn fish, but Logan and his dad were light. And after a few, there were no filters. Some of his most honest conversations with Garrett were over drinks. Logan's face grew a little numb and he took Kara's hand. She didn't pull away, just stared at him.

"Oh, are you two—" asshat started to ask.

"Sleeping together? Why yes we are, Stew." Logan grinned.

Kara choked on her wine and Logan lightly patted her on the back.

"If you'll excuse us, Stew. I'm just dying to dance with my girl here."

Stew held up both hands and sort of gaped at Logan like he was a crazed animal. And he was. Kara, still recovering, went with him toward the back patio, and when he pulled her into his arms, she did that thing he also hated. She assessed the room.

"No one is looking, princess."

"Oh, I beg to differ."

"Nanaism?"

Kara nodded still peering out of the corner of her eye as Logan turned to avoid crashing into another couple.

"What just happened?" Kara asked.

Logan held back a laugh, because he wasn't sure exactly how much trouble he was in yet. "I made an entrance. I wasn't going to sit there and watch you play country club with some guy who I'm pretty sure owns a blow-dryer. It's not how I work."

Kara nodded, looking unable to speak.

"No one, Kara? You've told no one," Logan confirmed.

"I told Grady. Jake knows. This is just—"

"Some other part of your world where your mother still sets you up and you play along."

"Yes, I guess that's what this is. I didn't ask you to come."

"And now we know why. Stew over there may have gotten lucky."

"Don't be an ass."

"I'm not. That was the Scotch Grady gave me talking."

Kara glared over at Grady, who held up his glass to both of them.

"Damn, that stuff is strong." Logan blinked his eyes and turned her again as they danced to avoid the edge of the patio.

Kara seemed to be considering something. Her eyes went to a crowd of women whispering out of the sides of their mouths and then, suddenly, Kara laughed. Full-body, pulsing against him with her face buried in his chest. It was the very best sound and when her eyes peeked up, still dancing with laughter, he saw her. Crazy-haired Kara was in there like a little girl playing dress up with far too much makeup on.

"Are we allowed to laugh?" Logan asked, smiling at her.

"Oh, Christ, who cares at this point? You just told my dad's top analyst that we are sleeping together." She laughed again. "The women we walked past are all in my mother's bridge club and my father has suddenly stopped his all-important mingling to sidle up next to Grady at the bar, no doubt sent by my mother. He's there to find out what 'in all things holy' is going on?"

Logan's brow went up, but before he could ask, she answered.

"That's a Momism, not to be confused with a Nanaism. Huge difference. I'll explain later. Anyway, she's sent my father to Grady to gather intel. I'm not sure why this feels so incredible, but it does. Look"—Kara leaned back—"my hands are shaking."

"Is that a good thing?" Logan pulled her into him.

"It is a great thing. Anything that is not, as my father says, 'perfect,' is right where I want to be."

He swayed her in his arms and his heart pounded in his chest as if it couldn't get close enough. It was heady, more powerful than the Scotch, which was thankfully melting out of his system.

"Can I kiss you?"

She didn't even do her "who's watching" thing. His heart opened and maybe his hands shook too; then she leaned up and kissed him. It was soft, a whisper really, and then the song was over. Logan took her hand and when his eyes drifted away from her beautiful face, he noticed Bindi Malendar standing next to her husband and Grady. The woman had a presence that Logan hadn't quite figured out, but his first thought was rather than everyone being scared of her, perhaps Kara's mother was actually the one who was afraid.

As Nana would say, it was "time to pay the piper," Kara thought squeezing Logan's hand a little tighter.

"Kara." Her mother's tone was quite familiar, as she and Logan joined everyone near the bar.

"Mother." Kara squeezed Logan's hand. "I'm not sure if you've met Logan Rye. He's a chef and the owner of The Yard, where Dad had the volunteer dinner."

Bindi Malendar scanned her memory and then her face filled with familiar. "Yes, of course, you have a hammer in the ladies' room, oh and you were in the newspaper dancing with our daughter."

"We do have a hammer in the bathroom and yes, I was dancing with your daughter. She's a great dancer by the way." Logan smiled.

"I don't think I got to meet you that evening at the volunteer event." Her mother ignored Logan's comment about dancing.

Bindi Malendar had a talent for sifting through and picking out only the pieces of the conversation she cared to continue.

"It was quite hectic with all of the people out supporting my husband. Dear"—she turned to the senator who was talking with Grady—"did you meet Logan at the volunteer dinner?"

"I did. I thanked him when we left that night and welcomed him when he showed up tonight. Kara's writing a piece on him and his restaurant."

"Oh right." Her mother's gaze shifted back. "Well, that's great. Logan, it is a pleasure to meet you."

She extended her hand and Logan took it gently, looking like he wasn't sure how much to put behind the shake.

"It's great to finally meet you too, Mrs. Malendar. I voted for your husband," Logan said, and Kara was sure he knew that he'd hit the money shot.

"Well, that's good to hear. You're a smart boy." Her mother reached out to touch Logan on his arm. "I hope Kara is treating you well," she said, and for the second time in one evening, Kara almost choked. Logan turned to her, patted her on the back, and gave her a playful smile that had nothing to do with the Scotch—it was all his own.

"Yes, she is treating me very well."

"That's good because Kara can be brutal. Have you read any of her reviews?"

"I have and she is tough. I'm lucky this is a feature and not one of her fear-inducing reviews," Logan teased.

"Oh well, that's good. Yes, very good. Patrick?" Her mother turned away from Logan in that dismissive, "we're done talking" way that drove Kara nuts. "Have they started with the coffee already? I see some people with coffee."

Her father glanced around and shrugged. "Maybe some people wanted coffee." He put his hand on her mother's shoulder. "It's fine. There's plenty of—"

"Logan and I are . . ." Kara wanted to get it out before ten minutes were spent discussing the timing of the damn coffee. She lost her words for a moment when her mother turned to her.

"Seeing each other. We are. We're dating."

Bindi Malendar seemed genuinely confused for a beat. "Really?" She raised her perfect eyebrow. "Well, I had no idea that"—she turned to Logan with a little more assessment now—"you were dating. That's lovely, isn't it Patrick?"

"It is. Logan's family runs Ryeland Farms." Her father was clearly pitching the case for Kara's new man.

Bindi smiled. "They run the farmers markets. There's one here, but I believe there's also one in the city?"

"There is. We started the one in LA a little over a year ago." Logan smiled.

"Well that's great." Her mother assessed her from head to toe. It had always been that way. One misstep or surprise and her mother took account of everything about her children. It was like she had a running list of positives and negatives. Kara smiled. There was entirely too much smiling going on, but at least it was out. Kara was certain there would be a few more discussions on the matter, but not tonight. Her parents both excused themselves and hurried off to work the room.

"Now that wasn't bad at all." Grady was still standing at the bar. Kara laughed.

"I'm not sure if I did well or if they hate me."

"It's hard to tell. There's a thin line between love and hate in the Malendar home, but I think you survived. Sis, your thoughts?"

"You were great." She suddenly wanted to leave, wanted to breathe. "Can we leave now?" she asked Grady.

He checked his watch. "You've been here for almost two hours. If you walk slowly to the door and take your time getting your coats, I think you will have been here for the obligatory time."

They all laughed.

"Where's Kate?" Kara asked.

"Sitting this one out. I haven't gotten her down the aisle yet, so I don't want to push it. Besides, she does this stuff all day. And she hasn't been feeling well, stomach bug or the flu maybe."

"That's not fun. Sick fiancée, surely that gets you out early, too?" Logan asked.

"You would think, but I get to meet some guy who wants to give money to the Roads Foundation. He's late, of course, so I'll be here for a little longer." Grady hugged his sister good-bye.

"I love you." She kissed him on the cheek.

"Me too." Grady hugged her and extended his hand to Logan.

"You did it, man, you survived. Wait until you have to do a sit-down dinner. They close the doors to the dining area and . . . well, that's when you really become a man." Grady laughed.

"Thanks for being a friend." Logan was so sincere, it felt out of place in the room.

"Anytime."

Kara and Logan said their good-byes and just like that they were a couple. Sure it was cursory acceptance, but the thought that she could be with him and have a life with him *and* still keep her parents where she needed them made her feel hopeful.

Chapter Twenty-Seven

Kara followed close behind as her mother opened the sleek black door of La Luna and exchanged double-cheek kisses with Monique and Cheryl. They were there to try on the dresses her mother had chosen for the spring social. Even though spring was months away, it was never too early for Bindi Malendar to get out the paper dresses and fold something onto her cutout daughter.

La Luna was an exclusive dress boutique in Old Town Pasadena. Her mother had used Monique and Cheryl for years, and by association, so had Kara, for special events anyway. Both women were probably in their mid-forties and from what Kara could tell, flawless. Monique had dark chocolate hair pulled tight into a tail that dropped, like silk, down the back of her slender golden neck. Cheryl was slightly shorter, but in higher heels, so they appeared the same height. She had a short crop of white-blonde hair that made her gray eyes look almost otherworldly. Both were perfectly manicured, pressed, and polished in black, "the only color of winter." It made Kara a little sick that she knew this, but like it or not, these ladies had fitted her for both proms and every other picture-perfect event since. They were part of her family. Kara was pretty sure when Hillary Clinton said, "It takes a village," that La Luna was not what she had in mind.

"Kara." Monique gave her a hug and ran her hand along the back of Kara's hair. She had left it down, forgoing the straightening iron. Mainly because when she'd slid out of Logan's bed this morning, she felt warm and wonderful. She didn't want to primp and polish that away. She wanted the smell of his sheets, the feel of him, to somehow help her through this day. When he kissed her, coffee on his breath, she no longer cared about "doing her face and fixing that hair" as her mother eventually said when she picked Kara up at 6:30 in the morning with matching espressos, the breakfast of Malendar women. Coffee, especially espresso, was sophisticated, her mother had preached for as long as Kara could remember. "Tea is messy and boring," she had once said. Kara worked at drinking coffee in college; it never took, but she tolerated it around her mother. It was simply easier than arguing. Monique was trying to be subtle, but Kara recognized the smoothing gesture. Her curls were always unruly and her mother hated them.

"Monique, lovely to see you too." Kara tried, but failed at sincerity.

"I like this beachy in February thing you are working here, darling. Someone's ready for surf lessons," she said, looking at Kara's mother whose annoyance was less subtle. Both women flashed that odd half grin that Kara hated.

Kara returned the well-rehearsed smile and gave her token response, the one she'd used since she was old enough to wear a proper dress. "Oh, I know, I'm just a mess."

"No worries, sweetheart. That's what we're here for." Monique took her coat.

Bindi and Cheryl were already chatting near the half circle of plush white couches and floor-to-ceiling mirrors. Kara glanced down at the boutique's wood floors as she walked to take her place next to her mother who was now gesturing impatiently for her to join them. As her mother looped her arm through Kara's and continued talking about someone, somewhere who was doing something inappropriate, Kara focused on the wood floors. It was the only warmth in the entire place and she'd never noticed them before. She thought of Logan. His morning face as he'd walked her to his door. His body, lumbering and then wrapping her up. She closed her eyes for a minute after looking out a nearby window. The sun was up and light spilled into the sterile shop. Kara could see her bare feet as they padded across Logan's wood floors, and as her mother rolled her eyes and continued to drone on, she wanted to run back to his bed.

"Kara!" her mother interrupted her perfectly lovely moment. "Are you with us dear, because I'd like to know what you think of your dress before we start with the fitting."

"Why?" fell from Kara's mouth before she could stop it. She could hear Monique's giggle and Cheryl's quick intake of breath.

"What does that mean?" her mother asked.

Kara turned her face away from the sunlight and back at her reality. "Nothing. Sorry." She reached out to touch the dress Cheryl was holding. "That's beautiful and a great color." Kara tried to smooth things over. She was not in the mood for confrontation.

"It will look great on you," Monique chimed in.

"It's your signature, dear. Everyone needs a signature color," her mother said for the thousandth time in her life, smoothing Kara's hair.

Raspberry. Raspberry had been her "signature color" since she was sixteen. Every dress from that moment on had been raspberry or was accented with the hue. How could someone possibly be given a signature color without her permission? Wasn't that the point of the word "signature"? Unique to that person? It was to the point that Kara couldn't even eat raspberries.

"Well, let's get it on you and see how it fits." Cheryl walked in front of the mirrors toward the back and they all followed her. *Sort of like ducks*, Kara thought.

"That's a good idea because I'm sure there will need to be some alterations," her mother started. "Dear, have you been following an eating plan because you seem to have put some weight on. We may have to—"

Kara grabbed the dress from Cheryl, ignoring her mother because she had heard the same speech dozens of times before. She could practically recite it herself.

In the changing area, Kara let out her breath. She knew it wasn't the same breath she had taken in when they had arrived, but it sure felt like it. She held the dress out in front of her, knew it wasn't going to fit, and smiled.

Chapter Twenty-Eight

*K*ara saw the note on Logan's door as she climbed his porch later that night.

I like you. Do you like me?

It was followed by two check boxes, one yes and the other no. Kara smiled. The note instructed that if her answer was "Yes" she should come on in and meet him in the backyard. Her heart fluttered giddily. She leaned forward and kissed the paper, leaving a faint impression of her lip gloss and indicating that yes, she liked him a lot.

Laughing at herself, Kara turned the brass knob and stepped into Logan's small home. She could smell him, his food, and centuries of old paint—life lived. She closed her eyes. She wanted this. This wasn't obtained by a decorator or purchased on a showroom floor. Kara ran her hand along the wall molding as she made her way toward the back of the house to the kitchen. What was coursing through her body was earned, not bought, from early mornings remembering to water plants, bake fresh bread. Those things made a life.

Kara walked through the white entryway of the kitchen and past Logan's stove which, like a painter's palette, was stained, dented, and used. The back door was open and she saw the glow of candles. She pushed through the screen door and stood, taking in the most magical sight she had ever seen, at least since becoming an adult.

Paper lanterns hung all around the back porch, and the steps and walkway that led to the grass were lined with candles in punched tin holders so the light came out as tiny dots along her path to a canvas tent. Soft music, she couldn't make out what it was, spilled off the porch and into the huge magnolia tree and endless greenery of Logan's backyard. She noticed a table to the right of the tent with covered plates, bottles of wine, and more candles. As Kara made her way to the tent, Logan was backing out on his knees. He heard her and turned.

"Oh, hey."

"Hey," was all she could manage as he stood, hair falling into his eyes. Logan wiped his hands on his jeans and pushed his hair off his face.

"So, I thought"—he moved to her—"since we were super adults the other night, dressed up and all, that we might try something a little—"

Kara couldn't say anything. She was pretty sure this was what stunned felt like. Logan must have noticed and misread, because he started to backtrack.

"Okay, maybe this was ridiculous, I just thought that—"

She reached for him and pulled him into her as if she was afraid he might disappear into the night. She held on and kissed him deep. She wasn't sure how to put everything she was feeling into words, so she showed him. When they pulled apart, he slowly opened his eyes and smiled as golden flecks sparkled from the candlelight.

"You see, I knew you were a closet nature lover, princess."

She laughed and he took her face in his hands.

"Just a little more," was all he mumbled before he took them both back under.

The sweet smell of spring surrounded them and when Logan's warm hands moved into the back of her white blouse, her skin knew his touch and welcomed it. His breath grazed her neck and then his lips found their way back to her lips. It was a slow dance of movement and Kara felt so safe, so wanted.

"Don't let go," she whispered and he pulled back and looked at her. He brushed her hair off her face, held her, and said nothing. He didn't need to. He knelt down, took her with him, and pulled them both into the tent. There among pillows and blankets, amid the soft lilting music and the chirping of nighttime, Logan made love to her, slow and timeless. As Kara let go, looking up into his soft candlelit face, she knew even if she wasn't allowed to have him, she would never be the same.

He could barely breathe. It hit him so hard he knew why he'd been avoiding this very thing for most of his life. He loved her. Brushing the hair off her shoulder, it was as clear as anything had ever been. He was stupid in love with the woman underneath him. Every-thing about her, even her prissy side—he loved that too. In that moment, as she slowly opened her beautiful eyes and a smile crawled across her perfect lips, he knew he was too close, too far to turn back. It wasn't something he often admitted, but he was scared.

"What's your tent story?" Logan asked in an effort to hang on to his stupid heart. He ran his fingers along her shoulder, down the bare velvet skin of her body. There were only a few candles left and dinner was surely cold, but Kara purred, opened her eyes, and his heart whispered she was everything.

"I love that you assume I have one. Does everyone have a tent story?" Kara asked kissing his shoulder.

"Eh, most people, at least the ones I want to know, have some version of a tent story."

"I've never been camping, Logan."

"Seriously?" His face fell. "Well, it doesn't need to be a camping tent. There are lots of different—"

He stopped mid-sentence when Kara rolled up to a seated position and held the blanket to her chest. She was laughing. So stunning, not traditional California-girl beautiful, Kara was intricate, sort of like the glass she made, he thought watching her laugh at him. A mixture of light and dark, pieces of so many things—he wasn't sure how he was ever going to breathe without her.

Kara touched his chest. "Oh, the look on your face was priceless. I have tent stories. Most of them are white cotillion or wedding tents, but those are boring. I do . . . " She ran her finger down his chest toward the blanket covering him. Logan's breath caught and she smiled and turned to face him, folding her part of the blanket around her body like a towel. "I have a fort story, does that count?"

"Forts qualify."

"Okay." Kara began her story like a little girl around a campfire. "My Nana was a big woman, tall and big. She used to wear these billowy tops with patterns on them. She must have gotten them all from the same place, because I remember every one of them had this pearl button closure at the back." She moved her hands to the back of her neck as if to demonstrate and then dropped her hands and smiled. "She used to pick me up and I would wrap my arms around her neck and play with the button."

Logan smiled, watching as the memory seemed to play out for her.

"Nana was a blast. There's no other word to describe her. She had a refrigerator full of real Coke. She loved candy bars, especially Snickers. We used to play cards and every afternoon she would nap. Grady and I would usually get into trouble during her nap time and she would chase us around her house with a fly swatter, laughing."

Logan could see Kara was right back there.

"She was great." Kara returned to the story. "So, pretty much every summer, she would help us build a fort. Not only did she help design and construct, but she would sleep in it with us."

"Was this like a bed, couch fort?"

"Nope. Living room, on the floor."

"Nice! Sheet?"

"Pretty much every one she had in her linen closet. I remember because the next morning she would say she hadn't seen this much laundry since 'Hector was a pup!'" Kara laughed the sweet easy laugh of childhood and Logan's heart nearly burst.

"Hector?"

"Yeah, I have no idea who Hector was, but it must have been a long time since he was a puppy because Nana always used that phrase any time something hadn't happened in a while. She was all about the quirky phrases."

"She sounds like a blast." Logan touched the part of Kara's leg that peeked out from under the blankets.

"She was. Grady and I used to argue over who knew more. I would never tell him, but I think he knows more of them. I guess it's our way of keeping her close. We call them Nanaisms, as you know."

Logan kissed her knee.

"Was she your mom's mom or your dad's mom?"

"Mom's."

Logan looked surprised.

"I know. They don't seem like they'd be related, but my mom was a lot more fun back then, too. Then she became all grown up and dressed up, but Nana stayed the same. She understood the little things." Kara was still wrapped in her memory, and then she was suddenly back. "Are you hungry? Why am I always hungry around you?"

Logan smiled and tugged his jeans on before he pulled her out of that blanket and showed her again why they were both hungry for one another.

"So, what's it like being Logan Rye, middle son of the owners and operators of Ryeland Farms?" Kara asked moments later while they were in the kitchen heating up the chili Logan had made for their camping trip.

"Very cute." He added both bowls back into the large cast iron pot on his stove and turned on the flame. "I thought we were telling tent stories. I've got one that involves Garrett and some man-eating raccoons."

Kara laughed, flipping open the cloth napkin that held the cornbread he'd made that morning. She took a bite and moaned.

"My God, how is this so moist?"

"Corn flower and fresh corn. They are the keys to making a woman moan like that." Logan unwrapped the cheese.

"So good. But, I'm serious, it can't be easy doing all of this"—she gestured to the meal, his kitchen—"and helping run the farm. Seems like you must have been born responsible."

Logan laughed and fed her a small piece of white cheddar as he grated more.

"Did I seem all that responsible when we were in Paris?" he asked.

"No, but that was just a flash, before I knew you."

"And you know me now?"

"I'm trying to, but you're a little closed up in there. You're great at talking about me, but I'd like to talk about you."

Logan sighed. "There's not much to say. You've met my dad, Garrett, and Kenna. They're all different kinds of pain in my ass, but I love them and we've been through a lot. The farm is work, sure, but it's all I've ever known, as much a part of me as anything else. Other than that, my favorite color is navy blue."

He laughed, Kara didn't.

"What are we doing, Logan?" Kara asked suddenly very serious as if she'd been building to this conversation.

Shit.

"Why didn't you tell me your mother left—that she didn't die?" Kara continued and Logan was now certain this was a conversation that had played in her head.

He was standing in his kitchen, no shirt, no shoes, still trying to get a handle on his heart that kept leaping with the declaration that they were in love and her eyes did that thing when she asked. He hated the eye thing people did when they brought up his mother. Everyone had problems. His mom bailed; that was the bad in his life. He had so much good, and he saw no point in dwelling on it. It hadn't affected his life. He was fine, so long as he was allowed a little distance.

"You never asked."

"I never . . . oh that's rich." Kara let out a painful laugh.

"You assumed and I let you. Not the same as lying."

"Really, well you never asked if I was a senator's daughter."

"No, but I did ask your name."

On that, Logan pinned her with his eyes. He had her, direct hit and yet he wasn't sure this was a game anymore.

"True, but the point is you weren't being honest. You kept this from me and would have continued keeping it from me. Why?"

"Because I don't talk about it and everyone doesn't know my mother left us. I don't share that part of my story. I don't see the point. She left when I was seven. I have no idea where she is and I haven't spoken to her. She may as well be dead. I'm not sure how the hell you found out, but now you know."

"When I interviewed Makenna, she didn't realize I was in the dark. Does it bother you that I know?"

"Does it bother me? I'm not sure. You just brought it up after what I thought was incredible sex. I'm making chili here, princess." Logan tried to slip back into their usual casual banter even though he was pretty sure Kara was not going to budge. "I'm not too keen on discussing my mother under most circumstances. I at least like to have my clothes on." He turned for the bowls. Admittedly, at least to himself, he was now annoyed that Kara knew about poor, sad, little motherless Logan.

He poured them both a glass of wine, his last attempt at bringing things back to normal.

"Can you believe this is a Syrah? It seems too much fun for such a serious wine."

"It's a good wine. Well done—are you changing the subject because it's uncomfortable for you to talk about yourself, or because it's none of my business?"

"Both? Is both an acceptable answer? Kara, I'm kind of boring, not much to tell."

Kara let out a breath she'd been holding since he said, "Both."

"Fine. Let's stick with food, wine, and my odd circus of a life. That'll be the extent of it. Forget the fact that I'm in love with you."

Logan could tell she hadn't meant to blurt it out, but there it was, her words floating between them. He loved her too, but she needed to back up a few steps. Unfortunately, he couldn't figure out how to do that without hurting her.

"Whoa, you love me? When did you decide that?"

Kara was struck. He could tell she was grabbing for a clever comeback, a pinch for his pull. That's how they usually played, but she said nothing and hurt poured off of her. Logan's heart squeezed and tried to reach out and help her, but Logan wouldn't allow it. One of them needed to survive this and it was going to be him.

"I'm sorry," Kara said and Logan's knees nearly buckled. Why the hell was she sorry?

"I didn't mean to say that and . . . I must have misunderstood what we were doing here." Kara turned toward the back door and then spun back around. "You know, isn't this all a bit hypocritical? I mean your issues with me have always been that I was fake, I was a liar—"

"I never said you were fake." Logan's eyes were still averted.

"Word choice, the point is I was billed a liar after Paris. I was hiding something when you found out about my studio, and yet your mother left, she's not dead, and you didn't say a word. What's that, Logan? Isn't that hiding? Isn't it a lie?" Kara asked now clutching her hands on the small chair in his dining area.

He wasn't ready to look at her, especially not after what had hit him less than an hour ago back in the tent.

"I'm not discussing this." He folded his arms across his chest like a sulking child. He warned his heart to shut the hell up because this was the part he knew was coming. This was the part where she would dig around and find poor motherless Logan instead of the man he'd become.

Leaving him in Paris was actually the best thing that could have happened. Sure, she always took the blame for Paris, but the truth was she left just in time. Before she got too close, before she wanted all the way in. Now she was standing in front of him, asking for something he couldn't give her. He didn't want to let her all the way in. He couldn't; he wasn't made that way, but looking in Kara's eyes, he knew she wasn't one for staying on the front porch. This was the part where she frantically gathered her things from his yard and left him anyway.

Kara left Logan's house and drove straight to Malibu. She cried all the way up Highway 1, so by the time she pulled into the driveway of the familiar blue beach cottage, she was only left with one question. What the hell was she doing? He was clearly not going to make a life with her. When had she turned into such a blithering, "love me, please," softy idiot? Her protective shell was long gone and Kara found herself left with nothing but a mushy middle.

The moment Logan closed up and she realized she wasn't going to reach him, the air grew so thick she felt like she was suffocating. All she thought about was running, saving herself, and getting to her beach house. She turned off the car and stepped out into the cold ocean air. The moon was full and she already felt better. Slightly.

She opened the door to the cottage Nana had left her a little over five years ago and started to cry again. She'd brought all of this on herself, she thought. She had asked to be found, wanted to feel, but now as the pain washed over her again, Kara would have given anything to go back into hiding. Being at Nana's was a start. She would hide out for a while, work on her glass, and finish the last of her articles. No Logan.

I'll find my way back, Kara thought, as she fell asleep on the couch listening to the crash of the ocean tide. She would survive, she always did.

The next morning, Kara almost fell off the couch reaching for her phone that was vibrating across the coffee table.

"Hello." She didn't fully open her eyes.

"Well good morning. Where are you, my favorite sister?"

"I'm your only sister." Kara sat up on the couch and cursed her scratchy, tear-swollen eyes. "Why are you calling me, Grady?"

"Let's go to dinner."

"No. I'm spending some time at Nana's beach house. I needed to get away. Alone." She hoped he would get the message.

"Great, a little relaxation is a good idea. Let's meet at The Rusty Nail—it's close to you and I'll drive up. Kate's coming too."

"Grady, I—"

"I'll text you the address. See you at five." He hung up before Kara could register what happened. Her brother was good at getting what he wanted.

Kara pulled into the gravel parking lot of The Rusty Nail. As she got out of her car and walked toward the onslaught of neon beer signs, she smiled because it was exactly her brother's type of place. She pushed on the door handle, which was, in fact, a large rusty nail.

Clever, she thought and was immediately hit by the smell of stale cigarette smoke and grease.

The cigarette smoke was most likely a lingering reminder of The Rusty Nail's heyday when shag carpeting and smoking indoors were still considered cool. Most of the floors were now covered in tile or linoleum or some combination of the two. Kara approached the dark wood hostess station and saw Grady and Kate already sitting in a booth in the corner. Grady stood as she approached.

Kara shook her head. "I'm sure they're famous for something, but I'm not even going to guess." She kissed him on the cheek.

"Chicken fried steak and they have the best mashed potatoes you've ever tasted." He sat back down and handed Kara her menu.

"And you're marrying this man?" Kara said.

"I am." Kate laughed. "Someone had to take him off the market. But, they do have pretty great mashed potatoes."

"Wait, he's taken you here before?"

Kate nodded.

"Hey, I'll have you know this place has an A-plus from the health department—it's just old. Old isn't always bad."

"I know, Grade, but you realize people don't eat chicken fried steak and mashed potatoes anymore, right? They're practically illegal." Kara laughed.

"That's ridiculous. Where's that boyfriend of yours, he'll set the record straight." Grady glanced at Kate when Kara's face fell. He seemed to be looking to his fiancée for help.

"Did something happen?" Grady asked, as a waitress, with something like a tiara in her hair, came and took their order.

Kara looked up at her brother and then to Kate, their hands clasped on the table. They were silly happy and Kara was not about to "piss on that parade," as her Nana would say.

"Nothing happened, I'm fine. It's just that Logan is not my boyfriend, so I was a little thrown by the title," Kara told them after they had ordered.

"Oh, so something did happen. Because you two seemed—"

"Yeah, well things change. Let's talk about you guys."

"Okay." Kate jumped in to save her. "Well, I would like you to be a bridesmaid in our wedding."

Kara set her menu down and started to cry.

"Shit, well done Galloway, now she's crying."

Kate reached across the table and held Kara's hand.

"She just needs a good cry," Kate said.

"What? Does your kind send signals to each other? How did you know she needed to cry?"

"Because any time a woman says she's fine, that means she's as far from fine as she can get."

"Right, note to self." Grady looked confused.

Kara started laughing toward the end of their conversation.

"Are you better now?" Grady seemed desperate to help.

"I am much better." Kara wiped her eyes. "I would love to be a bridesmaid. Thank you, Kate."

"I promise the dresses won't be hideous," Kate said as their food arrived.

"You can dress me up in anything, just please make sure it's not raspberry, I'm allergic."

They all laughed and while Kara didn't go into detail, she was pretty sure they'd both figured out she and Logan were finished, which they were. There were obviously parts of himself Logan was not willing to share. That may have been fine when they barely knew each other, but she wanted more now.

"Listen." Kara felt like she was going to burst if she ate one more bite of mashed potatoes. "I know I haven't always been the nicest person, but I want you both to know that I'm working on that."

"Great, you can start by telling me that I was right. This place is awesome, isn't it?"

Kara laughed. "It's not bad. I won't be back, but it isn't bad."

Chapter Twenty-Nine

$\mathcal{L}$ogan hadn't had a decent night's sleep since Kara left three days ago. His mind was spinning with her and his mother and how he'd managed to let any of this shit back into his life. He had put his mother and what she did in a compartment in the very back of his mind. That was where he kept her so the mess of her didn't define his life.

When Kara asked him and he realized that compartment was about to be opened again, something snapped and he couldn't let her in. He didn't want her there, didn't want anyone there. The fact that she now knew he was a complete hypocrite and the biggest liar of them all, was what got him into the shower and into work before the sun. Work was the only thing that made sense anymore. Yet since he'd arrived it had not been the rhythmic meditation that he loved, but instead one screwup after another.

"Table three just sent this back," one of the servers said in a flurry, sliding past Logan and putting down a plate of what appeared to be their cavatelli porchetta with no more than a couple bites taken. "The lady claims it's way too salty."

Logan grabbed a fork out of the bin and dipped into the pasta. He nearly saw spots the moment it hit his tongue.

"Travis!"

At his name, Travis looked up from the back room where he was prepping spinach and saw Logan's face through the opening that separated the back and front kitchens.

"How the hell did this get served?" Logan asked as he brought the plate back toward Travis.

Travis dried his hands as he approached. Logan threw his fork in one of the dishwashing bins and handed the plate to Travis who quickly took a bite.

"Holy shit. Who made . . ." His question fell as both of them turned to the young man swirling a pan over a flame. Todd did not notice either of them because his earphones were in and he was performing for whatever was in the pan that would probably send some poor customer into cardiac arrest.

"Comp this," Logan told the server who was still standing by the window waiting. "Apologize profusely and then tell them I am remaking it personally. I will be out to deliver it and talk to them ASAP." Logan plucked the earphones from Todd's ears and turned off the flame under his pan. The server nodded and hurried off.

"What the hell, man?" Todd turned on Logan and simultaneously pushed his bangs out of his face while grabbing at the waistband of his eternally sagging skinny jeans.

"'Man'?" Logan raised an eyebrow.

"Huh, sorry dude, but I was in my groove there." His smile revealed a glimpse at the gap in his bottom teeth.

Logan could feel the table waiting for him to rectify Todd's screwup. He didn't have time to argue; he needed the stove.

"Travis needs you in the back." Logan pulled an apron on and took the pan.

Todd said something about this new "righteous ragu" he saw on the Food Network and Logan almost punched him. With the table still waiting, he instead bumped him aside and pointed him toward Travis. Logan couldn't say he was sad to see him go.

He was a fair owner who recognized that everyone contributed something to the team, but Todd wasn't getting it and probably never would. Three weeks ago it was spinach salads that were stopped before they went out on the floor because they were drenched in dressing. That time, Todd explained it was because the new Linkin Park album had him all "amped up." Logan shook his head thinking about it now as he added olive oil to his pan and then the pasta. Besides, if the kid called him "dude" or "bro" or "man" one more time Logan was going to publicly lose it.

It was for the best that Travis was sending him home. And that was one of the great things about working alongside Travis—he knew exactly what had to be done at the same time Logan did. They were completely in sync. There's no way he'd be able to run this restaurant so well without him.

Logan turned out his version of cavatelli porchetta onto the waiting plate. He grated some Parmigiano-Reggiano on top, rimmed the plate with a damp rag to make sure it was perfect, and placed it in the window. He pulled the apron over his head and put it back on the hook as he entered the floor and grabbed the plate down from service window.

It turned out that the husband of the woman who returned her order had read Kara's feature on Logan and the restaurant. The day just kept getting better. Once Logan replaced her meal and she told him it was delicious, she spent at least another twenty minutes talking about the great picture of him and Kara. The whole damn table raved about her articles and asked about where Kara was.

Right when he felt like his head was going to explode, the woman turned to him and said, "You better lock that girl down with a ring before she gets away. You know what Beyoncé says: if you like it put a ring on it."

Logan smiled, it was part of his job to smile, and walked away both grateful that he'd cleaned up Todd's mistake and mystified that a woman old enough to be his mother was quoting Beyoncé.

The day continued on from there with the dishwasher breaking an entire basket of bar glasses, two of the burners going out on his cooktop, and a little boy who slipped while running out the door after his parents. Logan saw visions of the lovely family of three suing him for everything he was worth, but they were very nice and sort of blamed it on their son, which was fine with Logan. He'd had all he could take at that point and handed the last hour off to Travis.

"I'm going home. Can you handle closing?"

"Sure, it's slowing down out there. You okay?"

"No." Logan grabbed his keys off his desk.

"Do you want to talk about it?"

"No. I want to go home, go to bed, and not have to do something or take care of something for a week. I want to go somewhere tropical where I can swim in blue water and fall asleep on the beach. I want someone else to make decisions. I want someone else to cook."

"Okay, well my pool is really blue right now since I got a new pool guy. So, if you want to come over and sleep in the guest room, you're more than welcome. I'll cook for you and make all the decisions. You might regret giving me that freedom, but I'll take it for you, man."

Logan laughed and for a minute wished he was like Travis, carefree and pretty damn happy where he was in life. Travis wasn't always trying to prove something. He wasn't a rescuer, he was just a man and right then, Logan would have given anything to be the same.

"I'm fine"—Logan patted him on the shoulder—"but thanks for the offer. I just need to get some sleep."

"Tomorrow's Sunday and even the Lord rested on that day. Get some sleep and I'll shut 'er down tonight."

"Make me proud." Logan didn't even bother to say goodnight to everyone else.

"Will do. 'Night." Travis returned to the front.

Logan pushed through the door into the dark parking lot. He was out of control and he hated the feeling. He'd replayed those moments with Kara a hundred times and every time, he came out the asshole, but there was no way to fix it. She needed more from him and he wasn't going there. Ever. So, that was it. It was over and after a very long sleep, he would pick things up and get back to normal. He just hoped he could remember what that was.

Chapter Thirty

Kara spent the last few weeks at the beach collecting glass and reviewing a few local places Olivia asked her to try out once she heard Kara was in Malibu. Kara agreed to a couple, but she was mainly trying to finish the last piece of her feature. The other two had been well received and she wanted to finish strong. The last piece was interviewing Logan's father and getting pictures of Ryeland Farms.

Kara drove up to the farm all the way from the beach and immediately felt the weight as she met Logan's father at the door. She told herself she had a job to do and she was going to get it done. She had sent Jeremy and his crew to the barn because she wanted some pictures of their rooster and the other gorgeous chickens they had in their coop. Kara had no idea chickens could be so beautiful and healthy.

During the tour, Kara loved watching the animals. There were two goats and the most adorable baby piglets. Herbert Rye explained that the litter had been recently weaned and he was feeding them twice a day. He asked Kara if she wanted to feed them and she found that she did. Her family had a Yorkie when she was growing up, but other than that Kara had not been around animals. With Mr. Rye's help, she fed the piglets. It was amazing and her cheeks hurt from smiling by the time they were done. A little over an hour later, she sat at an outside picnic table with Logan's father, running down a list of her remaining questions.

"You're saying that today's chickens aren't the same as they used to be?"

Herbert smiled and Kara could see where Logan got his charm. "Very little in today's food production is like it was thirty years ago. Our country produces far too much food. Cheap food that is inhumane. It's downright wrong. Did you know that chickens mass-produced by these giant farms are bred for their breast meat? They're so top-heavy they can't even stand up. That's not a life," he explained and Kara agreed.

"So what is working?" she asked.

"Local farms. Places even smaller than our farm are popping up all over the place. People, all different ages, different walks, are choosing farmers markets and grass-fed beef. People are educating themselves and like Maya Angelou says, 'Once you know better, you must do better.'"

Kara smiled.

"I watch a lot of Oprah," Herbert continued. "Logan says I watch too much, but her show's on when I break for lunch. Smart woman, that Oprah."

"That she is." On that note, Kara asked a couple more questions about their dairy cows and she was done. "Thank you so much for your time, Mr. Rye." She packed up her things.

"You're very welcome, my dear. Thank you for taking the time to listen." He took her hands. "My kids always tell me not to butt into their lives, but when I see something that isn't right, I can't help myself."

Kara started to tell him he didn't need to say anything, but he continued.

"He's the best man, but he's been taking care of everyone else for so long that he's forgotten how to take care of himself. If he watched more Oprah, he would know that. She talks about self-care all the time."

Kara laughed because she was pretty sure she was in love with two Rye men at this point.

"I know. I'm sure he will figure it out." Kara looked into his eyes and knew where Makenna got hers.

"He loves you," Herbert said as she turned to walk away. "It's something I've never seen before, pretty powerful stuff, so I'm not counting you guys out just yet."

Kara turned back and kissed him on the cheek. "Thank you. Let's hope you and Oprah are right." She didn't have the heart to tell him the truth. Then she left him before she crawled into his lap and asked him to make everything better.

As Kara threw her bag into her car, Logan's truck pulled up and parked across from her. She found herself in a weird limbo where she wasn't sure if she should get into the car or stand there and wait for him to get out. She decided to wait. She was finished hiding at this point. She was ready to live her "authentic life" as Herbert and Oprah said.

Logan turned off his truck, sat there for a minute, and wondered how strange it would be if he just drove back home without getting out. *She must be here to finish her article.* He'd forgotten about the damn thing while he was trying to forget about her. His heart was racing, but he pulled it together and stepped out of the truck. She was standing outside her car as he approached the gravel path that led to the barn. His heart pounded in his ears and he knew if he could only get through this, make nice, and move past her, things would go back to normal. He needed normal at this point.

"Kara." That's what he went with. Her name. Simple.

"Logan."

Shit, and the volley began.

"You get what you needed from Dad for your article?"

"I did, thanks, he was very helpful. Sweet." Kara tried to smile. She caught his eye and he felt like he was going under.

The pause was painful. She shifted on her feet and then put her hand on the door to her car.

"Let me know how it goes." His mouth must have been on autopilot because he wasn't sure where the hell that last thing came from, but he was pretty sure he should brace himself for Kara's return.

"What? Let you know how what goes?"

Logan shook his head and backed up. "I don't know what I'm saying, Kara, okay? This is awkward. I'm glad you got what you needed and have a safe ride back."

"Fine." Kara opened her car door.

Logan walked past her.

"Just so we're clear, I'm not the one hiding this time. I'm not letting my parents, or how I was raised, dictate my future. I've figured myself out. This one is all on you." She slammed the car door.

He never turned around. He simply stood there with his back to her because the truth was he was scared to death. He wasn't going to be able to give her what she wanted, but he hadn't been able to find his way back to having order in his life without her either. So he was just going through the motions until something clicked. Today he was here to work and help his dad out. He knew how to do that, so he would work himself to exhaustion and hopefully collapse into a dream state that for once didn't include Kara's face, her body, or that laugh.

Makenna was in the kitchen when Logan walked into the house.

"I'm making lunch. Do you want a sandwich?"

"No."

"Coffee?'

"Yeah, I'll get it." Logan grabbed a cup. "Where's Dad?"

"He and Garrett just left on the quad. Said they would be right back."

Kenna sat down at the table next to him.

"Remember when Dad got that peanut butter grinder at a garage sale?"

The caffeine from the coffee was setting in and Logan smiled.

"Yeah, and he made like twenty jars of peanut butter a week and read all of the health benefits to us."

Kenna laughed. "God, to this day I can't eat peanut butter. Peanut butter and bananas, peanut butter with pickles, it was crazy."

"It was," Logan said. "What made you think of that?"

"I was making my sandwich and thinking about how you used to make our lunches."

Logan looked at her.

"They were good lunches, always on the counter when I came out for breakfast. You must have gotten up early to make those."

"Nah, you just got up late."

"Well, either way, it's a nice memory. Being in this kitchen brings back so many great memories, ya know?"

"I do. We have a lot of great memories here, Kenna. I'm glad our lunches are one of yours. I liked making them."

"I'm sorry."

"For what?"

"That I messed up and told Kara about Mom. I should have picked up on it and left her where you wanted her, dead."

"First of all"—Logan stood to get more coffee—"it's not your fault. I should have been honest. I don't want Mom dead, it was just easier than explaining."

"I know, but you and Kara can get over this, don't you think?"

"I don't think so. I'm just—I don't know what I am. I want to go back to the life I had before I bumped into Kara again. Things made sense, and now they don't."

"What if she needs you though?"

"She doesn't need me. Believe me, she's more than capable of taking care of herself."

Kenna got up and put her plate in the sink.

"We're all capable of taking care of ourselves, Lo, but sometimes it's nice. It's better when someone else makes your lunch, you know?"

Logan nodded. He couldn't say anything past the lump in his throat. His heart hurt for Kenna sometimes. Christ, was everyone in this house watching Oprah?

"Anyway"—she walked toward the door—"I'm sorry I wasn't fast enough to lie with you."

"That's okay." Logan turned to her, but Makenna was gone.

"She was sorry she wasn't fast enough to lie with him." That's what it was, wasn't it? No matter how he tried to move things around, he had lied to Kara. "Own it," Garrett would say, "once a liar, always a liar." He was in no position to point fingers.

Chapter Thirty-One

"I need your opinion." Kara opened the front door to Jake standing with his yoga mat slung across his chest.

"Well, hello to you too." He walked in and tossed his stuff on the round black chair by Kara's entryway. "Do you have any coffee?" he asked on a huff and even as Kara ran back to her bedroom, she could tell something was wrong.

"French press in the kitchen. Are you all right?" Kara yelled from above in her bedroom.

The upstairs of the house was open to the downstairs, so Jake grabbed a cup, the coffee press, and took a seat at her dining room table.

"Oh God, I need my yoga today. My chi or whatever the hell that woman calls it, is blocked." Jake sipped his coffee. "Can you hear me up there?"

"Yes, your chi is blocked. What happened?"

"It's nothing, stupid really. What kind of opinion do you need?"

"Your fashion opinion."

"Oh, so because I'm gay and married to a man named after a damn textile, my fashion opinion matters? I suppose we, the collective gay 'we,' all know about women's clothing, manscaping, and Cher? Well, I'll have you know that I've never manscaped a day in my life. I mean, sure I trim, but every man trims. Even the almighty heterosexual, he trims."

Kara, pulled a light cover-up over her tank top and slowly walked over to the half wall of her bedroom. She looked down at Jake who was now violently flipping through the paper.

"Jake, honey?" she said gently, because she had never seen him so upset.

He glanced up, tears welling in his eyes. She walked down the stairs, took him into her arms, and he started to cry. She held him until he pulled back, quickly wiping his eyes.

"This is so stupid. I shouldn't be crying, but I get so damn tired sometimes."

"Do you want to tell me what's wrong?"

Jake sat back down and Kara joined him.

"The Strickland School, they won't let Eloise in."

"What? I thought she was a shoo-in? References—and her tests. What happened?"

"Her father and I happened, that's what happened. We got the rejection letter in the mail yesterday and I called to find out why, you know? What went wrong? The woman in admissions told me on the phone that they didn't think Eloise was the right 'fit' for Strickland and that the children at their school were more 'traditional.' She paused before saying 'traditional.' The bitch paused, you know how uppity meanies do when they want you to understand that traditional means much more than just the word?"

"Yes, I do. I'm very familiar with uppity meanies. I'm sorry." She touched his hand.

Jake let out a breath of what seemed like resignation. "I'm just so tired of this. I get that we're not the norm, but we live a life like every other family. We have a house, we raise our daughter who we fought tooth and nail to even get. There's a whole group of people who would have rather seen Eloise raised in foster care than by two gay men."

"I know, but she's yours, Jake, and no one can take that away."

"But there's always more and more damn hoops. What am I supposed to tell her?" He started to tear up again, but dismissed it with a quick swipe of his hand.

"Jake, you're going to tell her what every parent tells their child when the world isn't fair. You'll tell her she's brilliant and wonderful and that sometimes people can't get out of their own way."

"Is that a Nanaism?" He smiled through his tears.

"Sure is. I'm telling you the woman was brilliant." She leaned over to hug him. "It's going to be all right. Not right this minute, but eventually."

"I know. Now, what was your fashion question?"

"Oh, well, it's not important now."

"Yes it is." He went up the stairs to her bedroom.

"And for the record, I ask your opinion because you're a good dresser. Do I even need to say that to you?" Kara asked.

"Oh, I know. I was just practicing my righteous indignation. Cotton thinks we should sue the damn place. I'm working myself up into the angry gay man." He laughed as they walked through the glass front door of Kara's bedroom.

Kara gestured to the bed. "Well, what do you think?"

Jake ran his hands along the material. "Silk?"

"Yes."

"It's gorgeous. A bit of a departure for you, but I'll bet Logan will love it. It's gorgeous, honey."

"Yeah well, it's not for Logan, it's for me."

"Okay." He seemed careful not to trip the dangerous wire that was no doubt lurking somewhere in their conversation. "So if this isn't a 'let's make up' date dress, what's it for?"

"Why it's the spring social, Jake." Kara batted her eyelashes. "You mean you weren't invited to the Bradburys' annual Hop Into Spring Social?"

Jake laughed. "Aw shit, did you draw the short straw?"

"Grady took St. Patrick's. He says it was because he was a family beer expert, but I'm pretty sure it was because I was . . ."

"A wreck?"

"Not quite a wreck. Let's just say I was working remotely from the beach. Indisposed, as my Nana would say."

"Whatever you say, sweetie. Eloise is still talking about the beach, so you can invite us up for dinner anytime you're indisposed."

Jake turned his attention back to the dress and shifted his head a little in surprise.

"The big fancy let's get the rich and powerful families together on Coronado Island weekend spring social, that one?"

"Yes, smart-ass. That's the one. Do you think it's too casual?"

"Not at all, it's nearly floor-length. Perfect for early spring and I love the tie at the back of the halter, but Kara this isn't the paper doll stuff you normally wear to these family events. Shouldn't you be down at Bitch and Bitchier, picking out some shapeless frock in sensible raspberry with a pineapple purse?"

"I probably should. Old Kara would, but I'm sick to death of her. This dress is me. It's a statement dress."

"And you're looking to make a statement?"

"I am."

"Care to share the statement?"

"I no longer wear pigtails and it's about damn time I dressed myself. Oh, and orange is my signature color. Orange, so back your shit up, Momma."

"Oh, that's a statement I can definitely get behind. It's perfect. Shoes?"

Kara pointed to the shoes sitting on the lush linen-colored carpet of her room. They were high, multicolored, and strappy. Jake gasped.

"Yes." He nodded and turned her to face him. "You will be, well, you will be vibrant, delicious you." He kissed Kara on her cheek and grew emotional again. "Now, silk is not forgiving, so we best get to yoga so you're all tight and dewy."

Kara laughed. "True. And there's still the matter of your blocked chi."

"Let's go beat the asshole into submission."

Chapter Thirty-Two

The following afternoon, Kara arrived at the Bradburys' house right on time. The silk of her orange dress swished past her legs and her sandals were not nearly as uncomfortable as they appeared. She felt great and even though it had taken her a while, she was on her own terms. Sure, it wasn't as simple as finally choosing her own dress, but it was a start.

The Bradburys had a large green yard complete with the longest white picket fence Kara had ever seen. She went to high school with one of their daughters and as she rounded the side of the house toward the entrance where the band was playing, Kara remembered when she fell off the golf cart at Crystal Bradbury's thirteenth birthday party. There had been too many of them in Mr. Bradbury's cart and when they took a sharp turn in the circular driveway, Kara had gone flying. She could still see the scar on her knee some days and especially when her legs started to tan in the summer. That was years ago, she thought, as she was now greeted by Crystal's parents. Kara exchanged niceties and was ushered over to the refreshment area while the Bradburys greeted their other guests. So much had changed since that birthday party. She wondered if Crystal still wore lavender; if she remembered correctly, that was her signature color. Christ, they really had been paper dolls for their mothers to play with.

Kara took a seat on one of the white chairs placed in little clusters around the yard. She sipped her lemonade.

"Where's Logan?" Grady asked thumping down in the seat next to her.

Kara stiffened at the mention of Logan's name and her brother, of course, noticed.

"I'm not sure. I thought you were sitting this one out. Why are you here?"

"I was all prepared to throw you to the bunnies here at the Hop Into Hell Social, but Kate thought you might need me. Crazy right? Maybe you'll tell me what happened now?"

She sighed. Her brother was relentless. "A lot of things have happened, Grade."

"Are you okay with that?"

She could tell he was being careful, trying not to push too hard.

"I'm good. I love him, but he won't let me in, so it's not going to work out. Turns out Paris was about as close as he was ever going to let me get. Oh, and his mother didn't die." Kara tried to get it all out in one swoop.

"Excuse me?" Grady asked crossing his legs and leaning in closer.

"She left them, ran away with some rich guy. She isn't dead, she's just gone."

"How'd you find that out?"

"Makenna. When I interviewed her. I mentioned something about their mother dying and she looked at me like I was nuts."

"Oh wow, that's rough. Is that all you're fighting over?"

"You know, I think I liked you better when you were sad, alone, and hiding. Being in love and finally running your foundation in the open has made you a little annoying."

Grady laughed.

"At what point do you start acting like my brother and defending me?" Kara asked.

"Um, okay well he should not be giving you such a hard time about your games, when he's playing one himself. Is that better?"

"Yes, much."

"However you want to look at it, this is all just garbage getting in the way, Kara. You two need to figure it out and clear this stuff up."

"I don't think that's going to happen. I haven't spoken to him in weeks. The last part of the article is due to Olivia at the end of next week. I finished the light fixture for the dining room at The Yard. I guess I'll have it couriered over next week."

"Have you gone down to the restaurant?"

"No. I'm finished. There's no need."

"Make up an excuse. What the hell, you're all Honest Abe now?"

Kara smiled at him. "Nana?"

Grady smiled back. "Yup, Nana. I can't stop. Kate thinks she's taken over my body."

"She always did like you better."

"True."

Kara shoved him.

"Deliver the light fixture yourself. Maybe he needs a little push. We're men, not the smartest of the species, you know?"

She nodded. "True, but I already tried pushing. He obviously knows what he's doing."

"Kara, you can't just let this go, can you?"

"I guess we should join everyone else and mingle." Kara grabbed her purse before her heart jumped out of her chest.

Grady seemed to pick up on her change of subject. He was a great brother, she thought as he offered his arm and Kara held on to him. They made their way across the moist spring grass toward their parents who were currently in animated conversation with another couple. Kara and Grady held back, sipping their drinks.

"We're quite a pair, you and I. A little bit hard to love, maybe."

Kara smiled. "We probably can't blame that on our parents for much longer. Time to grow up, eh?"

"We should have run away that night. You screwed the whole thing up with that damn cat of yours."

Kara laughed and Grady returned the wave of some guy in seersucker.

"I mean, just think, we could be seasoned circus performers by now," Grady said through his senator's son perm-a-grin.

"I thought we already were circus performers." She bumped his shoulder.

Grady put his arm around her.

"That we are, sis." He pulled her close and kissed her on the forehead. "You okay?"

Kara let out a breath and snuggled into her brother's shoulder. He was so happy, so in love, and she was becoming her genuine self. Long overdue, but standing there with him, she really had nothing to complain about.

"You need a haircut."

Grady laughed.

"Well played. I've taught you well. Dodge and evade." He looked at her, all that big brother magic in his eyes. "Make sure you figure it out, okay? Don't go back to raspberry again."

"Not a chance. Now go find a lemonade for that gorgeous woman walking toward us, before she wakes up or Mom gets ahold of her."

Grady laughed. "I love you." He left her side and headed toward Kate who looked fantastic in a green sundress.

Just as Kara was sure she'd stayed long enough to make her exit at any minute, her mother and father sauntered over in all their linen finery.

"Kara dear, this is certainly an interesting choice." Her mother touched her dress and somehow made it feel less luxurious than it did when she'd slipped into it earlier.

"Thank you, Mother." She kissed her on the cheek.

"You look great, honey." Her father squeezed her from the side.

"I wasn't aware you liked orange," her mother continued, still surveying. "It's actually not a bad color on you. I guess that's more of a burnt orange. Patrick, what color would you say that is?"

"I have no idea, my love. It's a great dress, we are at a party, could we please stop inspecting for a few minutes?" her father said playfully, but with purpose. He kissed his wife and then smiled at Kara.

Her mother raised her eyebrows, but softened at her father's kiss and once the microscope lifted, Kara started thinking about her exit strategy. She did want to talk to her father quickly before she left, so while her mother was rambling with two other women, Kara pulled him aside.

"Eloise starts school in August." She held his arm and walked with him toward the back of the yard.

"That's great news."

"Yeah, at first Strickland School wasn't going to let her in and then just last week they called apologizing and offered her a spot. Weird, huh?"

"Well, maybe something opened up."

"Dad." She stopped and turned to look at him.

"Yes, darling daughter."

"It was you or it was Grady. He says no, so that leaves only one person who loves me enough to help my friend deal with morons."

"It was your mother." He looked over at the children playing with Hula-Hoops.

"Excuse me?"

"You heard me, your mother called the school and, well, she's your mother. When she was done with them they felt exactly the way they should have felt."

"About as small as ants at a picnic? Huh, those skills are helpful in certain situations."

"She loves you, honey, and she wanted to help."

Kara looked at her father sideways, as if there must be more.

"Oh, all right, it didn't hurt that Mrs. Crenshaw, the admissions director, was one of your mother's sorority sisters. She never liked her, so she laid on the whole, 'What would the sisters think? Is this how we make the world a better place?' thing. Cootie caved once your mother said she was seriously thinking of contacting the chapter and that she would not be invited to our open house next year."

"Cootie? The woman's name is Cootie."

Her father laughed. "It's a nickname, I think. I hope."

"Hmm, well I'm grateful. And it's nice to see Mother using her powers for good instead of evil."

"Kara, your mother is—"

"Oh, Dad, like you said, this is a lovely party. Leave it. I'm thrilled she helped Jake and Cotton. Eloise deserves the very best. Like Nana used to say, 'Let's let sleeping dogs, lie.'"

They both laughed and her father did just that. They started walking again and he moved on talking about his first few months of work, the trip he and her mother took to Greece last month, and his next speech. The senator liked to discuss his life, which was fine with Kara because at the moment, her life was a bit of a jumbled mess.

"So, how are you?"

Damn, Kara thought.

"I'm good. Working and . . . just planted an herb garden."

"Really?" Her father waved to someone in the distance. "Logan help you with that?" he asked as if it was the most casual thing in the world.

"No."

"Huh." They started walking back because Kara's mother was looking over at them. "You know, I'm sorry your life has been a bit of a mess." Her father slowed down.

Kara was shocked and a little relieved at his candor, especially among the spring social set.

"We probably could have done some things differently."

Kara said nothing.

"Feel free to disagree." Her father's brow furrowed, but Kara just laughed and kept walking.

"I just think we've ruined your happy a couple of times with our . . . well, with my needs or the campaign's needs," he said. "I'm sorry about that."

Kara could feel her eyes filling so she glanced back toward where they'd come and quickly wiped a tear that managed to escape.

"It hasn't been that bad, Dad."

"Well, if you need anything . . ."

"Dad, I'm fine. I'm working on a life for myself, so if you and Mom could sit tight, I'd like to have my own happy for a while."

Her father nodded and put his arm around her. She couldn't look at him without breaking her no crying in public rule.

"I think we can do that. You go be happy, honey," he said and swallowed back what seemed like a lump in his throat.

And then before either of them could say another word, her brother in shining armor approached.

"My son!" Their mother walked over to Grady.

"My mother!" he mocked. Kara laughed.

"Run." Grady leaned in, pretending to greet her again. "I'll hold them off."

Kara laughed, kissed her father and mother good-bye, and did just that.

She had packed up her things from Nana's place before the party, so she drove home to her current reality and was working on a new lamp in her studio by sunset.

Chapter Thirty-Three

*K*ara turned in the last of the feature articles. It was good work, she was proud of it, and then she resigned. Olivia had a good cry, but Kara decided she wasn't cut out to be in the media. It was always sort of ironic that she ended up there in the first place. She'd learned a lot about herself over the past few months: most important was that she needed to be creative, not correct. She no longer wanted to pick other people apart; she wanted to be happy. Happy in her own skin and making something instead of tearing something down.

She drove past The Yard for the third time that week, but this time she pulled in. She felt powerful about her solution and had decided to take Grady's advice. The light fixture she'd made for the restaurant's private dining room had been wrapped up and in her car all week. It was time to give it to Logan.

Her old self told her she had no business being there as Kara got out of the car and noticed the storm clouds building. The air smelled of rain and Kara told her old self to shut up. She gently took the fixture, wrapped in burlap, out of the back of her car. She held it to her chest as if she could somehow squeeze a piece of herself into her last gift to Logan.

He'd made it very clear that he didn't want her, at least not for the long-term. Old Kara would have told him to go screw himself and moved right on. This Kara, the person she'd spent time with lately, was exposed, raw. Damn it, she hated raw. When she'd felt exposed in the past, she had crawled up into her tower, as Logan called it. But that didn't work anymore. She liked herself like this.

Maybe she would take Jake up on his offer to build a studio in town for her to showcase her work. She would drop the light fixture off and then it would be "Time to celebrate you"—that's what her Nana had said on every birthday when she'd arrived at the door draped in shopping bags. Kara's birthday was a few months away, but it was time to celebrate herself. With or without Logan Rye, she'd taken a journey and found her truest self.

She stood at the entrance to The Yard for a beat hoping her heart would stop racing. Just as she was having second thoughts, the door opened and a group of happy, celebrating people spilled out. Kara could hear the music and the hum of people enjoying their evening. She walked into the restaurant and her heart stopped pounding as it melted into a slow ache for what she couldn't make work.

"Kara." Summer smiled as she grabbed menus and walked a couple over to the "lover's cove" table. "I'll be right back."

"Oh, sure," Kara said, standing in the front of a restaurant that no longer felt familiar. They were busy and she would normally make herself comfortable or walk back to the kitchen, but now she stood there like a stranger.

Makenna came buzzing in from the patio area carrying a tray of dirty dishes. She stopped when she saw Kara.

"Hi." Kenna was clearly going for relaxed even though Kara could see her mind spinning with questions.

"Hi. I know you're busy, but I just wanted to drop this off."

"What is it?" she asked handing the tray to a passing busser and wiping her hands on a towel behind the hostess station.

As she met Makenna's eyes, Kara found that she couldn't quite speak, so she simply handed the bundle to her.

"Heavy, let's bring it over here." Makenna walked into the restaurant and set the fixture on the pizza counter.

Kara said nothing; she could smell the food and hear the kitchen activity through the service window. She let out a deep breath as Makenna started pulling at the twine of the package.

Kara glanced up, and her eyes found him. Logan was once again standing in his kitchen peering out through the service window at her. They'd come full circle, but this time, once the shock wore off his face, Logan gave her a cursory nod and then averted his eyes. He wasn't coming out of his kitchen this time. He was on one side of the narrow street in Paris and she was on the other, but unlike when they were younger, he wouldn't cross the street. He wasn't going to take her in his arms and kiss her, tell her he loved her. That wasn't what was going to happen and Kara had learned enough about herself to know better than to stand there waiting for him.

Makenna pulled back the last piece of burlap from the fixture and gasped.

"Oh, Kara, this is gorgeous. It's for the private dining room. I almost forgot," she said and must have seen something on Kara's face because she looked toward the kitchen for her brother.

"Thank you. It's finished and I thought I would bring it by, but I didn't realize . . . I need to go." Kara stared down at the fixture, unable to look anywhere else.

"Okay." Kenna touched her arm and brought her out of her trance. "I'll walk you out."

"Oh no, that's okay," she started to say, but Kenna touched her back and held the front door open. "How is he?" Kara found herself asking as a gust of the approaching storm hit her.

"He's a mess. Kara, I'm sure he wants to see you. You guys should—"

"No." Kara clicked her car open and the dim lights came on. "There's no point. I wanted to bring the light by. It turned out really nice. We, I, used the glass that was left over from the garage. I think he'll . . ." Kara's entire body felt like the storm above, and as rain started sprinkling, she pulled Kenna into a hug.

"Kara." Kenna's voice was thick with emotion.

Kara pulled back. "I'm fine. We'll both be fine. It's best to let it go."

"I don't agree. Neither of you look fine to me, but I'm certainly not one to give out advice. I'll show him the light fixture and we'll put it up tonight," Makenna said, sadness in her eyes. "Take care, Kara."

"Thanks, Kenna." Kara got into her car. As she closed the door, it began pouring rain. She watched Makenna run back into the restaurant. Kara turned her headlights on, wiped the tears from her eyes, and drove home.

It rained through the night. Kara woke early, made a Thermos of tea, and pulled her boots and slicker on. She wanted to get into her studio early to finish the lamp she'd started last week. The rain had made the tiles of the walkway a deep orange that contrasted so beautifully with the green of the grass, she stopped to watch. She loved her home, especially when it rained. She sat on the stone bench outside her studio. With the hood of her slicker up, she was dry while everything else was washed. She poured herself some tea into the twist cup of the Thermos and thought about all the times she played in the rain as a kid. With her friends after the Sadie Hawkins dance in seventh grade. Their cook had stayed late and made kettle corn and hot chocolate. They'd danced in the rain and then watched *The Princess Diaries* in the living room. Kara's childhood was sprinkled with spectacular moments of normal. She clung to them when she felt like she was drowning. The rain hit her navy-and-green rain boots as she kicked her feet in front of her.

Eventually, she stood and finished the rainy waltz to her studio. She shook out of her slicker and left her boots at the door. Once inside, she turned on the lights, lit a candle, and sat taking in her space. She loved it here and had often thought of making her whole house like this, but she wasn't sure she could achieve the same feeling in a larger space. Sometimes smaller spaces held on tighter. That was probably why children hid under the covers or babies balled up. Small spaces were manageable, safe. Kara couldn't keep out the memory of the tent in Logan's backyard. They'd been so in sync, so in love, whether he was willing to admit it or not.

Small spaces were safe, because as soon as she stepped out, wanted more, he shut her out. It wasn't fair, but Nana always said, "No one ever promised fair." Kara moved to her worktable and started to pull out a few pieces of glass that might work in the still-empty spaces of her lampshade. She turned her music on, letting it play softly so she could still hear the rain, and got to work.

A few hours later, Logan opened the door to her studio and walked in. He didn't care that he was dripping wet. He'd barely noticed, hadn't felt anything after Makenna and Travis hung her lighting fixture in the private dining area last night. They'd all gone home around one and he'd sat there staring at the flecks of light. He'd traced the reflections on the table with his finger, trying through scratchy eyes to figure out why he couldn't put her away. He'd done it after Paris, but this was different, deeper. He'd shut all the lights off in the restaurant except for the dining area and lover's cove. The light she cast over his restaurant made it hard to breathe. She was part of his place, part of him. He couldn't find a way to give her what she wanted and he couldn't find a way to let her go. After tossing around in his bed for a few hours, Logan decided he needed her and he would figure the rest out later.

He closed the door to her studio. She was sitting at her table and before his brain even engaged, his heart dragged him straight to her. He pulled her to her feet and kissed her. He moved to her neck and buried his head in her hair. He could feel his eyes well.

"The fixture is incredible. God, I miss you."

Kara looked stunned. She didn't move.

"I can't find my way back to before you." He was fighting for breath and clinging to her.

"That's why you're here?"

He could feel Kara stiffen, but he kept holding on.

"So what is this—a primal grab for something that's been taken away from you, Logan? Like a toy?" Kara unwrapped herself from his arms. "I'm past the point that this is interesting," she continued and Logan knew he should have stayed away. The pain in her eyes was unbearable. "This isn't a movie or a bad romance novel. I don't let many people into my life, but when I do, it's because I love and care about them. I love you, Logan. I'm sorry you don't know what to do with that, but I don't want to be some screw against the wall in the rain because you can't find your normal. As sexy as you are, and as much as I do enjoy wrapping my legs around that body, I want Bill and Rosemary."

He recognized the reference to the original owners of his house—their romance.

"Kara, what we had was great. Why can't we—"

"I want roots and a life," she said, "and I can't have that if you won't let me in. Let me see the parts of you that aren't all shining armor. I can have Paris all the time, Logan. But not with you if everything is at arm's length because you haven't dealt with your stuff. So unless you're here to tell me about you, to share the parts you are hiding with me, then just go, because I'll find that life without you."

"I've given you everything I have." He pushed the wet hair off his forehead and tried one last time to get them back to where they were before she wanted more. "The thing is, when you left Paris, when I knew you had lied, that worked fine for me."

"No it didn't. You were hurt. We both were."

"That's the thing. I was never going to give you everything anyway." He figured if he said it out loud, that would make it so. He was trying desperately to hide from his pain.

"I'm not an everything type of guy, Kara. Maybe you didn't pick up on that in Paris because you wanted me to be some lovesick guy left behind, but that's not who I am. I will always keep enough of myself for a full recovery."

"Really? Then why are you here?"

Logan was not in physical pain. He would have given anything to simply forget her because this was madness. "I have no fucking idea. I shouldn't have come by. The thing is, I'm not a long-term guy and I guess that's what you need."

"I think you're wrong."

Logan laughed because there was nothing left to do. "Oh really, what a surprise."

"I'm serious. Kenna put it perfectly: you're nothing but roots. They're all around you. You're not exactly proving to be the stereotypical guy who doesn't believe in commitment. I mean, you own two food processors, a vacuum, and your house has a porch. Look at your family, your father, there's nothing temporary there."

"That's different." He pushed back, feeling her prying again. The woman simply didn't give up. Didn't she know they were heading right back to the night she asked about his mother?

"You create all this security for everyone else. Who tucks you in, Logan?"

The question hit him in the chest. Why did any of this matter? He was a grown man; he didn't need anyone to tuck him in for Christ's sake.

"You've loved me, helped me find my own strength. Who does that for you? When you're not fixing and helping everyone. When you fall apart, when you're weak, who picks you up?"

"My father, my family, my friends, everyone at the restaurant. We hold each other up."

"What about me?"

Logan took a deep breath. "You're that too. I need you."

"As long as I stay right here, right?" Kara asked holding her arms out in front of her. "When was the last time you were weak, Logan? You run everything. Anyone needs something and you're right there. You kept your family together, gave Makenna purpose after she lost Adam. You are super son, super brother, and super chef. Hell, there's nothing you can't do. The farm needs you at four a.m. even though you closed at one the night before? You're there."

"That's enough. You're making me out to be some fucking martyr. It's part of being in a family. We help each other. Not all of us come from . . ."

"From where Logan? Go ahead and say it. I know my family isn't perfect. I'm not saying you don't have a wonderful family. You do. I love them. It's not them, it's you. I'm not leaving you, I'm not running anymore, and you don't know where to fit me in."

She was relentless and he felt himself going down. She was in control and appeared to know it. He could feel the panic rising up the back of his neck.

"That's it, isn't it Logan? You can't relax, count on me because God forbid if the indestructible Logan Rye ever needed me."

Logan's father had once taken him to a middleweight boxing match. He still remembered staring up wide-eyed at that tattooed man, eye swollen and blood dripping from his mouth as he hung on the ropes. On the way home he'd asked his father how a man could handle that much pain. His dad had ruffled his hair and said, "A man's wired to fight his way off the ropes and then other times there's nothing left to do but throw in the towel, son." Logan was on the ropes. He couldn't take anymore, so he took one last shot.

"You'll never have to worry about me needing you, princess. I can take care of myself. Always have."

"I know, and that's the problem. It's not enough. I don't want someone who's just going to take care of me. I want to take care of you. I want to hold you up, too. It's not fair if you're the only one who gets to be strong."

"Well, then I'm sorry. This is who I am—how I was raised."

"Unfortunately, you're right. I wonder if she knows the damage she's caused."

"Damage? There is no damage."

"Oh, Logan. Of course there's damage. We all have it."

"Don't climb in my head. I don't need a therapist."

"What is it you need, Logan?"

"Shit!" Logan threw in the towel and walked back out into the rain.

Chapter Thirty-Four

*A*s soon as Logan slid into the booth at Libby's on Wednesday morning and sat across from his dad, no Makenna, no Garrett, he knew what their meeting would be about.

"Not talking about it," Logan said.

"Fine."

"Good."

"You know, I've never said boo to you about how you conduct your business. Except I will say the music in those bathrooms at your restaurant is way too loud."

Logan peered over his menu.

"Says who?"

"Says me. Can barely hear myself think in there and that's what the damn bathroom is for. I've made some of my best decisions in the bathroom, so you might want to think about lowering it."

Logan shook his head. "I'll get right on that. Is that what this meeting is about?"

"No, I thought you might want to talk."

Logan said nothing. Both men sipped their coffee and Libby took their order.

"I'm having a hard time finding my way back, that's all. I'll be fine, I just need some time."

"What are you finding your way back from, son?"

Logan shook his head. He didn't know what to say. He tried anyway. "My normal—where I was before . . . Christ, I don't know. Nothing works anymore." Logan watched his father fold the paper wrapper he'd taken off his napkin. He didn't look up, so Logan went back to staring at his thick-rimmed coffee cup.

"Your girl's not your mom."

Their eyes met and Logan was sure the shock registered across his face. His father had always guided them, but he wasn't big on advice when they were growing up. He believed they needed to figure things out for themselves.

"I know." He was having a hard time breathing.

"You sure? Seems like you're bent on going it alone. You've got to know that's probably wrapped up in what your mom did to you. Women, they're not all her, Lo. I want you to know that."

The look in his father's eyes was too intense. Logan needed out.

"Boy, how much Oprah do you watch?" he asked and felt the pressure ease when his dad laughed.

Libby delivered their pancakes and for a few minutes both men passed the syrup and talked about Logan's new tomato plants.

"I'm serious," his father said, pulling the conversation back. "Sure, relationships are scary, but if you do the work they work. You've got your whole life. You don't want to be alone, Lo. You know when you were a kid, you used to hang out on the couch instead of your room like Garrett. You were a snuggler. You liked being around everyone."

"Dad—"

"Don't interrupt me. You're not meant to go it alone, but you're a little damaged. That's okay, so is she." His dad paused to take a sip of coffee. "You love her, she loves you. That doesn't happen every day. She's her own woman, smart. I like that. And her eyes are calm."

"Dad," Logan warned as his chest tightened.

"She's a good one, Lo. That's all I'm saying. It'd be a shame if you let her go." He sipped his coffee.

"You finished?" Logan asked.

He nodded.

"I know she's all of those things, but she wants things I'm not willing to give. Things were great, but now she's pushing. She's got a lot of this stuff with her family. She likes to talk and discuss things and I'm just not into that. I like to keep moving. I like to stay focused and with her, I lose sight of things. I start thinking."

"Thinking about what? Marrying her, giving me another grandkid?"

"Whoa! Where did the marriage thing come from?"

His father seemed like a little kid with a secret.

"I never said I wanted to marry her."

"Don't have to. It's clear as day every time you're around her."

Logan shook his head and wondered how the hell a man looked when he wanted to marry a woman. Did his dad make this shit up? Or maybe it was Oprah again. Tomorrow on our show, Five Ways a Man Looks When He Wants to Get Married.

"Back to what I was saying—I understand what you're saying, but I've got to call bullshit when I see it. Those are only excuses for you to keep yourself safe. That's not you, Lo. You drink up life, always have, but your mom messed you up. Whether you want to see it or not, that's what this is about. It's time you moved on."

Logan was pretty sure this was the longest conversation he'd ever had with his father that didn't involve produce.

"Okay, I'll consider what you're saying. Still doesn't mean things with Kara and me are ever going to work, Dad. I appreciate the—"

"The girl fed the pigs for Christ's sake. When she came out for that interview thing. Fed the pigs, yes she did. She's a keeper."

"Dad, that was a novelty. She's writing an article. The jeans she wore that day were probably hundreds of dollars."

"Oh, don't do that. She's not about all of that. Besides, my jeans are pretty pricey these days too. Kenna's turned me on to these Levi's 606 jeans. You heard of them?" his father asked, lifting up from the booth like he was going to show his tag.

Logan shook his head, again shocked.

"Well, they're vintage according to Kenna. I love 'em because they're made like jeans used to be made in the sixties and they're made in this country. That's important too, but the damn things cost me almost two hundred a pair."

Logan laughed. "You pay two hundred dollars for your jeans?"

"Have to. Seems that's what good stuff costs these days. It's not just food, Lo. Kenna's forever telling me to be responsible, pay attention." His father smiled.

"Good kids, all three of you. I got lucky." He looked up, eyes a little glassy, and Logan's chest squeezed again.

"Has nothing to do with luck, Dad. It's hard work and sticking around."

"So do the work then, raise your own family."

"I can't." Logan barely recognized his own voice. "I have this family. This works and I'm not willing to risk something—"

"Lo, we're all grown up now. All of us," his father said, looking right at him. "Love's all about risk. You don't get a guarantee, there's no contract, and sometimes you get stepped on. Doesn't mean it's not worth a try. Kind of like that running of the bulls thing you sent me when you were in Spain. Those people get in there and let the thing chase them because it's a rush. Son, that's what we live for. It'll break my damn heart if you keep yourself all knotted up in there."

Logan didn't know what to say. Libby cleared their plates and left the check on the same flowered metal tray. He felt like paying the check and getting the hell out or changing the subject back to something that made sense. Chickens, his salsa recipe, anything but this.

"I'm sorry your mom couldn't be, what's that Oprah says, 'the best version of herself.' She was just not cut out to be a mom."

Logan ran his hand over his face. He was so damn tired. "You know, I've heard that phrase before, that she wasn't cut out, and it seems like such a simple explanation for a terribly complicated thing. A mother doesn't leave her children, Dad. I don't care how hard it is or whether or not she's cut out for something. That's a bullshit excuse."

"It is. I won't argue with you, but a person can't do something they can't do either. What if she'd stayed? I've thought about it a lot over the years, and I'm pretty convinced she did us a favor."

Logan glanced up again in surprise.

"You didn't know her. I mean sure you knew her as your mom, but I knew her and she was a mess, Lo."

Logan felt the tears and put his palms to his eyes, as if he could somehow push them back in. His father reached across the table and took his hand.

"You did great, Lo. We made it and now it's time to let yourself be loved. She won't let you down, I can almost guarantee it."

Logan laughed. "Oh really?"

"She fed the pigs, Lo, and loved it. That's gold." His father slid the check over and took some bills from his money clip.

Logan let him pay; there was no sense arguing. They walked out of Libby's and the sun was trying to shine past the clouds that had been threatening rain since last night. Logan felt lighter. Maybe he'd been waiting for someone to tell him they were in the clear— that they'd made it. He would probably never understand, but he knew when his father said they were better off, even great, that something shifted. Maybe he had been taking care of everyone else. He loved them and trusted them above all else, but now according to his father, it was time. Time for him to go beg the sexiest pig feeder in the world to forgive him.

Logan walked his dad to his truck. His father pulled him into a hug.

"Thanks, Dad."

"Thank you, son. I love you." Then, his father did something he hadn't done since Logan graduated from college—he kissed his forehead. His father turned from him, a little glassy-eyed, and Logan knew this would be the very last time they spoke of this. They would put his mother, his father's wife, back where she belonged and move on. Logan watched his father drive past and wave, and not for the first time, he felt fortunate. Life wasn't always fair, but he lucked out in the father department.

Chapter Thirty-Five

*K*ara spent the morning reorganizing her closet and cleaning out her refrigerator. She even ran her usual route twice earlier that morning as the sun was rising. Lately, she found that two loops were the minimum to set her straight. She stopped by the farmers market on her way home, and now, putting her new produce in clean refrigerator drawers lined with fresh paper towels, Kara felt fine. Jason Mraz was strumming his guitar and asking her to live high, live righteously as Kara closed her refrigerator and hopped in the shower.

It was actually a little heady now that she knew who she wanted to be, she thought as the warm spray hit her face. She'd told her mother she would commit to campaigns going forward, but other than holidays, she would not be available for fundraisers or whatever other events Stanley managed to dig up. Her mother was put out at first, but eventually acquiesced. Kara was learning to be selfish with her time and even though she was pretty sure her heart would hurt for some time, she was moving toward happy. That was enough for now.

She got out of the shower, dried her hair, and started making lunch. She was cooking more now and managed to get Makenna to sneak her a few bottles of olive oil from the monks. Kara couldn't erase Logan, or the things he'd brought to her life, completely. She didn't want to. He was part of her and that didn't change simply because they couldn't make it work. She knew she would eat at The Yard again someday, and eventually seeing him would hurt less and less. Kara had just finished chopping zucchini and making her tea when her phone vibrated across the counter.

"Hi, honey. How are things?" Olivia asked.

"Things are good," Kara replied, tilting her head to hold the phone while she rinsed her hands from the zucchini.

"Perfect, listen I just got off the phone with Harold and I guess Logan Rye added some equipment to his yard at the house. From what we are hearing, it's pretty special and I was hoping since you handled the original stories so beautifully you wouldn't mind finishing this up for me?"

"Olivia, what's this about?"

Olivia did her dramatic sigh. "Help me out here, Kara. I've got a date tonight with Jeremy, otherwise I'd do it myself."

"Oh"—Kara smiled into the phone—"you two are dating?"

"Yeah, that's old news. Where have you been? Oh, that's right, you left me. We are dating and my God, let me tell you the man can—"

"So things didn't work out with the therapist?" Kara asked, cutting her off before Olivia made another comment that made taking photographs sound obscene.

"That was never going to work. He never shut up," Olivia said and Kara could picture her on the other end of the phone, feet propped on her desk with her head thrown back laughing at herself.

"Enough about amazing Jeremy. We'll pay you freelance to handle this last one. Believe me, honey, you're going to want to cover this."

Olivia knew something, but she was never going to tell Kara, so there was no point in asking. She'd just have to head to Logan's house and find out for herself. She was fine with that, might as well get it over with sooner rather than later.

"Okay, I'll go over tomorrow and get you something in the next few days." Kara prepared to hang up.

"Oh no, honey. This needs to happen right now. Harold, my boss, in case you've forgotten who he is, wants you down there like in the next couple of hours."

Kara sighed. "Fine, I'll go."

"Good girl," Olivia patronized. "Oh and you might want to put on the Jimmy Choos, maybe a trench coat. Yes, did I ever tell you about the time—"

"Good-bye, Olivia." Kara cut her off.

Logan was on his porch when Kara arrived a few hours later. She hadn't seen him sitting in the corner, but she heard his voice right before she knocked on the front door.

"After she left, we ate pizza every night for . . . it must have been two months. I turned eight that summer. I was watching something on TV after school one day and they were talking about how dinner—a meal—brings a family together."

Kara froze. She was afraid if she moved he would stop talking.

"As clear as I can remember, that's when I started cooking. I mean, I was only a kid, but I started giving my dad lists on loose-leaf paper. He thought it was just a phase I was going through. I started with frozen dinners and vegetables. I made canned soup and sandwiches. Kenna would set the table. I remember her insisting that the paper napkins be folded corner to corner and not in half. It was fancier that way, she would say. She was so damn cute. Pigtails and missing teeth. God, we were so young." Logan smiled and Kara's heart ached for all of them.

"Did you think it would bring her back?" Kara asked carefully and sat next to him on the porch swing.

"Easy, princess. I'm new at this delving into my feelings shit."

She laughed.

"I think I may have at first, but it was really about making sure we were all okay without her. You know?"

Kara nodded and let him continue.

"I could never get my head around it as a kid. I don't even get it now. My dad was out on the farm and she left during harvest. He was working eighteen-hour days. We were all at school. I remember because Jenny Nathan had cupcakes for her birthday. I got the frosting all down the front of my shirt and the school called home. No one answered. I didn't care at the time, just wiped my hands on it and went on with my day, but I was seven. Makenna was five. She had half-day kindergarten and no one picked her up. She sat in the office until two when Garrett and I got out. We all walked home together." Logan's eyes started to fill and Kara thought she might die.

"Shit." He quickly wiped his eyes. "I don't think I've ever actually said this out loud." He took a deep breath, turned to Kara and she willed herself to not let one shred of pity cross her face.

"Anyway, we walked home that day and the next day Dad told us she was gone. I guess she left a note."

Kara couldn't keep her tears back. They spilled down her cheeks. "What kind of person does that?"

Logan shook his head. "It's been the four of us ever since. We each took on a role whether we knew we were doing it or not. Kenna has always managed the money, well not when she was five, but by the time she hit junior high, she was telling us how much money we had, when we needed to cut back, which coupons I needed to use at the grocery store."

"What was Garrett's job?" Kara asked, so happy that he was talking and letting some of this out.

"Garrett has always been man number two of the house. He's the protector, fighter when necessary; he worked the farm with Dad while I went to school. He learned to speak Spanish in high school and at night courses after that, so he could manage a lot of our guys. Now, he pretty much runs the whole thing. He's a pain in the ass. You think I'm bad? He's an emotional misfit."

Kara laughed.

"And then there's you," she said softly.

Logan nodded. "And then there's me. The wife and mother."

They both laughed.

"I'm sure Oprah would say I'm the caregiver. I made sure forms were signed, that we ate, and that Garrett didn't wear the same underwear every day of the week." Logan looked at her. "This is where we all do the collective sigh and say, 'Oh, that poor family.'"

Kara shook her head, not quite sure she could speak. "I don't think so. It seems like you've done fine without her. I mean you had to grow up pretty quickly, pick up some slack, but everyone has shit. Yours actually doesn't seem that bad." She smiled.

"Oh really?" The look on Logan's face softened and he seemed so grateful for the break in what Kara was sure was painful. She loved him for telling her.

"Yes, really. I mean, sure you had some 'stuff' to deal with, I guess"—she rolled her eyes—"but I spent most of my childhood in junior assembly, cotillions, and ruffles. Lots of ruffles. I think it's time for us to return to poor Kara Malendar, misfit to US Senator Patrick Malendar, gorgeous brother Grady, and lest we not forget, perpetually perfect and disappointed Bindi, mother extraordinaire."

They both laughed as she stood and did a very deep curtsy. He pulled her into his lap and used his thumbs to wipe her tears.

"I'm so sorry. Nothing works without you, so here I go." Logan held her face. Kara could feel his heart beating against hers. He let out an uneven breath and his eyes welled again. "I love you. Come on in, take whatever you want, it's all yours anyway. Just please don't let go."

Kara kissed him, softly as if her lips could somehow caress away his hurt. She'd never known this kind of love. Sure it was romantic and she loved every inch of his body, but there was a need to protect and care for him that she didn't recognize. She'd only recently discovered how to love herself, but she would need to make room for this too because her love for Logan was lie-down-on-the-tracks, take-a-bullet kind of love. He was the very best person with the most tender heart, and here he was handing it over to her. There were no words for what was coursing through her, so she just kept kissing him.

Logan pulled back. "Does this mean I'm forgiven?"

"It does."

"Just like that, princess? This feels too easy."

"Too easy?" She laughed. "I'm exhausted."

"Really?" He stood up and pulled her into his arms. "Well, then we should get you to bed. Exhaustion is one of those things that you need to take care of right away."

Kara smiled and kissed his neck. "Do you know a lot about exhaustion, farm boy?"

"You have no idea. I believe in working very hard."

She laughed. "Wow, you and lines. It's a talent." She buried her face in his neck.

He backed through the door of his bedroom and she knew she had been fooling herself. When a man moves over a woman's body the way Logan did, it was near impossible to stand in a room with him and pretend to be friendly. He loved her until she was once again panting his name, and then he made her a bologna sandwich with Miracle Whip, and they started all over again.

Kara woke up the next morning in Logan's bed, but without Logan. She sat up with that startled sense she was supposed to be somewhere. What day was it? Sunday, it was Sunday. She lay back down and closed her eyes, remembering him and wanting more. She got up and put on one of his T-shirts. The house was quiet as she walked into the living room. God, she loved this house. She smelled the coffee and again wondered how she could love the smell of coffee so much, but not enjoy drinking it. She checked the kitchen—still no Logan. In the center of his small round dining table off the kitchen was a beautiful teapot. It seemed hand painted. Next to it was a delicate matching teacup. Kara lifted the lid of the pot and found hot tea. She closed her eyes. *Thank you, tea gods.* She poured a cup and stirred in one sugar with a dainty teaspoon she'd never seen.

She was starting to wonder if Logan had to go into the restaurant, when she noticed large dirt footprints. It was as if someone had tracked mud from where she was standing, out to the backyard. Maybe a pipe broke or something was wrong in his garden. Kara pushed through the back screen door.

She found him. He was sitting on the last swing of a three-swing, swing set. Coffee in hand, legs crossed in front of him. He smiled at her and Kara almost dropped the lovely teacup.

He said nothing, so she walked down the steps of his deck and took the swing next to him. She propped her feet out in front of her as she sipped her tea.

"New swing set?"

"Yup."

"I like it." Kara looked straight ahead, wondering what was going on, but at the same time enjoying the simplicity of sitting on a swing set with him. She reached out to one of the support pipes. "Feels pretty sturdy."

"Had them cemented in." Logan sipped his coffee.

Kara looked at him. "Pretty permanent."

"Yup, this sucker's not going anywhere."

Kara's heart began pounding in her chest. She finished her tea and set the teacup in the sand to the side of them. She was afraid to get up, afraid to change anything.

Logan dropped his cup too and held his hand out for hers. When she gave it to him, he pushed off gently and they were swinging. The morning air was crisp and Kara could feel goose bumps on her bare legs. The sun was beginning to fill the sky and the birds in the magnolia tree were now awake.

"I love you," Logan said.

"I love you too."

"I'm sure I'll screw up a lot before we make it to Bill and Rosemary."

At the mention of their names, Kara squeezed his hand.

"I'm sure I will too." Her throat felt thick.

When the swings slowed, Kara pushed off, still holding tight.

"I want the things you want. Our children in the garden, pancakes on Sunday," he said.

Kara couldn't breathe.

"I want the rooms of our house filled with your light, your refracted magical sea light. I want to wake up every morning wrapped around you," Logan continued and then his voice hitched and he stopped swinging.

He got off of his swing and knelt down in front of her. Kara let out a gasp. She was out of her body at this point. She jumped out of her seat and knelt down in the sand with him.

Logan laughed.

"Okay, well this is one way to do it. Crazy-haired princess Kara, I promise to try. I promise to cook for you and always keep bologna and Miracle Whip in the house. Please marry me and I will give you everything I have; it's all yours and I will love you all of my life."

Kara nodded. She couldn't speak yet, so she stayed there in the sand in nothing but Logan's T-shirt. Very undignified, her mother would say. Kara couldn't care less.

"Farm boy, I think I may have loved you from the very moment I met you. I'm certain I was gone once I tasted your hollandaise sauce, but nothing prepared me for imperfect you." Kara started to cry. "Thank you for letting me keep you safe." She held her hands to her chest. "I love you."

She held his face and kissed him.

"Is there a 'but' coming here because you haven't even looked at the ring. Is this going to be an 'I love you, Logan, but I can't spend every damn day with you' type of thing?"

Kara laughed and her eyes fell to the dark velvet box in his hand. The band was platinum, she could tell, and mounted on top was a gorgeous square stone, but it wasn't a diamond. It sparkled more with tiny intricate cuts. It had a wash of blue and reminded Kara of the sun glinting off the ocean. She loved it.

"Logan, it's incredible." She kissed him again.

"It's a white sapphire and the band is recycled platinum." He slid it onto her finger. "Kenna said I needed to get off my damn soapbox, because every woman wanted a diamond, but I couldn't do it. Have you seen *Blood Diamond?*"

Kara laughed and a breeze blew across her face, drying her tears.

"Yes, I have, and I'll climb up on the soapbox with you. I love it and I love you so much."

There they sat, kissing in the sand by their new swing set. Canopied by the magnolia tree and surrounded by Logan's garden. He stood up and gestured to his back. Kara hopped on and he carried her piggyback into his house, their house.

"Life was meant to be tasted," her Nana had told her over banana splits one summer. Kara smiled and kissed the back of Logan's neck. Nana really did know what she was talking about.

Acknowledgements

I would like to thank:

Katie McCoach, my editor, for just about everything.

My favorite restaurant, The Parlor, for being brilliant, gentle, and delicious.

Barb Froman and Barb Vitelli for reading, sharing, and supporting my work.

My family for putting up with my closed door, imaginary friends, and often absent mind.

Anyone making a small batch, growing a small patch, or finding a different way.

Tracy Ewens shares a beautiful piece of the desert with her husband and three children in New River, Arizona. She is a recovered theatre major that blogs from the laundry room.

Taste is her fourth novel, and the third in her *A Love Story* series.

Tracy is a horrible cook, wishes she could speak Italian, and bakes a mean Snickerdoodle.

Made in the USA
Charleston, SC
25 October 2015